Sugar, Baby

Sugar, Baby

Celine Saintclare

BLOOMSBURY PUBLISHING

NEW YORK · LONDON · OXFORD · NEW DELHI · SYDNEY

BLOOMSBURY PUBLISHING
Bloomsbury Publishing Inc.
1385 Broadway, New York, NY 10018, USA

BLOOMSBURY, BLOOMSBURY PUBLISHING, and the Diana logo are trademarks
of Bloomsbury Publishing Plc

First published in 2023 in Great Britain by Corvus, an imprint of Atlantic Books Ltd.
First published in the United States 2024

ISBN: HB: 978-1-63973-2-463; EBOOK: 978-1-63973-2-524

LIBRARY OF CONGRESS CATALOGING-IN-PUBLICATION DATA IS AVAILABLE.

2 4 6 8 10 9 7 5 3 1

Typeset by Westchester Publishing Services
Printed and bound in the U.S.A.

To find out more about our authors and books visit
www.bloomsbury.com and sign up for our newsletters.

Bloomsbury books may be purchased for business or promotional use.
For information on bulk purchases please contact Macmillan Corporate
and Premium Sales Department at specialmarkets@macmillan.com

For Artie

I will always be the virgin-prostitute, the perverse angel,
the two-faced sinister and saintly woman

—ANAÏS NIN, *HENRY AND JUNE*

A kiss may be grand
But it won't pay the rental

—'DIAMONDS ARE A GIRL'S BEST FRIEND',
GENTLEMEN PREFER BLONDES

Part One

INGÉNUES

Prologue

The town I live in was voted four times by WeLiveThere.co.uk as The Worst Place to Live in Britain, an admirably big reputation for a relatively small place. Personally, I call it The Wasteland, maybe because the longer I stay here, the more I get the suspicion I'm wasting my life. Just under an hour's train ride from London, The Wasteland is the sort of town that nobody ever seems to leave and certainly nobody moves to by choice, unless it's to one of the villages on the leafy outskirts. The villages have high hedges to obscure disagreeable views, and honey-suckle to combat the stench of the river that runs through the middle of town, carrying cigarette butts, condoms like phantom jellyfish and general miscellaneous nastiness along with it. Over there, in the hills, gardeners are hired for the upkeep of newly built Japanese rock gardens, sunken fire-pits and ornamental topiary. Polished black Jaguars take the corners slowly. The majority of my clients live in the villages, including Camilla and her daughter. Emily.

One

Emotional Damage

I t's May, baking hot, lounge around with a freezer Calypso in front of a whirring fan kind of weather, and I have three spacious floors to mop, approximately forty-eight cabinets to dust and a drain to unblock. Outside, Emily is lying topless on the grass like she's in a sun lotion ad. It is a private garden, I'll give her that—nothing but green and yellow fields out the back, a host of conifers lined up at the top of the opposite hill—but it feels like a lot for pre-noon on a Wednesday.

Just thinking of being outside without a top on makes me damp, and not in the good way. I feel a bead of sweat prickle at the skin between my shoulder blades, then run down the middle of my spine before it's absorbed by my knicker elastic. The sun is already pressing in at the windows and this house has a lot of them—by the afternoon it's going to be stifling, my regulation candy pink overalls soaked through.

In the kitchen, I fill up a plastic mop-bucket with detergent and warm water, hear one of the other cleaners getting the vacuum going in the living room. I can't see Emily from the kitchen windows, just the corner of the orange-and-white striped beach towel she's lying on. But I've seen her face before in a portrait blown up to A1 size, hanging in a silver frame in the hallway, a close-up of her feline green eyes, full lips, blonde hair thick and curling at her shoulders. And I've been inside her bedroom, white linen bed-set and heavy pink drapes, a French antique-style dresser and matching drawers with not much inside them (yes, I've looked, I always look—it's my right to make sure I'm not working for the next Jeffrey Dahmer). Her wardrobe is a whole adjoining room with six shelves of designer handbags: a little black Lady Dior, an emerald green patent-leather Gucci, a quilted Chanel flap bag with heavy gold chain detail, a red Celine, a beige Prada. The first time I came here I ran my lambswool duster over the faces of them all and wondered about the girl who owned them and now she's here, naked.

I ascend the grand staircase, bucket in one hand, mop-handle in the other.

First, I mop the master bedroom which belongs to Emily's mother, Camilla, until the dark hardwood is slick with water like the glaze on a chocolate cake.

Camilla is a white-haired, Toast-clad version of Emily, another six feet of sinewy limbs and implausibly good bone structure. She has the skin of a woman who holidays frequently, freckled with sun spots and crêpey in the folds of her décolletage. She has a lot of chunky metallic jewellery and something of a patronizing expression—you can't tell if she's looking at you like that because she's misplaced her glasses or because she just thinks you're really, really stupid. She's the type to tell you all about her safari in Kenya and her skiing trip to Val Thorens with unnecessary detail, little slips that betray her lack of awareness. 'The villagers were *so* pleased to see us, of course they live in *such* terrible poverty, it really means *so much* to be given the opportunity to share their culture.' That kind of thing.

Emily's still out there in the sun, resting bitch face behind gold-framed sunglasses, her tanned skin shiny from the lotion and gleaming in the sunlight. Her body is perfectly sculpted, two round breasts with nipples that both point upward, toes painted white. For a minute I try to search her taut, blemishless skin for a flaw, squinting at her through the window. Then she reaches for her bottle of suncream, feeling for it, stark white against the rich, watered green of the grass, and shatters the stillness. My heart pounds. I suddenly feel like a pervert and shift slightly out of view, but I keep watching her, sitting up and rubbing lotion onto her outstretched legs, her spine protruding slightly. This is the part of the ad where a voiceover would play. SPECIALLY FORMU-LATED FOR 24 HOURS OF HYDRATION. A close-up of the expensive, translucent, probably coconut-scented cream melting into her skin.

The vacuuming has stopped, there's just the birdsong and the crickets now. A bumblebee bumps around the cracked window for a few seconds before giving up on trying to get in.

I close Camilla's door behind me. Leaving my mop bucket in the hallway, I get a feather duster out of the airing cupboard and climb the second flight of stairs to Emily's room, head straight for the wardrobe. A whole room of its own, six metres in length, racks of gowns and mini-dresses and silk slips hung beautifully along the whole perimeter. Rows of colour-coded jumpers folded up and stacked according to cut and shade, enough to fill a boutique. A revolving cabinet, six feet tall and filled with lush velvet bags and gleaming once-worn shoes. Each compartment is tantalizingly lit so that its contents glow behind the glass.

Taking this in, I have the sudden urge to destroy something, to violate this girl in some way. To exact a little revenge. Putting my feather duster down, I open the top drawer of a large cabinet and find it filled with lingerie, carefully categorized with grey felt dividers—tulle, cotton, silk and satin, knickers rolled into rosettes, corresponding bras. A sky-blue suspender belt embroidered with daisies, which I put in my pocket.

I catch my reflection in her ornamental mirror. It has a black leaf design, a stem curling around the frame and crossing the centre. I run a finger along it and its velvet feel surprises me. My face is fragmented by the design, carved into pieces: a hooded eye, iris almost black, chin with a dimple in the middle of it.

At my eye level there's half a lipstick mark pressed onto the surface. It's faint, as though someone was admiring their reflection so closely that for a second they found themselves kissing the glass.

From out of the window I can see she's gone, leaving her towel twisted up on the grass. I shove the evidence down into the depths of my overall pocket, close the cabinet drawer, feel the sweat prickling at the back of my neck. Maybe she just got a little thirsty, maybe she was set upon by an army of fire ants.

'Oh, hey'—she's standing in the doorway, taller than I imagined and twice as beautiful up close. Her make-up-free face is glowing with perspiration and the early stages of a rosy tan. She's not naked, thank Jesus, but wears a cream babydoll dress, short and flared, showing off the full length of her legs, a silver anklet on her left ankle. I suddenly feel transparent, as though the suspender belt is flashing through the side of my overalls.

'I can leave,' I offer, reaching for the duster.

'You're all right.' And she just breezes in, smelling like clean sweat and rose perfume. She opens the cabinet where the loungewear is kept, starts lowering the zip on the back of her dress. I turn away and back into the main bedroom, feeling stupid for still being here.

'That's better,' she says a minute later, emerging from the wardrobe in pink velour trousers and a matching top. 'One of the cleaners?'

'Yes, but this is just a part-time sort of thing,' I tell her. 'It helps fund my passion.'

'What's your passion?' Clients love this sort of chit-chat, asking me polite questions. It makes them feel good about themselves.

'Taxidermy.'

Her green eyes widen. 'Stuffing dead animals?'

Here we go again. I swear I can't help it. Every time I feel backed into a corner, my mouth starts spouting bullshit before my mind can put a stop to it. 'Yeah. I'm working on this little scene right now, a Thorny Dragon lizard sitting and smoking a pipe in his study. I'm saving up to have his little suit made—tiny buttons, you'd be amazed how much it costs.' I look around at her wardrobe then add, 'Well, maybe not.'

Her phone vibrates in her hand and she scrutinizes its contents from a distance, holding her phone at arm's length as if she doesn't want whoever it is to be able to get at her.

'Men,' she says, giving me a knowing look, and I smile like I understand her, even though I know just looking at her that I never will. I was the only Black girl in my year at school. The only one. I know I still have damage from the whole blonde-is-better, Abercrombie-&-Fitch propaganda I was subjected to as a teenager, but anyone can see that Emily is the Dreamgirl, the beautiful blonde protagonist of every American teen film I watched growing up.

She leans over her windowsill and rests her forearms on the ledge. I get the feeling she wants me to stay and talk, and I oblige her because it's too boiling to do any more work.

'You've got a lot of bags,' I say, gesturing towards the wardrobe.

She smiles then, slowly, unsheathes her smile like a weapon, her teeth dazzlingly white. 'Presents, mostly.'

'From who?'

She shrugs.

'Your parents?'

'No.'

'Who, then?'

But she doesn't say anything, just winks at me before turning back towards the window.

Two

Abercrombie Bitch

My best friend, Jess, is getting ready in front of her make-up-dirtied wardrobe mirror. From the Polaroids stuck around the frame, dozens of faces watch her as she stands in a corset top and knickers and considers what to do with her hair. Some are overexposed by light and heat, nothing more than sunspots floating on the tops of shoulders, but in most of them I can make out the glitter paint and bucket hats of Glastonbury and Coachella festivals past. There is Xanthe, her flatmate from first-year halls, wetsuited on the beach at Newquay and posing suggestively with a kayak paddle. The netball girls on their European tour, drinking cocktails from three-litre barrels at a foam party in Malaga. I cringe when I see them now, after everything that happened in Year 13.

Jess and I don't have much in common. She has always been a go-getter, team player, teacher's favourite, whereas I've had about three friends in my whole life put together. I guess that's the reason we met—she was the new girl at school, just moved towns from Clacton-on-Sea, and the only empty chair in form room was next to me. 'I like your butterfly clip,' she told me. It was actually a death's head moth that I had pressed and laminated with the library machine, but I smiled and told her it was from Claire's Accessories. She wrote her name on her exercise book in green glitter-gel pen. She had scented erasers and a set of pastel-coloured highlighters.

We're getting ready to go out for my birthday. Well, Jess is getting ready. I put on my face hours ago and am currently lying on her bed holding my phone above me at a perilous angle to disguise the fact that I'm messaging Toby, who Jess thinks is a useless stoner.

While she zips up her jeans, our eyes meet in the mirror. 'When was the last time you took some pictures?' she asks coyly. Caging me in.

'If you want to get anywhere taking pictures you've got to show them to people—and I don't know any.' I pop a tab of gum and chew with deliberate casualness. Then I use the same hand to slick back some of the baby hairs which have emerged out of my high bun, now fraying at my temples like bits of tassel at the edge of a rug.

'God. What I wouldn't give for a bit of volume like you, Ag.' Jess has plugged her curlers in at the socket and is flicking her ginger hair around in the mirror. She does that sometimes—goes on autopilot, her mouth forming half a sentence before changing topics. She's well-meaning, just has a poor attention span.

'This hair ain't for the faint-hearted, darling,' I say, being generous because I'm relieved by the change of subject.

Jess is always pleasantly surprised by my changing hairstyles. She assumes it's like a magician's trick, oblivious to the long hours it takes to finesse my braids or put in my weave. She gets frustrated if she has to spend more than fifteen minutes on hair styling.

Her brow furrowed with concentration, she begins to wrap strands of hair around the heated tongs, then unfurls each curl with a tentative pat like it's something precious.

'But surely it's worth it if it's what you really want to do?' She's back on the Help Agnes Find Her True Purpose mission. Ever since I crashed out of Sixth Form in spectacular fashion, with nothing but a smattering of failed exam results and a bad case of anxiety to my name, Jess has been worried about me. When she and everyone else around me moved on, leaving for universities and apprenticeships, I started working for a cleaning company, and Jess's concern escalated to embarrassment—which she's now converted into this coy little life-coach act. 'I mean, is there anything you love more than photography?'

'Um . . . fucking?'

Jess turns around and waves the tongs at me. 'Don't make me use these,' she threatens.

'Look, I know what you're saying.' I sit up, readjusting my crop top which has ridden up to show the underside of my left tit. 'I need to stop cleaning houses, love myself, *manifest my dreams*. But cleaning isn't so bad.'

Jess rolls her eyes.

'Rude,' I say. 'I'm a highly employable professional, I'll have you know. We've got, let me see . . .' I start to count on my fingers. 'Attention to detail. Discretion. Exquisite client care, delivered with intimacy and understanding.' Jess is snorting now, but it's true. Nobody knows their clients better than I do. I've dusted stray hairs from their pillowcases with the back of my hand, wiped dried flecks of toothpaste from their bathroom mirrors, emptied their bins of scarlet tampons and shredded condom wrappers.

'Listen, Jess,' I say, getting off the bed to join her in the mirror. 'It's my *birthday*. I don't want to be serious, I just want to get off my face and enjoy myself. Can we do that? *Please?*'

My arm is around her shoulders, my face pressed up against hers. She's softening, I can tell. 'You look gorgeous,' I say, and kiss her cheek. She smells, as always, like Pantene shampoo. 'Just make sure you shake those curls out or they'll confiscate your ID, Shirley Temple.'

She pushes me away. 'The cocktail?' She has those cold hands that thin girls often do. She's an icy constellation of knobbly red knuckles and knees.

'The child actress, you airhead.'

'Hmm. You're not still talking to Toby, are you?'

'No.' I sit down and scroll intently through TikTok, because Jess is one of the few people who can usually tell when I'm lying.

Well, it's a half-lie. Talking requires a level of involvement on both sides. My recent WhatsApp chat with Toby is a single, uninterrupted column of messages with blue ticks.

'Why do you ask?' I mumble, not looking up from my phone.

'Well, the *retro* film reference for one. And I was just thinking he might be out tonight. Mightn't he?'

Toby's reverent awe for Woody Allen and his insistence that *Annie Hall* is the Best Film Ever Made hardly qualifies him as a cinephile. I have always been obsessed with Old Hollywood and went through a phase of illegally streaming every single Marilyn film ever made during quiet shifts at work, propping up my phone against the bathroom tap to use it as a screen.

'Does that matter?'

Our eyes meet in the mirror again, hers narrow and searching, mine wide and innocent.

'Ag!' she squeals.

'What?'

'You're sleeping with him!'

'I . . .' I bury my face in her pillow. 'I'm ashamed, truly.'

Something soft makes contact with the back of my head. It's Biffy, a bear with a pink satin bonnet that Jess swears she will never throw away, and has now chucked at me.

'What is *wrong* with you, Agnes?'

'Everything.' I roll onto my back and look up at the ceiling, arms outstretched, palms upturned. 'The dick is tragically good, Jess. Why is it the worse the guy, the better the dick?'

'I can't even talk to you about this.' She takes a deep breath and continues with her curling.

I don't tell her I've texted Toby to tell him we're going to town (Going out with Jess tonight, Wasteland central!), in the hopes that he shows up to wish me a happy birthday. I've been dropping hints for weeks but as of yet nothing's materialized.

'Now how do I look?' Jess asks.

Her red hair is coiled up around her face like springy telephone wire.

'Like the best poodle at Crufts.'

'Oh, shut up.'

'Blue-ribbon winner.'

She rolls her eyes then leans forward and rakes through her newly formed curls with her fingertips. The spirals loosen and lengthen into shiny waves.

'Better?'

'Better.'

'Right,' she says, clapping her hands. Her boots are ready and waiting by the door next to my battered Converse. 'Now down your drink, you're too sober.'

We are venturing by local cab into the rotting heart of The Wasteland. It harbours diverse local attractions such as Poundlands, Costcutters, betting shops, and the Three Butts, a pub outside which an old man once made the Nazi salute at me. The river that courses through its heart carries a sour, sulphuric smell.

Our taxi drives down Jury Road, passing Tasty Garden (an okay Chinese), Bengal Blue (a sub-par curry house), a garage lot filled with a sea of old Fords and Peugeots in varying states of decay, some with flaky green algae set into the roofing. The yellow light from the street lamps sparkles off the enamel on Jess's teeth and the highlighter on her browbone. As we pull up by an underpass, a homeless man watches us from the dark hollow under the bridge.

We downed shots of Tequila Rose in the last five minutes before the taxi got here, and as I swing my feet out of the vehicle I realize that I'm approximately one strong drink away from being wasted. Jess walks with purpose, like a girl scout, and I trail her past the Three Butts, down the cobbled main road with the big building that's been empty since Woolworths closed down. Our destination is a bar called, unimaginatively, the Joint. It is the only watering hole in town where we don't risk running into a member of the English Defence League or being enlisted into an impromptu line dance. It is the kind of place which plays a cycle of Cascada, Abba and Rizzle Kicks, has two-for-one deals on a drink called Purple Rain and pushes the tables to one side so people can dance after 11 p.m. It reeks of old upholstery soaked in cider, a smell I actually find comforting now. The one regular is an old man with a scraggly grey beard down to his stomach who sits at a fruit machine and shouts at it, absorbed in his own world, oblivious to the growing crowds.

It's a Saturday which means the Joint is packed tonight. Jess and I dance pushed up against each other in the middle of the floor. I keep looking around, hoping to see Toby's gap-toothed smile or shaggy brown hair lit up by the disco lights, but no such luck. I check my phone again.

'Stop doing that,' says Jess. 'Don't worry about that tonight.'

'But, Jess . . .'

'Fuck him!' she says. 'He doesn't deserve you.' I try not to wince at this phrase, drained of all meaning by the sheer number of times I've heard Jess say it to me over the last six months, and allow a quick nod.

'Let's dance.'

Jess looks pretty tonight. Prettier than me. Curled hair, false lashes, lips overlined with brown pencil. Her cheekbones are dusted with white glittery highlighter, a tiny silver star sticker under her left eye like a cosmic beauty mark. She gets talking to a couple of men—surprisingly decent, they both have all their hair and a full set of front teeth—tells them it's my birthday and they disappear in the fog of the disco before returning with a tray of cheap shots in fluorescent green plastic shot-glasses. They're all different flavours like 'Birthday Cake' and 'Cherry Bomb' and they taste like children's medicine.

My feet start to feel light in my sandals, even though I know the straps are cutting grooves. The bass of the music rattles my ribcage. I realize with a sudden, satisfied feeling that I'm drunk.

'You like to dance, huh?'

I turn to see who's speaking to me. A Lacoste polo tee done up to the top button, sweat-slicked hair lying flat along his forehead.

'Reminds me of bein' a kid,' he slurs, gesturing round at the sticky floor, the jittery neon strobes. His pupils are wide black holes.

'What? Were you part of the circus or something?' I reply, casting an eye over the undulating crowd.

He laughs, whisky breath. 'No, I mean the music, the dancing . . .'

'I wouldn't know,' I say flatly. 'I had a fire-and-brimstone, vengeance-and-Bible-verses kind of childhood. No secular music allowed. No pubs. Just church.' Then I quickly swivel round before he can look at me like I'm crazy.

I find Jess dancing with the man who bought the shots, their hips locked together as they grind to 'Waiting all Night' by Rudimental. That last shot I took is pulsing through my system.

'I need to go to the loo,' I yell into Jess's ear.

She nods though I don't think she can hear me. It has not escaped Jess's notice that she is my only friend these days, apart from my sister Marlena, and although she tactfully ignores this topic in conversation, I think it gives her leave to take my presence for granted.

Of course, she doesn't know about Emily. And I intend to keep it that way.

Ignoring the girls snorting keys next to the hand dryer, I fall into a cubicle, hit the green phone icon next to Toby's name and press my mobile to my ear.

'What?' he growls. I'm not deterred by this blunt opening. Toby is efficient with words, his text messages to me a continuous cycle of the phrases Yh, Wat time? and Ok x. In person, I always think he sounds a bit like a gruff old man, although he is twenty-three, handsome in a washed-out kind of way, sandy-haired and grey-eyed and lanky in football shorts.

'Toby, it's my birthday,' I say.

'Happy birthday, Ag. But listen, you can't be buzzing me like this. We've talked about it.'

The fact that this is an unusually high volume of sentences for Toby to utter in one go gives me confidence to pursue my mission. 'I know I'm drunk, but hear me out.'

'*Ag*, I—'

'I think I have feelings for you.'

'—don't want a relationship right now.'

My confession was muffled by his voice, thank Jesus, but the fact that he didn't hear me pour out my guts in real time is a paltry consolation.

'Look, Ag, we've been through this.' His voice softens. 'Just chill out so we can keep having fun, all right? Peace and love.'

The line goes dead. Before I can even register what's happening, let alone the fact that I have just been told to chill out by a man who sources his weed on a Reddit forum, a torrent of vomit is wrenched out of me and slops orange and chunky into the toilet bowl. I crouch down on the filthy floor with the piss and the splashes of vomit. My bare legs are coated in bodily fluids and fragments of discarded tissue. More vomit. I pluck a wodge of toilet roll and wipe my mouth with a shaky fist. Happy fucking birthday to me.

I hear a group of girls come into the toilets, three or four maybe. There's the click of a phone-camera shutter, and I imagine them gathered around the mirrors, staring down their reflections and snapping pouty selfies.

'She looks a right state,' says one of the girls. Her voice is kind of familiar.

'Imagine spending your twenty-first birthday here.' I *think* I hear that next part, but I also know I'm prone to paranoia when wasted, to hearing voices and thinking everyone is talking about me. One of the many after-effects of my wild ride through secondary education. I try to push back the inevitable thought spiral the way my CBT counsellor taught me when I was thirteen, and actually succeed for a few seconds—until I hear my best friend's name. Spoken loud and clear.

'Poor Jess, doing charity work.'

The bathroom swells with house music as they leave, their voices quickly fading to nothing. I turn the cubicle lock and stand by the sinks. I am sobered, overcome by a dark anxious feeling that stoppers my insides like thick tar and makes me feel as though I can't breathe. I use water and napkins to wipe the sticky stuff off my legs and dab some cool water on my forehead. They're right, I do look a mess. My liquid liner has run down my cheeks, turned to grey, and I'm sweatier than the Lacoste polo creep from earlier.

'. . . it must be in here.' The door swings open and Izzy Collins comes through it. I knew I recognized her voice. Abercrombie bitch. 'Oh.' Her mouth opens and shuts like she's an electrocuted goldfish.

In the sweepstakes of public humiliation, overhearing a bygone it-girl from Year 13 bitching about you is mid-level. Having them realize you have been eavesdropping is off the charts. For a second, I worry that maybe neither of us will move or say a word and we'll be trapped in this horrifically awkward moment for eternity. But then she wishes me 'Happy birthday' in a clipped voice, flushes bright red and leaves.

The lipstick she's come back for is left sitting by the basin in its pretty gold case. I take off the lid and appraise its colour, then slick it onto my lips before putting it into my handbag.

Three

Fire and Sulphur

I wake up in my own bed the morning after with a desert-dry mouth and an EDM beat drop thrumming on repeat in my ears. I have no recollection of how I got here. The last text message on my phone is from Jess.

> **03:36 am:** Couldn't find u to say goodbye! ☹ Guessing you had to get home before your Mum woke up. HAPPY BIRTHDAY text me when you get home xxxx

Constance and the church ladies are already in the living room casting out demons. I can tell from the murmuring, eerie chorus drifting up through my floorboards. Of course. There is no respite from the weekly prayer meeting.

I allow myself a few seconds of self-pity, gaze mournfully at the moth which has fluttered in and settled on the ceiling lamp. Resistance is futile, I think, then drag myself out of bed and into a top with a virginal collar, a floral midi-skirt that wafts primly at my calves. I splash some cold water on my face and scrape away the fossilized remains of last night's make-up.

Downstairs, soft gospel music plays on the kitchen stereo. I put the kettle on and lean against the countertop, focusing all my attention on trying not to be sick in my mouth. It's difficult because our house is hotter than a kebab truck in summer months, thanks to criminally small windows and a high concentration of neighbouring homes. It's a red-brick semi in an estate near The Wasteland's High Street, which Constance bought off a scheme for council-home occupants in the nineties. The front door opens directly onto the living room, accessed exclusively from the inside of the house by walking through the kitchen, which opens through a third door onto the staircase, leading up to our bedrooms and the bath. This odd structure gives the house the feeling of a tiny carpeted labyrinth, and means there is no discreet way to sneak out late at night except via the glazed window in the side of the kitchen. I have perfected the art of scrambling on my hands and knees over the gas stove without making a sound, nudging the latch open with my toe, making sure not to knock over the cactus pot and guardian angel statue on the sill, and dropping silently onto the asphalt patch outside.

The 11 p.m. curfew is just one of Constance's extensive list of rules—no make-up, no missing curfew, no going to a boy's house or having a boy over, 'holy' relationships only, no alcohol or drugs, no tattoos or piercings, and no fucking fun under any circumstances.

As the saying goes, strict parents make sneaky kids. I once had a massive lovebite above my collarbone and told Constance it was a bruise I got helping Yemi Oluwawe's son down from a tree. Every time I pop the morning-after pill, I get assaulted by pain and nausea for two weeks thanks to my useless gut, and have to come up with a new creative alibi. Last time it was bad tuna mayo from the train station café—a little light retching and a scoop of John West in brine flushed down the toilet and she's none the wiser. Jess's parents have begrudgingly agreed to lie for me on more than one occasion.

I really thought things would ease up when I was fourteen, or seventeen, but at the grand adult age of twenty-one I'm an expert-level escape artist who can do a full face of make-up in the back of a taxi and perform six different sex positions in a Volkswagen Polo.

At least Constance has the sleep schedule of a Benedictine monk. I rely, in desperate times, on the assurance for the most part that she's in bed by ten. If I'd arrived home after my birthday night out and seen the light on in the hall, I'd have legged it back to Jess's and texted Constance saying we fell asleep watching Netflix. Exhausting? I know.

The kettle burps out steam as the red light at the base flicks off. I make a black coffee, gingerly edging around the fruit cake with blue icing and silver balls that Marlena made for my birthday—naturally, my sensible and studious sister is at the library. But before I can make my bid for freedom up the stairs, Constance wordlessly opens the living-room door in a kaftan and stretches out her arm for me to join the prayer group. She looks like Nefertiti, with the kind of face that begs to be photographed. I can smell the coconut and hibiscus of her hair product as she draws me inside. Her curly auburn hair is drenched in sunlight, becoming a halo, and she coaxes me into the prayer circle. If other women are yardsticks who we measure ourselves against, my own personal metric system started with my mother.

'Did you have a good time with Jessica?'

'Yes.' No.

'That's nice.'

Constance is the woman whose beauty, humility and piety I never had a hope of living up to. She's closer to the source than the rest of us, you see, a mortal angel. If she ever found out what I get up to she'd double over and throw up on the kitchen tiles, then take the little souvenir vial of holy water down from the shelf in the living room and douse me with it. Her face is as beautiful as it is bare, and earnest as a slate roof tile. High regal cheekbones, deepset almond eyes with hazel flecks in the iris. When she fixes her gaze on you it's hard to look away. I notice it all the time in supermarket cashiers and cleaning clients.

There's something a bit unjust in having a mother that much more beautiful than you, unnatural even.

But as for the cowardly, the faithless, the detestable, as for murderers, the sexually immoral, sorcerers, idolaters, and all liars, their portion will be in the lake that burns with fire and sulphur, which is the second death. I can feel her breath on my face as she prays, now fervently uttering phrases in the strange, rambling language of tongues.

In the corner of the living room is a big burgundy sofa that's older than me, which Constance keeps covered up with a thick crocheted blanket to hide its thinning arms and sagging seats. I slump on it, watching the women sway with eyes clamped shut and arms outstretched to summon the Holy Ghost. Uko in her virtuous pastel cardigan, Phyllis with her stiff grey coiffure and Constance's auburn 'fro catching the light. They are the three staples of my childhood, iconic and stoic as saints—the only father figure I grew up with was the Big Man himself and frankly, he's yet to make an appearance.

I make the obligatory stab at praying—*Dear God, please save me from this hangover and please, please, please let Toby text me back.* I still feel heavy and sour, as if my stomach is pooling with battery acid. My head is empty except for the cursed, echoing vibration of the bass drop from the Joint.

Four

Test Rabbit

Toby's seeing someone else. I find out in the usual way: open Snapchat, check his story (like always), hear a girl's voice, replay it, replay it again, go to her page and check the comments on her pictures, find Toby's name and the trail of smiley-heart eyes he's left there, stay up until sunrise comparing myself to her FaceApped pictures and wake up with my teeth grinding and repetitive strain in my thumbs.

At work, I think about him. When I flick cobwebs, when I squirt bleach around the inside of a toilet bowl, when I scrub polish into the crevices of an ornate mirror frame with a toothbrush. My romantic yearning isn't dampened by the smell of disinfectant—if anything it's ignited—and I'm haunted by questions like, How will I know I'm alive without Toby to witness me? How will I know I exist without Toby to touch me? And crucially, who's going to eat me out now? These are not the questions a woman should be asking herself after her six-month situationship realizes she's catching feelings and dips out. I know. I should be inserting a rose quartz yoni egg into my vagina and reciting self-love affirmations in the mirror. But the fact is that without Toby, I'm living in a monotonous hellscape with no adrenaline to balance out the tedium of my everyday tasks.

Even Jess is gone now, departed on a two-month holiday to Thailand with her uni friends before the autumn term, leaving me to fester in The Wasteland for the rest of the summer. I was invited, of course, but both of us knew it was just a formality. I couldn't even afford the plane ticket. It adds an extra sting knowing that Olive will be there too— one of the girls from Gladwell Secondary. She begrudgingly tolerated me at school because of my association with Jess but I always sensed the condescension in her voice on the few occasions she deigned to address me directly. Now, she studies international relations at the same uni as Jess—so in a few years' time when this country sends their foreign news correspondents to Libya or Syria, amongst them will be a first-class cunt called Olive.

Friendless and bored, I do the one thing available to me to fill up my time and ensure my continued survival. I book all the cleaning shifts I can get, pull on my candy pink-striped overalls and catch the bus (Dayrider return ticket) to the northern boundary of town. To Emily.

*

Emily is sitting in the kitchen on her laptop when I arrive, dressed in tiny black jersey shorts and a cerise sports bra with sparkly trimming and ruching at the breastbone. She looks like an off-duty Victoria's Secret model on her way to Pilates in 2011. A pink Agent Provocateur parcel is on the floor beside her, its black ribbon intact.

'Lingerie,' says Emily without looking up, 'is the fakest gift on the planet. It's just a polite way for men to say they want to see you without your clothes on.'

'I wouldn't know,' I say with a sigh, 'no one's ever bought me any.'

I'm happy to see her. She intrigues me. I'd like to part her perfect skull down the middle, click it open like a clutch-purse, poke around inside the soft wet pink of her brain.

Emily looks up from her silver-grey MacBook and squints at me. 'You look . . . terrible,' she says, 'like you haven't slept in a week.' 'Strange,' I say, not missing a beat. 'I've been sleeping like a baby.'

Emily stirs Manuka honey into her green tea and tells me she wants to have 'a quick chat' before I start my shift. The formality of this request puts me on edge—has she noticed the suspenders missing from her drawer? Her face is more mischievous than angry, so I figure I'm probably okay. I am supposed to be doing the cupboards right now but I've stopped to give her my full attention, holding the lambswool duster across my chest like a bouquet. Emily is probably used to being attended to in this way, because she looks exactly like Margot Robbie's character in *Wolf of Wall Street*. She has definitely perfected YouTube hair tutorials with names like Easy French Twist Updo and Six Instagram Baddie Hairstyles You Need to Try; every time we meet, her blonde mane is pinned and tied into a new structure. Today it's Pam Anderson-esque with a wispy fringe, teased up at the crown and then messily piled on top of her head and pinned in place. It's not something the average civilian can pull off. It's definitely not a hairstyle that you ever see in The Wasteland.

Emily's a city girl to the bone, you can tell. She probably gets the train down here for the occasional weekend—delicately avoiding The Wasteland's high street, heading straight for the hills—to sleep off a hangover and make the most of her mum's Sky subscription and cupboard full of expensive herbal teas. Then when it's Sunday after-noon and she's sufficiently detoxed her insides, she rattles straight back into the hot core of London.

Sipping her tea while wincing at its heat, Emily tells me she's writing an e-book and she wants to publish it anonymously. It's going to be called *10 Easy Ways to Get a Man to Do Anything You Want*. She has expe-rience in this area, she says.

* * *

Emily started out just modelling, a job which she still does part-time. Male celebrities would meet her at events and then find her on Instagram or start contacting her agency to get a date with her, in increasing numbers. One afternoon in a low-lit bar in Richmond-on-Thames, a Bafta award-winning actor (his name kept anonymous by Emily for privacy) kissed her goodbye on the cheek and then put a white envelope in her hands, thanking her for the beautiful afternoon. It contained a large amount of cash and his phone number. She realized, then, that there was only the tiniest side-shuffle between posing for fashion lines and posing during a three-hour date.

'If a man's got money I can get it out of him,' she says. 'It's easy once you learn how. I could show you how to make a career out of lunches and champagne, Agnes.' She looks up at me from whatever she's been scrutinizing on the laptop screen, a flash of uncertainty in the form of an arched eyebrow. 'I mean, if you want. It's just . . . I was thinking, it might be good to test out some theories before I publish them, to make sure it all works.'

'So you want me to be like your guinea pig or something?' I say, stroking the feathers on the duster while trying to decide whether the proposition is flattering or demeaning.

'Not a guinea pig,' she says. 'Something cuter like . . . a rabbit. They have rabbits in test labs, right?'

'You don't have any friends who'd want to be your test rabbits?'

'My friends have already been involved in this shit for years,' she says. She's watching me and her eyes are doing something strange, dilating on demand, and her voice is lower, softer. 'So what do you think? Ready to make some real money, Agnes?'

'What makes you think I'd be any good at it? I can barely get a text back.'

'Well,' she explains, looking me up and down, 'you're a pretty girl, the right age, well-spoken. A blank canvas.' I don't know if I like the sound of that last bit. 'And you're a critical thinker,' she continues. 'Trust me. Being irresistible is easy when you know how.'

I put the feather duster down and lean with my elbows on the kitchen island, because the thing about Emily is, resisting her feels like spiting yourself.

*

First, she impresses upon me the importance of concealing my identity when meeting a stranger for the first time. 'You might meet a real creep and want to disappear. Keep your name a secret and vanish into the blue, easy-peasy.'

She lists a range of other tactics: order the second-most expensive thing on the menu to show you've got good taste but you're not out to take the piss, always negotiate an allowance before the end of the date, wear perfume with lavender, vanilla and pumpkin essence because these supposedly stimulate blood flow to the penis so the man associates your presence with arousal. Wear red, use sparkly eyedrops, lower your voice and talk at half the usual speed so they watch your mouth and lean in to hear you.

And then the golden rule: discretion is queen, but cash is king. If he has a nice time, ask for more money. If he wants you to dress up, ask for more money. If he wants to see you at short notice, ask for more money.

Another point Emily is very clear on. She is not an escort, not a prostitute, not a call girl. She is simply a participant in a mutually beneficial relationship.

'"Sugar baby" is probably the closest term,' she tells me, yawning and inspecting the nails on her left hand, 'but I don't like labels. It's better to think of it all as a business. We've got youth and good looks and they're commodities in demand, so we provide a streamlined service. Everybody wins.' She's matter-of-fact now, more monotone, less coaxing. 'Think you could handle that?'

I'm not sure if it's my week of cleaning and double prayer group with Uko and Phyllis making me feel desperate, or the fact that Emily's signature scent—a syrupy rose, like Turkish delight—makes it impossible to think straight, but I am seriously considering it.

The job that Emily is describing is not so different from mine, after all. Attention to detail. Discretion. Exquisite client care. The difference is that I'm an unknown entity to my clients. I walk their grand houses like a nameless ghost. Backstage, you know? What Emily is suggesting sounds like a performance.

Of course, there is another difference.

Escort. Prostitute. Call girl. What do these three terms have in common? I'm not a prude, obviously, but the idea of a blurred line between sex and business is kind of making me freak out.

'Would I have to . . . ?'

'There are *all kinds* of arrangements,' Emily says. 'Some guys literally just want a dinner date. Someone charming to listen to their conspiracy theories about 9/11 and make them feel clever for introducing you to Nick Cave's deep cuts.'

She raises an eyebrow. I can feel my face getting hotter.

'Okay, that's *some*. But what about the others?' I blurt out in a single breath.

'Oh, darling.'

As if on cue, I hear a soft clinking, and Camilla comes wafting into the room. Her love of metallic jewellery means you often hear her before you see her.

'Hello, Agnes,' she says, both her stern tone and her unimpressed expression making me rethink my slouch over the kitchen counter. 'I hope this one isn't keeping you from your work.'

Emily touches her hand lightly to my forearm. 'Agnes, Mum is throwing a party on Saturday. You should come.'

'Oh, what a lovely idea,' Camilla says evenly. 'Do come, Agnes. And you must bring your mother too.'

Constance is the regular cleaner at this house—Camilla *adores* her—but she can't do Wednesdays anymore because she's helping at the United Pentecostals soup kitchen or something so I'm covering for her.

We work together, Mum and I. She signed me up at Mrs Finch's cleaning agency when it became apparent I couldn't hold a retail job down. I think she wanted to keep an eye on me. Every immigrant parent's worst nightmare, but she didn't make me feel bad about it. Just gave me a speech about how careful we need to be in our clients' homes, how some things can never be properly clean again once they've gotten dirty, some things can never be fixed once they've been broken. I trailed her like a little pink shadow in my uniform.

By the time I've mumbled something about not wanting to intrude, Camilla's already halfway out the door again.

The way Emily is watching me now is like I'm a little project of hers, her chin resting on her hand as she looks me up and down, eyes glowing with mischief.

'We can chat more on Saturday,' she says, 'but I have so many things to teach you.'

'Like what?' I'm trying not to show how excited I am. Be cool, Agnes, don't smile like a fucking idiot.

Emily opens up her laptop screen and turns it round on the tabletop so I can see a title typed out in capitals:

CREATING YOUR CHARACTER

*

I'm staring at the phosphorescent stars pasted on my bedroom ceiling, Emily's words from earlier today running through my mind on repeat.

Trust me, being irresistible is easy when you know how.

I can imagine an upgraded version of myself, teeth whiter, salon-waxed, dressed head to toe in designer. No more scrubbing toilets, just rolling around in my black Rolls-Royce to beauty appointments, brunches and cocktail parties—in *London*. Everything paid for by a fleet of men who throw money at me just for being gorgeous. God, that sounds too good to be true. And there's a gnawing feeling in the pit of my stomach warning me that it probably is.

There are all kinds of arrangements.

I'd have to keep it from Constance, of course, another secret. And I suppose there might be a bit of moral resistance that I'd have to dramatically overcome. Some sleazy banker would take me for dinner then back to his hotel room where he'd hold out a wad of cash and ask for a sexual favour, I'd say no, we'd go back and forth in a charade of manners, notes stacking up until it became absurd to refuse and at last I'd do the deed. Then I'd emerge like Anne Hathaway in *The Princess Diaries*, two plain-Jane photographs of myself parting to reveal a high-fashion vamp, a premium creature of the night.

I'm surprised to find that thinking about it turns me on. Thinking about myself as someone confident, utterly shameless, and impossible to resist. I push everything off my bed—plush animals, decorative pillows—peel my thong off and drop it over the edge of the bed where it falls on top of my cherished Helmut Newton photobook.

I see God then, literally—I look up at the ceiling and see Jesus, white and blue robes, golden halo, floating above me shaking his head in disgust. He extends his arm, index finger pointing downwards, and I feel the lake of sulphur beneath me, the bottom of the mattress burning away. Sigh. He always shows up when it's inappropriate.

The thing about being raised in a strict religious household is that no matter how hard you resist it, a part of you will always see things as split into two. Good versus evil. Pure versus impure. Madonna versus whore. You're not a saint so you must be a demon.

Do you not know that your body is a temple of the Holy Spirit within you, whom you have from God? I've had so many Bible verses recited at me over the years that my mind just spits them out at the most inconvenient times.

When I need to summon enough arousal to compete with the guilt, it helps to think about Toby, which is really fucking annoying but needs must. So I focus hard, channelling a particular memory where he removed my pink overalls, pulled my underwear to the side and started to eat me with his fingers stroking at the inside of me. You know, the upwards motion thing that everyone knows about but hardly any guys can be bothered to do? And if they press down on your lower stomach with the other hand at the same time it makes you . . .

That's better.

*

Toby is on top of me, he's stripped me naked and now he wants me to beg. I love it when you're fucking a guy and his face gets all primal and he doesn't even really look like himself. I never liked polite sex, lovemaking. Is it too much to ask to be out of my skin and feel like an animal? Toby always understood this. Some people do and some people don't, it has to come from inside.

'I don't think you really want me to fuck you,' he says, teasing me with the tip of his cock.

He pushes half an inch inside me and then pulls out. I'm so wet it's not even funny.

Fuck it. I start begging. Please, Toby. I reach out and grab him, hold on to the backs of his thigh and pull him into me.

He grips my throat while he fucks me, and then when I'm done he eats me until I come again.

I look up at the ceiling, my heart pounding with relief, and see nothing but the glow-in-the-dark stars. Jesus is gone and I'm relieved, but I know he'll be back.

I should really message Toby. But as the euphoria of the orgasm dissolves, my self-respect floods back into my body. I put my phone on Do Not Disturb and try to go to sleep.

Five

Sugar-land

I checked the Free Press earlier today,' Constance is eager to tell me as soon as I come downstairs. She's switched off Transcendent Prayer Group Mum today and is embracing Hyperactive Control Freak Mum, because we are going to the party at Emily and Camilla's tonight, and any hint of fun makes my mother anxious.

'You know a pair a' sisters gone missin' on their way home from school?' she informs me luridly between crunches of cereal. Cornflakes are an acceptable meal for any time of day among Vincentians. 'Found some poor girl's body dumped in the river at Wye Park at the end a' last month.'

'That's great, Mum, thanks for sharing,' says Marlena.

Marlena is taller than both Constance and me, pointy-chinned, her hair braided back into cornrows. She is sitting on the sofa in the living room shuffling through cue cards while *MasterChef* plays on the TV—she claims the ambient sound helps her memory. She doesn't even twitch as I pass her, taking my milky tea over to the armchair. My stomach is churning with anticipation of the party later.

Constance kisses her teeth. 'No use bein' ignorant to the reality of the world we livin' in.'

The irony of this statement isn't lost on me.

'We'd better be careful, Lena,' I say. 'This serial killer obviously has a thing for sisters.'

'He took it really personally when that Tia & Tamera show was cancelled,' she adds, without looking up from her revision.

I laugh-snort tea through my nose. 'The revenge of Sister, Sister.'

Marlena shakes her head, smiling. Meanwhile Constance storms over with a handful of kitchen roll, mumbling to herself about how we never take anything seriously.

Then she says it. The sentence I've been dreading. 'You got make-up on, Aggie.'

'Barely.' I stand up to confirm this in the mirror hanging in the kitchen. I had tried to be subtle. A barely visible line of black pencil, a light coating of mascara, a L'Oréal peachy powder blush meticulously blended over the apples of my cheeks.

'You know the rules,' she says. 'You're beautiful as you are.'

I am aware of how this looks, a grown twenty-one-year-old woman reaching for the baby wipes because her mother tells her that vanity is a sin. But as long as I rely on Constance for bed and board I have to live by her rules. Plus there is a part of me, a small, aching part, that does actually long to be the pure, godly daughter she's always wanted.

Her reflection in the kitchen mirror next to mine—bare, devastating, a fair argument for the existence of a creator God—actually makes me want to cry at the injustice of it all. Of course she's against make-up, she doesn't fucking *need* it.

An expression of panic contorts her perfect features when she realizes the kitchen window is open and it sets her off on a crusade around the house to identify and eradicate every possible entry point, giving me the chance to slacken a bit on the make-up removal. As well as being a fanatic Pentecostalist, Constance has a morbid fascination with slayings and kidnappings and an obsession with keeping everything locked—I once watched her check the front door was shut, like, twenty times in a row. Last Christmas she put mace in my stocking, together with a fluorescent rape whistle.

I laugh a bit when I remember the other present she gave me, a book called *Legs Closed, Heart Open: A Guide to Christian Adulthood* with a wild-eyed woman called Wendy Okerede on the dustjacket. Then I scrub my cheeks over the sink with a flannel until they're pink and raw (may as well make the most of that natural blusher effect), getting a perverse pleasure out of the sting. I dab most of my eyeliner away with a wet tissue but leave a faint smudge, hoping I look a bit Zoë Kravitz. It gives me strength to know that the stolen lipstick is still with me, zipped up safely inside my handbag.

Constance has returned from her mission with her headscarf in one hand.

'Much, much better, gorgeous girl,' she says, smiling approvingly and stroking my cheek with the backs of her fingers like I'm a stray cat. 'Could you give me a hand with this, Aggie?'

In front of the kitchen mirror, I help Constance wrap her auburn hair out of view in a faux-satin headscarf. Soft pink against the freckled brown of her forehead.

'She is a nice woman, that Camilla. Nice of her to invite us.'

'It was her daughter,' I reply, while my stomach does somersaults.

*

Our bus stop is right outside the school for troubled youths. Constance delicately averts her eyes from the teenage boys who are smoking rollies on the pavement, shouting taunts at passers-by. OI, SIR, YOU WALK LIKE A PEDO! We catch the bus to the village, a journey we've both done many times before. I can predict the exact moment that Constance will tut and shake her head—when we pass the Catholic church, because Catholics are no better than Satanists in her eyes. As we near the top of the hill, the trees suddenly become more groomed, and there is honeysuckle, blossom, plants that are there on purpose rather than just randomly clawing their way out through the gaps in the concrete.

The bus turns into Camilla's lane. Through the gate's cast iron bars, I can see the shiny white paint of the front door winking at us, the tall pointy topiary lining the driveway which always makes me think of manicured acrylic nails, like some giant Instagram model is reaching up from under the earth. When we alight, we are passed by several people who look as though they're paid extras on a television drama about affluent, warring housewives. A woman wearing a floral tea-dress is carrying a bottle of wine. A middle-aged couple are taking their golden retriever for a stroll. They are walking in the slow, pleasurable way of people who have nowhere urgent to be.

I key in the entry code for the gate, cleaner's privilege, and we make our way down the footpath to the sound of Frank Sinatra. It feels eerie to be here as guests, Constance and I in our Amish 'party' dresses— ankle length, batwing-sleeved, shapeless enough to conceal a chastity belt. Polyester birth control. The colours of the garden are saturated by sunlight, potted yellow pansies and white-pink magnolias amplified to the point of unreality. I'm filled with dread or acid reflux, maybe both.

The front door is propped open by an ornamental stone. When we enter the house, we are politely ignored by the two people nearest us—a woman in a burgundy sort of kaftan, and a man in chinos rolled up around the ankles, with foppish hair and the kind of jawline I can only describe as villainous. They turn briefly over their shoulders, look mildly alarmed at the beauty of Constance's bare face, then return to their conversation.

Constance suggests we go into the living room and look for Camilla. I follow her reluctantly. There is a high percentage of Cathies—that's what I call them, as in Cath Kidston. An attractive, Russell-Group-educated white woman who reneged on her dreams of academic or artistic stardom, defected to suburban motherhood and now focuses the entirety of her mental prowess on her children's extracurricular activities and the latest in health-food fads. She develops orthorexia, and dresses almost exclusively in florals. There's nearly always something inexplicably heavy metal lurking in one of her bedside drawers or the bathroom cabinet, like a plastic bottle full of baby teeth or a round brush matted with a decade's worth of hair.

I come across many Cathies in my line of work.

We drift through the main reception room and my eye is drawn to a silver tray, a white tablecloth laid with crudités, glistening tomato-topped bruschettas dusted with finely chopped basil, at the back of the room.

'They've got food,' I say to Constance, and start to pick my way through the milling crowd, energized by the idea of having something to occupy myself with.

Constance sucks her teeth. 'White people and they cold food. Why everyt'ing always got to be ice cold?' Her Vincentian accent is more pronounced, channelling the soft barrelling tones of her mother, as it always is when she uses one of Grandma's sayings.

I feel an elbow in my back as someone pushes past me, the man with the villainous jaw from earlier. He throws his hands up in a mime of defencelessness but doesn't say sorry, only narrows his eyes in momentary confusion at Constance and me. He is talking in wry, knowing tones to a man called Spencer about a wine called Txakoli, which needs to be poured at a 90-degree angle, from a height, he says, in order to release its flavour in tiny silvery bubbles.

I stand with my back pressed up against the wall. There's no sign of Emily. Maybe she's forgotten that she invited me and flitted off to London at the last minute—making me her apprentice was just a silly whim and now she's found something else to entertain herself with. I feel the familiar ache of revenge, consider poking a hole through one of the Cathies' summer dresses with a toothpick. Or slipping something in my bag. I cast an eye over the silverware on the buffet table but nothing gets me excited.

The French doors are thrown open on to the back garden, which has clearly already become the refuge of the heavily intoxicated. A couple are sitting on the brick wall smoking intensely, the man's brow furrowed as he exhales reprimands at his girlfriend. Her eyes are closed blissfully, pointed chin turning one way and then the other. Beyond them, up on the sloping grass, a guest sits in a deck chair, hands clasped over his belly.

Constance begins to grow agitated, her usually placid face folding up into a frown.

'Where's Camilla?' she says, turning to look over her shoulder at the door.

I can catch titbits of chatter from the crowd of guests, phrases lingering in the air between the jazz music and the laughter.

Have you met Liz's brother-in-law? He's black but he's really lovely.

If I've told you once, I've told you a hundred times, the whole point of having an au pair is so the kids can be bilingual.

But they're not speaking French, Tony, they're speaking broken English with a Haitian accent.

Camilla glides into the room in white linen trousers. She is the antithesis of a Cathy. Rather than defining her life's purpose, her children are simply inconveniences and treated as adults from the moment they can walk and talk. Women like Camilla believe life should be lived: one should travel regularly, spend freely and drink voraciously. I had a similar client who jetted off to a meditation retreat in Malaysia for two months, leaving her twelve- and fourteen-year-old sons to fend for themselves with nothing but a crate of expensive bottles of port to give as thank-you gifts to their friends' parents for feeding them. I told the boys they'd better call the agency instead when they tried to pay me with a bottle of forty-year-old Portuguese Kopke.

At the sight of Camilla, the faint lines on either sides of Constance's mouth bend into her signature smile. 'Finally,' she says, 'I'm goin' to say hello to Camilla.' And she begins to push her way through the crowd of guests with a brusqueness she usually reserves for the privacy of our home.

Camilla has a soft spot for my mother, most women do. Once they get past the beauty they tend to find her old-world piety fascinating; a half-hour conversation with her gives them the same feeling as a spiritual retreat or a reiki healing session. But they especially love to hear her talk about her island days, the years she lived on St Vincent. Her voice sounds richer, she almost falls into a trance as she describes it.

Auntie Deb on the seabed, sayin', 'Watch out for barracudas!' And the sea warm as a bath.

Agnes, the island I called home was all kinda colours, but most of all it was green. Rows and rows of proud green sugar cane crop . . .

Emily enters the room, jolting me into the present like a shot of espresso's just been mainlined into my veins. She wears a black shift mini-dress and a patterned hair-scarf, silver bracelets stacked on her dainty wrists, silver anklet. She offers her mother's friends a tight, mask-like smile by way of greeting. When she spots me, she waves frantically and mouths at me to *come upstairs*. As I pass by I overhear a bit of the conversation between Camilla and Constance. My mother is holding forth about the nature of forgiveness and Camilla is watching her face with a bemused, starry-eyed expression like she's witnessing the Second Coming.

'This is so fucking boring,' Emily says to me as I follow her. 'I can't believe I let her drag me down from London for *this*. The annual Look-at-Me-I'm-Camilla-Canon-Party. I *hate* these people. In an hour they'll all be outside lying on the grass and someone's going to suck off someone they shouldn't in the downstairs cloakroom.'

'You're joking,' I say. My voice sounds flat when I hear it come out my mouth and I realize: I'm disappointed. Emily didn't really want me here. She just didn't want to suffer alone.

'We like to think people get wiser with age but a lot of them just get more stupid.'

'If it's so bad, why did you invite me?' I blurt out.

'I didn't invite you here, stupid,' she says, turning over her shoulder to look at me, 'I invited you to where we're going next.'

And just like that, the nervous flutter in my ribcage is back. 'Where's that?' I say, trying to sound chill.

'I'm kidnapping you,' she says brightly. 'You *do* want to get out of here, don't you?'

Of course I do. I want to go down the rabbit hole into Emily's world, Agnes in Sugarland! But I live with a dictator and I either broach nights out at least two weeks in advance if I want a shot at approval, or weave a convincing web of lies. I'm out of time for both options.

'I've got . . . I have to go to church tomorrow morning. United Pentecostals kicks off at nine a.m. sharp.' She narrows her eyes at me, and I quickly add, 'Not by choice. One of the conditions of living rent-free with Constance.'

'We won't stay out too long. Just a few drinks.' Tempting. 'Come on, I'll introduce you to some of my friends.'

'I only have this . . .' I say, gesturing downwards.

Emily looks at my long, pink, Constance-approved dress and tells me she has things I can borrow.

This is not my first time in Emily's wardrobe but every time I come back I can't believe the size and luxury of it, the kind of thing you'd expect to see on *The Real Housewives of Beverly Hills*.

'You need something sexy,' she says, 'none of this small house on the prairie crap.' She rifles through the racks and holds out a strapless red dress. It is dangerously short. 'This is what you're wearing.' She rolls her eyes at the bewildered look on my face. 'Come on, it's Valentino, for God's sake.'

She doesn't hand the dress to me, just stands dangling it by the coat hanger, an expression of expectation on her face. I realize she is waiting for me to get undressed. I pull the dress I'm wearing up over my head and stand in my mismatched cotton briefs and T-shirt bra, my left hand twitching compulsively at my side.

The red dress is heavier than it appears, with boning stitched into corset to create a severe hourglass shape and padding in the bra to add cleavage. I hunch over in the corner and pull my T-shirt bra out of the top of my dress like some kind of sleazy magician. Emily zips me up, runs her hands over my taut, scarlet hips and tells me I look like the sixth Kardashian sister. 'Look at you. Who knew.'

I like how the dress manipulates my body into a caricature of itself, forcing me to stand up straighter.

While I'm staring at myself in the mirror, Emily sits at the dressing table in a pale pink dressing gown, taking out her make-up brushes with the ritualistic reverence of a shaman preparing for a healing ceremony. As she sharpens a lipliner, I remember the stolen lipstick in my handbag and take it out to apply it, leaning over her shoulder in the dressing-table mirror.

Emily sighs and holds her hand out. I press the lipstick tube into her palm, pleased to be able to contribute to the process and show her I'm not a total lost cause. She wrinkles her nose at the brand name, but turns and applies it to my lips with a quick, expert series of tiny dabs, holding my face by the chin.

'This is nice lipstick, Agnes,' she says, squinting at the result. 'But it's all wrong for you. Too safe. It's not *saying* anything.' A gleeful pitch has entered her monotone. 'Your *brand*. I've got it!'

I laugh too, more uncertainly. 'What do you mean, my brand?'

'Your aesthetic, your character. It makes it easier for the men to compute.'

'I didn't realize we were going to meet any m—'

'Agnes, you are the exotic femme fatale,' she says, eyes sparkling, 'red, black, leopard print and . . .' She pulls open one of the dressing-table drawers to reveal approximately forty tubes of lipstick, lined up like toy soldiers in a blue satin-lined case. She holds one up with a flourish. 'Blood red lipstick.'

With the final touch applied, Emily beckons for me to look into the mirror. A better, sharper version of myself blinks back. My face is somehow transformed, whittled into something new. My eyes are more feline, my cheekbones more pronounced, my lips are glossy and plump.

'Where's your phone?' she asks me.

'Umm, over there, why?'

'You want some pictures, right?'

I pretend I'm not into it at first and then give in to the photoshoot, smiling and pouting while Emily yells praise from behind the camera like Kris Jenner at Kim Kardashian's *Playboy* shoot. 'You're doing amazing, sweetie!' and I feel my heart swell with pride at how easily we've slipped into friendly familiarity. Her laugh is surprisingly childish, high and twinkly, like a wind chime.

Emily sends me the pics immediately on WhatsApp, and I upload one to Insta in the hope that it will make Toby jealous or if not actively jealous then at least a bit regretful. I choose the picture where my face is slightly out of focus in a way that makes my lips and eyes look luxuriously, impossibly huge. I caption it with a moon emoji, a wine-glass emoji.

Emily has taken a little plastic baggie out of her dressing-table drawer. 'You don't mind, do you?'

I tell her to go ahead.

A sharp, businesslike sniff and then she pinches at the pink velvet of her nostrils.

'Do you want some?'

'No, thanks.'

I've got to be on my best behaviour tonight, impress Emily with my brightest, sharpest self, and I'm not good with gear at the best of times.

'Suit yourself.'

Six

It's a Ratio Thing

S even thirty pm. The taxi driver keeps looking at Emily in the rear-view mirror, his cloudy eyes lingering over her tits in her low-cut dress. He's in his late forties, greasy hair combed over the balding crown of his head, hair crawling out of his nostrils like he's got a pair of tarantulas stuck up there. It's strange, that a man who would normally repulse me can, at this moment, make me feel so inconceivably jealous that he isn't looking at me.

Maybe my insecurity is palpable. I look over at Emily, her confident posture, shoulders pushed back.

Why does it even matter? I know I look hot. Why do I need a man to turn that knowledge into a fact?

Also, why do I have this nagging, sickening feeling that I've forgotten to do something important?

'I didn't say goodbye to my mum,' I realize out loud, feeling instinctively for the door handle even though the car is in motion.

'Send her a goodnight text,' Emily says.

> **Me:** Hi Mum, just left for some fresh air with Emily. She'll pay for a taxi to take me back. Don't wait up for me x

I know, not exactly my best work.

We arrive at Piccadilly Circus. A flashing rickshaw carrying a hen party is pedalled down the street by a weary biker in a helmet, his speakers blasting out 'WAP' by Cardi B. People are looking at us. A man in a baseball cap stops by a news-stand and aims his phone at us, a minor non-criminal act that somehow crosses a boundary, becomes an eerie violation.

'He thinks he's slick,' Emily says before I'm almost knocked off my feet by a group of football lads piling out of the Angus Steakhouse. I lose her momentarily then spot her again by a roped-off door at the side of a club, her blonde hair like a beacon.

'This is the place,' she says.

'There's no sign,' I say, craning my neck to look around.

'Obviously,' says Emily.

A tall security guard unclips the velvet rope, giving her a sidelong, inscrutable glance. I feel that old, familiar prickle of anxiety, but push it deep inside my stomach and follow her inside.

The woman sitting at the desk wears a green velvet dress in the same shade as the carpet. With the kind of practised smile which is indigenous to people in boutique customer-service jobs, she greets Emily as 'Miss Canon'. Japanese cuisine is in the Red Room, she says, and French in the Aviary. This sounds like something out of *Twin Peaks*, which makes me think of Toby, wonder if he's seen my photo yet. If it made him miss me, if the sight of my black-rimmed eyes gave him flashbacks to the mother of all blowjobs I gave him for his birthday back in February. (Yes, he's a Pisces.)

The wallpaper on the foyer ceiling is covered with cherubs. Fat-armed and sullen-faced, they are knock-off Raphaels posing with garlands of flowers, an arrow, a trumpet. The concentric swirls of the blue sky behind them creates the illusion that they're moving, bobbing around in a counterfeit mosaic heaven.

God sees everything, Constance would always remind me on bad days, when I had come home with swollen eyes after some dickhead in Set 2 Maths had poured Fanta down the back of my shirt, or I was the only person left without a partner in Drama. A comfort that's cooled to a threat with age. God sees everything.

I have that roller-coaster, anti-gravity feeling like I'm upside down. 'Agnes?'

'I was just . . .' I glance up at the ceiling.

Emily tilts her neck half-heartedly. 'I'm starving. Come on.'

We follow the Stepford Wife down the corridor, her hips swaying in green velvet, a black seam in her stockings. She is flawless except for the soles of her Louboutins, which are so worn that the red paint has rubbed off in places. The angels watch us from the vestibule.

'Ever had snails before?' says Emily.

'Never.' But I'd try them, I add silently, thinking of the Year 9 Biology class where I sliced through the slimy spotted belly of a frog with my blue acrylic uniform jumper pushed up to my elbows. Or the day I blew down a foam pipe to inflate the sheep's lung our science department had procured from a local butcher, while the other girls retched in the corner with cries of, 'Miss, the *smell*!'

We have arrived in the Aviary. The first thing that strikes me is the enormous tree in the centre of the circular room. It's not real—there are no roots disturbing the mosaic floor, no fallen leaves or soil debris. It stretches towards the domed ceiling, where coloured lightbulbs have been formulated to cast a dawn-like glow over the room. A quartet of violins fill the air with melodies, and a dreamlike video of flitting birds, blue finches and lilac lovebirds, is being projected onto the ceiling.

'I'm half-expecting Lumière and Cogsworth to jump out with a two-metre jelly on a silver platter,' I say to Emily.

'Who?'

'Grandfather clock and dancing candlestick? *Beauty and the Beast?*'

Emily did not watch Disney cartoons as a child, she tells me. Camilla's hatred of musicals combined with a succession of moody teenage babysitters had her graduating straight to noughties reality TV classics like *The Simple Life.*

A waiter greets us, dressed in a pale yellow waistcoat, white shirt, black tie. He's short and has the childlike hands that I find perverted on a man.

'Hello, Miss Canon,' he says.

'This is Agnes Green.'

'A pleasure, Miss Green.' He shakes my hand, gripping it with his tiny fingers. 'This way, please.'

He leads us to a table made of shining brass, elevated on a podium that we have to climb to reach the seats.

Emily tells him we want champagne and it arrives a minute later. There's the whole ceremony of popping the cork. I have a sudden stabbing panic about how much this is all going to cost, but I drink the champagne anyway. It's too late to stuff the cork back in.

The waiter returns, brandishing a big round platter.

'You like oysters?' Emily asks me.

'I've never had them.'

'Oh, really? They're an aphrodisiac *apparently,*' she says with an eye-roll. 'Try one with some of the mignonette.' She points to a gory-looking sauce. When she goes to the loo I wrap one of the oyster shells in a napkin, emblazoned with 'Club Number Seven' in golden lettering, and put it in my handbag. The oysters are whisked away and small dishes of curled grey-green shells arrive in their place, tiny three-pronged forks placed at their side.

I have never eaten snails before. They look alarmingly like the commonplace garden molluscs I used to prise off the pavement as a kid. I liked the feeling of suction on the back of my hand, the mouthlike sensation against my skin.

'That's garlic butter,' says Emily, tapping the ceramic pot with an oblong of green-speckled white inside it.

I cut a little butter with my fork and stab the snail flesh out of its shell onto my tongue before I can overthink it. The texture is strange, a mixture between fat and cartilage.

Emily reaches for the champagne bottle but our waiter emerges with slightly frenzied efficiency and whisks it out of her hand.

'I do this for you, madam.'

He tops up our glasses, replacing the ice in the bucket with a rattling pour. More dishes arrive, things I've never tried before but find delicious. As we eat, Emily tells me their names: wild turbot, chicken leg stuffed with duck foie gras, pappardelle with grated truffle. My mind does a quick calculation of the numbers in my bank account, flicking through recent payments like a jukebox. This dinner is probably going to cost hundreds. I might just have enough to cover it, if I'm careful and only eat tinned chickpeas for lunch for the rest of the month until payday.

'So what's yours?' I ask her, emboldened by the alcohol and feeling entitled to something from Emily now that she's almost certainly put me in debt. 'Your *brand*, I mean.'

'You can't tell?'

She swills the last of the champagne from her glass then uses it to point towards her outfit. She is wearing a white mini-dress with fluttery bell sleeves, muted pink sandals with silver embossed butterfly wings on the backs of the heels, a Tiffany's silver heart chain bracelet around her wrist. Her eyebrows are fluffy and brushed up with clear gel, then a little bronze eyeshadow, a soft brown wing, a touch of cream liner on her lower lash line. Her lips are soft pink, outlined with matte pencil, a little dab of gloss in the centre.

'I don't know,' I say. I'm looking at her bracelet, thinking about when Jess got a Tiffany's necklace for her sixteenth birthday and I was so jealous it literally burned me inside. 'Angel, goddess, supermodel? All of the above?'

'I'm the Princess.' She delivers this line without the slightest hint of irony, her eyes wide and unblinking. She sighs, examines her nails and continues her explanation in her signature monotone. 'Sexy-on-accident kind of thing. Hyperfeminine, always put together, and a little bit bratty when the occasion calls for it. Some men love a girl who's hard to please.' She sips on her champagne. 'Yeah, I think that's it.' She puts down her glass and takes out her mirror to confirm she looks perfect.

'So working with your mum, what's that like?' she asks me. 'If I had to work with Camilla I'd be locked up by now. We can do about five minutes a day in each other's company before we get into a screaming match.'

I shrug, mutter. 'It's all right, not like it was the plan or anything.' I feel the old sense of panicked uncertainty about the future wash over me. By compulsion I reach into my bag, flick the napkin open and run my fingertips over the ridged oyster shell.

'No?' She tears apart a chunk of bread from the basket between us on the table, and starts massaging one half of it into a ball of condensed dough. 'What *was* the plan?'

'The Olympics,' I sigh, unable to help myself. 'I was a gymnast. Really good, you know? On track for great things but I, um, tore my ACL trying to rollerblade. Like Lana in the White Dress music video. She actually broke an arm doing that, you know?'

Emily sinks her teeth into the doughball and stares at me. She chews her mouthful a little and then swallows, doesn't break eye contact. Her green eyes are boring into mine and I realize I've been staring back when my own start to sting and water. I lose the game blinking at my reflection in the butter knife.

'You lie sometimes,' she says, 'about stupid stuff. Why?'

'What?'

At first I feel like I've misheard her. I don't know what to say. I feel shame warming my cheeks and I know I've gone red. It's embarrassing for someone like Emily to look straight through me.

'It's okay,' she says, laughing her twinkly windchime laugh. 'I lie too, to men all the time, especially when I'm drinking. Spinning a yarn of bullshit and seeing how much of it they'll eat up—have to entertain myself, you know. But I mean, taxidermy? Come on.'

My entire body feels hot. I don't know how to save this. Deny? Admit? She's looking at me with this expression on her face like she knows she has me. She's a bitch, yes, but somehow, I feel I love her.

'I uh . . . I don't know,' I mumble. 'I can never tell my mum the truth about stuff so I guess I've just got into the habit of throwing things out there. I don't know.'

'Well, you need to get better at it,' she says, raising an eyebrow. 'It's amazing you've gotten away with it for so long.'

I shrug.

'How about you tell me something true?' she asks me, her voice low and seductive.

And before I know it I'm telling her all about Toby. My voice catches in my throat when I explain what happened on my birthday, the Snapchat story, the hours spent scrolling his Instagram account.

'I hope you know you deserve better than that Tony guy,' she says, her words slurring slightly. She is looking at me like I'm a work of art, somewhat reverently.

'Toby,' I correct her, 'but thank you.'

'You're young and that counts for a lot,' she says. 'And you're pretty. It's like currency, like . . . a bunch of casino chips in the game of life. You can keep them locked up in the back of a drawer and waste your time with guys like that or you can use them.'

'I want to use them,' I say without thinking, like a reflex.

'Good girl,' she says, winking. 'Welcome to the dark side.' If we were in a TV show this would be the part where she holds out an open palm and offers me a nondescript pill.

'I know where I'm taking you,' she says, clapping her hands, giddy with delight at her own brilliance. 'The only place to be on a Saturday night. Come on, let's go.'

I can't hold it in any longer, the worry I've been stifling, and break out in a cool sweat.

'We need to get the bill, right?' My face and fingertips are hot, pulsing with shame. 'How much do you think we've spent?'

It seems absurd to spend so much on something and have nothing to show for it but a full stomach.

Emily blinks her lovely eyes at me, turquoise in the artificial dawn light. 'It doesn't cost anything,' she says.

'H-how do you mean?'

'We don't *pay*,' she says. She chuckles as if the mere suggestion is ridiculous, beyond comprehension. 'It's a club. Club Number Seven,' she explains. 'Men pay, women don't. It's very, very exclusive. You have to be nominated, seconded and then approved by a personal meeting with the founder.'

Naturally, Emily Canon was approved on sight.

'I think we met for a reason, Agnes Green,' she says in her serious voice. 'I'm a big believer in fate and destiny and all that shit. I think the stars aligned for us.' She grabs my hand across the table. 'Get up, we're leaving.'

She texts relentlessly during the whole Uber journey, filling me in on the contents of the messages while switching between apps with expertly quick fingers: an after-party at the Mayfair Hotel, a friend of hers DJ'ing at Tape later, some people she knows going to Cirque, a guy she's seeing begging her to come to Home House. I wonder how it must feel to have so much going on, every phone contact unfolding endless possibilities, to be known and wanted everywhere, each night fizzing with potential. The only text on my phone is from Constance, a stream of consciousness telling me to write down the taxi driver's number plate, reminding me of the dead bodies in the Wye.

It's past midnight. The word HADES is printed onto the black canopy outside the club, in such dark letters that it is impossible to read unless lit up by the headlights of a slow-moving taxi. There's a woman there wearing a black rollneck and a pair of heeled booties, clutching a clipboard. She seems to be denying entry and changing the ticket price on a seemingly random and nonsensical basis, her pitch high and falsely apologetic.

Right, girls, suuuuuper busy tonight so it's going to be forty pounds each, too much? One millisecond passes. *No worries, have a nice night.*

Hi, angel, nice to see you again. Ten pounds each, please. Pay Riccardo and IDs ready. Have a greeeeat night, hun.

There's a clustery queue of about thirty girls lined up against a railing in front of the black canopy, noticeably white, all in fast-fashion minis and midis, block heels with the clear Perspex straps. There are no men.

'It's a ratio thing,' Emily mutters, following my gaze. 'Join the queue for two seconds. I need to call Eduardo . . . Hi, Eduardo, darling, we're here, outside. Hurry up, will you, it's getting cold.' She leads me by the forearm to the back of the line, then skips up to the entrance, to the visible fury of thirty bodycon-wearing women.

With a swish of the black velvet curtain, Eduardo emerges from the dark mouth of the club. He's good-looking, dark-haired and wearing all black, and he's texting away, the silver ring on his thumb flashing in the white phone light, stopping only to look up and smile occasionally or mutter clipped answers and instructions. Next to him is a man wearing a layered assortment of vests, long-sleeved tops and polo necks, all made out of black fishnet. Soft black liner rings his watery grey eyes. He looks like a strange kind of techno Viking.

'Emily!' Eduardo calls out softly, in a thick Italian accent. 'Emily, come! Quickly.'

She embraces both of them and beckons for me to join her.

The girls watch with envy as we bypass the queue. The clipboard woman turns away to hiss something into her walkie-talkie while Eduardo slips two tiny gold cards to the guy in the payment booth. I assume that's our tickets taken care of.

'That's Eduardo,' she whispers into my hair, as I join her at the front of the queue, 'my promoter. And Sebastian, he's a photographer.'

'So good to see you, darling.' Emily kisses Eduardo's cheeks again. 'This is Agnes.'

'Well, hello.' He presses his cheeks against mine and makes a 'mwah' sound each time. His breath is gum-masked whisky. 'Welcome.'

'Look, guys, sorry but I've got to shoot off, my taxi's here.'

The Viking pushes past Eduardo out onto the street in search of his Uber.

Emily turns and pouts after him, 'Already? We've just got here.'

'I'll call you tomorrow,' he shouts back, climbing down off the kerb and into a Mercedes.

'Usual table?' Emily asks Eduardo.

'Yes, champagne and vodka there, anything else you want just ask . . .'

'Just ask Terrence, yes, yes, I know,' says Emily. Then turning to me, 'Let's go, come on.'

Under a maelstrom of red and indigo lights, Emily passes me a drink which tastes aniseedy and is strong and soon makes me feel as though I've made it to the centre of the world, to the white-hot core of everything bright and beautiful. 50 Cent's 'Candy Shop' is pulsing through me when a man with shoulder-length hair and yellow tinted sunglasses grabs my hand and twirls me like a toddler. I am floating on a river-tide of champagne and Valentino. I catch sight of myself in the mirror: my corseted, plumped-up chest, my eyes in the crimson strobes, my lips like a knife wound, red on red on red. I feel something stirring in me. A unity of inward and outward. A sense of rightness.

Emily entertains the men who approach her—for a while. She smiles sweetly, holds their hands and two-steps with them to the beat before dismissing them with a blown kiss, like a tap on the end of a lit cigarette to dispel the ash. They hold out their phones for her details. Number? Instagram? Email? She shakes her head and they sigh dreamily, still a little giddy when they eventually give up and skulk away.

Cardi B's 'I Like It' is playing and we are spinning. Emily's blonde hair whips my face. Her perfume is Delina La Rosée. She reapplies it liberally whenever she nips to the loo for a coke break. It smells edible, like rosewater macaroons or jelly gourmet sweets.

At around 4 a.m. the ceiling begins raining with glitter. And . . . paper? Aeroplanes or little origami parachutes or something. I reach down and pick one of them up off the floor to inspect it, turn to Emily and say in disbelief, 'Someone is throwing money.'

There are twenties and fifties falling all around us, blowing about on the booth seats in the breeze from the air conditioner, clinging to the moist bodies of the ice-chilled Grey Goose bottles. Emily, laughing, stoops to grab a fistful of notes, then stuffs them down the front of my dress. It feels sharp and ticklish against my skin, like a cluster of dried leaves.

She grabs my tits with both hands. 'You've got implants!'

I pull the money out from the top of my dress and zip it up in my handbag.

A man in chef's whites with a tattooed neck is kissing Emily's hand. He is in love with her, she explains to me. We're in a steel kitchen with cold light, a couple of ravers crouching in front of the fridge, considering some clingfilmed pizza slices with pointed acrylic nails. I vaguely remember descending a neon flight of stairs to get to this room.

Chef's Whites is holding Emily's forearm between his thumb and index finger, turning it towards the naked bulb and delicately brushing his lips against the fine blonde hairs that cover it.

'He's in love with me,' Emily says to me again, before grabbing his face and shouting, 'We want crack babies!' into his ear.

He grins, stares at her mouth and licks his lips. 'All right, Em, anythin' for you. You'll have to move for me, darlin',' he says to the model with a buzzcut who's sitting on the counter. I assume model, because even though she's clearly wasted she looks like she's in a heroin-chic photoshoot, her smudged black eye shadow, razor cheekbones and extravagantly high Versace heels giving her an air of sultry dignity. A man with pink hair and several rows of chunky silver rings puts his arm around her and kisses her shorn head.

'Dude,' Chef's Whites barks at him. 'Come on!'

Pink Hair puts his index finger up to hush him. 'Give me five minutes, okay. Come on, man.'

The chef throws his hands up. 'Ay-yi-yi!' He pulls Emily in by the waist. 'Five minutes, gorgeous, all right? I'll get the stuff.'

Emily bats her eyelashes at him as he leaves. I'm starting to notice how she acts around men to get what she wants out of them. Her alertness and directness become camouflaged, and a watery hypnotic glaze replaces the laser focus in her eyes.

'You good?' she asks me, taking her baggie out and snorting off the tip of her pinkie fingernail.

'I'm good.'

The chef returns with a bottle of passionfruit vodka, gripping three shot-glasses between his scarred knuckles. Emily's hand disappears into the fridge and comes back cradling a cold magnum of Veuve like a newborn. She uncorks it, sprays everyone in a rocket of white foam. The sound of popping champagne draws attention, and a cluster of people descend on us from the staircase like a plague of thin and fashionable gnats. A raven-haired girl in an Oh Polly mini-dress picks up the bottle and drinks from it. A couple of men, their hair combed in a way that indicates they're not native to these parts, have followed her and her friends, lured by the overpowering smell of Baccarat Rouge, and stand nearly close enough to press their suited crotches up against the raven girl's satin-covered bottom.

The girl turns around in protest, catches a glimpse of the watch on one of their wrists, then turns her attention back to the champagne bottle with a casual kind of resignation.

'See?' Emily whispers. 'It's a ratio thing. We show up and the men with money follow.'

In amongst all this I notice that the chef has a boner. I can't tell if Emily notices, her glazed eyes betraying no emotion.

Emily wants to go upstairs and watch the sun come up from the rooftop, but I need to pee.

'Hurry up,' she says, 'I don't want to miss it.'

The toilet attendant is asleep with her face on the countertop. I put one of the £50 notes into her tip jar, then collapse onto the toilet seat, too tired and tipsy to do my usual squat-and-hover.

Scrolling through Instagram while I pee, I check Toby's profile for a final time. One of the recent photos is of him sitting on the sofa in his living room. There is a deliberate composition to it—an angle that flatters his cheekbones, light coming in through the blinds and casting warpaint stripes across his face—which makes me suspect it was taken by a female hand. I know this room well, and the picture strikes a pang in my heart, not quite of fondness but of familiarity. The bong full of cloudy water on the coffee table, the grinder, rolling papers, a half-drunk bottle of Lucozade, an empty plate with the gravy practically fossilized on. I bet that reggae was being played at an ear-shattering volume in the background—he's *that* kind of white boy.

Emily comes into the toilets calling my name. 'Come on,' she chastises.

I press the Block button on impulse. There is no crescendo and no dramatic finale, I just know in my heart that I'm done. 'I'm coming,' I call through to Emily. 'I'm coming.'

I follow her up a long metallic staircase that creaks with each step, through the heavy Alarm Activating Door which Emily reassures me will absolutely not activate an alarm. Up out onto the flat roof which is cold and breezy. There are a couple of bartenders and waiters with their shirts unbuttoned at the top collar, the women out of their shoes, smoking roll-up cigarettes. Emily puts her arm around me and we huddle close together against the chill and watch the sun come up. We look down at slate grey tiles on the roof of the nearby building, lilac in the dawn light. Rows of terracotta chimneypots and dark satellite dishes. A black cab crawling sleepily like a beetle down the street. Silver skyscrapers in the distance, the ghostly London Eye, and a hundred jagged cranes. The first chimes of birdsong.

Seven

Pimps and Hoes

I am rushing, tiptoed and hunchbacked, along the back row of the United Pentecostals congregation in the direction of the toilets. I almost trip over Yemi Oluwale's feet on my way. Pregnant and beaming, with a lot of black box braids piled up in a scarf on the top of her head, she hauls her snotty-nosed toddler up onto her lap to let me pass. He glowers at me, a spit bubble between his parted lips.

I weave past the worshippers, their eyes closed and arms outstretched like zombies I need to avoid in a video game. Phyllis and her stiff grey coiffure are staring me down from across the aisle with a look that could freeze water. I mouth 'period' at her and clutch my stomach.

I almost apologize to my own reflection when I walk into the toilets, not recognizing the bare-faced girl in a shapeless cream dress. I turn the lock hastily and answer Emily's call with my back pressed up against the cold cubicle door.

'Well, if it isn't my little it-girl in training,' she says. 'You made it back all right then?'

Barely. Constance was waiting downstairs when I got back at half six in the morning, having napped, tactically puked, and downed several Ibuprofen in a train carriage where I was the only passenger. There would have been hell to pay if she hadn't fallen asleep in the armchair. Like I said, her sleeping patterns have been a real saving grace for my social life. This morning, I told her I was home three hours earlier than I actually was and she couldn't prove otherwise.

'Mhmm, what's going on?' I'm so hungover my brain feels like it's swimming in my skull.

'I've been working,' she says. Her voice somehow *sounds* fresh and spritely. I do a mental calculation of all the lines I saw her snort last night, the champagne, and begin to doubt whether Emily is actually human.

'*You?*' I tease her. 'Working?'

'Don't rub it in,' she says. 'I had to be on set at nine a.m.—it was a last-minute. Where are you?'

Of course, Emily's "working" is different to mine—hers involves make-up artists and manicurists and designer clothing, not biohazard spills and scrubbing.

'I'm at church.'

'Oh, yeah, forgot it was Sunday. Ever since I started doing the image thing at Cuckoo on Wednesdays my whole week's been thrown out of whack.'

I sigh, imagining a life where I don't remember what the days of the week are.

'I'm actually calling to invite you to lunch tomorrow.'

And suddenly I'm sobered up. 'Mhmm, where?'

'London.'

'Emily, I can't *leave* The Wasteland in the middle of the day. I've got shifts.'

'Agnes Green, when are you going to wake up?'

I lean forward to look at my bloodshot eyes, dark circles, sallow cheeks in the bathroom mirror, and manage a whimper. Good question.

'Do you know,' Emily continues in a steady voice, 'how much money I made by going out to lunch last month?'

I do not.

'Eight. Grand.'

'Eight . . . thousand . . .'

'Precisely,' Emily says. 'It's no joke. These dates, they aren't just for fun. They're a payday. Come on. You have to admit, it'd be better than cleaning.'

She's got me there. 'Not hard to be . . .'

'Exactly. Meet me tomorrow at one p.m. I'll send you the address.'

She hangs up and I make my way back into the foyer, still too wrecked to process what I've just agreed to. Worship is over, the keyboard music twinkling on softly as Phyllis reads off a PowerPoint slide, hand gripping the microphone, hairsprayed grey bob vibrating from her over-articulation of each word.

A wife of noble character who can find? She is worth far more than rubies.
Her husband has full confidence in her and lacks nothing of value.
She brings him good, not harm, all the days of her life . . .

I linger in the foyer feeling uneasy. Sometimes, listening to Phyllis talk, I get paranoid that she knows my secrets. As her eyes scan the congregation, her voice trembling with all the gravitas of an American Megachurch preacher, my heart rate ramps up so high I can hear the blood pulsing in my ears. It's so deeply entrenched in me, the Fear of God, so much more strongly than the belief.

The congregation spills out of the door for tea and coffee in the playground, served from a big metal boiler into squeaky Styrofoam cups. The United Pentecostals host their church services in a local primary school. Across the road is a council building with green sea-glass coloured windows and blinking CCTV cameras, a cement mixer tilted up on its hinges in the car park like a dog on its hind legs. The children sprint towards the jungle gym, which I personally think looks more like a prison yard, with its weathered heap of tyres and metal bars propped up in the bark pit. May slid easily into June today, and it's warmer than ever.

Constance emerges beside me.

'Cousin Louise called me,' I say, surprising myself because the words come out before I've made up my mind to say them. 'She wants to see if I can babysit tomorrow, there's something she needs to do. Do you think I'll be able to get holiday from Finch?' Finch—or, Mrs Finch, as she insists on being called—owns the cleaning agency which employs us.

This babysitting alibi is a dangerous one because it's easily disproved and relies on Constance not talking to Cousin Louise for the rest of the month. High risk, high reward and all that.

She agrees, unsurprisingly. The only time my mother ever encourages me to skip work is if I get the opportunity to look after babies instead. I think she hopes that I'll catch some maternal urges and decide to settle down with a local youth leader who plays the ukulele and is saving himself for marriage. 'I don't see why not,' she beams. 'Any trouble and I can cover for you, darlin'.'

The next day

My wardrobe is stuffed with the polyester and acrylic of high-street sale racks past, nothing to compare with the red Valentino. It's hot and humid but I think it might rain later. All of this adds up to an inevitable conclusion.

> **Me:** I have nothing to wear to lunch
> **Me:** Not a joke Emily. Please help
> **Me:** Emily I need to get the train soon please answer

If don't leave now I'll never make it on time. I'm wearing a black midi-skirt and a white shirt, unbuttoned and with the sleeves rolled up in the hopes of looking a little less library-work-experience and a little more London-Paris-Milan.

On my way out, I decide to check on Marlena, and push the door open to her bedroom. It adjoins mine but I haven't heard a peep out of her since revision season started. Sure enough, she's hunched over her desk with her back to me, armed with a green highlighter. Pinned to her corkboard are equations written out in her boxy scrawl. A3 posters with titles in neat bubble writing. Electronegativity. Shapes, Polarity and Intermolecular Forces.

'Busy,' she says.

'Can I come in?'

Silence means yes. I edge in past the wardrobe and crouch on the floor—there is nowhere else to sit, as her bed is folded up against the wall in the daytime to make room for her desk. Seeing her having to study in these conditions breaks my heart a bit. It didn't matter for me—I was barely capable of conscious thought when A levels came round—but Marlena is different. Marlena deserves to study in a huge, oak-panelled library with rolling spiral staircases and vintage bureaus. Constance can't afford a laptop for her, so she has to use her smartphone to look up facts and copies everything out using biro and paper. The clump of banknotes from the Hades dance floor is currently stashed in my drawer. If I can find £250 more, she's getting a MacBook.

'Lena . . . ,' I am trying to keep my tone light. 'Is it obvious I've got a two-day hangover?'

'You don't have to get quite so drunk every time you go out, you know?' she says, eyes pointedly fixed to her textbook. 'One of these days Mum's gonna catch you.'

'Not for you to worry about, Lena,' I say quietly.

She sighs. 'Do whatever you like—I just don't want to deal with the drama. I've got to focus this year.' She looks at me over her shoulder, taking in the outfit and my full face of make-up. 'Babysitting for cousin Louise, are we? You can't fool me, I've got an IQ of one hundred and forty-four, remember?'

'My little genius,' I say. 'It's just a little white lie told for the greater good. I promise. And Lena, I am proud of you.'

'Oh, really? What am I planning to study?'

'Natural Sciences,' I tell her, my heart swelling a little. 'At Cambridge.'

'You remembered.'

'Of course I remembered. Go on—test me on something else. Test me on . . . respiration.'

'Very funny,' she says. 'I'm busy now, thanks for dropping by.'

Already lost in her work, she doesn't turn back to see me blow her a kiss before I pull the door closed. My head is pounding.

On my way to The Wasteland's train station, I stop in the pharmacy and buy a red lipstick from the NYX Lip Lingerie line using my cleaning money. Matte liquid, in the shade Untameable. I can't tell if I'm being para or if the woman at the checkout desk really does have a concerned look on her face as she handles the lipstick tube like it's a stick of dynamite.

'Dress-up party,' I mutter, 'for my friend's birthday. Pimps and Hoes.'

She nods, 'Makes sense, love,' and asks if I'd perhaps be interested in some red stiletto-shaped press-on nails.

I politely decline—my nails are bitten down to stubs these days—and tap my bank card on the reader.

Emily: Sorry angel I just woke up
Emily: Something classy, doesn't really matter
Emily: Remember we're meeting at Nobu, in Hyde Park

Me: Already en route, I hope this is okay
[Photo Attachment]

Emily: Lol you look like you're cosplaying as a sexcretary

Me: Is that bad? It's the best I could do

Emily: Actually no
Emily: You know what? He'll probably like it

Me: Wait what
Me: Who will like it?
Me: Emily
Me: Emily, who?
Me: Fuck you
Me: I'll be there in an hour

London. The Tube is criminally muggy and reeks of BO, hence the accusatory side-eye glances being hurled along the carriage aisle. Even worse, 'Or Nah' by Ty Dolla $ign, ft. The Weeknd, is filtering loudly through someone's headphones, which basically qualifies as public masturbation. I apply the lipstick using my phone's front camera as a mirror and feel better with it on, not as invincible as when Emily made me up but less vulnerable than before. I look up to see a man in a suit watching me. He has a weak chin, blending without distinction into his neck. I tilt my chin down and blink up through my eyelashes at him, hold his gaze. The Look.

He raises his eyebrow and tilts his head towards the overhead poster. It's commissioned by Transport for London and has **Staring is Sexual Harassment** blazoned across it in hot pink capitals. I duck my head instinctively, then realize . . . he's flirting with me. He smiles, holds up his left hand (wedding ring noted) and points at the Tube route mapped out above my head.

He mouths, *Which stop?*

I hold up three fingers.

When we arrive at Hyde Park Corner I oblige him, tap eleven random digits into his phone keypad and tell him I hope he calls. Then I climb the Tube steps up into the daylight.

*

It's the kind of airless, intensely sunny day that compels Londoners to undress by virtue of some DNA hardwiring. I pass a protein-shake bro, presumably on his way back from a training session judging by his gear and beetroot flush. His muscled hands twitch at the hem of his gym shirt as he resists the instinct to strip it off. I'm telling you, it's primal.

I spot her outside Nobu, the blonde dressed head to toe in white, and call out her name. 'Emily!' She waves at me, her eyes shielded behind cat's-eye sunglasses with white rims. I walk through a red light in my impatience to get to her.

'You look amazing,' I say. I almost bite the words back before I say them because surely Emily doesn't need to be told this. The words must have become trite and lost all meaning to her.

Cursive letters reading *Angel* rest on her collarbone, harnessed by a fine gold chain. She wears high white trousers and a see-through white top with no straps. The porelessness of her skin is unsettling, the kind of perfection that only exists in glossy Los Angeles TV series where the high schoolers are played by models in their thirties. I had always chalked the secret of their glowing complexions up to post-shooting edit-room wizardry but now I'm being forced to reconsider.

'Thanks, babe. Nice lipstick, by the way.' She points to a man who I had assumed was a lingering passer-by, ogling at her under the guise of waiting for the lights to change. 'This is Matthew.'

So this is him. Actually quite attractive in a dapper upper-class alien sort of way. A cross between Matt Damon in *The Talented Mr. Ripley*, adding a decade or so to his age, and Benedict Cumberbatch in, well, anything. An angular skull with a cubesque forehead, thin lips but pleasingly high cheekbones. The thick square glasses of a middle-aged man who considers himself more fashion-conscious than his peers. He wears a beautiful navy suit with a white shirt underneath, no tie, and carries a dark brown leather laptop case with the letters MCM mono-grammed onto it. He must be the only man in London who looks completely unflustered by the heat, a quality I've always admired in people.

Emily offers no more details by way of an introduction, and neither does he. He could be her stepbrother for all I know, though it seems unlikely based on the way he presses a hand to the small of Emily's back as we enter the restaurant.

We appear to be inside a spaceship. The waiters, dressed in sexless navy pyjama-style suits, are serious, free of make-up and tall. They move gracefully between the open kitchen and the tables, depositing plates with the precision of contemporary dancers. We're sitting right up against the floor-to-ceiling window, which presents a vertiginous drop down to the street below. A couple seated nearby—nondescript, grey-haired, in latticed leather sandals—keep turning to look at us. It's not exactly unusual for people to stare at Emily, but when my eyes meet the woman's, her liquid blue irises in yellowing whites, she puts her hand over her mouth and whispers something to her husband.

'You've got to have a cocktail,' Emily says, oblivious to the old couple watching us from two metres away.

'Oh, yes. Do have whatever you like,' says Matthew. His voice is achingly posh and sort of slouches over the vowels, as though it's a great effort to manoeuvre his lips around them. He flags down our waitress with a languid wave of his hand.

I look helplessly at Emily, because we both know that these days I like whatever she tells me I should. 'Two lychee martinis,' she tells the waitress without looking at the menu. 'What are you having, Matthew?'

'Just a water for me. It's back to work after this,' he says.

'So what do you do . . . Matthew? Do you work in . . . fashion?' I don't know how to talk to him except to ask mundane questions like I'm playing Guess Who with Constance and Marlena.

Emily and Matthew look at each other and laugh, hers twinkly and involuntary, his low and matter-of-fact.

'Law,' he says neutrally. 'And luxury goods, I suppose, where this one's concerned'—he glances at Emily, straight-backed in her chair, indecently beautiful.

What the hell does that mean?

'Well, you do have great taste,' replies Emily, resting her chin on her hand, all coy and sanguine. She starts counting out a list on her left hand. 'Restaurants, women, shoes, women, handbags, women—did I miss anything?'

Oh. That's what it means.

He reaches out and gently taps the gold bracelet on her wrist. 'What about this old thing? Though I preferred the platinum.' He's slung his suit jacket on the back of his chair and rolled up his shirtsleeves and I can't help but notice his beautiful forearms. Elegant but strong and knotted with veins.

'Maybe you'll have to take me back there,' she says. She shifts a little closer to him on the curved leather cushion. I turn over my shoulder and see that the beige woman is watching us unashamedly.

Our drinks arrive, two martini glasses with soft, fleshy lychees impaled on dangerous-looking metal skewers, an empty glass and a tall bottle of water.

Matthew takes a swig from the glass of water the waitress has poured. 'Sorry, Agnes, nothing terribly exciting, I'm afraid. She's teasing you. I work in law.'

I think maybe Emily's in some sort of trouble. I try to catch her eye but she's looking at Matthew, doing her come-hither drowning-siren eye thing. 'What kind?'

Emily gives me a stern look. I know I'm scraping the conversational barrel but I'm actually interested. Well, suspicious.

'Mostly corporate,' Matthew says, tearing his eyes away from Emily for a few seconds to respond to me.

'Stop being boring, Agnes,' Emily says quickly. 'No one wants to talk about work.' She refocuses, her voice becoming as sweet and runny as the honey she spoons into her tea. 'I think you should have a drink,

Matthew. I love it when you drink. Remember how much fun we had at the Arts Club that time?'

'I remember,' he says pleasantly, 'and don't think I don't know what you're up to. I *also* remember that subsequent trip to the Dior shop.'

'They gave us so much champagne.'

'They didn't want *me* to see the bill. They were probably in on it—you called ahead.'

'Come on,' she urges, her hand grazing his thigh. 'Have a drink with us, just one.'

Matthew smiles and shakes his head. 'All right, all right. You order for me then. Happy?'

'You know me, Matty, I'm never satisfied.'

'And what about you?' Matthew makes a noticeable effort to stop gazing at Emily and acknowledge me. 'Do you like giving us men a hard time like Lady Emilia here?'

I don't know how to answer him, because I give men an *easy* time, the easiest, replying to their texts in seconds and memorizing their desires so I can repeat them back by rote like an obliging cocktail waitress. Maybe I've been going about things all wrong.

'The black cod, we've got to have the black cod.' Emily orders food for the table. 'And the yellowtail jalapeno, popcorn shrimp, lobster tempura with the honey sauce.' Just when I think she's ordered everything she possibly can, she spots something else on the menu and says, 'We'd better have that too.' But when the dishes come she takes a bite from each of them and then mashes up the remains on her plate with the spears of her fork like it's an art project.

Halfway through the meal, Matthew takes a white envelope out of his pocket and puts it on the napkin next to Emily. She smoothly drops it into her bag without taking her eyes off her plate. I remember her words in the kitchen the other day. *Discretion is queen.*

'I'll be just a minute,' she says, excusing herself.

Then Matthew and I are alone. We are alone and my mouth is full of silky cod. I understand now why Emily decimates her food into tiny nuggets—it's hard to look seductive with hamster cheeks. I try not to panic, don't want to choke to death all over the white tablecloth, then chew so fast I almost run out of breath. Swallow, smile. Perhaps I've been a bit over-zealous with the food—it feels as though the honey sauce from the lobster is curdling in my stomach.

In the minutes since Emily left, Matthew has relaxed back in his chair. His jaw is tilted like he's about to say something important, and he's studying my face. 'I'm glad Emily brought you along today, she said I would like you.'

'She did? What did she say?' I mentally kick myself for making it so obvious that I'm gagging for a compliment.

'Just that you're attractive. Funny. And new to all this.'

As I suspected, this lunch is an induction into sugaring. Baptism by seafood. I imagine Emily and Matthew dressed in priestly robes, dipping their hands into the font and sprinkling my face with spicy garlic seasoning from the scallops . . . Speaking of hands, his are beautiful, and I'm suddenly distracted by an overwhelming desire for him to touch me with them.

'I like your clothes,' he says, gesturing at my white-and-black Zara get-up. 'It's classic. Very Anna Karina.' Emily was right.

'I'm a sucker for a French film,' I say, and by the way his eyes warm a little, his jaw muscle relaxing, I can tell that this reference was a test and that I have passed it.

'I tell you what, darling,' he says. I feel a subtle but growing hint of excitement in my belly at the word *darling*. It truly is sickening how easily I'm won over by a term of endearment spoken by a man I find attractive. 'I'll give you my number. We'll go for lunch sometime. We'll go to Isabel, or wherever you like. Whatever kind of food you like. I should warn you I'm a gift giver,' he's watching me closely, the grin on his face widening. 'Look at you. I'll have to take you everywhere so everyone can see how gorgeous you are.'

How am I supposed to say no to that?

When I imagined this moment, I had expected a drastic internal battle, a dark night of the soul. But this—this feels second-nature. This feels easy. This feels like something I want.

'If it's fine with Emily, it's fine with me,' I say. The last thing I want to do is piss her off and I don't know how these things work. Do we *share*? Is it the more the merrier?

He holds out his phone for me to put my number in and then he calls me beautiful. I can barely look him in the eye.

Beautiful. In school, being blonde was a prerequisite for beautiful— we were culturally still on Paris Hilton and not yet onto Kim K, so I was never even in the running. The way Matthew's looking at me, attentively, admiringly, it makes me feel as though I'm a girl like Emily or even one of the women in a Helmut Newton photograph—supremely confident, powerful, as though I too can suck all the colour out of a room and draw people to me like a magnet.

Emily returns with her sunglasses on. 'Time for a bit of shopping, Matty?'

The bill comes with three shots of vodka which we down, while the beige woman from the nearby table watches us leave, her lips pressed tightly together. I meet her gaze and she flinches, reaching for her glass of water. As we're leaving it suddenly strikes me, she reminds me of Phyllis, disapproval wafting off her like a high-silage perfume.

We hail down a black cab to the Gucci store on Old Bond Street. While Emily looks impassive behind her sunglasses, I sit with my nose pressed up against the glass, watching out of the window like a tourist. I've never driven by car through central London before. It turns the volume of the bustling streets right down to mute, makes me feel like we're inside a snow globe, a silent glass orb protecting us from the fever-pitch swarm of Piccadilly. Money makes everything soft, I think.

The store smells like the fresh paper of newly assembled gift-boxes. Shoes and bags are displayed on plush burgundy cushions. Jewellery in the red, green and gold hues of the Byzantine era gleams behind glass museum cases like the crown jewels. The sales assistants are on us from the moment we enter, following each of us around at a measured distance, like well-groomed shadows in their black uniforms.

Emily spots something she wants in the first five minutes, a white leather handbag with a Bambi-esque deer embroidered onto the top flap. She hooks it over her shoulder and arches her back in the full-length mirror to see the effect against her all-white ensemble.

I drift to the rack nearby. There's a beautiful blood-red leather bag dangling from a ceramic mannequin hand—and I mean *beautiful*, bag-of-dreams, a bag that you want to wear like an extension of your own body.

I peek at the price tag out of curiosity. £2,800.

'Everything all right, madam? Is there anything you'd like me to get you?' a willowy shop assistant croons.

'I'm fine, absolutely fine, thanks. I'm just waiting for my friend,' I say very quickly, and wander back to the mirror, swinging my hands at my sides and feeling like a spare part.

Matthew returns from his exploration of the mens-wear department. 'Looks like Emily's already fallen in love with something,' he says. 'Agnes. You don't want to try anything on?'

'It's all so . . . tasteful,' I say. 'Elegant, gorgeous, etc. Not my style at all.'

'Oh, really? I think I'd have to disagree with you there. Go on,' he whispers mischievously into my ear. 'Whatever you want. Don't even look at the price tag.'

He has to take a call. He crosses over to the corner of the shop and turns back to wave at me, smirking.

I wave back. Emily glares at me and I know she's trying to tell me to *rein it in, play it cool*. I gather myself. Remind myself to play the part. The Femme Fatale. What does *she* want? I stroll back to the manne-quin, pausing again by the red leather bag on its heavy gold chain.

'Let me get that for you.' The assistant, who is petite and red-haired, picks up the purse and presents it by the handle, gestures towards one of several tall mirrors attached to the shop pillars.

I see that Emily's bag is packaged and ready to go.

'I love it!' she calls out. 'You should get that. It's perfect.'

I join her at the counter while the assistant goes off to fetch a fresh bag from the stock room.

I watch Matthew round the aisles with the alert, edgy moves of a snow panther. When he spots us waiting he strides over and unceremoniously hands Emily a Montblanc leather cardholder, pausing his phone call briefly to mouth *Amex* at us.

*

We kiss Matthew goodbye and watch as he clambers into a black cab, shielding his eyes from the sun.

'He's such a nice guy, isn't he?' says Emily, closing her bronzer with a snap and tossing it with the brush into the carrier bag. 'Come on, let's get a taxi to my place. I want you to meet my flatmates. You'll love them, especially Sara.'

As she takes off in the direction of the Uber meeting point I jog after her. 'Emily, wait, *what the fuck* was that? You have to explain.'

'Explain what?'

'Well, what the fuck just happened? Who *is* that guy? And why didn't you tell me about him beforehand?'

She stops in her tracks then, takes her sunglasses off, and looks at me. I'm reminded of Camilla and her indecipherable gaze. Patronizing or short-sightedness? In Emily's case I think I know the answer. 'Why does it matter?' she says, with an easy shrug. 'I wanted to meet you for lunch. I fancied sushi. And then I thought, naturally, why spend our money when we can spend his? You had a nice time, right?'

'Well . . . yes, but . . .'

I keep thinking about his hand on my upper arm as we kissed goodbye, fingers pressing into my flesh.

'Then we're good,' she says. She takes out the white envelope that Matthew had passed her at the restaurant. 'Oh, and before I forget— here's your lunch money.'

'My *lunch money*?' I snort. 'What, like, for sandwiches? Milk and cookies?'

She checks her reflection in a jewelled pocket mirror. 'No, you idiot,' she says, deliberately missing my sarcasm. 'It's the money he gives me for going to lunch with him.'

Cocking her head to the side, she produces a bronzer compact and a little portable kabuki brush and starts applying it to my cheekbones.

'Good colour on you,' she pronounces. 'Well, go on and open it, for God's sake.'

Inside the envelope is £300.

'No fucking way.'

Why am I so surprised? This was the deal all along. I just wasn't expecting it to happen so suddenly—the suited man, and now this crisp white envelope which is starting to make everything feel just a bit too real.

'Stop screwing up your face and stay still,' she says, giving my cheeks a final swipe with the bronzer. 'There—all done! I'd split it,' she says, 'but, seeing as you're a first-timer . . .'

'So he pays for the lunch, buys you a gift then pays you *as well*?'

'Obviously. Matty's like an old friend, you know,' she says slyly. 'We've been doing this for a year. Same old story with him, trapped in a loveless marriage and all that. Don't believe a word of it but it makes them feel better to set the scene, we can all pretend we're good people then, blah, blah, blah. Fun, right?'

'Emily, it's *loads*. Three hundred pounds for an hour of eating at a nice restaurant.'

She seems buoyed by this statement, and adds, 'Five hundred if he's really feeling generous. It's not like winning the lottery or anything, but it's hair money at least.'

'Hair money?'

'The highlights and the Olaplex and my blow-outs. Plus I like it too, you know, the attention. Most of these guys are somebodies and you can have them by the balls—I could call in favours from all kinds, trust me. I was seeing this guy from the Home Office for a while—two gin martinis and he'd start running his mouth, I started getting worried they were gonna Marilyn Monroe me.'

'*Jesus.*'

'Yeah,' she says, smirking. 'But the thing is, these guys have way, *way* more to lose than we do so they're super discreet. You don't have to worry about anything getting out.'

I nod, taking it in. This is reassuring. I feel less like I'm about to make the most terrible decision of my life, and am starting to think this might just be the best thing that has ever happened to me.

'Congratulations, Agnes Green,' Emily says, putting her sunglasses back on with a flourish. 'You just survived your first sugaring date.'

Eight

Off to the Races

The flat Emily rents with a group of models is part of a tall, Victorian-looking block in South Kensington. There are dozens of flights of stairs and no lift, a thin wooden banister and frosted windows on each landing, which rattle in their panes like there are ghosts following us on the way up.

She turns the key in the lock and ushers me in. 'Have a seat. You want coffee?' she says, talking to me but gazing at herself in the mirror on the wall by the front door. 'We have a machine.'

I say yes please and sit down on the cracked black leather sofa in the living room while Emily goes to make drinks.

'Hey!' A tall, thin girl with ice-blonde hair walks energetically into the room. 'I'm Sara, you must be Agnes.'

She sits down on the sofa next to me and I notice that she smells of something chemical, like nail varnish remover or medical-grade skincare cream. Constance would say 'she looks like she eats a slice a' toast for supper'. Bony legs in flimsy grey jersey shorts, thick dark Cara Delevingne eyebrows, fluffy white hair with black roots and fraying ends. Though she's a model like Emily, she could also be any English Literature student from King's College, sitting on that sofa nursing a hangover with a plummy accent and chipped black nail polish.

'I'm feeling a bit shit after last night,' she tells me in a mock-whisper. I realize that the chemical smell I noticed earlier isn't nail varnish remover, it's vodka. 'Emily said you're coming out with us later, right?'

I nod. 'I'm surprised *you're* feeling up to it.'

She points to her face. The skin on her lower lip is white and peeling. '*This?* Oh, no, all I need is an espresso and to dunk my face in a bowl of iced water. We're going to have so much fun tonight. Did Emily tell you about me?'

'She didn't,' I confess.

'Typical,' she says with a forced giggle. 'That little bitch. We met on a photoshoot four years ago. God, what was it . . . some lingerie line. It was so embarrassing because I'd forgotten to shave my pits and I was asking around the models, like, "Help! I need a razor, like, now." And Emily had this whole little, like, kit of a razor and hair removal cream, and wax strips, and I was like, "this bitch", and we've been friends since.'

'What is she going on about?' says Emily, coming in with a tray of two mismatched mugs and an espresso cup.

'Just telling Agnes the story of how we met and fell in love,' says Sara, taking her dainty white espresso cup off the tray and pressing it to her lips.

'Oh, you mean the day you started stalking me on Instagram and leaving comments on all my stories until I caved and invited you to drinks?'

'She's right,' says Sara through slurps of caffeine. 'I am pretty much obsessed with her.'

'Everyone is,' replies Emily evenly.

'Good morning, beautiful people,' comes a serious voice from the doorway. It's a girl with dark brown skin and thick hair to her waist. She is wearing a 1920s vintage lace chemise the colour of a duck's egg, and has a matching ribbon tied around the crown of her head in a big bow.

'It's the afternoon!' Sara says, dissolving into slightly manic giggles as the girl squeezes in next to her.

'This is Yomawu,' says Emily.

Yomawu stretches out her hand. Formal. I give it a gentle squeeze. She has enormous eyes, high full cheekbones, doll's lips, a long lithe neck. I realize I've been staring, avert my eyes.

'Nice outfit. Very . . . preppy,' Yomawu says, referring to my secretary look. 'Where're you from?' Her accent is faint but I recognize in it the unmistakable melody of Ghana.

'I'm half Caribbean. My mum is from St Vincent,' I say. 'She moved over here in the nineties.' There is the other half of my lineage to explain, but of course, I leave that part out. The only thing I know about my father is that he was biracial and left when I was still a baby.

Yomawu nods placidly, not seeming to register my omission. 'Where's Kiki?' she asks.

Sara tells us Kiki is sleeping. Knocked out on diphenhydramine and melatonin. Not to be disturbed till nightfall. 'That means she's not working,' Sara's voice, which was trembling with delight till now, steadies itself. 'Kiki works nearly every day. We have the same agent but they've all got fucking favourites.'

'You know yesterday she actually told me I might get lucky one day and start getting direct bookings like she does?' Yomawu rolls her eyes. '*Gucci?*' She spots the white carrier bags propped up on the floor by the coffee table.

'Yeah,' I say, blushing inexplicably. 'Just a new bag.'

'Let's see it.'

I unfurl my Gucci bag with its blood-red leather and double-G emblem. It is the most expensive thing I've ever owned and it was bought for me by a stranger on a total whim.

'Oh my God, it's heaven,' says Sara.

'I got one too,' Emily tells them, nodding sagely.

'Oh, yeah? Who was the lucky sponsor?'

'Matthew McKinnon,' Emily answers.

'Fitting in already.' Sara winks at me.

Forty-five minutes later. The *Born to Die* album is playing off someone's laptop while we get ready to go out in Yomawu's room. Everybody knows the words. It's one of those albums that is branded onto
my brain. Jess was never a Lana fan. Everyone in my secondary school
was big on third-wave-feminist pop like Avril Lavigne, you know?

Late afternoon sun is streaming in, warming the lilac duvet. Sara's
GHD straighteners and Emily's hair waver are radiating heat, adding
to the room's almost sub-tropical climate. The smell is not especially
fresh, more like hair and skin, eyelash glue, the acidic musk of the over-
flowing laundry basket. A tampon kissed with a spot of red-brown lies
in a fistful of tissue in a little plastic bin. Both windows are flung open
to keep us from suffocating in perfume mist.

A heap of party dresses writhe in the corner of the room, sequins,
sparkles, feathers. No one seems to know or care which clothes belong
to who. The models are stripped naked and pass garments back and
forth between them. Amongst all the bare breasts, legs, arses, I don't
know where to look. It's weird to see so many beautiful people in one
room, even stranger to see them all naked—it tips over into the feeling
of a fashion editorial or some kind of live performance piece. I haven't
even seen Jess this naked.

Sara sits up against Yomawu's pillows with a plush white rabbit in her
lap. She's wearing a pair of black mini-briefs, the low-rise kind I never
wear because they dig in and leave a line. She's smoking out of the open
window, tipping ash into the glass lid of a heart-shaped jewellery box.

'Look at that,' she says, pointy chin aimed at the street.

The room vibrates with thunder and a cool breeze comes in from
the window as it starts to rain. Sara puts her hand out to feel the
raindrops, extinguishes her cigarette on the outside of the window
frame and then pulls the window closed.

Nine

Hunting Ground

3.37 a.m.

We outnumber them. That's got to count for something, right? Blue Shirt opens a bottle of champagne with the slightest nudge of his thumb. 'Hell in a handbasket!'

He is swearing because there are only two glasses in the room. Picking up the oyster-coloured landline phone from the bedside cabinet, he calls for additional glasses while the bottle of Dom—we're on a first name basis now, baby—spurts white froth onto the carpet.

We are in an executive room at the Dorchester, overlooking Hyde Park. It is aggressively air-conditioned. Yomawu exclaimed in delight at the satin yellow drapes hanging over the headboard when we entered the room, and to be fair to her, they do look like something out of a fairy tale. I was more concerned with the sound of the door closing behind us, the turning of the lock. The journey has sobered me up and I can't escape the feeling that I'm out of my depth.

'And anything else you want, Yummy,' says the man in the pink shirt. The phone still clamped to his ear, he puts his hand on the back of Yomawu's neck.

She wants cherries and strawberries and vanilla ice cream. They're all drunk, starting sentences they don't finish, laughing before the punchline. Blue Shirt pulls up Spotify on his phone and starts playing Duran Duran, the sound coming out distorted and tinny. 'Hungry Like the Wolf'.

'Here we go,' says Sara.

Emily, who is gazing down at the black expanse of Hyde Park through the window, turns over her shoulder to watch me. *Follow my lead and you'll be just fine.*

*

Eight hours earlier

The thunder has stopped. We have moved from Yomawu's bedroom into the living room, where Emily pours drinks and Sara plays music and everybody takes selfies and candids of each other for Instagram. We are like actors skulking around off set, acclimatizing to our costumes and practising our lines. Sara starts making a TikTok and the same seven seconds of a song play over and over about fifty times until I feel like I'm going insane.

I meet the legendary Kiki when she emerges from the bathroom in real mink eyelashes, lipstick the colour of a bruise, a sparkly jump-suit that plunges in the front and the back. She must have arrived an hour ago and got ready on her own; this kind of look doesn't come together in five minutes. She'd look like an ice-skater if it wasn't for her shoulder-length black hair, which is brushed out in a voluminous cloud. Kiki's character is the Bombshell, I decide. Larger than life. Intimidating.

'Hi,' I say to her, with what I hope is an easygoing smile.

'Hello . . . new person,' she says. Her accent has a musicality to it—Sara told me she's from Rio—but her tone is disarmingly blunt.

'An-agnes,' I manage. Stuttering my own name, a new low.

Kiki gives me a wry, uninterested smile.

'Don't pay any notice,' says Sara into my ear. 'She's all bark, no bite, well . . . well, maybe one time, but don't worry about that.'

I give her a '*sorry, what?!*' expression and she winks. Sara looks like a rock star's girlfriend, which doesn't strike me as much of a reach for her. Leather dress and cream fur, no lipstick, bitten-down fingernails. Her hair is like something out of 1996, crimped into a delightful mess. For a model she's awful in heels, wobbling around in a pair of studded Valentinos like Bambi on ice.

A bit shaken by my first Kiki encounter, I mainline wine until my jaw feels loose, my laugh getting increasingly louder. I spend most of my time on the sofa talking to Sara, but find my eyes keep wandering to one person in particular. Yomawu. She took the longest to get ready, then hovered around in the periphery of the group photos like she didn't want to leave evidence of her existence behind. I've noticed that she's gone to the bathroom about twenty times to touch up her make-up, and when she returns she's quiet, not really present in the conversation. I feel a pang of recognition watching her, and the next time she heads for the bathroom I surprise myself by following her, touching her gently on the wrist before she shuts herself inside.

'What's up? You look great.'

'*I know,*' she says.

'I love your dress,' I tell her, persisting. 'It suits you.'

We glance down at it simultaneously. Electric blue, strapless, a figure-hugging bodice, a slit up her left thigh. It is the furthest thing possible from the nightdress she was wearing when I met her earlier, which floated around her body like water.

'It's not my style,' she says quickly.

'Then why are you wearing it?'

She doesn't answer. Then she says: 'Are you coming in?'

I close the bathroom door behind me and Yomawu takes down a white ceramic vase from the shelf above the mirror. It's the kind of thing you'd expect to find locked in an elderly lady's display cabinet, together with painted plates and porcelain figurines of Edwardian ladies with parasols and cocker spaniels. She takes off the lid, painted with pale pink flowers and sage-coloured leaves, and removes a plastic baggie of powder.

Her eyes flash up at me, wide and curious for my reaction, and when I give none it seems to relax her. She giggles, licks a finger, dips and sucks.

'Microdosing,' she says, holding the baggie out for me. 'A little bit before the alcohol kicks in, and a line later on if we start lagging.'

'I'm okay,' I tell her. The truth is, I'm reluctant to take narcotics on the best of days but today is like my trial run—all eyes on the test rabbit—and the last thing I want to do is get out of control and embarrass myself. I don't know how to say that to her without sounding deranged so I stay quiet.

'I know what you're thinking,' she says solemnly, as she replaces the baggie and puts the vase back on the shelf. 'You're thinking this girl's been hanging around white bitches too long.'

I burst out laughing. 'White girls do love a bit of Molly. And anal.'

'Yes,' she says, grabbing my forearm excitedly and snorting. 'What is *that* about?'

I can hear Emily calling our names, 'Agnes! Yomawu!' Her voice grows louder as she comes strutting down the hall in new stilettos.

Emily opens the bathroom door, tilts her head at us. Her hair is held high in a pony and the thick Russian hair extensions make it swish out behind her like the heavy corners of a theatre curtain. Her eyebrow raises suspiciously at our close proximity, Yomawu's hand still wrapped around my arm.

'Come on, the Uber's here,' she says. 'You can carry on licking each other out later.'

The street is shiny as a newly minted coin after the downpour, the air balmy. Why is it that rain only feels beautiful in unfamiliar places? Rain in The Wasteland makes me think of limp, wet burger wrappers. Of the dead branches of trees wafting like tentacles around purple For Sale signs.

I almost trip on the steps down in my platform heels—courtesy of Sara's wardrobe. I've got my new, blood-red, sickeningly expensive handbag hooked over my arm, my old crossbody bag discarded some-where in Yomawu's room. I snapped a picture of Matthew's gift earlier and sent it to Jess (your girl's coming up in the world x). I hope Olive sees it over Jess's shoulder while they're on a tourist boat cruise and promptly throws up with jealousy into the Mekong river.

Sara sits in the front of the taxi and jabs at the radio buttons as the driver stares at the road ahead with blinkered focus. She passes through Katy Perry, Beyoncé, Olivia Rodrigo in quick succession before landing on Ariana Grande. '7 Rings'. She cranks it up to a deafening volume.

Yomawu gives me a sardonic look. 'He's going to rate us one star,' she mutters. But even she can't resist flicking her hair back and shim-mying in her seat.

Our night starts at a bar on Sloane Square, just across from Venus Foun-tain. I like how that sounds, 'Venus Fountain', like a Helmut Newton photograph or a black-and-white Italian movie about a bored heiress who falls in love with her chauffer. The bar itself is grove-like, full of exposed brick, with a regrettable Día de los Muertos aesthetic—white skeleton masks with red flower garlands and antlers everywhere.

'Ladies.' A beaming man whose nametag reads *Carlos, Assistant Manager* approaches us just as a trio of guitars strike up, and the very best table at the bar is instantly available, separated from the dance-floor by swathes of blood-red fringe.

Waiters bring us extra side plates for our platter of nachos, extra pork tacos because Kiki tells them they're her favourite, a spicy guacamole for Emily, some sliced sourdough and salted butter for Yomawu. *Anything else, anything at all that we can get for you ladies, please just let us know, and thank you again for joining us this evening.*

'This beats nights out in The Wasteland,' I say, thinking of that local crackhead outside the burger van who would ask every time he saw me, without fail, what mixed-race pussy tastes like while I was trying to eat my chips.

Plus, everything here is on the house, including the frozen margaritas that I'm finishing at a rapid rate. Get it together, Agnes, for fuck's sake.

In the booth, Sara spills crushed ice from her margarita onto her lap. She keeps trying to speak Spanish to the staff. '*Señor! Vamos hacer la fiesta.*'

'This reminds me of Peru!' Sara shrieks, oblivious to Kiki's death glare. She reminisces about the six-week trip she took to South America after Sixth Form, where she ended up working for a club owner-cum-drug dealer who signed her up on his payroll as a 'secretary' and paid her thousands of dollars a week on the condition that she use the hot tub topless for twenty minutes every night. It was the final straw when she found a hidden camera in her bedroom.

She's already wasted, flicking her crimped waves around like a horse's mane. Emily gives her the side-eye, then shifts closer to me on the cushioned seat. Rose perfume, like always. She begins to deliver a crash course on how to 'separate the sugar from the Splenda' of the male species. She has a simple three-step formula for identifying moneyed men: Watch. Shoes. Jacket.

'First you look at the watch. And the shoes. An amateur like you probably couldn't read a jacket yet—that comes later. Enormous watch face equals a fragile ego, and God help us if it's diamond-encrusted.' She turns and tips her glass to a couple of men who won't stop staring at her from across the bar.

Yomawu is in her own world, swaying a little to the Latin music. The crystals must be kicking in. She looks unreal despite the hated dress, the smooth skin across her sharp collarbone like velvet over wire.

Kiki gets up to dance, but Emily wants to go for a smoke so I follow her cloud of Delina rose and vanilla up the stairs.

'I don't know where we're going to end up tonight—' she puts two menthol cigs between her lips—'ber eh cunyajump jonight jwo jhousand hounds.' She lights them both on the same flame and passes one to me.

'I didn't catch that,' I say.

'I *said*,'—blowing toxic peppermint mist into my face—'I can't go home tonight without two thousand pounds.'

'Two thousand? What for?' I suck my menthol without really inhaling.

'A Capucines bag,' she says, baring her teeth at me and then at her reflection in the tinted nightclub window. She screws up her face in disgust. 'Veneers, too.'

'How the hell are you going to get two thousand pounds out here?'

'You'll have to wait and see, darling girl,' she says.

Cigarettes neatly extinguished under heels, we head back inside, passing a group of young women being turned away at the door. They look a bit like the girls from my secondary school, like Jess before she went to uni and discovered Depop and Bella Hadid. Skinny jeans and black crop-tees and a lost, hungry look about them. They glare at us with furious envy and I remember being eighteen and feeling certain that there was some amazing party going on somewhere that I wasn't invited to, and might never be invited to. I want to rush over and tell them I'm just a tourist here, that I usually get drunk for four quid at a local pub with a sticky floor. But then I remember that I'm wearing Sara's dress (black, dangerously low butt-crack-skimming back) and jewellery (gold snake bangle, upper arm) and that Emily has done my make-up (signature liner, red lips to match my new Gucci). I wouldn't believe me either. I watch them turn their backs and slope off sulkily across the square.

As we descend the staircase to the bar, I blurt out: 'Matthew gave me his number.'

'Oh, did he?' Emily's tone is bright, eyes sparkly, cogs turning.

'Yes, well,' I'm shifty on my feet. Why does this feel like a confession? 'He asked if I wanted to go to lunch sometime.'

'Why didn't you tell me earlier?' She maintains eye contact with me while reaching into her bag for her pocket mirror.

'I don't know.'

Shit. I start to panic. Have I fucked up? I feel as though I've broken an unspoken rule and the sugar baby volturi are about to slide down from the ceiling on a firefighter's pole made of Chanel-branded ribbon.

'Do you want to see him?' she asks, squinting at herself, clipping the mirror shut.

'I mean, I wouldn't mind. I had a nice time . . .' And his hands! 'but I wouldn't want to . . .' And his hands.

'Go,' she says, pulling a travel hairbrush out of her bag. She rakes it through her ponytail and feels with her manicured fingers for any bumps. 'I have plenty more where that came from. But ask for four hundred at least.'

We rejoin the girls at the table and Emily leans over to whisper something into Yomawu's hair. I wonder whether or not I've just fallen out of favour with Emily. Surely not. This is what she wanted, right?

Sara hands me another margarita and clinks her glass against mine.

'Hurry up,' says Emily, raising her voice against the Spanish music, 'we're going to Palm Beach.'

'What the hell is Palm Beach?' I ask Sara.

Her pointy pink tongue chases a globule of tequila-soaked ice around the bottom of her glass.

'Ooh,' she says, a picture of glee. 'Palm Beach is a hunting ground.'

'"Drunk in Love"!' Sara shouts at the DJ, almost spilling her lychee martini. 'Can you play "Drunk in Love"?'

Palm Beach, as it turns out, is a Berkeley Street casino. Plush velvet sofas in chromatic deep purple, mirrored stairs, faux-gold detailing on the countertop, that kind of thing. We are greeted by a man in a suit who immediately signs me up with membership by taking my picture on the lobby webcam and presenting me with a gold card. 'You ladies look fantastic,' he declares, though by this point I find the compliments are beginning to lose their lustre, the accompanying stares a by-product of being out with the models that I'm starting to take for granted.

Kiki has commandeered one of the waiters, putting him to work as her own personal photographer. Not that he seems to mind, dark eyes lingering over her chest in her sparkly jumpsuit as he suggests different poses and locations and mutters things like 'that's right, queen' at ten-second intervals. To be fair, she does look regal.

'What time is it,' Yomawu asks, back from one of her loo breaks and visibly restless.

'I don't know, but it's been ages,' says Sara, turning pointedly in the direction of the DJ's booth, 'and he *still* hasn't played "Drunk in Love". Look, let's just get on with it already—'

Emily, who's in the middle of recording a video clip for her Instagram story, holds her free hand out to prevent Sara from getting up.

'Not yet,' she says. 'You have to wait half an hour more.'

'Whatever you say, *boss*.' Sara collapses back into her seat and smiles at Emily, wonky and childish. Emily gives her that magnanimous Margot Robbie grin and wipes a stray mascara speck from underneath Sara's eyebrow with her fingertips.

Constance: Agnes there is leftover rice in the fridge for lunch when you get home tomorrow. Give the babies a squeeze from me and don't stay up all night watching nonsense on the TV.

Fuck. I'd completely forgotten about my babysitting alibi till now and this has spun me out. I put my phone on flight mode so she'll think my battery's died, just in time for a crowd of men to filter into the seating area, passing chairs around to accommodate their group. Velvet jackets galore, thick pomaded hair, enough Tom Ford to get me at the back of the throat from four metres away . . .

'Okay,' says Emily. 'I think now is good.'

'You sure?' Sara hauls herself up to her feet, taking a few seconds to find her balance. 'Who do you want?'

'Bring me the Dads on Tour,' says Emily, reaching out and slapping her on the arse. 'Gettem, cowgirl.'

Yomawu looks up, hiccups softly. 'Aww,' she says, 'I know who you mean, they look like it's their first time away from home. Personally, I love a dad bod.'

'Yomawu,' says Emily, 'you're an exceptionally beautiful woman. Get some standards and don't let them con you with their lazy bullshit.' Then she sighs. 'Isn't it just *so* obvious their wives have packed their cases? Sitting ducks.'

There are indeed a pair of harmless-looking men in their early fifties hovering at the bar holding full glasses of whisky, eyes flitting around the room as if waiting for someone to tell them what to do.

'How do you know they're from out of town?' I ask her.

'It's obvious,' Yomawu answers.

'How?'

No one responds. We are watching Sara approach them, beaming, pointing us out, and like clockwork all three of them start towards us.

'Ladies,' says one of them, stubble on his cheeks, cheeks striped white-and-raspberry from the day's sun. 'How are we tonight?'

'Thirsty,' says Kiki.

The men laugh because they think she's joking, and we laugh because we know she's not.

'You're American?'

'From Boston,' says the one who hasn't spoken yet. 'We come back and forth a lot for business.'

'Emily's American too,' Yomawu says, surprising me.

'Oh, you are? What state?' He has nice facial structure, but his cheeks are beginning to loosen from the bone like meat from a well-cooked lamb shank.

'Half-American,' she says. 'My dad's from Maryland but he lives in LA now.'

'You ladies mind if we join you? Your friend Sara told us you'd be okay with that.'

'Wouldn't want to interrupt your evening,' the other one says.

'Not at all,' Emily purrs.

The men pull up seats and sit down like puppies waiting for their treats. They're decent enough looking in their crisp shirts (one blue, one pink) and their fresh haircuts, but there are better-looking men around. These two meet Emily's own personal criteria, however. One wears a bulky rectangular-edged watch—Tag Heuer on the right, Emily types on her phone with lightning speed, angling it towards me discreetly—and the other has on a silver bracelet (Omega on the left, bingo.) I write the brand names down in my phone, paying attention. I've mentally labelled one of the men Blue Shirt, and the other Pink Shirt, for clarity.

Pink Shirt talks intently to Yomawu, pawing at her bare leg to emphasize his words. She sips her drink and evenly meets his gaze. I can hear occasional fragments, 'thirty thousand dollars', 'what they didn't realize about bitcoin', 'these guys were making a killing'. Yomawu endures his conversation with a geisha-like grace.

As Blue Shirt fawns all over Emily and Sara, Kiki complains of a headache and orders an Uber.

'You're leaving already?' I ask her.

'Going home,' she says. 'I need to make some content.'

I get the feeling she's bailing out of wherever this is heading and start to feel uneasy. Emily doesn't seem to notice; she is clutching Blue Shirt's hand. 'We *have* to do tequila shots,' she tells him with urgency. Her pupils dilate like black ink spilled on a seafoam-coloured napkin, bleeding out into the fibres—and there it is, he's a goner.

'What do we know so far?' Emily asks Yomawu while he gets the drinks.

'They're staying at the Dorchester. Here till the end of the week.'

'The Dorchester it is then,' she says decidedly.

Yomawu fiddles in her handbag and takes out a stick of chewing gum. 'I'd rather just go to bed,' she says quietly. 'This guy's so boring and the colour of this dress is giving me a migraine. It's so *bright*.'

'You'll be happy tomorrow when you check your bank balance,' says Emily. 'And just think of the dress as a costume. Men don't get your whole frills and lace soft girl thing—and the kind of guys that do are *not* the kind we're trying to attract. Trust me.'

Yomawu leans back against the sofa seat and groans. 'It honestly offends my soul.'

Emily offers her a sip. 'It'll be over before you know it.'

'Wait, what's going to happen?' I ask helplessly. Something about the resigned way that Yomawu just shrugged is making me panic. I am so tired of playing 20 questions with Emily, but my very real fear of dying is overtaking that.

'Shh, they're coming back,' she says. It's too late, she's doing her watery siren eyes again, putting them under like a seasoned hypnotist.

Shots are lined up. Blue Shirt raises his in a toast.

'To London,' he says, his tongue curling around the word, savouring it, anticipating an evening of well-deserved debauchery.

'To London.'

The tequila goes down smoothly, it doesn't burn the back of my throat like the stuff in The Wasteland. 'Drunk in Love' starts playing and Sara squeals and stands up to dance on the sofa with the heels of her Valentinos digging into the cushions. Emily dances with sexy control like a model in a music video, all slow-motion hip-rolling and pouting, touting her glass like a prop, working her angles.

'So do you live near here?' Pink Shirt asks me.

'Yeah,' I say, emboldened by my third shot, 'we live together in South Ken.' It's a wishful lie, but nice to say. It's like that manifestation guru I follow on TikTok says. Imagine it, achieve it.

The earlier crypto talk aside, he watches my mouth when I speak with an attentiveness that I might find sexy. Is it sexy? He walks me to the bar with his hand pressed lightly to the small of my back and the skin-on-skin contact makes me tremble, just slightly. It's been a while since I've fucked anyone.

Maybe it's not him, the attentiveness. Maybe it's all coming from me.

I look at Pink Shirt as he leans his forearms on the bar, tapping his black Amex card on the counter. The slight razor burn on his neck. I try and picture what it would be like to have him on top of me. His Hermès belt cutting into the flesh of my lower stomach, his hand unpicking the single button at the halter-neck of my dress. Maybe it's the power imbalance that turns me on. It must be that.

'Here you are, honey. Thought you might want a margarita as well.'

From then on it's the taste of salt and tequila and the sharpness of the lime juice on my tongue. More shots, more dancing. I join Sara on the sofa, almost fall off and break my neck. Blue Shirt grabs me by the waist, catches me and spins me around. He's sweating, and I grasp on to the back of his neck which is slick with it.

'Put me down,' I say and I'm giggling at first, but then I have to shout it into his ear because he can't hear me over the music. '*Please*, put me down!'

In the taxi to the hotel, Sara and Yomawu slump a little in their seats, tequila-weary, but Emily is bolt upright and enduring Blue Shirt's chatter. We're in a big six-seater, meaning there's room for all of us in the back (Pink Shirt rides shotgun, I think out of some kind of chivalric urge to protect us from any advances the cab driver might make). Before we pulled away from the casino, I caught Emily studying my face, perhaps looking me over for signs of weakness.

Blue Shirt is rambling, a bit incoherent, staring less and less guardedly at the smooth skin on Emily's chest. I watch her reach out and press her fingers into the trouser crease on his inner thigh. I gasp—it just feels weird to look at, like something that shouldn't be seen. Pink Shirt keeps craning his neck from the passenger seat to be sure Yomawu is still there. I catch his eye while he's mid-staring at her.

'Is Yummy all right?' he whispers.

I nod. 'She's fine.' My whisper comes out hissy and irritated.

Sara rouses from her half-sleep and nudges me, her fluffy white blonde head picking up the lamplight. 'You're not worried, are you?' she asks in a soft hoarse voice.

'I mean,' I lean in closer, whisper, 'they're strangers.'

'Chill,' she says, and closes her eyes again. 'What's the saying from that Angelina Jolie film? The one where she keeps getting her tits out. "Too beautiful to die."'

This is not comforting. '*Gia*?' I offer, hoping Yomawu will wake up and give me moral support.

'Yeah! Precisely!' She chews her bottom lip thoughtfully. 'That's us. Everyone fucking loves us, we're too beautiful to die.'

I pause for a beat. 'Sara, Angelina Jolie's character passes away from AIDS at the end of that movie.'

'She won a . . . a Golden Globe,' she says dreamily, 'and then she jumped in the pool like *splash!* I used to be obsessed with those old clips of Angie. I did some photos just like that one she did in the nineties. Like, really thin brows, dark lippy and just wearing a bra, straddling the toilet seat backwards . . . so fucking cool. My ex took the pictures.' Her eyes flutter open as we pass by an electric billboard, a close-up of glossy female lips wrapped around a fried drumstick. 'Fuck, I'm wasted.'

I end up thinking about all those headlines Constance was so fond of wheeling out every time I threatened to put lip gloss on. Part of me really thinks I'm going to wind up as *Woman, 21, murdered by men she met in Mayfair bar.*

'Don't be scared,' Sara whispers, surprising me—I thought her mood was going to take a dark, silent turn after the comment about the ex, but her fingers with their chipped black nail polish are stroking mine. Like Jess, her hands are constantly a bit cold, her body heat not quite making it out to her extremities. 'You're with us. Nothing bad can happen.'

She takes my hand and tucks it in with hers in the warmth of her fur coat pocket.

Ten

Hail Satan

Now

3.38 a.m.

Sara collapses next to me on the bed, puts her leg over my waist and nuzzles my neck. There's a mirror on the ceiling. I look up at Sara's milky thigh against my black dress, her fur sleeve under my neck. Emily lays her head on the pillow, Yomawu shuffling onto the other side, and we all look up at our reflection in the mirror.

'I'm really glad we met you,' Sara says. Then she makes a soft little 'Mmm' sound as if she's cosying down for sleep, and I know it's just the tequila running through her bloodstream, but still, I feel warm love spread through my body.

'Me too,' says Yomawu.

Emily says nothing, just stares up at her own reflection, shifting her chin left and right for the imaginary photographer.

'If you're angry at me, I'd rather you just tell me,' I turn and whisper into her neck.

'Huh? Why would I be angry?'

'I don't know.' Heartbeat in my ears. 'The Matthew thing.'

She smiles. 'Oh, sweetheart, I couldn't care less about that. I was just wondering whether I should try out threads or not.'

'Threads?'

'You know . . .' She puts two fingers either side of her temples and pulls in an upward motion. 'What do you think?'

'You look like the cat lady.'

Her high twinkly laugh. 'Look, Agnes, it's business, you know? I wouldn't have introduced you to him if I minded. I'm not precious about these things.'

'Room service!' The waitress politely ignores us tangled up on the bed. I can't imagine what kind of horrors hotel staff get to witness on the night shift. The girls ignore her too, barely stirring, except for Emily who sits up against the headboard and watches her steadily.

Blue Shirt is glowing with pride, pressing his palms together. 'Hope you girls are hungry,' he says, and I notice the back of his shirt is dank with sweat.

The more I drink the more handsome he gets, the more fuckable. I hate myself for feeling a twitch in my chest when our fingertips touch as he passes me the champagne flute. I envy Emily's cool detachment.

Sara whittles a melting scoop of ice cream with the tip of her metal spoon. When 'Girls on Film' starts playing, she holds out the bowl for Blue Shirt then stands up on the bed and starts dancing.

'Go for it, girl,' says Blue Shirt, his face shinier as he holds out his arms for her, 'come on.'

Sara leaps down from the bed, wraps her arms around his neck, her legs around his waist, her leather skirt crinkling up around her hips to show a black cotton thong. He spins her around until she yelps, 'I'm gonna be sick!' and then he puts her down carefully, one spidery leg and then the other.

Pink Shirt sits down on the edge of the bed so heavily that the mattress bounces. He puts his hand onto Emily's shin and wraps his fingers around it like he's testing the bone for a fracture.

Emily looks up at me and I smile. She reaches for Pink Shirt's hand, gently guides it higher up her leg, above her knees, between her thighs and then she takes his other hand and puts it on my leg so he's touching both of us.

'Are you okay with this?' she whispers.

I nod, surprised to find that I am more than okay with this, I want Pink Shirt to keep touching me. But then Emily grabs hold of his hands and pushes them away playfully. He holds them up in surrender.

'Okay, okay,' he says. 'May I get you some more champagne, ladies?'

'Why, thank you, sir,' says Emily, resting her head back on the pillows.

I cross one leg over the other and hope no one can tell that I'm wet.

As Yomawu idly picks a champagne-soaked strawberry out of the bottom of one of the glasses and eats it, Sara is sitting in Blue Shirt's lap on the armchair, one hand fiddling with the cuff on his shirt. They both start as Emily flicks her Barbie-doll ponytail over her shoulder and gets up with an almighty sigh.

'Right, girls, we've got to go.' She claps her hands. 'Come on, we've stayed out too long as it is.'

Blue Shirt and Pink Shirt protest in unison as Sara and Yomawu obediently go in search of their shoes, dutiful and swaying.

Blue Shirt dabs the sweat on his forehead with the napkin the champagne bottle came wrapped up in. 'Oh, come on, you guys just got here. At least have another glass of champagne, I'll call down for another bottle.'

I'm perched on the edge of the bed watching the commotion like I'm at one of those immersive dinner plays. I don't understand what we came here for.

'We really can't stay,' Emily insists. 'Can we?'

'No,' says Yomawu, a little tremor in her voice. 'We have to work tomorrow, we're going to be in so much trouble if we can't.'

It's the first I've heard of any job.

'What's that, Yummy?' Pink Shirt sidles up, puts his hand around her waist.

'We're really, really behind on our rent,' says Sara.

'We could be evicted,' says Emily. 'We would love to stay and have another drink with you, and y'know, whatever else, but we just can't. It's a six a.m. start.'

'That's a real shame,' says Blue Shirt, looking Emily up and down. She holds her bag against her chest, ready to leave. 'Say, how much are they paying you girls tomorrow?'

'Fifteen hundred each,' says Emily, without a pause.

'Well, that doesn't sound like bad business to me, your rent must be insanity. Where are ya staying, girls, Buckingham Palace?'

'Come on, girls,' says Emily. 'This is silly, we should have gone home to bed hours ago.'

The men share a glance, then Pink Shirt says: 'Now look here, girls, the night is far from over and we've been having a real good time with you. How about we pay you what you would have made tomorrow and you stop worrying and relax?'

'We're not in London very long,' Blue Shirt adds. 'What do you say?'

Emily says to Blue Shirt that they should go into the room next door and make the bank transfer before they get too drunk and forget about it. Pink Shirt stays behind—he has his hand inside Yomawu's dress and is kissing her neck. She moans softly and spills champagne from her glass, her wrist limp.

I sit down next to Sara on the sofa. Her legs are crossed, skirt rolled up practically to her waist, any sense of decency gone with the last drink. She rests her head on my shoulder.

'They're just giving you all that money?' I whisper to her.

She's grinning. 'Giving *us*,' she corrects me. 'You'll get your share.'

'I haven't done anything.'

'Doesn't matter,' she slurs.

'Are you gonna fuck them?' I ask her.

I look at Pink Shirt's hands as they wander freely over Yomawu's body. Pink Shirt, blue dress. I'm too shy to ask Sara if they're about to have an orgy.

'You never have to do anything you don't want. If they expect it it's their own stupid fault.'

In Constance's list of forbidden activities, orgies probably come above murder and drug-dealing.

'They won't be angry that we're, like, leading them on?'

Sara shakes her head. 'They might be, but don't worry—I took karate—' she squeezes her lithe little bicep. 'I can fight.' Her eyes roll shut briefly as she battles a wave of dizziness. When they flicker open, she does a double take then lets out a squawking laugh. 'Yoyo, what the *fuck* are you doing?'

Yomawu has stripped totally naked except for her heels, revealing long tapered limbs, tiny ribcage, stomach as taut as a drum, pointy dark nipples in the centre of small breasts. She's a Helmut Newton photograph in action.

'I fucking hated that dress,' she says over her shoulder at us, hooking her hands around Pink Shirt's neck. They kiss. His hands stroke down the indent of her spine, grab hold of her high round arse and dig into the meat of it, roughly.

This seems totally out of character for Yomawu, the most reserved of the group despite her molly habit, but then again I've only just met her. Sara seems to be taking it lightly, eyes gleaming like a kid at a birthday party.

Yomawu comes over, puts her hands on the arm of the sofa so that her hair falls forward and tickles my shoulder. 'We're going next door to the other bedroom for a bit,' she says.

I put out an arm to steady her, she's wobbling. I look at Pink Shirt waiting behind her with his thumb hooked through his belt strap.

Sara rolls her smudgy eyes. 'I've already told you,' she says resignedly. 'I've already told you, Yoyo, I'm not fighting you, love.'

Yomawu hushes her.

'Are you sure she's okay?' I whisper to Sara.

'I want to go with him,' Yomawu says, stamping her foot.

Sara shrugs and tells me to let her go. 'It's her own fault if she regrets it. It's just Yoyo being Yoyo.'

The front door opens a crack and Emily calls out. 'Sara, Sara, can you come into the next room?'

Sara stands up, stretches, yawns. 'She wants reinforcements. You wanna come?'

Do I want to come? *Do I want to come?* I don't know. I walk out with Sara into the corridor. She gives the unlocked door a nudge, and I see a second's worth of bedsheet and bare leg before it clicks shut again.

'Think I'll just wait for you guys back in there,' I say.

'No worries.' I hear muffled giggling, a male voice, Emily's wind-chime laugh. I return to the original hotel room and sit down on the armchair. I'm alone.

*

I wake up in Sara's room, white ruched duvet cover, blue pillows, the sun raining in because we forgot to pull down the slatted blinds before collapsing into bed. Sara's next to me, sleeping on her front like a newborn. My heart beating and my blood pressure starting to rise, I reach for my phone in one quick reflex and . . . exhale. The clock reads *11:14*. I know Constance is on a cleaning shift all morning, which buys me time to locate my secretarial outfit and my bank card and my old handbag and leg the hell out of here.

But there's a tantalizing smell of coffee wafting in from the kitchen, and I realize . . . God, I'm fucking hungry. My stomach is churning for McMuffins, fried tomatoes, baked beans and sausage, Greggs' steak bakes, cheese melted onto toast under the grill and slathered in Worcestershire sauce. I need carbs and cheese and I need them right now. At the sound of cracked eggs hitting the frying pan I swing up out of bed and Sara stirs.

'Wait for me,' she says, climbing out of bed. In order to leave the room, she has to navigate a tangle of clothes, shoes, empty tobacco packets, a half-eaten bag of cheese-and-onion crisps, a Peruvian flag and a tennis racket propped up against the wardrobe. She picks out a Martin Garrix T-shirt from the pile and slips it on. I sit upright, inhale deeply, it smells like . . .

'Is that sick?' I ask, wrinkling my nose.

'For fuck's sake, I've done it again!' She picks up her plastic waste-paper bin like it's an unexploded bomb and rushes out of the room, her bare feet slapping against the tiles. 'Always a bin, never the toilet,' she groans.

My need for cheese-loaded carbs having become almost medical at this point, I shuffle into the kitchen. Emily, in a seafoam-blue silk pyjama set, is making coffee in a moka pot on the stove.

'Oh, hi,' she says, beaming, 'thought you'd never get up.' She looks me up and down. 'Feeling all right?'

'How do you look so *fresh*?' I ask her. I can see she's got eggs and bacon frying in a pan, the good thick bacon. 'I'm starving,' I say pleadingly.

'Food will be ready in a minute,' she says, pushing down the lever on the toaster. 'As for looking fresh—' she checks her reflection in the blade of a butter knife—'half a litre of water before bed, magnesium, vitamin C, zinc and 5-HTP supplements with a banana first thing in the morning, more water, an espresso shot. And if all else fails, nothing brightens the complexion like a quick dunk in some icy water.'

She's like somebody's trophy wife, blonde, claw-clipped and full of the joys of spring while I sit Gollum-hunched on the kitchen chair, my hungry stomach groaning a symphony. *Just fifteen minutes for breakfast and then I'll leave.*

As Sara shuffles meekly out of the toilet in her T-shirt and sits down at the table, Emily begins to plate up the toast, bacon and eggs, pouring the coffee into assorted mugs.

'Did anyone check on Yomawu?' she asks, drinking her cup of coffee standing up by the window like she's about to buckle us up in the minivan and take us on the school run.

Sara, mouth full of buttered toast, shakes her head. 'Em, you know what she's like.'

'Go and tell her I've made her a coffee and she might as well come and get her money, mightn't she?'

Sara re-emerges ten minutes later, followed by a barely visible Yomawu, who is wrapped in the biggest, fluffiest pink dressing gown with the hood pulled up over her head and a clutch of shredded tissue in her hand.

Sara gives her arm a squeeze. 'Yoyo, want some toast?'

Yomawu shakes her head.

'You should eat something, sweetie,' says Sara.

Emily puts a cup of coffee in front of Yomawu. 'Drink,' she says, 'and you'll feel better before you know it.'

Yomawu is staring into the bottom of her cup of coffee like she wants to drown in it. I feel a stab of protectiveness.

'Is everything okay, Yomawu?' I ask her.

'She's dramatic,' Emily says.

'I'm not,' says Yomawu quickly, and from the look in her watery eyes I feel instinctively like pulling my knife further out of her reach.

'Where the fuck is Kiki?' says Sara suddenly.

Silence.

'Hang on.' Emily picks up her phone and sits down at the table.

She opens up Instagram and we all lean in to look at the screen. Kiki's Instagram story shows her boarding a private plane—there's a boomerang of her holding her glass up to the aeroplane window, sunlight sparkling on the ocean.

'Looks like she's doing all right,' Sara laughs.

'Fucking bitch,' says Emily. 'She never shares.'

Yomawu smiles, still teary-eyed. 'You're not jealous, Em?'

'Of our resident camgirl? Don't be ridiculous,' she says. 'Right, we need to divide up the money from last night. Agnes, send me your details?'

I almost choke on a bit of stringy bacon fat. 'Are you absolutely sure? I mean, I didn't . . .'

'You were there,' says Emily.

'And we like you,' Sara beams.

'Yeah,' Yomawu sniffs and offers me a weak smile, cheering a little bit as the caffeine hits her system. She gets up and starts to reassemble the moka pot for another batch.

'Put your bank details on here.' Emily gets a wad of Post-its and a ballpoint out of one of the kitchen drawers, shoves them at me with her manicure-tipped hand.

'Two secs.' I go to Sara's room to get my purse out of the new red handbag, sit back down at the table, squinting at my Metro bank card and writing the numbers down.

Emily jabs at her phone screen in the breeze of the open kitchen window, making the transfers. Then she rolls a bunch of cigarettes and we smoke squashed up together over the sink, tapping ash into the dirty dishes and the pan with its globules of shiny bacon fat.

'Don't start a grease fire,' Yomawu warns. She's shed her thick dressing gown and is sitting up on the kitchen counter in a lilac slip with her feet on the window ledge.

Sara takes some strawberries out of the fridge and opens a little bag of sugar, starts dipping the strawberries in and then eating them. She passes around the punnet and the bag. I lick the sugar off mine while I check my bank app.

It's there. £1,500 for doing nothing. For being young and pretty, for whatever Emily and Sara and Yomawu did behind closed doors.

'Be right back,' I say shakily.

I cross the hall and lock myself in the bathroom which is frankly less than clean—a faint grey ring of grime around the bathtub, a cloudy, water-specked plastic shower curtain that's suspiciously green around the bottom edge. I'd start with some baking soda and lemon juice mixed up with Fairy liquid, just the way Constance taught me. The skirting boards are dusty enough to be fluffy and the toilet could use a good dose of bleach, maybe a jet-wash.

I look in the mirror. There's something different, something of the Femme Fatale still lingering around my eyes even now my make-up's rubbed off. I take a cotton pad and the Garnier Micellar Water from the sink, and run the soaked pad over my eyelids one more time. It comes off clean. Then I squint in closer at my reflection under the single strobe with the pull string. I look like *her*, the vixen in the red bandage dress, the woman I turn into with the first swipe of liquid red, as though she's possessed me.

Constance used to warn us about demonic possession. Anything could trigger it. Evil spirits were suspected—were assumed, even—to hang around in movies and bad books and pop music. When we were little, Marlena and I watched a lot of YouTube videos where they played Jay-Z and Beyoncé songs backwards. Illuminati. Hail Satan. 666. Kill yourself. We clutched each other, screaming, under the covers. Constance had to anoint our bedroom doors with holy oil and buy a night light for the hallway.

Fuck.

Constance.

The time on my phone reads 11:47, which means she will be on her way home from her shift, floral brolly hooked over her arm, in exactly five minutes. I have to get back to The Wasteland. There's no way I'd be coming home this late if I'd been babysitting.

I find my outfit from the lunch with Matthew and yank it on, buttoning the white shirt crookedly and shoving up the zip on the black midi-skirt halfway. I sling my old crossbody over my shoulder and grab the red handbag. When I come out, the girls are all sitting at the kitchen table looking at a laptop, Sara's monkeyish feet in Emily's lap and Yomawu's legs tucked underneath her. They're scrolling holiday destinations, talking about booking a girls' trip.

Sara climbs up when she sees me and hooks her cool fingers between mine. 'You're coming with us!' she says.

I imagine the four of us playing blackjack in Vegas, riding jet-skis in Miami, tossing coins into the Trevi Fountain.

'I can't,' I say, a pang of sadness mixing in with my panic. 'Family thing. Got to run.'

'Come back soon,' Sara says. 'Promise!'

'I will.'

Yomawu raises her empty coffee cup.

*

Before I can turn the key in the lock Constance pulls the door open for me. Her hair is wrapped up, she wears one of her kaftans. Her eyes flicker between the handbag I am holding, glaringly obvious with its gold crisscrossed Gs, and my face. Her beauty is muddied with worry, jaw clenched, puckered folds on her brow like punctuation marks.

'Can I . . . come in?'

She doesn't move.

'I spoke to Louise.'

Fuck.

'I thought we were through with this, Agnes.'

Eleven

Fucking Cousin Louise

When Constance concluded I was defective at the age of thirteen, she sent me to a child psychologist. It was a short course of counselling, seven hours free on the NHS. The psych, a recovered agoraphobe, wore cork sandals with a red suede strap and silver toe rings. She always looked as though someone had just grabbed her by the shoulders and given her a shake—wild, brassy blonde hair, eyeliner that floated around a couple of millimetres too low under her lash line. She was tired, which meant she followed the book. She had a little flip calendar on her desk with her retirement date highlighted.

After the sixth appointment she drew her prognosis. The fantasies—my obsession with Hollywood starlets, my deception of Constance, the lies I spun for my schoolmates and teachers about being the secret offspring of a famous actor—were all a response to Dad leaving. Dad was the reason I had low self-esteem, a fragile sense of identity, a crippling fear of abandonment that made it virtually impossible to make friends. That was her conclusion and even back then I had enough sense to know she was wrong, but Constance seemed satisfied, probably relieved not to be the main culprit for my issues, and I didn't want to answer any more questions so I kept my mouth shut. She sent me off on my way with a leaflet about the benefits of positive thinking, mindfulness and exercise.

'You a good girl, my good girl, my good little Agnes.' Constance, glowing with pride, squeezed me like we were long-lost family members reunited at the end of a daytime TV movie. She was always a big believer in affirmations, *the power of the tongue* and all that.

I don't know why but it made me so angry, Constance's joyfulness about me being all fixed up. It felt unfair, like I was a prop. It didn't matter whether I was happy as long as I was *good*. Later that night, I took my Sunday Best church dress out of the wardrobe. It was pale blue, with little puff sleeves, and covered with tiny embroidered bows, the kind of old-fashioned thing the adults went crazy for when I wore it to church. I got my craft scissors and I cut a hole through the underskirt. The scissors were for kids so they were blunt—they came as part of a scrapbook-making kit—and I had to hack at the white skirt layer until I'd made the tiniest tear, and then I poked my finger through to widen it a bit and then I grabbed either side of it with my fingers and thumbs and I tore it, right up to the seam where it joined the bodice so there was no way of hiding that it was ruined because the ripped underskirt hung down below the blue top layer. Then I panicked. I screwed the dress up in a ball and put it in my book bag and then I squashed it into the bin outside the school gate.

*

Constance is quivering with anger, her delicate nostrils flaring, her hands balled up into tight little fists like she wants to beat the Devil out of me. She pulls the front door shut behind us and follows me into the living room.

'Where did you go, Agnes? Where have you been?'

She's been speaking to Cousin Louise. My alibi has been debunked. I'm trying to compute the risks and rewards of doubling down on my lie versus coming clean, but my hungover brain isn't working as fast as it should. The game's up. I don't look at her, just stand feebly beside the sofa, fixing my eyes on the soft crochet blanket. I feel Constance's glare burning me with its fury. I want to lie down.

'Tell me!' she says. 'What have you been doing all night?'

It's like a horrible slow motion, stomach churning, out-of-body thing. My mind goes empty.

'Agnes, look at me!' She's still shouting but now her voice crescendoes into this high-pitched hoarse cry. 'Where did you get this?' She points at the Gucci-emblazoned bag.

'I was at Emily's. We went out last night. I'm just borrowing it.'

Finally I can get some words out, not that it especially matters from the state of Constance's face, which is red and screwed up in disgust. I can practically hear her pulse racketing up to a superhuman level.

'Out . . . partyin'?'

Fuck it, rip the band-aid off. 'Yes.'

She takes in an enormous breath. She's so angry that she's smiling—that's the expression she used to get on her face before she'd smack us as kids. A kind of righteous biblical rage. I feel like she might really hit me now, open palm across my face.

'Agnes, you really been pushin' me to the edge, Lord Jesus give me strength. You livin' like a heathen, ignorin' my rules which are there for your own protection.'

'A heathen?' I look her square in the eye, suddenly calm with indignation. 'What year are we in, 1705?'

Her eyes sparkle with rage. 'You know *very* well what a heathen is, Agnes. Not a Christian. Someone of the world, a sinner. You been in church all your life, remember?'

'Not by my own choice,' I say quietly.

I wait for it. The Caribbean Mother Slap that this time *I know* is coming. But it doesn't.

Her breathing is ragged. 'I've tried, Lord knows I've tried to be reasonable with you, Agnes.'

'Reasonable?'

She closes her eyes, holds up her right hand, puts her left over her chest like she's making an oath or maybe checking for a pulse. She even looks beautiful now, for fuck's sake, like a Grecian sculpture. 'Please, shh. If you can't follow my rules, if you can't respect the beliefs of the household, then you need to leave.'

I look around at the room. The two armchairs on either side of the sofa, both pointing towards the TV, the artificial sunflowers in the teal ceramic vase, the paint-by-numbers canvas of Jesus holding a child's hand and walking towards a coastal horizon. Suffocating. But there's also a photo of Marlena, Constance and me taken a few years back, I think it was at a church brunch. Marlena's the tallest in the family and she towered over us even then, glasses reflecting the light from the flash. It didn't always feel this strained between us.

'So . . . you're kicking me out?' I feel like I'm in a dream.

Constance doesn't say anything, just sits on the window ledge with her arms crossed, looking down at the street.

'Mum?'

Nothing. The silent treatment, Constance's final refuge.

'Fine,' I say. As it always goes in the precise moments when you don't want to cry, my tear ducts are burning and my cheeks are twinging uncontrollably.

I fill a backpack with things and start off for the train station. Constance isn't downstairs when I leave, she's shut away in her room. I slam the front door as hard as I can manage, so the house shakes. It's here. The day of reckoning. I've finally been excommunicated.

The sense of freedom that is rushing through my body is terrifying, like coming up on a pill. I turn back to look through the window at the living room where the picture of Jesus is swinging from a loose nail on the wall.

I make it to the underpass by the Three Butts before my lungs give out, then crouch down in an unidentifiable puddle of muck, violently shaking. Getting out my phone, I try to call Jess, momentarily forgetting she's in Thailand, but the line is dead. Then I call Emily. She picks up on the second ring.

Part Two

STARS

Twelve

Seventies Pornos

I was raised to believe premarital sex was an unforgivable sin but it only took one orgasm, probably given—in hindsight—quite accidentally by a drunk skater kid called Aaron, to ruin me for ever. It was the winter before Year 13, early February. I remember because there was a chill in the air and you could see my nipples through the jersey bodysuit Jess had convinced me to wear without a bra. It was at Maddie Hartley's house party, and like all party tag-alongs, I planned only to stay for two hours. I could leave once Jess had seen the boy she was after and strategically ignored him for half an hour before making a move (unlikely) or until she was sick in the kitchen sink (more likely) and needed to be escorted home. But Aaron surprised me. I knew him, vaguely, I'd seen him before outside the boys' school and thought he was cute. He saw me mainlining spirits and instead of coming over and saying something patronizing like, 'I've never seen a girl drink whisky before', he held out an empty mug and asked to join in.

Behind the first door we tried upstairs we found Maddie's parents sitting straight-backed on the bed surrounded by a heap of rolled-up carpets and fragile vases that had been cautiously stowed away, looking at us like they'd been busted and not the other way around. When we eventually made it into an empty bedroom we were both laughing and I grabbed his hand and pushed it under my skirt so he could feel that I was freshly shaved, as per a tutorial some girl gave via biro illustration on YouTube, and wet, as per the hour we'd just spent dry-humping against the side of the sofa downstairs.

The orgasm itself was like a turning point for me, something spiritual. I'd never been able to achieve it on my own, backing down from the climax as if I was afraid of what it might do to me.

I had no idea that this same body that I hadn't asked for, that marked me out as different, that pained me and ached me and made me bleed every month could also make me feel that fucking fantastic. It seemed absurd not to make the most of its potential for pleasure when the pain came guaranteed.

I taught myself everything I needed to know. I learned to give head by following advice off a website called YouQueen. I wanted to be good at it—you might say that I was obsessive about it. I thought if I was going to burn in hell for sucking and fucking then I'd better at least make it worth my while. Then I graduated on to Pornhub, clearing my search history over and over again, and feeling my heart in my mouth any time Constance called my name for the next two weeks.

I practised riding my pillow, arching my back in doggy position in the mirror—because, as all the websites said, it absolutely had to be arched. I would consult Reddit constantly over each new bodily anxiety, because the prospect of sex provided a whole new list of criteria that I needed to live up to.

Do I get too wet?

Are my nipples too big?

What does the perfect pussy look like?

I spent whole nights scrolling through the comments.

The first few times I thought I could counteract the sex with prayers and fasting, spend a period of time I deemed appropriate grovelling to God on my knees by the side of the bed. After a while, I learned to compartmentalize a little better. It's always been complicated. It's like there's this flame of desire that burns blue with ecstasy for a brief moment before it cools down, solidifying to a shame I carry around with me and put my hand into my pocket to feel. I imagine it dark and smooth like one of those massage stones.

*

Texting Matthew is a group exercise for which every- one, apparently, needs to be present. We're gathered sombrely around the kitchen table, Emily, Yomawu, Sara and I, like we're about to begin a seance. Since moving into the Kensington flat last month, I have become accustomed to doing everything as a unit. Every text, outfit, breakfast decision is filtered past the atten- tive ears of the flatshare. I even share Sara's bed with her. At first, I found this co-dependency unsettling. I'm used to skulking in and out of Constance's house like an urban fox, not bound by anything outside of work hours except my own whims and the extent of my bank balance.

I got used to it after a while.

Sara suggests using the Gucci bag as WhatsApp fodder. 'Be like, "Oh, I just remembered I never messaged to thank you!"'

'No,' says Emily immediately. She's fresh off the train after a weekend break to her mansion in the village, to work on her e-book and raid her mother's pill cabinet probably, and she's pinging with repressed energy. I try not to think about whether Constance might have cleaned her house or seen her at the train station. Doesn't matter if she has, I tell myself, Emily would have known how to play it.

'The trick to messaging a man,' Emily continues, 'is to always imagine that he's having the most boring fucking day and then *bam!* A message from you, and suddenly he's got something to wank about during his lunch break.'

'In other words,' Yomawu translates, 'it's got to be sexy.'

Yomawu is painting her nails with Essie nail varnish in the shade Ballet Slippers. No fluffy dressing gown today, she's in good spirits.

'Okay,' I say, 'sexy like what?'

'Ooh,' Sara pipes up again. 'Say: "Hey, sexy, you know I had a dream about you last night." '

'You really are a lost soul, aren't you?' says Yomawu to Sara. 'It's meant to be *irresistible seductress who always gets what she wants*, not like you've been stuck in someone's basement with nothing but a stash of seventies pornos to watch for the last five years.'

Emily nods in agreement. 'You've got to lead him to water,' she says, 'then hold his head under it until he drowns.'

'Umm,' Sara giggles, 'that's definitely not how the saying goes.'

'Oh, you know what I mean,' says Emily, holding out her hand. 'Give me the phone.'

I hesitate so she sighs and snatches it from my grasp. She types the message out with a determined look on her face and then slides the phone across the table to me.

'Read it and weep.'

I clench my jaw. 'Emily, I really will weep if you send this.' I have never been one for flirting via the written word. I mostly only date non-verbal stoners like Toby, and tend to just mirror their one-word responses with streams of yeahs and lols, all punctuated with that single lower-case x. The text that Emily has written is kiss-less. It is provocative, kind of mean, and mortifyingly direct.

'I don't talk to guys like this,' I protest.

'You do now,' she says, taking back the phone with a shrug. 'I've just sent it.'

> **Me:** Matthew
> **Me:** I have a new outfit and nowhere to wear it so I think you should take me out tomorrow. You choose the place.
> **Me:** Don't be disappointing

I toss my phone onto the sofa seat like it's a grenade and cover my face with my hands. I think of Matthew with his dignified expression, his beautiful hands and exquisite suit, opening my message in his plush-carpeted office, his lips curling with disgust, his—

The notification whistle goes off.

As Sara cheers, Yomawu grabs the phone, smudging her still-wet nail varnish in the process.

'What does it say?' asks Sara.

Yomawu aims the screen at me, attempting to unlock it with facial recognition.

'Agnes Green doesn't exist any more,' I say to my phone. 'I have passed away.'

Emily stands up and gets behind me, laughing, lifts my head gently, with a palm pressed to either side of my cheeks. Yomawu takes a lunge forward, holds the phone out like a taser.

'It worked!' she shrieks.

Sara claps her hands, giggling.

'Dun, dun, dun, Agnes Green. You've won a date!' she says in a booming gameshow presenter voice. 'Tomorrow afternoon at Green Park.'

They bundle me up into a rugby tackle of an embrace.

After phoning Emily outside the Three Butts, I went straight to the models' flat and haven't left since. Sara was still in her Martin Garrix hangover T-shirt when I arrived, buttery toast crumbs from breakfast in the corners of her mouth. Emily, face shiny from an oxygen facial, pointed me in the direction of the bedroom without making a big deal about it, and that was that.

In the first days, Emily took me to Harrods and we went to the sushi bar, sat with our elbows on the glass looking down at the googly-eyed fishes, the bright food-hall lights making rainbows in their scales. She took me along to her appointment on Harley Street and I watched a woman whose name badge read *Clara Drayton, senior aestheticist* pierce her already plump lips with sharp needles. Emily looked perfectly serene but she was crushing a dog-shaped stress ball in her lap the whole time, tugging its head between her thumb and forefinger. Clara pointed out my flat cheeks and offered me a syringe of my very own—4 ml to make a visible difference, she said, touching my face to show where the injections would go. Her fingers were hard and cold through her gloves. I told her I'd think about it.

Walking back through the clinic felt like being in a spaceship, the blue glass walls and artificially clean air. *It was like another planet.* That's what Constance said about her early days in England, when she first arrived from St Vincent in the 90s. Thinking about this, I longed for some food that wasn't lobster or a French export. Maybe some of Constance's semolina porridge with strawberry jam or a big warm bowl of rice with black peas, served up with baked chicken and home-made onion gravy.

*

With a final swipe of lip gloss, Emily sends me on my way.

'Remember everything I told you,' she says.

I check my reflection in the hall mirror on my way out. Hair curled with the barrel wavers, a softer version of my signature eyes, glossy red lips. Silky black pussy-bow blouse, flared black jeans, high heels. I'm wearing the specially formulated lavender, pumpkin and vanilla fragrance Emily orders from an aromatherapy shop in Portugal. I need all the help I can get, she tells me.

I'm actually starting to get a bit anxious at the state of my life—my somewhat dwindling bank account, new status as an adult orphan (practically), and now the fact that I'm about to be thrown into my first solo sugaring date without as much as a pat on the head from Emily. There's a good chance I'm going to fall flat on my face.

'Do you have any final words of wisdom?' I call out, and she emerges from the kitchen.

'Hmm,' she says, 'try to sound light, pleasant and sort of placid. Like you've had a lobotomy.'

'A lobotomy?' Is she joking?

'Yeah, but one of the better ones. Go on, the taxi's waiting.'

*

Marilyn Monroe had a manual on how to walk, something about pretending you're hanging from a cloud. I have this in mind as I approach Matthew outside Henry's Café, imagining myself dangling from the white cirrus wisps that hang in the sky overhead all the way from the Tube station.

Henry's Café is a quiet and dimly lit restaurant opposite the Ritz. The kind of place people might choose for a discreet working lunch, less ostentatious than the surrounding venues, and I'm glad because I'm nervous enough as it is—the last thing I need is to feel even more like a fish out of water. Matthew greets me with a kiss on each cheek and as we follow the waiter to our table, I glance at our reflection in the murky gold-coloured metal that wraps around the bar. We look good together. He's in another beautiful suit, still carrying his monogrammed laptop case, still cool in the heat although it's nowhere near as hot as it was when I saw him last.

'Was nice to hear from you,' he says, flicking open his napkin and placing it in his lap. There's something anticipatory in his face, like he's waiting for me to do something extraordinary. 'I like a girl who can get to the point.'

His eyes take me in, rove over my blouse. His glasses have slipped down his nose a bit and he nudges them back into place with the tip of his middle finger. Wedding band noted. I wonder how he manages to make sense of it all, trying to picture his brains inside his cubesque forehead. Separate compartments for Wife, Mistress, Girlfriend.

'How was your week?' I say, struggling for the right words now that Emily isn't here to write them for me.

'Murder at work.' He pushes the ceramic pot of olives towards me. 'You look delectable.'

Delectable.

Everything I do from this moment on—the way I put my bag on the seat next to me, run a finger down the wine list, cock my head to the side—is a concerted attempt to deserve this description. I'm channelling Emily's watery siren eyes, distant and intense. The trick, she told me, is that you have to think of sex—really good sex, the bit right before the orgasm—and then you slow your breathing, and you blink slowly, and let your eyes glass over. I don't know how it works but I think it does something to dilate the pupils.

I'm not sure it's working. Matthew seems distracted, fiddling with his spectacles. 'Excuse me,' he says, 'I don't know what's wrong with me. Need another coffee maybe.' I am the worst love witch in the world.

'So what's . . . why's work been murder?' I stammer.

He makes an exasperated sound. 'Let's not talk about all that. We're here to have a nice time, aren't we? You don't want to hear about authorized capital or convertible instrument, do you?'

I shake my head. I'm failing. I bite through the firm salty flesh of a black olive then realize there's no elegant way to spit out the pit and panic. I dart two fingers into my mouth and pluck it out, push it away from view under the rim of my plate.

'Are you enjoying your new bag?' he asks me. 'You know they'll clean it for you for free, any time. I mean, it's not exactly Hermès,' he says, looking me up and down with an amused smile, 'not quite yet anyway.'

'You don't think I deserve Hermès?'

Fuck. Was that rude? But, to my immense relief, Matthew laughs.

'I think you'd suit the perfume. Vingt-Quatre Faubourg, have you heard of it? It's an elegant scent, orange blossom, makes you think of silk scarves. That can be your next present. The perfume and a Hermès scarf, and every time you see me, you've got to wear it tied around your neck like an air hostess. How does that sound?'

'Sounds like I can guide you to the exit, sir,' I say.

He smiles. 'That's good. Funny.'

I exhale.

I like Matthew. The calm sense of worldly authority that permeates the air around him puts me at ease. And he called me delectable! Who gives a shit about the opinions of little boys when I have the adoration of a man like him? I'm really hoping he might call me delectable again. I *need* to be called delectable a thousand times over.

'Shit, fucking-fuck,' he says and abruptly puts his fork down.

'What, what is it?'

'There's someone from the firm over there,' he says through gritted teeth. 'I think he'll come over.'

I try very hard to sound nonplussed and chill, gabble out a *No worries, I'd love to meet your colleague*, but Matthew doesn't answer. My hands are clammy and trembling.

The man—about five-four, curly grey hair, round glasses— approaches with a gleeful troublemaking look on his face. He reminds me of the actor who played Bottom, in the production of *Midsummer* at the Globe we went to on a school trip. I half-expect him to lunge, rest his elbow on the table, announce: *You see an asshead of your own, do you?* But he doesn't, just claps Matthew on the back.

'Matthew, hi! How are you? How's Carol?'

So it's Carol, is it? It feels weird to give her a name.

To his credit, Matthew does a good impression of someone answering a completely harmless and unthreatening question. He leans back in his chair, crosses one leg over the other. 'Tremendous, thanks,' he says. 'She's been getting into knitting, of all things. So whoever I get in this year's Secret Santa can expect a handmade scarf. A Carol Original.'

'Brilliant, brilliant. You normally just send Mol out to Sainsbury's, don't you?' says the man with a wink. 'And how's little Oliver?' He looks at me out of the corner of his eye.

'Ha, you know what it's like, Dean, by the time the holidays come around I'm already too high on gingerbread and mulled wine fumes to think straight. I do whatever Carol tells me and just pray I live to see the New Year. Oliver's good, teething, poor little guy.'

'And . . . ?'

Matthew gestures casually in my direction, without looking me in the eye. 'This is Agnes, she's my friend's daughter. She's second year at Bristol, thinking of taking a law conversion.'

'And you're selling her the dream, correct?'

'No, I'm trying to convince her to save herself and give up while she's ahead.'

The man laughs at this. 'Agnes, hello. I'm Dean.' Bottom's eyes sparkle as he stretches out his hand for me to shake.

'Lovely to meet you.' I shake his hand chastely.

His glowing eyes scan my outfit, my face, my hair, even the surface of the table, like he's looking for condoms or Class As.

'Well, enjoy your lunch,' he says, slapping Matthew on the back of the shoulder again. 'See you back at the office, you old rotter. And don't let him put you off, Agnes—if there was ever anyone who loved his job, it's Matthew McKinnon.'

Matthew maintains a stiff smile until Dean returns to the bar out of earshot.

'Sorry about that,' he mutters. 'Thank you for . . .'

'Don't mention it.'

I feel for him though I probably shouldn't. Seeing him caught off-guard has made him seem more vulnerable, which is only adding to his appeal.

We eat slowly and talk in quiet, drawn-out sentences. Matthew asks me about my plans for the future. 'There must be something you'd like to do?' He sounds like Jess.

I hesitate, then tell him the truth. That I used to love taking pictures, that I wanted to take a course.

'What kinds of pictures?'

'Portraits, mostly. I like beautiful faces.'

'Me too,' he says, laughing again.

I tell him about the Helmut Newton photobooks stacked on my desk at home—*Polaroids* and *Sex & Landscapes*. He's watching me closely, so I keep talking. I tell him about how looking at a Helmut woman makes me feel. How whether they're clothed in black or jewels or even naked, the effect is always the same. Your eyes are on them. And somewhere in between the grain, the high-carat jewellery, the liquid shine of patent leather, there is a moment of truth captured, a snapshot of a fictional life.

He looks at me the same way he did after he compared me to Anna Karina, and once again, I feel the smug glow of having passed some kind of test. I remember something Emily said to me the night at Palm Beach. *Men choose a sugar baby over an escort because they want to pay for a girl who's not for sale. We're supposed to be educated, a girl he can have an intelligent conversation with. They want to think they're some sort of mentor.* A mutually beneficial relationship.

After he pays the bill, his hand moves across the table and I instinctively lean in, thinking he wants to be affectionate. Between his beautiful fingers is a small white envelope that blends in almost perfectly with the snowy tablecloth. He takes his hand away, and the envelope rests there between us.

That was much easier than I'd thought it would be.

Thirteen

Gentlemen Prefer Blondes

I've spent the last couple of nights since my date with Matthew watching reruns of *Live at the Apollo* while downing pink gin and tonics. I greet the girls as they come home in the early hours like some kind of alcoholic boarding-school matron on the night shift. We haven't gone out together since Palm Beach but Emily promises we will soon. 'Don't worry, we're only just getting started,' she'll say in the kitchen while passing me a menthol cigarette. She has repeated several iterations of this phrase to me over the past week. 'We'll have fun.' 'Next month it's going to be a wild one.' I am realizing that Emily likes to impress me, her little tourist, and that any lack of wide-eyed wonder from me concerns her. But the occasional late-night loneliness aside, I'm pretty happy watching the girls flit in and out of the house for castings and lunches and photoshoots.

*

'Hello prodigal sister,' Marlena answers my FaceTime call with her typical deadpan tone. She's lying in bed, screen light bouncing off her spectacles and making her eyes into glowing white rectangles. 'What have you been up to? Where are you?'

'Chill Nancy Drew, I'm at a mate's.'

'Jess?'

'No, you don't know her.'

Marlena's long face comes closer to the phone camera. 'But you don't have any other friends.'

'Well, I made some.'

'Fair enough,' she says, a little dazed but evidently not worried enough to challenge me. 'Are you coming back on Monday?'

'Lena, I'm not coming back.'

She snorts, 'What are you talking about? Of course you're coming back, just apologize to Mum and everything will be fine.' She's growing frantic, getting up and changing into a comfier position on the bed. I see a flash of elbow, her buttoned up pyjama top and then Marlena's distorted face, chin up close to the camera. 'How do you even have money without a job?'

'I have a job,' I say, without thinking, 'at a restaurant . . . I'm a waitress.'

Silence.

'Well,' Marlena's voice is quiet, barely more than a whisper, 'I think you should make it up with Mum, that fight was pathetic.'

'It wasn't pathetic, it was necessary and a long time coming.'

Neither of us says anything.

'What did you do today?' I ask her awkwardly, like I'm a distant aunt.

She yawns. 'Just revision at the library. Need to use the computers.'

I feel a familiar ache in my heart. 'What happened to that laptop the school lent you?'

'It was so slow, basically on its last legs anyway, it packed up,' she says in an indifferent tone, then sighs. 'I'm really tired, Ag. I'll text you in the morning or something.'

'All right, my love,' I say. 'Sweet dreams.'

* * *

Sara came back with the sunrise yesterday, her pupils wide as a hentai doll's. I'd been having a nightmare about Constance, her face reflecting silvery moonlight as she searched for me in a woodland full of tall pine-trees, the branches spiky against my skin as I hid in the darkness. I woke up with a start—and Sara was there, propped up next to me on the sofa, chattering away on the phone. She reminds me a bit of Edie Sedgwick when she's like that, blonde and loopy and absolutely steaming.

*

Emily says it's time for me to get in touch with Matthew if I want to solidify the *arrangement*. She sits beside me to help with the wording though it's easier now to ask myself, 'What Would Emily Do?' and act accordingly. I'm way more confident dealing with men when I have a framework to stick to.

> **Me:** Liked seeing you, I want to do it again.

Matthew's response arrives in seconds.

> **Matty:** Should we make it a regular thing?

> **Me:** What I'd really like is a monthly allowance and weekly meets.

> **Matty:** Monthly allowance is no problem provided you stay the night with me every fortnight. Good with you?

> **Me:** Fine by me.

> **Matty:** How much?

> **Me:** 2.5k

Matty: 2k

Me: 2.4

Matty: 2.2k. Final.

Me: Agreed.

Matty: That's perfect. Send me your bank details.

Two minutes later he sends me the details of a hotel room booking.

I do my make-up in the bathroom, pleased that my winged eyeliner technique is improving. Sara's there to wave me off, pink-cheeked and tipsy after meeting some property tycoon for lunch.

'What's the plan for tonight then, sweet-cheeks?'

I get out my phone to show her the screenshot of the reservation but I can't find it and I feel my face getting hot as I scroll up and down my camera roll.

'You're nervous,' she says.

'No . . . yes.'

Don't get me wrong, it's hardly my first rodeo but it's never been like this before. Formal, an official transaction. I've been selling a dream and now it's time to deliver.

She shrugs, grinning. 'Don't be. You've already sorted out the money side of stuff, right?'

'Yeah.'

'And you're happy?'

'Yeah.'

But Sara doesn't know me well enough yet to realize that monosyllabic responses are my way of avoiding the question. I don't know how I feel about it yet, only that I'm going to do it.

'Then you're all good,' she says. 'It's no big deal. You like Matty, right? He's decent-looking.'

'Yeah, I like him,' I say. And then, 'Did Emily ever . . . ?'

'Sleep with him? Hmm, I actually don't know. Others though, obviously.'

'Obviously.'

'Did she ever tell you about the five Ms?'

'The what?'

'Oh my God, it's this genius schedule to get the dude to come like, super-fast. But not *too* fast.' She starts to count on her fingers. 'First massage him—neck, shoulders, arms, hands, whatever. Kiss him here and there to break it up. The second M is masturbate—as in touch yourself in front of him . . .'

'Yeah, I know what it means, thanks.' I'm surprised at the edge in my voice, the nerves tightening the muscles in my throat.

'All right, bitch, chill out,' she says warmly. 'The whole idea is to get him really worked up at the start so you don't have to put too much work in later. It's just more efficient.'

'Okay,' I sigh, 'makes sense. What's number three?'

'Move,' she says.

'Sara, I have had sex before. You know that, right?'

'Ha ha,' she says. 'Well, you know how to move then. Respond to every touch. When he's fucking you in doggy or whatever you should fuck him back. A lot of girls don't, you'd be surprised.'

'Okay, no playing dead. I get it. What's next?'

'Number four, umm . . .' She puts her hand on her hip, and her eyes flicker up to the ceiling as she tries to remember. 'Mirror! That's the one—use a mirror. Blow him in front of it or get him to fuck you from behind so he can see himself. Men are visual. Oh, and the fifth one is moan. You've got to really amp up the noise towards the end. Not like a fucking porn star or anything, but a well-timed, well-pitched moan really does something to the reward centre of a man's brain, like a dog whistle. I had this one guy so well-trained he would come in time to my breathing. Got him down to like four minutes. Now that's efficiency.'

'What if it's not good enough to make me moan?'

Sara rolls her eyes. 'You're a girl. You know how to fake it. Now let's hear you.'

'Pardon me?'

'Agnes Green, let me hear you moan.'

I laugh. 'Get the fuck out of here, absolutely not.'

'I'll do it,' she says, closing her eyes, tilting her head back, running her hands through her feathery white-black hair. 'Mmmmmmm, *Matthew*. Uh, yes! Yes! Fuck me just like that! I'm gonna ride the glasses off of you. Ughhhhhhh.'

I nudge her in the tummy. 'Sara, stop.'

'Your turn,' she smiles.

'I'm not doing *that* but I'll try out your little routine,' I tell her, 'but only because . . . only because I'm a *tiny* bit nervous.'

On my way to the Tube, I get a text from Emily.

> **Emily:** Let me know how it goes with the five Ms, it's a big section of the e-book.

(I didn't realize she had been in the flat, or within earshot of us.)

> **Emily:** Don't worry if you forget though, there's only two things you HAVE to remember no matter what.
> Stay in character.
> And whatever you do, never mention his wife.

Vodka soda with lime, sipped slowly because I don't want to bloat. I have no idea what to do with my hands. I get up Pinterest and add new pictures to my Femme Fatale board, which I started after that very first night out with Emily at Hades. I don't know why Matthew chose this place, an unsettlingly eclectic hotel bar, you know the type. A faux bear's head over a shiny teal-coloured fireplace, paintings of pigs and fruit and pilgrims with pitchforks. Bartender with a ridiculous moustache. Maybe Matthew wanted to be sure no one he knew was going to see us. My God, I'm fucking nervous.

I'm wearing a black shift mini-dress, chosen for its easily accessible zip. Matthew puts his hand on my thigh as I reach the bottom third of my second vodka soda. We haven't even kissed yet. I do want him, it just feels so strange. My nerves are partially eroded by the vodka and there's just the sense of being in unchartered territory and I get the paranoid feeling that I'm being recorded—which is ridiculous, right? I can admit that I feel guilty—the guilt is lukewarm and buried under the soft soil of my determination, but it's there. Matthew doesn't display the slightest indication of nerves, he's more like a child waiting to trade in his tickets for a fairground prize.

He's already checked in, he tells me—he came straight from work, showered, ate in the restaurant while he was waiting.

'Was it good?' I ask him, a half-hearted stab at conversation while I try to remain calm with three-seconds-in, three-seconds-out nasal breaths.

He shakes his head. 'Dreadful.'

Doesn't really bode well. I can't decide whether I should have another vodka. I'm probably at my limit if I want to remember the four Ms (or five Ms? Fuck) and give a memorable performance but on the other hand I'm tempted to knock back a few shots for the sake of confidence.

'Do you not want a drink?' I ask him, putting the inflection on the word *you* to make it sound like our little in-joke. Really, I'm spooked because he's unset- tlingly sober. I like my men a little off balance—it's less intimidating.

He orders some Scotch whiskey on the rocks, sips it. He toys with the hem of my dress, traces my kneecap, the top of my shinbone, with the backs of his fingers. As he drains the watery amber-coloured whisky at the bottom of the glass I tell him I want to go upstairs. I can't take the suspense for a minute longer.

I follow him down the hall to the lift. Once he's pressed button 2 for our floor he puts his arm around my waist, a hand behind my neck grasping for my hair.

I flinch. 'It's a weave,' I say, softly. 'Don't pull it.'

'I won't.'

He puts his hand around the front of my neck instead, holds me gently by the jawbone, gazes into my eyes. *Ping.* We've arrived at our floor. Shit. I'm nervous. I should have had the shots. I can't remember the last time I was this nervous to fuck somebody. My knees feel like they're going to buckle. Now he takes me by the hand, pulls me behind him. Unlocks our bedroom door with the key card. What are the five fucking Ms? Moan, move . . . mirror? Use a mirror? Mirror what? Um, masturbate, I know that's one of them.

We sit down on the edge of the bed like two awkward teenagers on prom night. But it's a good kiss, not one of those clumsy first kisses when you don't know the dimensions of each other's mouths and end up knocking teeth. He slips his tongue in at just the right moment and I moan, no faking required. I take his hand and guide it between my legs.

'You're wet already,' he whispers. He takes off his trousers, then his soft grey boxers. He still has his shirt on. 'Come here.'

I unzip my dress and it slips down my shoulders. I step over the tangle of fabric that flops around my feet.

He stands by the side of the bed, facing me. Oral. This wasn't on the list. He's a pusher, I *hate* that. But I oblige him. He's pretty big, my jaw's already aching.

I sit back, apologetic. 'Can we . . . can we change?'

'Sure,' he says. He looks down admiringly at my face, wipes my chin with his thumb. 'Turn around.'

Agnes, don't you dare. I can already feel it, the embryonic feeling in the pit of my stomach that unfurls ever so slightly and murmurs 'maybe?'

Maybe, just maybe he feels something? No, Agnes. We don't do that anymore. Keep your head in the game.

I shuffle around on my hands and knees, taking too long apparently because he grabs me by the ankles and drags me back. I lose balance momentarily then get back onto all-fours. 'Look at you. You gorgeous creature.' Creature? Doesn't quite feel like a compliment.

He pushes inside me. It's good, a little painful, which isn't necessarily bad. I kind of thought it might be like this—one well-rehearsed motion after another. I imagined he'd have a set menu in mind, his greatest hits, because if you're paying why wouldn't you? Oh damn, I've forgotten to move. I grab fistfuls of the bedsheet for stability and push back hard, his balls slapping against me.

He groans, 'Fuck, that's good.'

Okay, I can do this. This is nothing new. Actually starting to feel a bit pleased with myself, I can feel my cheeks twitching with the smile I'm fighting to contain. I keep going, reach back and fondle him, tugging his balls gently. He groans again. For fuck's sake, that's *my* job. It's frankly a bit off-putting. The whole thing lasts five or six minutes and then he finishes dramatically and collapses on top of me, stroking my ribcage delicately.

'That was great,' he says, smiling with his eyes closed. 'Did you, darling?'

'No,' I say, 'but that's all right . . .'

He's shimmying down the bed, pushing my legs apart. I won't stop him. It's nice but too slow and lazy for me to get going. His head rests against my thigh, and I think he falls asleep for a second with his mouth on me.

He crawls up beside me and kisses me on the lips, a long kiss. He strokes my cheek.

'You're so pretty,' he says.

'Thank you,' I say, looking away because the gaze in his eyes is so intense it's threatening to burn me. God, this was easier when I didn't have to look at him, so much less . . . personal. I press my lips together because this is the part where a much younger, less experienced Agnes would spit out, 'I love you,' like it was some kind of reflex.

As we lie side by side I luxuriate in the feeling of having done a very adult, very forbidden thing and not feeling bad about it. There's no sign of Jesus. I think God's finally given up on me.

Matthew falls asleep spontaneously. And I feel quite powerful, like I'm a succubus that's drained his life force. He's still wearing his shirt, the white tails splayed over the tops of his thighs like one of those Victorian nightgowns.

Emily's awake when I get back, using her NuFACE infrared light, stretched out on the sofa. It's pitch dark apart from the TV and the red light that reflects in her eyes and makes her look demonic.

'Did you do the deed?' she asks me.

'Yeah.' I head towards the bathroom. For the first time since moving in, I feel impatient to be alone.

'Nice, how do you feel?'

I stop to think about it. 'Awake. Wide awake.'

*

The morning after, the first thing I do is go to Curry's, order the most state-of-the-art laptop I can find and have it sent to Marlena first class. They let me include a note with the parcel and I write, *May as well get used to the MacBook life now—can't have you sticking out in the Cambridge lecture halls. Love from your prodigal sister x*

I find myself—in the quiet moments spent queuing at the payment desk, waiting for my Uber, moisturizing after my shower—fighting hard against any romantic notions of Matthew that threaten to pop up in my brain. It's always been second nature to me to start fantasizing about the guy I'm sleeping with, to panic that they're going to lose interest in me, that I'm going to do something, or maybe have even already done something to fuck it all up. But this isn't like that Agnes, this is just sex, remember? This is a transactional relationship.

Mutually beneficial. And after the fourth or fifth time of reminding myself, it starts to settle in and I feel calm and in control of myself again.

I go to an expensive Black salon in Forest Gate and have a new weave done. The place smells like coconut, Dark & Lovely lotion, and lye vapour from relaxers. There are posters of black models pasted high up on the walls like deities, not a frizz or kink or curl in sight. I don't even know what my natural hair looks like, to be honest—it's been relaxed or braided or woven away since I've been about six years old. Constance never seemed to mind what I wanted to do with my hair as long as it looked natural, the look on her face when I asked her once if I could get pink dip-dyed extensions.

Swiping oil from the back of her hand with her index finger, the stylist dabs it along my rows of braids, gait swaying. The braids are too tight and I almost let it slide but decide not to, decide to ask her to undo them, and she begrudgingly starts again. She reaches into a box and comes back holding a fistful of glossy golden caramel hair, striped with platinum blonde highlights, like she's just scalped a Texan beauty queen. When she pulls the thread, stitching me together like a doll, I don't even flinch. I let my mind drift, dissociate from the pain.

Gentlemen Prefer Blondes.

Let's test the theory.

This café is really something. It's the kind of place I would have idolized when I lived in The Wasteland but, now that I've become accustomed to grand Mayfair lounges, looks try-hard and chichi. Fake pink flowers cling around the entrance archway and pigeon-toed influencers wander around underneath it on the balls of their strappy high heels. Emily sucks on a watermelon vape outside, a Dior saddle bag in the crook of her elbow.

'You look like a movie star,' she tells me, laser-beam eyes scanning me over.

'I know,' I say. 'I'd better, I fucking paid enough for it.'

'Honest. You look so striking.'

There it is. 'Striking'. Emily uses this adjective to describe me a lot. 'Striking' is not quite the same as 'beautiful' or 'gorgeous'. There's a subtle edge to it, a difference. It reminds me of the way that Camilla and the other Cathies would make cooing sounds at my mother's radiant beauty, saying how *exotic* she looked, extolling how lucky I was to have benefited from her excellent genes, how my skin would never age or crease.

But somehow, I can't bring myself to care. She means it as a compliment so I'm taking it as one.

When we're shown to a table, I have spied my fresh gold tresses in roughly thirteen reflective surfaces, including mirrors with 'Smile, You're Beautiful' printed on them in cursive, and I'm in such a good mood I don't even mind that the place is overcrowded and our lavender matcha lattes come grainy and cold. Emily throws her card down onto the bill and it clangs against the little metal dish.

'Let's take a picture together,' she says, holding the phone at arm's length and aiming the camera down at us. 'Maybe one of these cunts will help us get a paid post sponsorship. Come on.'

I bite the insides of my cheeks to make my cheekbones pop, tilt my chin so my face is under the light at the right angle. Pout my lips, give the camera 'fuck me eyes'. We look good. I look good, like better than ever.

'Send that to me,' I tell her.

'Done and done.'

I post it to my Instagram with a singular strawberry emoji in the caption, for mystery.

*

Me: Heyy, Jessica

Me: Hope you're having a good time on your travels?

Me: [photo attachment]

Me: What do you think of my new look? Eeeeeeeek, crazy
right? So different?
Me: Love you, speak soon xx

I'm trying to accept the fact that Jess has been unashamedly airing my
messages since she went on holiday. I know she'll be back in a couple of
months, excited to brag to me about full moon parties on the beach and
discovering turtle eggs or whatever it is you do in Thailand. She won't
ask me any questions about myself out of politeness, assuming I have
nothing to share and that my life's in the same standstill it was when she
left. I have to admit, I'm excited by the prospect of proving her wrong.

A waiter walks by staring at us and trips over a pram—thankfully
it's empty.

I shake my head. 'Poor guy.'

Inside me, little eight-year-old Agnes claps her hands and turns cart-
wheels. We are beautiful and the whole world knows it.

Emily wants to hear more about Matthew. 'Was it weird? Him being
your first proper S.D.?'

'It didn't feel like anything,' I sort-of-lie. 'It was almost too easy, you
know? I was nervous before, but once it started it was . . . normal. It
makes me a bit paranoid, that's the only thing, like I'd hate for people
to find out about this, can you *imagine* what they'd say?'

She nods. 'I know. But it's cool, like I told you before, they've all got
way too much to lose to broadcast any of this, and in five years I'll be
married up anyway, some old man's trophy wife, fucking my tennis
instructor.' She laughs, high and twinkly.

'Isn't that a little bleak?'

She shrugs, checks her reflection in her jewelled pocket mirror. 'I
actually think it sounds kind of delightful. I'll live on a huge estate with
a pool and a sauna and a wardrobe the size of a shopping mall, I'll bump
into the husband every so often but apart from that I'll be a free agent.
I'll do whatever I want and not have to worry about a thing. How about
you, what's your plan?'

'I don't know.'

I wish she'd move on from this. I hate people nagging me with their expectant smiles, hoping I'll cough up a plan, a goal, a dream. My plan is having no plan. For now.

'You don't know what you want?'

'I told you,' I say, 'I have no idea.'

'Do you want kids?'

'Probably not,' I tell her with a sigh. The thought of having a relationship with my kids like the one I have with my mum, a scam on both sides, makes me want to vomit. 'How about you?'

'Not if I can help it,' she says.

I half-expect her to ask what happened with my mum but she doesn't. I think she takes it for granted that mothers and daughters don't get along. She doesn't miss Camilla so why would I miss Constance? And I don't—well, maybe a little bit. But not really, not as much as I should.

I take her hand and we leave the campy influencer café, wait for our taxi outside. No neck remains unturned. They grin at us. They take in our designer outfits, flawless skin and shiny hair approvingly. Some of them scowl, or acknowledge us with a blank stare. Who cares? We're being noticed.

'Let me buy you a drink,' says some guy who's just passing. He wears a silly insincere grin and a beanie hat, too young to be serious.

'No fucking chance,' I tell him.

He looks back at us with a mock puppy-dog pout.

Emily cracks up. 'That's my girl.' She puts her arm around me and I lean into her cloud of rose perfume.

I see Matthew again a couple of weeks later. I needed to wait for the swelling from my cheek filler to go down. We drink in the hotel bar, have sex for fifteen minutes and then I stroke his hair and listen to his rambly stream of consciousness until he falls asleep. I'm making almost double my monthly salary as a cleaner from sleeping with a guy twice a month who I'd quite honestly probably sleep with for free. And the sex is okay. It's not earth-shattering but it's nice, you know?

I realize we're supposed to be different from escorts but when it comes down to it the difference is basically cosmetic—not that Emily would ever admit it. But I can. And it's not so bad. I don't feel the burn of hellfire flames at my feet. Maybe I feel flames inside of me but in a good way, as though the dark, craggy recesses of my soul are being lit up with candles, as if I'm free to be as naughty as I like.

And it *is* getting easier. When I think of myself in those terms, as a girl for rent, it's easy to get out of the bed and put my dress on, to shake Matthew awake and tell him he needs to be going, to hop in an Uber and not worry about when he's going to text me next. It's easy not to miss him or make it any more than what it is. But he always texts, of course. He can't help himself. He can't wait for the next time, he tells me. I'm getting the hang of this.

*

Toby: hey, did you block me on IG?

Toby: idc it's just a bit over the top, no

Toby: look, I thought we left things on a good note

Toby: well anyway, you obviously don't wanna talk rn but I just wanted to let you know you look really good

Toby: my mate Mo showed me your profile

Toby: 🔥 🌝

Toby: are you still in The Wasteland?

Fourteen

Bambi on Ice

I've brought back a carton of eggs from WholeFoods as my contribution to today's hangover breakfast, golden yolk. I still find it strange shopping there, with the roomy aisles and soft-spoken cheesemongers, but the sugar babies favour fancy organic supermarkets so I follow suit. I suggested going to Tesco for nibbly bits last week when all the other shops were closed and Sara looked at me with wide-eyed horror.

I've decided to start a new, additional secret Insta- gram account to document my sugaring dates and gifts, for no other reason than it's interesting to keep a record. *sugarbabydollxo9*. It's anonymous, no selfies, just vibes. The girls all think it's a cool idea and follow me back.

'Maybe it will blow up,' says Yomawu. 'You'll be a mysterious, anonymous internet celebrity.'

'I hope not,' I say, nauseous at the thought.

We listen to the opening strings of 'Honeymoon' on Sara's record player—she actually buys vinyl for it at this shop in Brick Lane. Yomawu is making pancakes—she mixes drops of pink food colouring into the batter and fries up hearts and bunny heads.

I've been getting to know Yomawu much better in recent weeks. Yoyo, as Sara calls her, is the only one of us with a university degree.

She puts it down to strict Ghanaian parents, tells me she would have preferred au-pairing or travelling in Vietnam to the four years of law she did at rainy Leicester. But the essays on stop-and-search gave her an interest in life beyond the high gates of her exclusive all-girls boarding school. Into the lives of poorer Black people in the UK, she tells me, picking her cuticles. She didn't participate in any of the Black Lives Matter marches or protests because she had no one to go with, but left an 'okay' anonymous donation.

Yomawu has a unique and highly specific sense of style. She's an aesthete. She favours pastels, vintage 1960s babydoll dresses. She keeps her hair ribbons tied to the rail across the foot of her bed, which reminds me of a wishing tree. For shoes, she likes simple black pumps and white embossed tights which look like icing on a cake. On her desk is a gold-edged notebook covered in pink satin, and a white fountain pen, kept carefully aligned with the edge.

I'm not sure why Yomawu does it, the sugaring. Perhaps a belated teenage rebellion. Perhaps she simply sees it as part of the London model package. In any case it doesn't seem as though she actually enjoys it much. Like she's a Charlotte trying desperately to be a Samantha out of a performative commitment to sexual liberation.

After every night out Yomawu spends the next morning burritoed in her lilac bedcovers and crying. Then Sara comes in saying, 'Yoyo,' in a sing-song voice and wedges herself beside her in bed. Emily makes no effort to hide her disdain for the whole charade. She can't understand the lack of control. Even her wild moments are carefully orchestrated.

As morning becomes afternoon, the air turns smoky from exhaust fumes and the burning meat of a thousand barbecues. Emily mashes the rest of her pancake on the end of her fork and dips her finger in syrup.

'Should we go up to Freya's later?' she says.

Freya is one half of the thirty-something couple who live above us. They have a roof garden that we are informally permitted to use, by virtue of some crack in the tenancy agreement, when the weather's good. Their apartment is exotic to us, a curious trove of adult accoutrements like potato mashers and fabric softener.

'Won't they be at work? It's Monday,' Sara says.

Yomawu shakes her head at Sara in disbelief. 'You really live in total ignorance of the standard English calendar, don't you? Today's a bank holiday.'

Dressed in our bikinis and cover-ups, with oversized sunglasses like we're ready to dodge the paparazzi, we begin the procession upstairs. Emily, Yomawu, Sara and I. The last I saw of Kiki was an Insta story she uploaded yesterday, specks of sea foam hitting the lens as she filmed herself from the back of a jet-ski.

Emily bangs on the door and Freddy answers it. He's wearing Birkenstocks. He smells a bit boozy and he's squinting at us as though his eyes are readjusting from being outside in the bright sunlight. He's a writer, allegedly, don't know what for. Sara's always drooling over him because he looks like an unwatered plant with a coke issue.

'Can we come in?' asks Emily. 'And use the roof?'

Freddy looks us over, his eyes darting across our bikini tops. He has really pointy incisors, I notice, and a bit of a weak chin despite his thinness. Maybe he'd look better with a beard.

'Sure,' he says. He steps aside and gestures for us to enter.

'Oh, hi, girls,' says Freya, who doesn't look pleased to see us but maintains a frosty politeness. I have never seen Freya in socks or shoes—her feet are constantly bare. She's got the kind of round Nordic face it's easy to picture in a fur hood and looks like she would have healthy, immaculate organs. 'How are you doing? Come to use the roof? Go ahead.' She's in the middle of a painting and there are a lot of thick white sheets everywhere to protect the wooden floors.

The other girls pass through the French doors out onto the roof. I linger by Freya.

'What are you working on?' I ask her.

I never had the patience for painting in school, preferring the instantaneous rush of snapping something with a camera, but watching Freya work makes me wish I could do it too. Something about the labour of the process, the shades and the textures coming together slowly, makes the final picture all the more enchanting.

'A commission,' she says, straightening up from the canvas and smiling at me, a warmer smile than the one she gave us when we entered the apartment. She takes her palette knife and daubs off some paint, the colour of sunflower petals.

'I love that yellow,' I sigh, then think, it's been a while since I said the word 'love'. 'How long did it take you? To get this good, I mean.'

She laughs, shrugs. 'Well, my parents are artists. So maybe it's in the blood,' as she says this last word, she reaches out and nudges me in the side of the ribs. 'A lot of practice and a degree at St Martin's helped a bit too. But at the end of the day,' she crouches down beside her canvas and squints at it, arching her neck as she takes it in from another angle, 'you're basically just trying to get other people to see the world from your point of view. That's all. And if you can do that, you're an artist.'

To get other people to see the world from your point of view. I want to stay and ask her more about this, but I can hear Emily calling my name from outside.

'I'm sorry,' I say helplessly, because I can't tell her what I really mean, how fascinating I find all of this, her work, how watching her brush ochre onto her canvas makes this crazy bud of hope open up inside me. 'Sorry—for intruding on your afternoon, I mean.'

She winks. 'Well brought up, aren't you?'

The rooftop looks like it's waiting for the rain to come. A hanging flower basket with a shrivelled-up purple flower inside, a patio with rock-hard soil and a pile of cracked chimney pots in the corner. Freddy is propping up the last sun lounger for me to sit on, Emily watching him as she applies suncream in a fine mist out of a pink can to her outstretched forearm.

'Fred,' she says, placing a delicate emphasis on the letter 'd', 'have you got anything to drink?'

He scratches his chest. 'We've got, um . . . Pimm's or Aperol? You guys want a Pimm's?'

'The old-people drink?' Yomawu says with a grimace over the top of her sunglasses. 'Do you have any pink gin?'

'Nope.' Fred is one of those white boys like Toby who doesn't speak in full sentences, instead preferring to communicate entirely in one-beat answers, like every syllable he chooses to utter is a precious gift to humanity.

'A jug of Pimms, thanks,' Emily says in the same voice she uses with bartenders. She tilts her face up at the sun, then inspects the skin on her forearms, her movements precise and rhythmic as the minute-hand of a clock.

'Thank you *soooooo* much, Freddy,' says Sara, flashing her wonky grin. God, she is such a soft boy magnet. 'I'll come and help you.'

'Cheers, babe.'

She uncrosses her coltish legs and follows him back downstairs.

'Have you spoken to your mum yet, Agnes?' Yomawu asks me. Her head is resting against the sunlounger cushion, so her question is directed out at the street, to the steaming tarmac. 'Only if it was my parents I'd ghosted for a month, they'd have already sent the whole of the London Constabulary to drag me home.'

'Pffft,' Emily laughs. '*Your* parents are probably tracking you as we speak, they've got your location on GPS.'

'No,' says Yomawu, 'they promised me they deleted that app after First Year. They were just paranoid.'

'You believed them?' Emily shakes her head. 'Look, if you ask me, Agnes has won the jackpot here.'

'What do you mean?' I ask her shakily. This conversation is really throwing me. I'm trying to expel thoughts of what Constance could be doing right now, probably in her faux-satin headwrap making a bowl of coleslaw or something, swaying to Hillsong Worship on the CD player.

'The big fight, independence from your mum forever! You don't have to play happy families around the Christmas lunch table when you all know you really hate each other's guts. Win, I say.'

'Yeah, but it might get a bit sad,' says Yomawu, her eyes watching me steadily to see whether she's upsetting me or not. 'Not having any family to have Christmas with and that.'

'We're her family,' says Emily sharply. 'We're basically sisters.'

I have a sister, I think but don't say out loud. I can't remember whether I told her about Marlena and she's just forgotten.

Up until now, I hadn't considered the consequences of leaving home, had sort of seen it like an extended holiday in the city. There was always a vague shadowy picture in the back of my mind that I'd be reuniting with Constance and Marlena at the end of it. I slosh out Pimm's into my glass as soon as Sara puts the jug down on the table and drink it fast.

As Freddy smokes, leaning over the balcony, Sara slips her long-sleeved black mesh dress off and stretches out in her bikini like a cat in the sun.

'Sara's birthday soon,' says Emily. 'We should go out.'

'Ooh, okay,' says Sara. 'How about Egg?'

'No,' says Emily, without a moment's breath.

'Phonox?'

'No.'

'Fabric?'

'No,' Emily sighs. 'You know what? I'm gonna message Eduardo and see what he can put together for us.' It's been established by now that Eduardo is her superstar nightclub promoter—every promoter needs a socialite model and every socialite model needs a superstar promoter. They're yin and yang. She reaches for her phone from her bag. 'Maybe a steak or sushi dinner, rooftop cocktails and then he can get us a table somewhere good.'

'Okay,' says Sara. Her expression is cheerful but there's something dutiful in her tone. 'Thanks, Em.'

Emily smiles.

'How are your parents, Sara?' asks Yomawu. 'Do you reckon they'll send you one of those Fortnum's hampers again? Because those truffles were to die for.'

'Oh, maybe.' Sara perks up. 'They're at the house in France right now, I think.'

'Well, why don't we go there?' Yomawu suggests.

'And stare at a bunch of fields?' Emily groans. 'I'd rather get shot in the head.'

I turn onto my stomach on the sun lounger and watch Freya through the French windows. She's been painting in a hypnotic frenzy for the last five minutes and now stops for a break, wipes her nose roughly with the back of her hand and drinks from a glass flask.

The rest of the evening is wasps, olive tapenade, ambulance sirens, suncream, condensation drops on the glass of the Pimm's jug, cold chicken drumsticks and vinegary potato salad. We play Cards Against Humanity and Emily wins every time. Freya passes around blankets when the air gets chilly, and Freddy is sent out for Coronas and dessert. Somewhere an owl is cooing.

'Something lemony!' Sara calls out.

He returns with a Sainsbury's bag full of a big strawberry trifle, two little lemon mousses, and a pack of Corona, his puny arm muscles twitching under the strain. We sit until Sara zonks out, clutching a half-finished pot of lemon mousse, and starts whimpering in her sleep. Emily shakes her awake.

When we leave, Freya gives my arm a squeeze and says, 'Take care, lovely, come back any time.' As I climb into bed, still tipsy, I think how pleased I am to be the one that she likes because she is older and an artist, so her opinion counts for something. I fall asleep easily, happily.

*

Matthew: Hi Agnes, I'll be in Devon for the next couple of days. I shall message you when I return. Will have to get by with just the thought of your delectable body for now.
Matthew: Please don't contact me, I'll contact you. Take care.

Some of these men like to think they're 007, I swear to God.

*

Kiki returns unannounced with a jam-packed Louis Vuitton suitcase and her glossy lips tightly sealed on account of the NDA she's signed. She breezes in around lunchtime on a cloudy Thursday morning, the driver following her up to the flat with his arms full of Dior shopping bags. I can understand Emily's dislike of her, to be honest. The superior way she wafts into the flat, sun-bronzed and smelling of salt breeze.

'You brought the fucking rain back with you, did you?' Emily is on the sofa, holding a UV teeth-whitening device to her mouth.

Kiki pays her no mind, beaming triumphantly. 'Just leave them there,' she says to the perspiring driver.

Sara's performing a downward dog on the rug. All the blood has drained to her face and her silver necklace dangles between her lips. 'How was Greece?' she says, collapsing. 'Did you have a good time with the mysterious Mr X?'

'Who's Mr X?' I ask.

'No one,' says Kiki. Emily rolls her eyes and removes the bulky UV device from inside her mouth, drawing a trail of spit between her lips and the tool like a strand of wet cobweb. 'He's no one now, but when you get drunk you can't wait to tell us all the details.'

'I *don't* get drunk,' says Kiki. She falls down on the sofa with a dreamy, 'Ahhh, it was amazing.'

'Ow.' Emily pulls her legs out from under Kiki's butt, squishes herself up against the armrest.

Sara crawls over and puts her cheek on Kiki's leg. 'How did you find Santorini? So lush there, isn't it?' She looks at Emily, then they both look at me and burst out laughing. It's become a bit of a running joke, all the places I haven't been. *Not even Mykonos? Ibiza?*

Jess still hasn't responded to my last message. Even though I'm sure it's just a signal problem on whatever Thai island she's floating around, I can't help feeling hurt. Like I'm clutching onto a friendship she wouldn't miss. I wonder if I've crossed her mind at all since she's been gone. Since I've been gone.

*

Marlena's calling me, so I wander into Sara's room and sit down on the edge of the bed. When was the last time we washed these sheets? It smells like musk and cigarettes in here.

'Hey Lena, how's it going?'

'I just had a delivery, I wonder if you had something to do with it,' she says, her voice high-pitched and racing the way it used to be on Christmas morning when we were little.

I chuckle. 'What makes you think that?'

'Well,' she says, and I can hear the soft thud of her feet on the carpet as she races up the stairs and the click of her closing door. 'You know how much I need a new laptop, and it's a huge present so who else would send me a bloody MacBook, unless I have a secret stalker . . . Oh my God, do you think I have a secret stalker?'

I laugh again. 'No, Lena, I reckon you're all right.'

'So I thought it *had* to be you but then I questioned it because you can't possibly remember where I live, right?'

'Very funny, Lena.'

'You know I can actually hear you rolling your eyes on the phone.'

'Fucking hell.'

'Don't swear,' she says.

'Jesus Christ.'

'Don't blaspheme.'

'Hang on a second,' I say, lying back and looking up at the ceiling. 'Weren't you calling to thank me?'

'Thank you, Agnes, seriously. I'm really, *really* grateful,' she says, and her voice is rarely as sincere as it is right now.

'You're welcome,' I tell her. 'And I want you to know that anything you need from now on you just have to ask me, okay?'

'What kind of restaurant are you working in? They must be paying you a stupid amount.'

'I've been doing bottle service in clubs as well,' I say. 'They tip you loads, you can make hundreds a night.'

'Oh cool. Well . . . thanks.'

'You don't have to keep thanking me, Lena.'

'All right,' she says, a smile in her voice. 'I've got to go now, Mum's gonna go crazy if she gets back and I haven't put the potatoes in the oven.'

'Take care,' I tell her, holding the phone very tightly against the side of my face.

'Bye, Ag.'

I lie there for a minute, picturing Constance and Lena having dinner together without me. I wonder if Constance misses me. I teeter between guilt and resentment: on the one hand, I should probably call her. On the other, it's not like she's tried to contact me, is it? Plus, if I were to call her I don't even know what I would say. How do you tell someone that they make you feel like a morally and physically inferior being, that the beliefs their life's foundation is built on are bullshit? You don't. You accept that you can't choose family. You try your best to keep moving.

Tonight, we're going out for Sara's birthday. Yomawu has decorated the living room with pearlescent pink balloons and bought all the stuff to make sugar baby cocktails. It's a drink the girls invented as a joke and wheel out for special occasions, a twist on the crack baby. Vodka, St-Germain, champagne, a glacé cherry and sugar on the glass rim.

Sugar babies must be served in a champagne coupe, Yomawu insists, and not a martini glass. 'It's more feminine,' she says, holding up a sugar-dipped coupe triumphantly.

'They're *so* good.' Sara is hovering in the kitchen, eating glacé cherries directly out of the plastic pot.

We sing 'Happy Birthday' and Sara blows the candles out on a custom-made triple-tier cake with a lemon curd and cream filling. The yellow icing is decorated with crystallized candies in the shape of little lemon slices. Sara eats three segments and the icing off the top of Emily's. While Yomawu's mixing more sugar babies, Kiki gives Sara a crystal—a carnelian for strength, she says—and also a Dior purse which she pulls out of one of her many shopping bags and presents with a flourish. Then we take an Uber to Aqua Kyoto on Regent Street where I slide into a champagne trance and don't emerge until the morning.

Sara wants me to keep her company while she takes a bath. A month ago, I would have found it so strange to be sitting and watching my friend bathe, but it feels perfectly natural now. The bathroom door is always open, the girls always floating between rooms in a state of undress. In the loo, Emily wipes between Sara's legs with a fistful of tissue when she's too drunk to do it herself. And when they're drinking they trade kisses like they're trying to top up each other's lip gloss. It's intimate rather than sexual, though I suspect maybe in Emily and Sara's case that line has been crossed.

They're professional models, after all. Their bodies aren't private property in the same way that an average person's is. They're used to being looked at, to being naked, to having their hair and limbs moved around by strangers. It starts to rub off on me and before I know it I'm lotioning up after a shower in Yomawu's room and rifling through her drawers looking for a comfier bra than the one I've got on.

With her wet hair slick to her neck Sara looks younger, even more boyish. Her ears stick out. I sit on the edge of the bath and trail my fingers in the water.

'Did you have a good time last night?' I ask her. 'I know the Mayfair scene isn't your favourite.'

'Mm-hm,' she says, grinning, eyes glazing over with pleasure, because the best part about being hungover is mentally replaying the good drunken memories, the group of us crammed in the DJ booth. 'I had fun. Do you have any idea where Yoyo went when we got to the club?'

'No, she was off on another planet.'

'Typical.' She lowers her voice to a conspiratorial whisper. 'You know, I've got the biggest fucking crush on Freddy. Don't kill me, Agnes.'

My heart sinks. I don't know why. It's not like it's bothered me before, men being taken. Maybe it's because their wives have always been some kind of yeti-like myth and I actually *know* Freya, and I like her. She's not part of any superficial game, not out for what she can get. She's trying to create something, and I bet her relationship with Freddy is the same. We should leave them alone.

'I know, I know.' She clears some bubbles aside and slides down into the tub so her mouth is below water level, like one of those sirens from *Pirates of the Caribbean*.

'Don't go there, Sara,' I say steadily. 'It's not worth it.'

She makes an 'Mmm' sound, like she's considering what I've said, or imagining fucking Freddy—which I honestly don't think would be that fantastic. He doesn't look like he's got enough energy in him to get on top of you—it's definitely a girl-on-top kind of situation—and after he comes you'd probably have to give him mouth-to-mouth.

I reach into the bath and pick her fragile wrist up out of the water. White with a band of purple at the bony part, fading to yellow around the edges.

'Where'd you get these bruises?'

She shrugs. 'Don't remember.'

'They don't concern you?'

'Not really, you know what I'm like after a couple of drinks,' she says. 'What did you call me?'

'Bambi on ice,' I say and we both laugh. 'Emily's in a bit of a mood since Kiki's come home, isn't she?' I ask her.

Sara curves her neck backwards to dunk her hair into the water. 'They've had this kind of rivalry from the start,' she says. 'They're strong personalities. Type As.'

Apparently when Kiki first moved in, she washed her underwear by hand in the basin and hung it up to dry over the shower rail, and Emily took a picture and posted it on her Instagram story with a poll about whether it was gross or not (34% voted yes, 66% no). By way of response, Kiki emptied her entire underwear drawer into the bathtub, ordered luxury lingerie packages to be delivered to the apartment every day and paraded them around in front of Emily for a week. After that it was checkmate. Emily didn't mess with her again.

'She's a witch, you know,' Emily confirms later on, as we're sitting around in the living room, waiting for Kiki to emerge so we can all go out to the rooftop. 'She's probably in there cutting the head off a chicken or something.'

I giggle, uncertain. 'Oh, come on, I very much doubt it.'

'Witchcraft's big in Brazil,' says Emily, shrugging. 'She's got candles, crystals, salt, bones, all kinds of shit in there.'

We all look toward Kiki's closed bedroom door like it's the portal to another world, Emily and Sara trying to stifle their laughter. Yomawu mutters something about the colonial mindset. Then Kiki comes out in a neon yellow string bikini, oblivious or pretending to be, and we all get up to leave.

These tense moments come and go without much digging down into the root of them. It's not worth splitting up the group for. We're stronger together. 'We're social beings,' Emily explains, 'so we're perceived as more attractive in groups. It's like we elevate each other, it's sort of dazzling. People don't know where to look.'

Freya's hair is damp, and she opens the door with a cigarette in hand. The sun-loungers are set up. Freddy is barbecuing lamb skewers, beef burgers, halloumi and corn cobs doused in butter and wrapped up in tinfoil. He forks the cooked meat onto a platter and takes it inside to Freya who's gone to chop up bread and make a salad, then comes back outside and flicks through a copy of the *New Yorker*, drinking canned beer. The sun is about to set.

I like their life, Freya and Freddy's. I like their apartment and the way they operate, not squashed up under each other's armpits but comfortably orbiting each other. And when they do collide, Freya presses her cheek to Freddy's and he puts his hand absentmindedly through the belt loop on her jeans, they have a quick kiss and then they move on.

'They're swingers, it's obvious,' says Emily, lighting her cigarette.

'Shh,' Sara hushes her, 'she'll be back in a minute.'

'Oh, let her hear. Why do you think they always want us up here sunbathing?'

'Maybe they're just nice,' says Yomawu, though I can see the cogs turning.

Kiki unties the string on her bikini top, dusting a little fluff off her breastbone. 'I like this roof,' she says evenly. 'If hipster Ken and Barbie want to see some titty, I say let them have it.'

'It's taking advantage,' says Yomawu.

'Well, who's really taking advantage of who?' I ask.

They turn and blink at me.

We sit out until it's dark, chewing on cobs of barbecued sweetcorn under the almost-full moon, prising hairs from between our teeth with the tips of our tongues. At some point, I decide to rouse myself from my Aperol-induced stupor and go help Freya with the dishes, washing off remnants of sun-dried tomato hummus under jets of pressured water.

'Thanks, love,' she says, 'I appreciate it.' She has a face that especially suits smiling.

I go to place a glass jar on the side of the sink but it slips through my fingers and smashes into pieces on the kitchen tiles.

'Fuck, I'm sorry.'

In my frantic rush to clean up the mess, I kneel on a shard of glass and pierce the skin on my knee. A stream of blood erupts, rolling down my shin.

'Don't worry,' says Freya. 'Don't move.'

She fetches a green First Aid kit out of the cupboard under the sink, mops me up with an anti-bacterial wipe then applies a plaster. Her hands are proper artist's hands—you know, nails cut short, calloused knuckles, little scratches and indents from the hard wooden ridges of paintbrushes and pencils. It's sort of charming the way she touches me so delicately with her beat-up hands, smooths out the plaster with her fingertips.

'Thank you, Freya.'

Fifteen

More Male Humiliation

Emily is already at the restaurant waiting for me. She's not alone but I'm used to this by now—the unannounced male guest, the wallet. However, the man beside her is younger than I'd have expected, dressed all in black. As I get closer I can see that his nails are painted with indigo varnish, and coming face to face with him I take in the dark kohl lining his eyes. They are sitting together at a metal table outside under the awning.

'This is Sebastian,' Emily introduces him. It's the man from that night at Hades. The layers of black fishnet and the silver rings.

He holds his hand up in a wave and, unexpectedly, flashes a tattoo of a pug in the centre of his palm.

'Seb's a photographer,' she says.

I sit down at the table, the metal chair cold against my bare legs, and Seb produces a bag of tobacco and some rolling paper. Before long he's puffing away, the three of us looking out at the road as a woman pedals by, a Pomeranian in her bicycle basket.

When I ask Sebastian about his work, he reels off a list of obscure names, edgy online magazines and the capsule eco-friendly labels of some Hollywood progeny or other. His tone is superior and he barely makes eye contact. Emily mentions a particular model who they both describe as bitchy and not anywhere near as pretty in real life.

I ask if he'll show me some of his work, at which point he looks at me with surprise in his dark brown eyes—as if he's shocked to hear I'm genuinely interested and not just trying to make conversation. Of course I'm interested, more than interested, part of me wants to climb across the table, grab him by the collar and scream at him to TELL ME WHAT YOU KNOW.

He holds out his phone with his Instagram page up. The pictures are fashion magazine editorial quality and some of the faces are famous.

He's waiting for my consensus, fingers full of silver rings tapping the tabletop, anxious for my approval.

'These are beautiful,' I tell him, honestly.

As he takes the phone back from me, his nonchalant air returns. I feel something stirring in me that's been dormant for a while, and ask him if he's in need of an assistant.

'I didn't know you wanted to be a photographer,' says Emily, a sharpness in her voice that makes me think I've pissed her off.

Sebastian shrugs. 'Sure. You ever been on a shoot?'

'No,' I say. 'But I wouldn't get in your way, I swear. I just want to watch and learn.'

He looks at me, tilts his head to the side.

'What kind of pictures do you take?'

Oh my God, he's really thinking about it.

'It's been a while,' I say, 'but I like film.'

'Yeah,' Sebastian scoffs, tapping off ash into the ashtray, 'it's trendy again these days, isn't it?'

I agree with him. Too shy to tell him that the grain in a film photo makes me think of life itself, of the hands that set the ISO and the aperture and shutter speed, that took the film out of its canister and tended to it in the red glow of the dark room, birthed a photograph in the dark water, fingers against the silky paper, hung it up to dry, watched it form—edge by edge, piece by piece.

He tells me he's got a beauty photoshoot for some new Manuka honey skincare line next Tuesday at a studio in Camden, and I'm welcome to come along and observe.

'You might learn something,' he says before turning back to Emily and asking her whether a different model, Tatiana something, still has a raging coke habit.

And just like that, I'm closer to my dream of photography than I ever imagined I'd get and I'm so fucking chuffed I have to stop myself from grinning like an idiot. Sebastian and Emily don't notice though, it's just another day for them.

Everyone I knew growing up worked as a cleaner or a hairdresser or in insurance or telesales or something—no one had one of those childhood-dream jobs, but Sebastian does. He takes pictures for money, like enough money to buy artisan coffees and concert tickets to bands no one's heard of, hideous pieces from every new Supreme drop because they're 'collector's items'. If he can do it, I can do it, surely. All I need is the opportunity to learn how. I really think I can do it, get other people to see the world from my point of view. Be an artist like Freya, like Sebastian.

*

Matthew is in a state of post-coital paralysis beside me in the hotel bed and I'm talking to myself in the dark, thinking out loud.

'And this Sebastian's a real photographer, is he?' Matthew asks me, his eyes half-open, his fingers tugging on my knicker elastic. 'It's not just some ploy to get you naked and take dirty pictures of you?'

'He's a *real* photographer,' I say, though it comes out sounding more defensive than I'd intended. 'I'm going to help him out at the studio this week.'

Matthew pulls me towards him with a hand at the back of my neck and kisses me gently.

I rest my head on his chest and look around at the hotel room, our very own time portal, the curtains pulled shut on the midweek bustle of the city streets below. There's a deck of cards in a pile on his bedside table—he tried and failed to teach me gin rummy for all of twenty minutes. A wine glass with the dregs of what he assures me is a good Rioja in it, a flower-shaped bowl that they sent the chips up in.

As Matthew strokes the length of my back, I think to myself about how much I actually enjoy these meetings. It's nice to be intimate with someone, to lie next to them in the dark—and then, once you've left the room, to find your life is your own again. And I'm surprised to find that as in a normal relationship the sex has greatly improved. We've learned each other's bodies with time, and Matthew cares about pleasing me, he's not one of those men who doesn't give a shit.

'You're gorgeous,' he says, 'fucking perfect. I wouldn't blame this Sebastian guy if he tried it on with you, I've got half a mind to film you myself. Keep you on a disc in my desk drawer.'

'No.' My heart is pounding, I push his hand away. 'No videos, ever.'

'I was just kidding, sweetheart.'

'I thought you hated modern technology anyway,' I say, embarrassed by my overreaction to his joke and trying to play it off with a wink. 'Wouldn't you rather draw me or something?'

'Sure,' he says, taking my hand and kissing it. 'I'll bring my sketchpad next time.'

Video. That's a mistake I'll never make again. Not that I personally got my phone out and decided to record, but more the series of little mistakes that built up to the gigantic one, like the wood and paint and steel that went into building the *Titanic*. Without photographic evidence you can deny, deny, deny but when someone's got you on video, you're done for. I envy people who grew up during the 1970s or whatever, in a time when the word 'screenshot' didn't exist. Now everyone's just waiting for the opportunity to put you online, for better or worse.

I live with the silent fear of that video somehow going viral. I don't speak about it, don't ask about it, it's my own personal Voldemort.

*

In Camden, everything is open and sunlit. I pass a stall making fresh orange juice, a market selling crystals and loose-leaf tea, a man sitting on the wall in front of the lock with a giant mohawk dyed pink at the edges, holding a sign that says HELP A PUNK GET DRUNK. A cluster of tourists queue up to get photos, hold shiny pound coins out in their palms. I navigate it all feeling dazed, my anxious stomach turning over in circles. Agnes, get it together.

I arrive at the studio and press a buzzer. 'It's Agnes, here for Sebastian,' my voice comes out a little strangled from the nerves.

The lock vibrates and I run up two flights of stairs without thinking about it. I pass the receptionist who doesn't look up from her phone, following the sound of the music, thumping and relentless.

Sebastian hasn't seen me, he's talking intently with a middle-aged woman in cut-off jeans and a white shirt with the collar turned up, a thick woven necklace on her tanned décolletage. She reminds me a bit of Camilla.

I'm trying and failing to catch Sebastian's eye. I feel like an idiot and am filled with the certainty that this was a stupid idea. But after five minutes or so, Sebastian comes over to where I'm standing by the snack table. Seemingly oblivious to my bad mood, he himself already has a face like thunder.

'I hate it when the fucking clients show up,' he says. 'They just don't let you do your job.'

Based on the pictures I've seen, I would say that Sebastian's artistic arrogance is somewhat justified.

The model emerges from a pop-up changing room—she's willowy, brunette, with a high forehead and enormous, almond-shaped eyes.

Before, the sight of such a beautiful model in the flesh would have stunned me, but not these days. She stands patiently while a make-up artist drips honey on to her face with a paintbrush.

Sebastian turns to me. 'Just black,' he says, 'three sugars.'

'Pardon?'

He's joking right? This is some sort of hazing thing, it must be. Next he's going to give me a list of impossible tasks to complete and a bunch of fake numbers to call.

'The coffee,' he says, eyelids hanging low as if he's bored of me already.

'Hang on,' I say, 'I didn't come here to just . . . make coffee.'

But he's already gone, wandering over to the monitor set up in the corner of the room and I'm left feeling slightly dazed. I could walk out, fuck it off, go home. Or I could just make the guy a coffee and see what comes of it. I made the effort to travel here, after all, and isn't that what it's supposed to be like? Starting at the bottom and all that? I remember Jess did an internship last year and they made her staple two thousand leaflets together and then unpick all the staples again because someone forgot to print out a double-page ad that was supposed to go in. Her hands were like claws for days afterwards.

I look back at the table of snacks but there's no sign of any coffee, no sign of any hot water for that matter. A woman wheels in a rack of clothes and glares at me.

'You're in the way.'

'Sorry,' I say, springing back.

The receptionist doesn't look up from her phone until I clear my throat and say, 'Excuse me, can you help me with something?'

Even she waits a little longer, scrolling down further on her Instagram timeline until she can bear to pull herself away.

'Yes?'

'Do you know where I can make a coffee?'

She rolls her eyes and points me in the way of the kitchen, where I'm pleased to find a kettle and a jumbo jar of Nescafé Gold.

When I return to the studio, Sebastian has a camera in his hands and is testing out the flash. The model stands waiting in a flesh-coloured bandeau and a pair of leggings, hands on her jutting hips. The owner of the skincare brand is skulking around by the monitor, ready to sound out her critique the moment the first image comes through.

'Thanks, mate,' says Sebastian, throwing me a quick and somewhat panicked glance. 'Hold on to that for me, will you? You managed to use the machine all right?'

'What . . . machine?'

'The espresso machine,' he says, casting a disgusted eye at the mug in my hands. 'What's in that thing?'

I have the feeling I've made a grave mistake, 'Nescafé.'

His one-note chuckle is bone-chillingly sinister, 'What did you say?'

'Nescafé *Gold*,' I say, as if the gold part might just be my saving grace.

He doesn't acknowledge my statement with a response, just carries on as if I'm not there.

I press my back up against the wall. As time passes I feel the mug of coffee grow cold in my hands.

The first images come through and the brand owner calls Sebastian over, her voice hushed and insistent. Sebastian storms over to the lightbox and shifts it closer to the model, tilting it upwards. The tension is palpable. More images come through, the model moves smoothly, her hands framing her face, the make-up artist arriving with more honey. The owner calls Sebastian over to the monitor again.

This time, he stands by me to fiddle with the camera settings, murmuring to himself under his breath.

'Can I help with anything?' I ask him.

He snaps, 'I doubt it,' then to emphasize his point shows me the last few pictures. 'She wants more shine here, and less there. I would take it out in post but I don't want the honey drips to look cartoonish.'

'Have you thought about trying another light?' I ask him.

'What?'

'An additional light at this sort of angle.' I show him with my hands. 'Perhaps you could set the foreground light back to a flash and then leave this one in the background.'

'Fine,' he says, 'we'll try it.'

He points me in the direction of the spare lights and I discard the mug of cold coffee, screwing the additional lights together under the burning glare of everyone in the room. When we're ready I hold my breath for the first shot but it flashes up on the monitor and the owner turns to me. 'Much better,' she says.

Sebastian calls back at us, 'How's that, Geri?'

'It's great,' she says, 'keep going.'

My excitement is tempered with dread when I start thinking maybe Sebastian's going to be angry that I got involved, might think I was trying to show him up or something. When he announces it's a wrap I think about making an excuse and dashing out the door but he walks right over, looks at me and says, 'I've got another beauty shoot next week. Friday. I'll text you.'

There's no mention of money but that doesn't matter, everyone knows you start off with free labour, that's how it works. That's why all the creative industries are dominated by kids from rich families, right? You've got to be able to afford to work for nothing and now, for the first time in my life, I can do it too.

My desperation to tell everyone I know about working with Sebastian overrides my hesitancy to keep messaging Jess. Fingers crossed she gets signal soon so she can send me the gushing congratulations this news deserves.

Me: hey Jess, hope your trip is going well
Me: GUESS WHAT
Me: I'm gonna be working with this amazing photographer in London
Me: So exciting
Me: [sent link]

Me: that's his page, let me know what you think
Me: you were right, I feel like photography is the path for me
Me: safe travels, message me when you can xx

*

Okay, Jess doesn't need to know the nitty gritty details but a part of me is just so excited to be able to tell her that I've got something positive going on for once. It feels fucking good and I hope, *pray*, that it continues.

Sixteen

It's Feet Only

A ny plans for the week, Agnes?' Matthew asks me, refilling my glass with champagne from the ice bucket. 'I think we should go away.'

By now, I've come to learn that Matthew is extremely particular. This is *his* fantasy, *his* vision. I can feel the warmth of it like a spotlight on my face, my body, my hands, and I know I have to perform. In the bedroom or at the bar. Matthew's Agnes is elegant, sharp, agreeable. A multi-orgasmic woman without any messy, unwieldy feelings. Passion on, passion off.

We're back at the eclectic hotel bar, as usual the nibbles we ordered come served in a plant pot.

'Away like . . . where?'

'Like abroad. I'll book something,' he says. We are the perfect pretend couple because each of us knows our part and plays it well. He's the organizer, the instigator, the leader and I'm the obliging companion. Good job I had my passport on me when I left home. It's never travelled further than London, but it looks like that's about to change.

'I've got you a present,' Matthew continues. 'Something I hope you can use in the near future.' He puts a gift box on the table which I open.

It's a Leica M6. The Holy Fucking Grail of film cameras.

'Are you serious?'

'You've been enjoying working with your photographer friend so much,' says Matthew, 'and I know you said you were into film so I asked my PA to do a little research. Was it a good choice?'

'Perfect,' I say, fingers trembling slightly as I stroke the camera in its casing. 'In fact, I think it's too good for me. I haven't taken any pictures in so long, I don't know if I can do it justice.'

'Well, this trip will be the perfect opportunity to try it out,' he says. 'You like portraits, right? Perhaps we can hire you some models.'

'Ah, I know plenty of models,' I tell him with a grin. 'Enough to open my own agency.'

'Well then. That's that,' he says cheerfully.

*

Elated by the camera gift, I fuck him with a little more than the usual vigour tonight. I let him tie my hands behind my back with the Hermès scarf he's bought me. He's still a pusher, he gets excited when I gag. I've learned to fake it. When it's over my ears are ringing with rapturous phantom applause.

*

Sara and Yomawu wave me off when the car arrives to take me to the airport. Emily's gone for one of her suburban detox weekends at Camilla's, but she sends me a cryptic text with a photo of her French dresser mirror—the sight of which makes me shudder when I think of the pink-striped chastity dress sack I was wearing the last time I saw it. I'd rather saw off my own arm than ever put something like that on my body again.

The trip is only three nights long and I've packed one of Emily's hand luggage cases with all the essentials—a lot of different dresses and a shitload of lingerie encased in protective bags with pouches of lavender in them (Yomawu's idea). Oral: floss, toothpaste, mouthwash. Physical: waist-training corset, under-eye cooling patches and a jade roller. Cosmetic: black eyeliner, red lipstick.

It's a cool day, with the grey threat of rain hanging overhead. I'm wearing a black tweed mini-skirt and a matching cropped black jacket with gold buttons, black Chanel pumps, like a nineties supermodel.

Matthew's sitting in the back of the car, pats the seat next to him. It reeks of his cologne.

Yesterday, Matthew WhatsApped me an attachment. A boarding pass. The accompanying message read: 'We're going to Paris.'

Paris! My stomach was fluttering with excitement.

But also . . . Paris? The Most Romantic City in the World? When I'm out in public with Matthew, I walk two paces behind him. We've only ever kissed behind closed doors, I've never slept in a bed with him till morning. I was expecting a beach destination, some isolated anonymous cove where we'd stay in bed until noon and then lounge around under the late sun drinking cocktails. Paris is for couples, not pretend ones, *real* ones.

In the taxi to the airport, Matthew tells the driver where we're flying to. 'Can you play some music to get us in the mood? A bit of Édith Piaf or something. Cheers, mate.'

As 'La Vie En Rose' comes warbling through the speakers in the back, Matthew slides his monogrammed laptop case out from under the seat in front and unzips his laptop, squinting up close to the screen. I stare out of the window all the way.

We arrive at the Hôtel Castille on Rue Cambon which is opposite the Ritz. What does it mean that I always seem to be opposite the Ritz and never inside it? It's a busy street, Chanel, Dior, eggshell buildings with black ironwork balconies, cream shutters. Paris with a capital P.

'Is that where you're taking me later?' I ask Matthew in the coquette voice I've learned from Emily, pointing at the Chanel store as the driver unloads our bags onto the pavement.

'Not far to carry your purchases, is it?' He's scrolling through his phone, searching for a contact. 'Bear with me,' he says, 'I need to make this call.'

There's a vague sense of panic about him that I haven't seen before. It's unsettling to see Matthew this way, like walking into your living room and finding that all the furniture has been shifted around by a poltergeist. He paces back and forth under the black awning outside while I head into the lobby with the driver.

'Fancy hanging around Paris with me for a few days?' I ask him. 'My date's a bit preoccupied.'

He doesn't crack a smile. 'Anything else, miss?'

'No, that's fine, thanks. That man will pay you.'

How easily those words come out of my mouth, now.

We both look out the window at Matthew, who appears to be hissing threats down the phone like Liam Neeson in *Taken*. The driver sighs and slowly trots outside for a smoke. As I sink into a velvet couch, I'm starting to think Matthew has a thing for quirky interiors. The lobby walls are blue-green and there's a polka-dot couch across the way.

A woman in a black blazer with long dark hair and a unibrow comes swishing past the sofa I'm sitting on and teeters around on her heels behind the desk, tapping something into the computer.

'*Anglaise?*'

'Yep.'

'Would you like to check in, *madame*?'

'Sure.' I haul myself out of the seat, dust down my skirt with my hands. 'The room's under McKinnon, three nights.'

'Just one moment, Mrs McKinnon.'

What an absolutely terrifying thought.

She wants me to sign something, I hand over my passport for her to scan. Matthew arrives just in time to put his card details under the room.

'Everything all right?' I ask him in a concerned tone, thinking that if he's basically absent for the entire trip then maybe he'll feel bad for neglecting me and send me off to Chanel with his black card and no spend restrictions.

'Everything's fine,' he says. 'Why don't you go ahead with the small bags, darling. Oh, and if you could hang up my blue shirt for tonight I'd *greatly* appreciate it.'

I'm beginning to feel like an employee—next thing I know, he'll have me going through his work schedule while he's fucking me from behind, laptop propped up on the hotel pillows.

I have never been one of those girls who's always dreamed of Paris. Of being proposed to at Disneyland, getting trussed up like a Christmas cake on their wedding day, of a nice white kitchen with a French bulldog. It must be nice to want everything you're supposed to want. If I were one of those girls, maybe this trip would feel different to me. Still, I like the faded grey beauty of the Seine, the evocative glamour of the tall buildings.

And yet. When we drink hot chocolates outside the iconic Café de Flore, Matthew wrinkles his nose at the sweetness of it and orders a standard coffee with cream. He's still in his business-wear even though it's baking hot—pale blue shirt, inky blue suit trousers, black brogues. He complains about the internet connection and groans at my request for pictures for Instagram. 'Can't we hire someone for this shit?'

I take pictures of the Arc de Triomphe when we circle it in our taxi, craning my arm out of the window to try and get a better shot.

'Can we go to the Louvre?' I ask him.

'Mhmm,' he says, eyes glued to his phone, presumably answering an email. 'Whatever you want, I'll organize someone to take you.'

'You don't want to come?'

'Well, I've been so many times, Agnes, you know how it is. I wouldn't be good company.'

This trip is turning into a washout. I wasn't expecting declarations of romance, getting lost in each other's eyes or slow dancing by candle-light, but a bit of decent conversation wouldn't go amiss. When we return to the hotel, Matthew tells me to go on up to the room and start getting ready for dinner, as he's got work to do outside.

I strip down, put on the hotel dressing gown and watch YouTube tutorials for my new camera, fiddling with the settings until I'm exas-perated. I don't remem- ber it being this complicated. My phone is buzzing against the bedcover and I mentally curse whoever's taken it upon themselves to actually ring me up instead of just sending a simple message. Grab my phone. It's Marlena. Fuck.

'Hi, Marl,' I say, getting up and walking into the bathroom. 'It's been a while. How's it going?'

I'm flooded with guilt. I've been a shit big sister lately—I didn't even call her back when I promised I would, just a few stingy texts here and there wishing her good luck for her exams.

'Are you okay?' I ask her. 'Has something happened?'

'I'm fine,' she says though she sounds a little uncertain. 'Everything's fine, I just . . . missed you. Don't take the piss, okay?'

'Awwww, you missed me?' I croon.

'I said don't take the piss,' she replies quietly.

'Okay, okay. Listen, I'm sorry I never called you back, I've been absolutely up to my neck in it. How are you celebrating acing your A-Levels?'

'Up to your neck in what? I'm not celebrating anything until I get the results,' she says.

'Oh please, with all that studying you've done? You definitely smashed it. Oh, and nothing crazy. I've been working as an assistant for a photographer.'

'No way, really? Congrats, Ag, that's amazing!'

I'm smiling like an idiot in the mirror, allowing myself one unguarded moment to imagine an Agnes Green exhibition with trays full of twinkling champagne flutes and legions of gushing fans.

'Also,' Marlena continues, 'when were you going to tell me you're in PARIS?'

Oh. I forgot about the picture I uploaded to my personal Instagram account, the view out of the window when we landed in Orly captioned *Bonjour, Paris!*

'It was a surprise,' I tell her.

I lean in to study my reflection in the bronze-rimmed mirror. My eyebrows are microbladed, my teeth whitened. My skin has been benefiting from regular oxygen facials and the occasional peel.

'Who are you with?' she probes.

'Just this . . . guy,' I say. Marlena still doesn't know anything about my sugaring exploits.

'Like . . . a *boyfriend*?' She whispers it like it's something forbidden.

'Mmm, not quite. He's . . . older.'

'Agnes—' she's using that same scolding tone she's used on me since we were young, like she's my big sister and not the other way around— 'how much older?'

'A bit older. But, he's cool.'

I look over at Matthew's suitcase, his ironed colour-coded boxer shorts folded into little squares, his socks slotted into a portable felt organizer.

'What's going on with you?' I ask her, trying to steer us away from potentially rocky waters.

'I need to talk to you about Mum,' she says.

'Oh, yeah?' I get that old pang of guilt and resentment and shame, start picking through the complimentary toiletries in the bathroom to distract myself. Make a note to try the lavender shower wash later.

'Mmhm. She's been getting worse,' Marlena says. 'She's got a headache like all the time, she only leaves the house for work. She hasn't held a prayer meeting or gone to United Pentecostals in the last . . . probably two, three weeks.'

'She's probably just been overworking herself,' I say, trying to keep my voice steady. 'Sounds like she needs to go to the doctor,' I say.

The only way I can stop myself from spiralling at this news is to eliminate all doubts, get the facts clear. And there's no doubt in my mind that Constance wants me to feel guilty and ashamed for leaving. It makes sense that she would start acting up now, to worry Marlena and get at me that way. She's hardly going to cave in and be the one to contact me first.

'Yeah, I agree,' says Marlena, 'but I don't think it's medical.'

'No?'

'No, I think it's mental, psychological.'

Regardless of the time she caved and sent me to the child shrink, Constance doesn't really believe in *mental health*. She believes in good old-fashioned prayer. Jesus is the greatest doctor of them all, she used to tell me.

'Why don't you call up Phyllis or Uko? I'm sure between the pair of them they can talk some sense into her.'

'You don't think . . . you don't think you could give her a call?'

I can't help laughing. 'Me? You want her to get *better*, right? Lena, she doesn't want to hear from me, trust me. Call up Uko.'

'Mmm, all right, maybe you're right,' Marlena says in her trademark 'considering-what-you-said-ultimately-unconvinced' voice. She doesn't want to push me any further.

I switch the phone to speaker and put it on the basin rim. I pull my skin tight either side of my eyes, thinking out loud. 'Maybe I should get threads.' My voice feels strange to myself, like it doesn't belong to me.

'What the hell are threads?'

I hear the electric buzz of the key card unlocking the front door.

'I need to go,' I tell her.

'But wait, Agnes, I'm not—'

'I'll call you later, promise!' I blow seven kisses into the phone and hang up.

Matthew comes striding into the room, looking like his spirit has been renewed.

'You seem . . . brighter,' I venture, slightly unsettled by the sudden change.

'Work trouble,' he says. 'All sorted now. Come on, hurry up and get ready! I'm taking you somewhere special.'

I put on a black slip dress with a gold D&G chain belt that fits snugly to my waist. My earrings are gold medallions, like coins, and I wear a dark ruby on a fine gold chain, a gift from Matthew, around my neck. The chain is so fine, it's like the jewel is just floating there on my collarbone.

'You look divine,' Matthew says. He is *staring*. 'Like a goddess.'

I apply Black Orchid liberally and then I'm ready to go.

The driver calls us an elegant couple when he drops us off on a sparkling street, one of many identical sparkling streets. Matthew looks pleased with himself, even though his black velvet blazer looks a little heavy for the balmy summer night.

We eat at Le Bristol, where the set menu is over €400 a person, and I devour my way through black beads of caviar, langoustines, truffled pasta, salmon, a delicious hard smoky cheese, buttery brie and a cheese-cake with cherry compote. We drink champagne. Always champagne in Paris, Matthew insists, quite the romantic now.

I took peppermint oil tablets in preparation for the havoc I knew this trip would wreak on my gut but regardless, my stomach is poking out in my dress, a little black satin bump.

Matthew's in a good mood. 'We can't go home yet,' he says, slotting his Amex back into his card holder before beckoning for the waiter to lean in closer so he can whisper something in his ear.

I'm presented with a Chanel box. Big, white and wide, it barely fits on the table, so the waiter whisks away our glasses and the tall bottle of water we've barely touched.

'What . . . Matthew?' I can't stop smiling, my cheeks are twitching. I'm a sucker for Chanel and he knows it.

'Surprise,' he says. 'Go on, open it.'

A black Chanel flap bag. Its heavy gold chain is bigger than necessary, swinging around from the clasp like a demolition ball.

I thank him profusely, of course. It's beautiful. I love it, Matthew.

Afterwards, we sit at the hotel bar on seats which fan out at the back like oyster shells, and order champagne and St-Germain cocktails. A few chairs down, a grey-haired man with a silk paisley necktie looks me up and down, lips curling around his fat unlit cigar. Matthew's arm tightens around my waist. We drink three or four cocktails each, and then shots of vodka, gin and tonics, champagne.

'Let me set you up in an apartment of your own,' he says. 'You shouldn't have to share.'

He puts his hand around the back of my neck, grips it gently. His eyes are full of watery stars.

'Very funny,' I say. 'Let's discuss it at breakfast, see if you change your tune between now and then.'

'More champagne,' he says to the bartender.

The cork pops, two fizzing glasses slid across the counter.

'You're so sexy, Agnes,' he says. 'Every bloke in here is jealous of me tonight, and you're smart, funny . . . you're . . . I should have married a girl like you.' He lifts his glass in a toast. 'To girls like you—you make life worth living.'

I clink my glass against his. 'You're drunk,' I say.

He shakes his head, downs the content of the glass and wipes his mouth with the back of his hand. When he pulls me closer by the waist and starts nuzzling the back of my neck with his open mouth, I put my hand to his cheek and tell him we should go.

*

I wake up to find Matthew pressed up against my body, his arms around me. In the light, I notice that his eyes are even smaller without his glasses, a little swollen from the late night and the alcohol. He reminds me of one of those red-eyed white rabbits.

'You're awake,' he sighs, shifting closer like he wants to kiss me.

I put my hand over my mouth and giggle. 'I haven't brushed my teeth yet.'

He slides down so his head's at my waist, kisses my stomach, parts my knees with his hand. Outside the window I can see a corridor of mauve sky between the shuttered windows and slanted roofs of beautiful old buildings. Then the birds start, one after the other. I come easily, maybe because I'm sleepy. Matthew wipes his mouth, climbs up next to me and falls asleep again. When he's really tired he sleeps like a dead man—it's almost impossible to wake him.

The shower is heavenly this morning, my post-orgasmic euphoria not quite worn off. I put on the plastic hair cap and use the lavender shower wash, which lathers into an velvety foam. I pretend I'm inside a tropical waterfall, the stream of hot massaging my back and cascading over me. It's a good day to be Agnes Green.

I rub out a circle in the soft fog of condensation on the mirror, and see that my skin is glowing. Then I smooth on rose-scented body butter. I don't much feel like getting into character this morning, so I reluctantly slip into a lingerie set then put a loose-fitting black maxi-dress over it, something that'll feel comfortable in the heat. I leave my face mostly bare, pull my hair back into a simple ponytail.

Matthew is awake, lying in bed on his phone. I sit down beside him to put my sandals on.

'Do you fancy breakfast?' I ask him. 'I'd love a proper pain au chocolat.'

'Mmm,' he says, glancing up at me for a second. 'Why don't you get ready and then we'll go?'

'I am ready.'

Matthew puts his phone down, looking at me for the first time. 'But Agnes, you're not going out like that, are you?' My cheeks turn hot as I realize: he's *smirking*.

'What do you mean?'

'Well, you don't . . .' He lowers his voice, which has risen a few decibels. 'You just don't look very *glamorous*, do you?'

'I didn't know I needed to look glamorous for breakfast.' I'm laughing but I feel as though I've had a door shut in my face.

'Well, that's . . . that's sort of the point, isn't it?'

'The point of . . .'

He says the words plainly, unashamedly. 'Of you.'

Agnes Green, don't you fucking cry. Emily drummed this into me from the beginning—*stay in character, always stay in character, men fall in love with concepts, with ideas*—but I somehow managed to screw it up. I'm fuming. I look at Matthew, eyes glued to his phone screen, scruff of hair on his bony chest—so contained, so content, so self-absorbed—and I feel this overwhelmingly violent urge to hurt him. To sink my acrylic nails into the sockets of his eyes, and pop that condescending glare right out of his head, watch his eyeballs roll across the carpet like a pair of bloodied marbles.

But I don't, of course. I shut myself in the bathroom and take my make-up bag out of the cupboard. I squeeze my NARS foundation onto a sponge, too much of it, so that it melts over my face like a mask. The eyeliner comes out clumsily, in a smudgy bold outline like a panda smear. My lips are a blood-coloured stain.

I drag my suitcase into the bathroom behind me and slam the door, pulling out dresses and nighties and shoes, scattering the lavender-scented lingerie bags all over the tiled floor. I put on my shortest dress, a black silky shirt dress that I'd typically wear over jeans or tights at a push. If I lean over even slightly it's going to show the bottom of my arse, a peek of Kiki de Montparnasse. I sit down on the toilet seat lid so heavily it creaks and tie up my spiky six-inch Fendi heels.

'Oh, for fuck's sake,' he says, like I'm his unruly teenage daughter. All I need to play Lolita is a couple of milkmaid plaits and a paper bag of bananas.

'So now it's too much make-up, is it?' I say, widening my eyes and raising my voice a few decibels.

'You know exactly what you're doing,' he says, teeth gritted, 'with the dress too.' But he takes me by the wrist—come to think of it, he really does look a bit like Jeremy Irons—and leads me out of the apartment.

There's a flush of dark satisfaction in the pit of my stomach. It blooms like a spiky black tea flower in the moment that you pour hot water over it.

I follow him down the corridor, into the lift where he refuses to look at me. I have to practically skip after him as he speed-walks down the hall. We sit on the terrace on dark wicker seats, opposite a pastel wall with a stone fountain. White tablecloths, little orange fruits on potted plants. The waiter approaches us carefully, already sensing the tension buzzing electric in the air, and discreetly backs away after offering us menus.

There are three or four men, nervy tech start-up types, sitting across from us with their laptops out. As I always do now, I check them off against Emily's criteria: shoes, watch, jacket. Office, Casio, non-identifiable. Basically unimpressive. Still, it doesn't stop one of them, red hair, checked shirt, from looking me up and down like he wants to know the nightly rate. You couldn't afford it, my love.

I order a large selection of pastries with relish. He says he just wants a coffee, black. What happened to cool, unruffled Matthew with his beautiful shirts? This one's sweating like a whore in church. When the order arrives, I immediately pick up a pain au chocolat and finish in a couple of bites.

Matthew's staring at me, somewhat disgustedly. I pick up another pastry, snap a photo of it, then take a bite so big it makes my jaw ache.

'I don't know what's got into you,' he says, frustrated.

'Today's always a rough one for me,' I say.

Matthew looks down at his watch. 'Wednesday?'

'July the sixteenth.'

His brow wrinkles up into a frown. 'Why?'

'It's the anniversary of my dad's death,' I lie, looking down mournfully at my half-eaten pain suisse. 'It was a skydiving incident gone wrong—a strong wind blew him out over the M40 and *bang*, he went down over the road, squashed like a bug on a lorry windshield.'

Matthew is stunned. 'I'm . . . I'm sorry, I didn't know.' He clears his throat, suddenly twitchy and self-conscious. 'Maybe you'd better go upstairs, wash your face and we can start the day over. I was going to take you to the Eiffel Tower this afternoon, seeing as you've never been.'

Mm, that's a difficult one, because I really do want to go. It's one of those things I've always wanted to do, no matter how lame it seems. I've got to get a selfie in front of the Eiffel Tower to at least show the girls. But I agree to tone down my make-up and change my shoes. Matthew watches me leave with a pitying, constipated smile.

Up in the room I post the picture of my pain suisse to Instagram.

> **@agnesgreen:** Dreams do come true and there's nowhere more dreamy than Paris.

Under the Eiffel Tower I tell him I want an increase in my allowance, which doesn't go down too well. When the street-hawker comes by with an armful of red roses, Matthew tells him gruffly that I'll pay for my own and the poor man raises his eyebrows, looking hurt and confused. We go to a seafood restaurant for lunch and Matthew spends most of it texting, hiding his phone under the table and smiling at the screen like an idiot. I can tell he's talking to other girls. I order a prawn paella and deliberately slop some out onto the floor, splash it on my skirt. A waiter emerges, napkin in hand. '*Madame!*'

'Don't worry about it,' I beam. 'I like being dirty.'

Matthew shifts in his seat, refusing to engage. I sit picking the translucent pink shells off the langoustines, twisting their heads off, beady black eyes, antenna-like arms. Flecks of shell and white gummy flesh under my fingernails, hands covered in grease.

In the taxi back to the hotel, I post a picture I took at the restaurant of my single rose against the white tablecloth.

@agnesgreen: They say Paris is a city for lovers

*

'This behaviour stops now,' Matthew says, turning the lock on our hotel room door.

I undo my belt, kick off my heels, unbutton my dress and stand there in my black-and-pink rosebud lingerie.

'Or what?'

He's staring at my body. He approaches, eyes shining. 'I've had enough of you acting like a spoilt little brat.'

'This isn't what you want?' I say. 'Come on, baby, I'm waiting. This is what I'm here for, right?'

He grabs me, turns me against him so my back's pressed to his chest, my thighs against the edge of the bed, his hard dick jabbing into the top of my arse.

'You're embarrassing me,' he says, breathing heavily.

'I know,' I say in a low, soothing voice. 'I know, baby.'

He pushes me forward by the shoulders and I bend over, put my hands on the bed. He feels up between my legs, grunts as he meets my wetness, puts his fingers inside me.

'You think I'll just let you get away with it?' he says. I hear his trousers unzipping, hoarse breathing, condom fumbled out of the bedside drawer.

'Why don't you show me? Why don't you teach me a lesson?'

I yelp when he grabs onto my hair. I take hold of his hand and sink my teeth into the flesh around his thumb.

'Fuck,' he says, pulling his hand back and slapping my arse with it. 'Disgusting little whore. Filthy slag.' He's exciting himself, I can feel him throbbing inside me, harder with every name he calls me.

How do I feel? Vindicated, in control, disappointed. Yes, disappointed most of all.

He turns on the TV, I turn on the shower.

I'm ready for dinner and when I emerge from the bathroom it's as though Matthew's eyes are going to pop out of his cuboid head. He takes his glasses off like he can't believe what he's seeing. A Honey Birdette black satin corset with harness straps that cross over my chest, a black leather mini-skirt, ridiculously high Louboutin heels.

'Agnes, no.'

'But you like my tits,' I say, pushing them up in the mirror. 'I think it looks good.'

'You're not seriously going out like that?'

'Matty, this is *Paris*, okay? They understand fashion, they're used to seeing people dressed up like this, all the time.'

'You look like you belong in an Amsterdam window,' he says, a twitch in his jaw.

'And that's the look of the season,' I tell him.

He's sweating again, I've got to him. The ravenous monster inside me wants to be fed with male humiliation. If he wants a proper whore, he can have one.

We eat in the hotel, probably because Matthew doesn't want to be seen with me anywhere else. He's quietly seething, sipping his wine and answering his emails. I flirt with the waiter, stroking the glass stem between my fingers. I flirt with the waitress, licking the cracked sugar off the top of my crème brûlée.

'Let's go back to the room,' he says.

'But I'm not finished,' I say, scrolling my finger down the dessert menu, hunting for the most phallic-looking thing I can find.

'You've already had dessert,' says Matthew.

'I'm still hungry.'

'Agnes—' he stands up, his chair scraping loudly as the legs drag across the floor—'we're going.'

I get down on my knees on the hotel room carpet. He looks at me, his eyes burning with a mixture of lust and hatred as he undoes his trousers, a growing erection in his black boxer shorts.

I know I'm good at sucking dick. I've read enough advice websites and watched enough POV porn to be a certified expert.

I press my lips to Matthew, stroke him with my tongue, take him into my mouth as far as I can. I suck gently, massaging him, moving my hands and lips in tandem. When I look up, I see he's enjoying it a bit too much. I graze him with my teeth, then softly ask: 'How does Carol do it?'

I've really done it now, broken every last one of Emily's rules. Mention the wife and it's game over. His eyes gleam. For a minute I'm worried he's going to backhand me.

'Don't you dare mention her name, Agnes.' He's gasping the words out.

Yeah, yeah, we get it, you're a family man. *You want to hit me? Go on and hit me.* But you're not going to, are you, Matty?

I take him back into my mouth and he moans again like a little bitch. I lick him all over, his balls on my tongue one after the other. He's getting closer, stiffening, he's going to come soon.

'When was the last time you came in Carol's mouth?' I ask him sweetly.

He grabs hold of my head and jerks his cock into the back of my throat, his semen like warm glue on my tongue. I push him away by the tops of his thighs, refuse to swallow it, let it leak down my chin and onto my bare chest.

He grabs for a tissue from the side of the bed and stares at me.

'Don't forget yourself, Agnes,' he says. 'You don't mention my wife *ever*, that's a non-negotiable rule. She's my *wife*, do you understand?'

I stand up, pull a handful of tissues from the box. 'Fuck you.'

'Excuse me?'

'Fuck you, fuck you, fuck you,' I say, my face and neck burning hot.

'You don't talk to me like that.' Matthew dashes his soiled crumpled tissue on the carpet and stands with his hands on his hips. But he looks ridiculous, cock softening, hanging between his legs like a sock on a drying rack.

'I want three and a half grand a month,' I say when it's over, disappearing into the bathroom for my obligatory post-sex pee. 'Or I'll never touch you again.'

'Fine,' he says, too weak to argue.

I knew he'd agree. I'm starting to get it. I never saw Matthew as truly pathetic until now.

He dresses brusquely while I put on my dressing gown and go out onto the hotel balcony to smoke. I hear the front door slam shut. It's going to rain, I can smell it in the air. I look at the roof tiles and think of Lux Lisbon in *The Virgin Suicides*. We studied it in Year 11 English Literature and for once I didn't skip straight to watching the film adaptation and actually read the whole book, cover to cover. I always remember that description of her. Rainwater collecting in her collarbone like a basin. She was so young, deteriorating to nothing, and no one even cared. The only guarantee was that she'd continue to be desired until death.

It always amazed me how the boys couldn't figure out why the girls killed themselves when it was so blindingly obvious.

While he's gone and I've finished smoking, I take all the miniature liquor bottles out of the fridge and tip them down the sink. I take a packet of gourmet crisps that are listed on the mini-bar menu as €6.99. I crumple one between my fingers and scatter the crumbs on Matthew's side of the bed. That should add a few euros to his bill, not that it especially matters. It's therapeutic to channel my spite.

It's fascinating, the ease with which a man can both despise and desire you. We fuck when he gets back, urgently, still clothed. There are no tender looks, no cheek-stroking. He kisses me with an open mouth, puts his tongue in forcefully.

There's something about hateful sex that makes me feel closer to nature. All the niceties and pretences are shed away like old snakeskin, leaving behind something raw. It's a sort of colliding. I scratch at his back, bite his shoulder through his shirt, grip his hair tight in my fists. I come just from penetration. What does it say about me that I enjoy this, sex with a man who doesn't respect me whatsoever?

*

No more sunrise kisses the next day, just the sharp tug of the duvet being pulled back. I open my eyes and see Matthew standing by the bed, his arms folded. Instinctively, I stick out my tongue.

'Mature,' he says. He wrinkles his nose, as if disgusted by a smell.

'You want mature?' I say, stretching my arms out then flopping back in a sprawl across the pillows. 'Maybe don't go for girls two decades younger than you.' I am trying my hardest to set the girl in Matthew's head on fire, to deviate so far from the script that he can never control me again.

He's shaking his head, eyelids heavy with disappointment.

'I was wrong about you,' he says.

'You'll survive,' I say, keeping my tone arch.

'You can forget about the arrangement,' he says wearily.

It's so strange to think that at one time I was consumed with the idea of pleasing Matthew, the power his words had over me. It was like being in the court of a king. But now he seems ridiculous to me, and weak.

As for the money, I'll figure something out. There are thousands of Matthews wandering around London, attaché cases in hand, an expression of perpetual confusion in their eyes that you might mistake for calm if you don't look too closely.

*

For the rest of summer, London is plagued by an onslaught of shitty weather—it's miserable and wet for the last weeks of July and most of August too. Everyone flees the city, at least everyone with money does, and that's everyone I hang around with these days. Sebastian tells me he's leaving for Los Angeles. When I ask how long for, he puts his hands through his hair and shrugs. Anchorless and trust-funded. He tells me he can't wait to get back into the sun, to party in the Hidden Hills and drink in Hollywood sunsets from rooftop pools. I wish him all the best, swallow my tears. He tells me, 'Hey, I'm sorry I couldn't stay longer. You've got a good eye, keep at it,' and I tell him I'll try. He updates his Instagram story to the wing of the plane and his continental breakfast in First Class. He takes my photography dreams off with him across the Atlantic, for now anyway.

I'm alone in the apartment; the girls are making the most of the quiet summer months to visit family, escape the endless days and nights of rain. The grass is so green it's taunting.

Matthew's on ice. As the days go on and I find myself sleeping more and eating less I force myself to admit two things: the first is that on some level, at some point I really fucking liked Matthew, and the second is that I was very stupid to allow myself to develop any kind of feelings for him in the first place. I won't let it happen again. The next time I even come *close* to caring about one of these guys I'm going to have Emily zap me with her epilator, which is as good as any medieval torture device.

I have the bed to myself for the first time and it feels like a desert. I bury my face in Sara's pillow, smell her perfume and cigarette smoke, then start feeling like a perv and put her pillow back in place on the other side of the bed.

I call Sara. The phone rings out. Then Yomawu—her phone's off. But Emily answers, after a couple of rings. She's in the suite Camilla's booked her in the Bahamas, and switches to Facetime to show me the hot-tub she's got in her bathroom, and I'm left wishing that I never called her at all.

It's clearer than ever how different my situation is from the other girls. Sugaring is just a pit-stop on their way, a chapter that will one day be forgotten, eclipsed by the more significant and impressive events of their gilded lives. But what about me? I've got fewer options.

For me, this could really be the final destination. I could do it for real. Graduate from sugar baby to escort. Increase my client base, get the whole thing more streamlined and efficient. I could do it if I could keep my mind in check, a tight grasp on my expectations.

My pictures from Paris are blowing up with likes and comments, more than I've ever had.

> Icon
> I'm so jealous of your life
> Omg gorgeous
> Love this
> Enjoy Paris beaut

I look at all the crap on my bed, the accoutrements and tools that I've accumulated through a summer of living with the sugar babies. The lube, the stretchmark concealer, the hair-removal cream. I arrange it all a bit more artfully, add some framing here and there with an opened lipstick, my satin rosebud slip.

I open up my secret Instagram and have a quick scroll up and down the pictures I've already posted, handbags and dinners, initials like *M* or *X* in the caption so I can remember who paid for them. Then I upload the photo as a draft, writing a caption to go with it:

How does a sugar baby survive? She cuts out the feeling part of herself and strangles it dead. She doesn't expect to be comforted in a world that denigrates sexual women, so she must create her own comfort. She buys expensive dressing gowns, scented candles, silk pillowcases. She goes out late and sleeps in. She's Holly Golightly, dreamy, zany, fun. (Because you may as well have fun.)

She keeps her men on a roster, sometimes she drops one just to prove she's unattached, and if she really misses him she goes down to the dermatologists or the waxing salon and gets the pain out of her system.

She's willing and women aren't supposed to be willing, not readily anyway. They're supposed to be initially reluctant, and then convinced. But not her. Not me, that is. If you want me, I'm yours.

I read it all through four times, checking for spelling mistakes. I always struggled with essays in school but for once the words flew out of me with so much fluency it shocked me. I don't know exactly what I'm hoping to achieve by doing this, perhaps it's just the opportunity to see myself from the outside. Perhaps that's all any social media post really is, an attempt to claim authorship, to make it all look deliberate.

Part Three

ICONS

Seventeen

Good Girl

Jess: Aggie! I'm back from Thailand, girl.
Jess: Sorry I haven't been in touch, got my phone stolen on the first leg of our trip so been having a digital detox lol
xxxxx

I don't know if it's my vodka hangover but I am having to channel Mother Teresa to not be pissed off by how chipper she sounds. It occurs to me that I probably haven't even crossed her mind while she's been away and meanwhile I've been filling up our WhatsApp chat like it's my own personal diary.

Me: Hey Jess
Me: No worries, I thought you were having too much fun to reply!
Me: How was Thailand?
Me: Would be really nice to see you actually, let me know when you're free to catch up

Would be really nice to see you? I don't recognize my own texts, they sound so businesslike and formal. Looks like I've become too used to messaging 40-something men.

> **Jess:** YAY! We're going out tonight, everyone's home for the summer—pls come xxxx

Fucking hell, this does not sound like a good idea.

> **Me:** Sounds fun, thanks for the invite Jess
> **Me:** Who's everyone?

> **Jess:** the old gang xxxx
> **Jess:** Olive, Malin, Tina xx

In other words, Jess's friends who politely tolerated me because they saw me as an embarrassing extension of Jess. I shudder at the thought of a night out in The Wasteland, the sticky-floored dive bars we used to skulk around in, the drinks we paid for ourselves, the deep-sea creature locals with nothing to offer us but fags and venereal disease.

> **Jess:** Pre's at Olive's for 9?:) She lives in the villages now,
> girl has moved up in the world
> **Jess:** AGNES
> **Jess:** Am I just talking to myself
> [Missed call: Jessica Waters]

Fuck's sake.

> **Me:** Sorry was in the shower
> **Me:** I'll be there xx

It might be fun for old time's sake, in a kind of sick masochistic way. As long as I don't bump into Constance. The thought alone is raising my blood pressure. I imagine her walking straight past me in the street as if we were strangers, her beautiful bare face turned away from me in denial. The halo of her auburn hair rounding the corner by the Three Butts before disappearing from sight.

Jess FaceTimes me while she's getting ready, for approval on her outfit.

'Jesus,' she exclaims when she sees my face on the screen, 'you look like a celebrity.'

'Hardly,' I say, nerves clouding my delight. 'I think the green top looks better.'

'All right.' Jess props the phone up on her dresser as she strips out of one crop-top and into another.

'Your shoulders look a bit red, Jess,' I tell her.

'I know,' she says. 'Factor fifty, my arse. There. How's that?'

'Much better.'

'Cool,' she says, and I feel my muscles slightly relax, just for a second, at the familiarity we've slipped back into. 'Ag, how's your mum and Marlena?'

Time to come clean. 'I have no clue.'

'What do you mean you have no clue?'

'I mean I moved out.'

'What? When?'

'About a month ago.'

'AGNES! Where to?' She picks up the phone and holds it so close to her face that I can see the tiny droplets of glue holding her fake lashes to her lids.

'London.'

'What . . . What?' Her internet connection malfunctions for a second, a portrait of confusion frozen on the screen. 'With who? Or did you win the lottery and just forget to tell me?'

'With some new friends I made.'

She sighs in disbelief. 'My God, I've missed a lot. And the photography stuff? How's that going?'

'Uh, well, it's not really going anywhere right now.' Understatement of the century. 'I had to put it on pause.'

'Oh, sorry.'

'It's all right,' I say, desperate for a change in subject.

'You want me to pick you up from the station?' she asks, warmly. 'You're coming by train, right?'

'Yes, please, Jess.'

'Cool. It's gonna be fun I think,' she says.

'It's gonna be interesting, that's for sure. I haven't seen any of them since Year 13,' I tell her, 'at . . . Gladwell's.'

A shiver runs through my body at the thought of it.

'Oh, you mean the night when you—'

'Yep,' I quickly cut her off. 'That night exactly.'

'Well, that was so long ago,' she says, chewing on her bottom lip. 'They're all over it. Probably don't even remember.'

How could anyone forget?

Once I get over my initial nerves at going back to the original site of teenage self-loathing, I start to feel a bit excited. It's a tempting prospect, showing up after all this time with my dramatic glow-up, looking like a celebrity. Jess said it, not me. My vanity gets the better of me and I dry-brush my entire body, exfoliate in the shower and help myself to Emily's Laura Mercier body crème from under the sink. I dress up in a black long-sleeved mini-dress, my Chanel flap bag, winged liner sharp enough to kill. Honestly, if I was still chilling in The Wasteland and someone walked in like this I'd hate their guts.

But as I leave the models' flat and make my way to South Kensington station, I can't shake the feeling that it's all a big conspiracy that even Jess is involved in—nobody's been at uni or Thailand, they've been holed up in an underground bunker for the last four years plotting my final humiliation. Nah, not really, not Jess. There's maybe three people I really trust in the world and Jess is one of them. I can't wait to see her sun-burned little face.

The Wasteland looks more barren than ever before. At the train station, a pigeon is dancing around with a bit of bread from a takeaway kebab and the black clouds overhead are starting to leak rain, which always brings out the sewage stench from the river.

As I put my ticket into the slot at the gates, I start to panic. I imagine Constance again, passing through town on her way to the bus station, weathered camel trench on top of her pink uniform and floral brolly hooked over her forearm. I don't know what I'd do if I bumped into her, what I'd say.

When I come out of the station I almost turn left on instinct and start walking home. Then I remember myself, and feel a sting behind my eyes like I'm going to cry.

*

'Where are you running off to?' Jess pauses in her Fiat 500 at the train station entrance, rolls the left side wheels onto the kerb. I slide into the passenger seat and put my arms around her. She smells like she always does, of Pantene shampoo. The skin on her forehead is speckly with a peeling burn. At the sight of her, this strange wave of nostalgia washes over me and I can't decide whether I'm happy or sad. I'll probably never feel the same kind of happy that I used to feel years ago, at a time when getting into Jess's car felt like the start of some grand adventure, the pinnacle of the week—Capital XTRA playing on the radio, the windows down as we drove to the park or into town to the cinema. Those little things, ordinary things, might never make me happy again. Not now that I've had the champagne and the velvet ropes.

Jess pulls back from our hug and gets a better look at me. 'Who are you and what have you done with Agnes Green?'

'You little bitch,' I say, play-punching her on the shoulder. 'Are you saying I used to be ugly?'

She grins at this. 'Nope, you're definitely still Agnes. And you were never ugly. You just didn't look like a *Love Island* contestant before. How are you feeling about seeing everyone?'

'How do you think?'

'Nervous as fuck,' she grins, 'but you shouldn't be.'

'You know I had nightmares, every night for a year, before I just blocked the whole thing out.'

'Good,' she says. 'Forget about it—who cares? People get up to worse.'

'I know that.' I roll down the window to try and get some fresh air. 'It's just the thought of a video floating around out there, that—'

'I still think that was just a rumour,' Jess says. 'I've never seen any video.' She tries to sound easy-breezy but she's got a neck twitch.

I feel the door handle under my fingertips. 'Of course *you* haven't,' I tell her. 'They know you'd tell me who took it.'

'You really don't remember anyone filming?'

'I was a bit preoccupied, Jess,' I snap at her. Feeling too hot in my black dress, I lean back against the headrest and close my eyes. 'Maybe this was a mistake.'

'Are you kidding?' she says. 'You look like a goddess. Agnes, no one remembers that night. It was years ago. Trust me.'

Her eyes are on the road and she's gone into Jess autopilot mode, not listening anymore, barely allowing time for me to respond. I always made excuses for her—short attention span, just a bit scatterbrained— but as I listen to her words now, tumbling meaninglessly out of her mouth, I can't help but wonder if it's not carelessness, but just that my opinion is totally irrelevant to her.

Olive's house is perfect for a party, or a murder. It stands alone down a little country lane on a generous stretch of land, a couple of streets away from Emily's house. You can see the same conifers from the back garden. As we roll up the drive, I can hear the thump of the music's bass. The house is a new-build, symmetrical and white with a slate-grey door and matching window panels. I can hear the metallic clang of the garden gate left swinging on its hinges.

'I'm so anxious,' I say in Jess's ear. 'I feel sick. You said this was just supposed to be a little pre—you know, low key.'

Jess shrugs. 'I guess word got out. Look, don't panic, okay.'

The garden is packed. People mill about like bumblebees, buzzing from one little cluster to another. It's not just the girls from school but some of the boys they used to hang out with and plenty of new faces too. A congregation of about a dozen or so have gathered around the garden table, the plastic cups organized in a beer-pong formation. Another group play music from portable speakers, bobbing their heads like strutting cockerels. It's trippy, seeing faces from my old form room milling along the low garden wall, almost identical to the one at Emily and Camilla's house. I'm used to seeing these people in houses with scratched pebbledashed walls, huddled smoking joints in a corner.

'Oh my God! Hey, guys!' Olive approaches us with a bowl full of cheese puffs the size of her head in one hand and a disposable red plastic cup in the other. 'So glad you could make it,' she says, pressing her cheek first to Jess's and then mine. 'You look so goooooood,' she says, blinking like a stiff wind's just blown a gust of sand into her eyes.

'Thanks.' My jaw's wound so tight I can barely get the word out.

This was a mistake, a big mistake. Trapped in a room with a bunch of people from my school that I can't stand and have happily lived without contacting for years. If everyone has a personal hell then this is mine, right here and now.

'There's Jäger for everyone,' she says. 'Help yourselves.'

'Thanks, Olive,' I say, taking one of the cups from the table and pouring myself the weakest Jägermeister and Coke I can manage, my hand shaking so I almost pour Jäger all over the floor.

The red plastic cups are an aesthetic choice, inspired by *American Pie* and the like, the films we grew up watching and couldn't wait to emulate. A funny choice for such an eco-conscious host. I don't follow it but I've seen Olive's Instagram account—niftythrifty777—where she posts handy little tips on planet-friendly living to the overwhelming support of her fans who practically fall over themselves to suck her dick in the comments section.

Olive beckons us into the living room. 'Girls, come on, we're playing "Never Have I Ever"—bring your drinks!'

Oh brilliant. How original. Good to see how much everyone's grown since sixth form.

'See,' Jess nudges me—she loves a drinking game. 'I told you it wouldn't be so bad.'

Olive takes the prime seat in the middle of the big sofa, Tina to her left and Malin on her right, a girl I don't recognize perched on the arm. Everyone mutters their greetings, and we huddle together so we can hear each other against the noise of the party. I sit on the floor next to Jess, who's silently wiggling to the music.

'You go first, Jess,' says Olive, cracking open a tin of G&T.

'Hmm, okay.' She screws her eyes shut and breathes deeply like she's about to recite a mantra. '*Never have I ever* . . . uh . . . cheated.'

Tina takes a sip and Malin flashes her a judgemental look.

'What?' Tina says. 'It was ages ago.'

There's an outburst of male laughter in the kitchen—the former white stoner group from school have produced a bong and are blowing competitive smoke rings.

'Agnes, your turn,' says Olive.

'Okay.' Coming up with a juicy detail isn't hard, but I have no desire to share any intimate details of my life with this lot, and there's nothing I care to know about them either. '*Never have I ever* kissed a girl.'

'Boring!' says Olive, swigging from her can and looking pleased with herself. She's wearing leggings and a spaghetti-sleeve vest top that comes down to the top of her thighs. She's a hip belt and a back-combing brush away from the fashion nightmare that was 2008, and I'm tempted to tell her as much.

'Okay, okay, my go,' says Olive, shifting in her seat. Eyes glistening, she looks around at each of us to make sure we're all paying attention. '*Never have I ever* had sex for money.'

No one moves or says a word. Tina's looking at me with her mouth hanging open.

'God, Olive—' Malin forces out a dry little laugh—'you didn't have to bait Agnes out like that.'

Jess turns to look at me so hard and fast I'm worried she'll have got whiplash.

'What?'

Olive is smiling, clearly invigorated by the chaos. 'No, but let's talk about it. Why not, right? She posted it on Instagram so it's not like it's a secret.'

Jess whispers to me. 'Posted what on Instagram? Ag?'

What . . . I don't understand. How did they find the secret account and how did they figure out it was mine?

Malin, sensing Jess's bristling concern, nudges Olive in the thigh. 'Stop, Olive,' she hisses.

But Olive ignores her. 'It's not supposed to be anonymous, right? Like, you know it's linked with your other Insta? It comes up as a suggested account. Plus, you can see your face in the mirror of the hotel room you posted. You *did* know that, right?' I can't breathe. Can't speak. Can't do anything but think: *Get out of here now.* 'So . . . what's it like, Agnes?' she asks, hands clasped as if she's politely enquiring about my health. 'Or should I say sugarbabydollxo9?'

'Do you have a pimp?' Tina pipes up, giggling.

'A pimp?' Jess's eyes are wide with horror. 'Agnes, what are they talking about?'

'Oh, Jess, you didn't know about Agnes's adventures? I thought you guys were close still,' says Olive.

But I can't say anything. I'm paralysed because I'm seventeen again and on the verge of a mental breakdown. I always fucking hated Olive, could never see why anyone liked her. Who can understand the mysteries of teenage popularity, what traits a cohort of thirteen-year-olds deem exceptional, who they choose to crown?

'Did anything happen to set you off down this path, do you think?' says Olive in an especially cunty way, even for her.

She wants to re-enact some kind of *Call Her Daddy* episode, some kind of *Red Table Talk* about young women and sex work.

I'm frozen. I literally want to die at the realization that they've all sat sniggering and scrolling through my account.

'Agnes,' Jess whispers to me, 'what the fuck are they talking about?'

'Chill, Jess,' says Olive.

My God, I want to smack her in the mouth.

'No, I agree, it's, like, not a big deal at all,' says Malin. 'Like, Tina has an OnlyFans!'

'Shut up,' Tina says. Then she adds quietly, 'It's feet pictures, only. Everyone does it.'

Jess pulls up my Instagram, clicks on to the sugar baby account and reads the post. She holds the screen up to her nose, green eyes staring intently.

'So this is what you've been doing in London?' She turns to me. Her tone isn't accusatory but it quivers with injury.

'Jess, stop slut-shaming,' says Olive. 'I just want to hear about how Agnes's past has led her to this lifestyle.'

'What *past*?' I say, uncertainly.

'Your, like, hyper-sexuality,' she says.

Malin nudges her again but she's unperturbed.

Jess is fuming beside me and it's only my anger that's stopping me from storming out of the door in a flood of tears. 'My what?'

'Well,' Olive goes on, 'Year 13. The party, the video.'

I knew it, I fucking knew someone was recording. Jess looks up, alert. Her hand twitches on the carpet beside me and I know she's stopped herself from reaching out and grabbing my hand. My heart is pounding in my chest—I feel as though I've been electrocuted. The music is too loud, it's echoing inside my head and all I can hear is laughter. I imagine them all, laughing at the video they've passed around behind my back.

'Who has it?' I snap. 'Do you have it?'

'No way. Omg,' Olive's laughing, 'only an idiot would still have it. People were seventeen in that video, it would be child pornography. Can't risk that,' she says, flicking her hair over her shoulder. 'I'm going to have a job in government.'

Fucking hell, why didn't I think of that? I can breathe. One less worry from my addled mind. I take a swig of my drink—the ice has melted and it's lukewarm from being almost crushed between my thighs.

'But even that night, for instance,' she continues, 'I don't know what happened. You went upstairs with one of them and then what? You just offered to suck them all off? Six guys, Agnes.' She presses her hand to her heart. 'I was so worried about you when I heard.'

There weren't six guys, there were three, maybe four. It was just oral. And even after the incident I was still technically a virgin. I've heard worse stories than mine. These things happen, at teenage house parties.

At the time, I didn't think much of it. Just fooling around. But the morning after I woke up with a pounding head, the night started coming back to me in flickering black and white, and I felt regret, as bitter as a lemon rubbed onto a fresh wound. I got down on my knees by the side of my bed and started to pray that if God was real he would rewind the last twenty-four hours so that I could undo it. I was paranoid. I heard the sounds, the shadows, smelt the skin, sweat and vodka cokes of the night before, even as I was tucked up in bed. I made a frantic call to Jess, who listened in hushed silence and feebly reassured me everything would be fine. I wanted to believe her, but she was wrong. My psychosis lasted for months. I was going crazy from shame. A teacher found me walking barefoot around the science department with a battered copy of the Old Testament in my hand, and called my mother in for a meeting. What happened next is blurry, but I dropped out of sixth form of my own choosing, buried the memory as deep as I could and avoided everyone at the party for the rest of time. Until tonight.

Jess is clearing her throat—she looks irritated, scratching the back of her left hand with her right.

Olive is still looking down on us from her seat on the plush sofa, one hand over her heart like she's taking an oath. 'I realize it's not the time or place,' she says, 'but I want you to know I'm someone to talk to, if you ever want to.'

Jess says loudly, 'Fuck off, Olive.'

'Excuse me?' Olive looks as though she's been slapped right in the mouth. And I'm suddenly in the room again, having previously floated right out of my body.

Jess gets up from the floor. 'It's pathetic,' she says, 'trying to humiliate Agnes all these years later. It's not her fault you don't have shit going on in your own life. Agnes, let's go.'

I trail Jess, my best friend, my only friend, through the kitchen and out into the garden. I don't speak and I don't look back.

When we get to the gate, I break the silence. 'Thank you for—'

But she cuts me off. 'Look, I need some time, all right. I just need some space.'

'Jess, please.' I follow her helplessly down the drive-way. My black dress looks extremely out of place here, with the garden gnomes and the conifers in the distance, but the air is cool. I can breathe, finally.

Jess shines the white light of her phone in the direction of her car.

'Why didn't you tell me about any of that . . . that sex work stuff?' Her face is red with anger.

I find myself stuttering like an idiot, 'I . . . I don't know.'

'Yes, you do,' she says. A ginger curl has escaped from her clasp and fallen into her eyes, she impatiently pushes it back. 'You knew I'd tell you. *Hey, Agnes, are you sure about this? Hey, Agnes, maybe don't put yourself in dangerous situations. Hey, Agnes, maybe think about the impact this could have on your future.*'

'You're shouting,' I say. 'You're talking to me like an idiot.'

'Maybe because you *are* an idiot.'

'You don't have to be so judgemental,' I tell her, feel my own anger rising up to meet hers. 'Maybe this is why I didn't tell you. You're always on my case, making me feel like shit.'

'Look,' she says with a sigh. 'I'm going, can you call yourself an Uber or something?'

I watch as she gets into her car. Her expression is a sad one and I hate to see Jess sad. The last I see of her is a pair of watery green eyes in the wing mirror, reflecting the lights on her dashboard as she turns on the ignition.

Eighteen

The Mean Reds

I wake up on Marlena's results day with a knot in my stomach. I mean, I always wake up with a knot in my stomach these days, but today it's triple-tied. I help myself to a shot of tequila while I languish in the flat waiting for a phone call.

I'm five shots in on an empty stomach when my mobile starts buzzing with a FaceTime call. Marlena is shrieking and holding a piece of paper up to the screen. I jump to my feet and squint at it. A results certificate.

'It's all blurry,' I tell her, starting to panic. 'It's all blurry Lena, what does it say?'

'It says I'm going to Cambridge!'

She's screaming, I'm screaming. Her goofy smile and glasses take up the entirety of the screen.

'You did it, you did it, you did it!' I'm grinning like an idiot.

'I did it,' she says, echoing me in the way she used to when we were small.

She tells me she's going out for dinner with Constance to Pizza Express as a well done.

'I guess you don't want to come?' she asks me, voice wavering.

'Best not to,' I say softly. 'We'll celebrate another time.'

'Okay, well speak later.'

'Proud of you,' I say. 'So, so proud of you.'

She holds the phone up close, 'Agnes are you *crying*?'

'No,' I say, defiantly. 'Now fuck off out of here and enjoy your day.'

She sticks her tongue out and hangs up.

I try not to think of her and Constance, raising their mocktails and beaming ear to ear, celebrating a dream the three of us shared coming true. Without me. I take two more shots of tequila then fall asleep on the sofa.

It's nearing the end of August. Back in The Wasteland, people will be defiantly pretending to have fun at miserable mud-slick parties and leaky barbecues, smiling like maniacs for the Facebook photos. The girls return from the four corners of the globe with topped-up suntans, souvenir shot-glasses and fridge magnets. It feels as though the gulf between us has widened. They've got stories to tell, pictures to show me and I've done nothing but sit in front of the TV and order in Deliveroo. I haven't even touched my camera. When I tell Emily what happened with Matthew, she sends me a bunch of website links. SeekingArrangement. SugarDating. WhatsYourPrice.

'Back on the horse,' she says. 'Come on, Tracey Emin.'

The sugar babies thought my Instagram post was some kind of edgy joke, found it fucking hilarious—thank God—and have started calling me Tracey Emin on account of her iconic bed photograph with all the condoms and stuff spread out on her duvet. They howl in protest when I announce I'm deleting the account.

I could always try and get signed with a modelling agency—height doesn't matter, they tell me, not for commercial. Sara takes some Polaroids of me in a black long-sleeved T-shirt and a pair of leggings. I look alarmed and uncomfortable in all of them.

'These are so shit.'

'Send them off anyway,' she says sunnily. 'You never know.'

'You're not spending your Saturday like this?' Emily comes into the living room. Her face is smeared with an orange mud mask that brings out, with unsettling sharpness, the green of her eyes.

'Weather's shit, running out of money, tired.'

Emily flicks the empty packet of Doritos that I've demolished off the sofa seat next to me onto the floor, and sits down with a sigh.

'How have you been getting on with the websites?'

'Meh.'

'Show me.'

'What?'

'Come on, Agnes, you're going on a date.'

I roll my eyes, unlock my phone and pull up Google Chrome.

'You know, it's an actual crime that you've hardly used that Chanel flap bag,' she says, scrolling up and down through my inbox on Seeking-Arrangement. 'If you don't go out tonight you can hand it over to me in the morning—I'll give it the life it deserves. Ooh, what about this guy?' She enlarges a profile picture and shows it to me. 'He offered to take you for dinner.'

'I'm not interested.'

'Too busy? Exciting plans for a Saturday night?'

I groan and take the phone from her. The man looks decent enough, kind eyes, his profile description is spelt correctly, good grammar, it looks like he's going through a red-Porsche-and-cigar-habit kind of mid-life crisis. Nothing wildly out of the ordinary.

'Use it or lose it, babydoll,' says Emily, itching with her pinkie finger at the edge of her drying clay mask. 'You'll be thirty before you know it.'

Jess: Look, I thought everything over and I have to say honestly I'm sorry
Jess: I may have overreacted like it's not your fault I've been unreachable all summer

Jess: Give me a call or we can get a coffee or something xx
Jess: When you're free, no rush
Jess: Love you, little pornstar

I laugh at that.

Jess: sorry, is that too soon?

The Uber arrives for my sugaring date before I have a chance to reply.

His name is Ryan. His text instructs me to walk to the end of the restaurant when I arrive. He'll be sitting at a table to the right.

My heart beats hard and fast but there is a bit of a thrill in being *her* again. The femme fatale, the perfectly groomed seductress, dressed to kill. The corsetry of my dress holds my spine nice and straight. When he spots me, he can't stop himself from smiling. It's just like Emily says, like a stage actress returning to a favourite role after years have passed—it all floods back. My arched posture, rolling hips, lips pursed, slightly lifted chin. Confidence, that's all it is.

'Hello, my dear.'

Ryan stands up to greet me with a kiss on the cheek, which is a stretch for him as he barely reaches my shoulder. Faded blue polo shirt, grey checked suit trousers, orthopaedic shoes. He has a prominent nose and dark eyes behind frameless glasses, and he looks harmless. No ring.

'What was your name again, my dear?'

'Abigail,' I say.

We play the normal game of ethnicity bingo. I'm beginning to feel like some kind of exotic horse and Ryan is a stable owner who wants to add me to his collection. But the femme fatale doesn't mind, the femme fatale wears bondage, gets on her knees and makes eating a carrot look erotic.

We order gin sours, I eat a Caesar salad, Ryan orders two coffees. He passes me the envelope, I tuck it away in my bag. He pays the bill and we go outside to hail a couple of taxis. I have to bend down and hunch over in order to present him with my cheeks to kiss, and he smells like coffee and body odour.

'Next time we can go to a hotel, yes?' He hands the cab driver a bunch of twenties to pay for my fare. What a nice gent. 'I'm into Shibari—is that something you might be interested in trying? I'd be happy to introduce you.'

'What's a Shibari?'

'Japanese rope bondage.'

Absolutely not a chance in hell. Maybe I'm not as ruthless as I thought.

I wave out the back of the window at him like I'm Lady Di, then inexplicably collapse into hot, embarrassed tears as the cab turns the corner. Goodbye Ryan, see you never.

Next there's Hugh. His suggested meeting place is unusual, a café hosted inside a church near Bank Station. He's waiting for me outside the ivy-strewn stone wall, flicking his watch to check the time as I approach. He's trim, tall. I sense a streak of meanness in his face, but maybe it's just good bone structure. His silver wedding band is winking in the light.

The church is old and ornate with high white arches. It's been a while since I've been in a church; United Pentecostals was nothing like this. I find myself face to face with a stone figure of the Virgin Mary, baby Jesus cradled in her carved arms. An eagle painted with gold accents sits on a presentation table beside them.

We pass through the foyer into the hall where the café is held. He asks me if I want a coffee, in a voice which is cut-glass and commanding, the kind of voice that makes questions sound like threats. Three months ago, I'd have worried about somehow fucking it up, ordering something embarrassing like a chai latte. It doesn't faze me now.

'You're twenty-one, right?'

'Yep.'

'That's right between my sons,' he says, Cheshire-cat grin. 'One's twenty and the other one's twenty-two.'

'Oh.' I rack my brain for an appropriate response but I can't find one. I've heard some odd things from guys before but this is a first.

'Shall we get down to business, then?' he asks me. 'I was thinking once or twice a week, midweek in a central hotel. Is there anything you're into that you might want to tell me about?'

Definitely not sitting in a church pew being sexually propositioned in front of the altar. It's almost too neat for words. If this were a scene in a film, nobody would believe it.

I look Mary in the face and start giggling like an idiot. 'I think there's been a misunderstanding.'

'What are you talking about?' He's indignant, puffing up his chest.

'I'm not . . . I don't know what I'm doing here, I can't . . . We're sitting in the front of a church. Jesus is right there.'

He looks around like he hasn't even noticed. 'Oh, are you religious?'

'I don't know what I am.'

'We can discuss it over text then,' he says. 'I'd better get back.'

Sitting in that church, I felt certain that I was being watched. Maybe I'm paranoid. Or maybe God is torturing me, I think, remembering the way I suddenly erupted into giggles in the pew. No, not God. It was Constance's face I saw in Mary's serene expression.

When Hugh texts, I can't bring myself to message back. I'd always end up associating him with that horribly unsettling feeling of two worlds colliding.

God sees everything.

*

'You struck out with a few, so what?' Emily is sitting on the end of the bed. 'Plenty more fish in the sea.'

Sara is still sleeping beside me. She came home last night (this morning, rather) at about 7 a.m. I feel deflated and defective. I'm airing Jess's texts not because I'm mad (okay maybe I'm still a tiny bit mad, but I *am* planning to reply at some point), Marlena's pissed off that I won't make up with Constance, dream photographer Sebastian's never coming back. I want nothing more than to hide under the covers for the rest of the week and have Sara collect my McDonald's delivery when the driver arrives.

'I think I need to get a real job,' I say. 'I don't think I can take this, I need some . . . consistency, a bit of stability. If I worked at Tesco's or whatever I could show up with no make-up on, my hair in a bun, *imagine* that.'

Emily's eyes look like they're going to pop out of her head. 'Are you fucking kidding me? What kind of masochist would choose to slave away for minimum wage when they could make thousands for a few hours' work? Look at you,' she says. 'We did all this work, and for what? You're giving up too easily. You've got to use the machine-gun approach—go on a bunch of dates, eliminate the duds, narrow it down to a quality roster.'

With Emily breathing over my shoulder I give in and open the laptop. I look for potential new guys on the internet, with my alias as Abigail Rogers (the name of my primary-school bully) and a blurred-out picture. My profile is full of promises and so are theirs. Thousands of strangers all over the country, all over the world—yearning for something that humdrum everyday life can't give us. In a lot of ways it's like any dating site—more honest, actually, only the currency is sex instead of love.

I'm sick of the married ones and that's what they all seem to be. After days of fruitless exchanges with semi-literate frauds, I find Christian. He is six foot three, or says he is, and has the flag emojis for Iraq and Sweden on his profile. It's full of pictures of him, posing on a rooftop bar, holding a champagne flute in a dimly lit restaurant, flashing snow-white teeth onboard a yacht in the Mediterranean. The woman by his side has a blurred-out face in every picture, as if to say, 'This could be you!'

A couple of flirty messages and selfies back and forth and he asks me out. If he looks like his pictures I'm going to sleep with him, I decide before I leave. I have a hot bath and spend ages shaving, massaging body butter into my skin, applying Emily's custom pumpkin and lavender scent to my breastbone, lower stomach, tops of my thighs.

A chill has set into the air so I borrow one of Sara's trench coats for our first date—I haven't had time to buy my autumn wardrobe yet. Christian takes me to the Riverside Café. He's clean and smells nice and is not a catfish; if anything he's more beautiful than in his photos. He even says 'Please' and 'Thank you' to the waitress and makes eye contact, instead of dismissing her with a wave. Christian is the Holy Grail of sugar-daddy dates and as I watch his lips move I know we're going to fuck later. We don't speak much—we don't need to—just polite observations and enquiries that trail off into nothing, swallowed by ambient restaurant noise. The sexual tension is thick in the air like on a hot day when the humidity's about to break. I stroke his leg with my foot under the table and he watches me with hungry, appreciative eyes.

He wants to go out clubbing on Park Lane, I suspect because he's booked a room at the Hilton. I can tell he's the kind of guy for whom nights out are serious business (work-hard-party-harder-yadda-yadda). I lose track of him on my way back from the cloakroom, but spot him at the bar, his shirt under the blue lights. We do vodka shots and then dance—he's a hilarious dancer and I very nearly get the ick. I grab hold of his hands to stop him waving them about and put them on my hips instead.

In the smoking area, he puts his tongue in my mouth very gently and on it I feel the powdery edge of something edible.

'Just a little something to keep the beauty going,' he says into my mouth.

'You don't have to explain,' I say, 'I'm game,' and swallow it down, kissing him back with even more force.

With his arm around my waist and an anticipatory half-smile on his lips, his hand slides down my back, grabs at my arse.

'No underwear?'

I shake my head, savouring it. The feeling when two people are about to fuck and both really want it is like a rare planetary alignment.

'Let's get our coats,' I say.

In Christian's apartment, I'm not even worrying about Emily's rules or the fact that the pill he gave me was definitely a dud, because he is here and has golden eyes and a mouth that I want to worship and he is looking at me, looking so intensely that I could almost melt. He tells me to sit down on the end of the bed—the bedcovers are a deep, rich blue. He kneels on the floor in front of me so that we are eye to eye for a minute and I take in the beauty of his face—there's an ancient cast to the heaviness of his brow, his strong arrow of a nose. He applies kisses down the length of my legs, takes off my shoes, nuzzles my feet, runs his hand up the inside of my thigh. His hands on my skin are warm, firm. He spreads my legs, licks me. Presses his open mouth between my legs like he wants to devour me whole.

'Fuck.' He's hard, stands up to take his clothes off and put a condom on, doesn't take his eyes from me.

I'm still—waiting, watching him. He's making me wait for it. He knows what I need, somehow, someone to make me surrender.

'Take your dress off,' he says.

I pull it over my head.

'Spread your legs wider.'

I stretch so far that it aches.

'Good girl, now touch yourself for me.'

He climbs on top of me, takes my wet fingers from where I'm rubbing at my clit, and puts them in his mouth, sucks them and then kisses me.

'You like how you taste?' he asks.

'Yes.'

'Good girl.'

He pushes into me, and I gasp. It's perfect. The way he acts (like he owns me), the way he smells (woody, spicy, citrusy), the way the air is warm but also pregnant with rain, the crisp cool white bedsheets, the expensive panoramic view out of his apartment windows, the obvious disparity between our size and strength and the way he's kissing me now. He scoops me up off the bed and pulls me closer, fucks me harder like he needs to be deeper in me, like he wants to feel more of me, like we'll never be close enough. Then I'm sitting on top of him, knees bent, feet on the bed—Lotus position I think they call it—and my thighs are trembling from the strain of it, and the growing intensity of the orgasm whose heat and light I can almost feel, like the sun coming up over the horizon. His hands are at my hips, fingers gripping flesh as he guides me.

'Let me help you,' he says.

I'm shaking. With one hand he grips my jaw, pulls my face so close our lips are almost touching but he doesn't kiss me. Instead he says, 'You'd better ask me before you come.' My muscles clamp down around him, flex around his cock, it's involuntary. He grips my jaw harder. 'Don't you dare.' Pulls me closer.

'Please, Christian.'

'Please, what?'

'Please . . . please, can I come?'

Or maybe what makes it really perfect is that he's just the right dominant to my submissive, without discussion, without practice, like he can see through my skin into my soul and somehow know what I need.

He pulls me forward onto his chest, wraps his arms tightly around me, fucks me so hard and fast that the air is knocked out of me and when I orgasm I see black for five seconds. My ears are ringing—I've been holding my breath.

'Did you come?' I ask him.

His eyes are half-closed, he has a contented smile. 'Yes, just now.'

I collapse down next to him—my legs are too knackered to get up and go to the bathroom to pee. I decide to bite the bullet and risk the UTI. In any case it was worth it.

'That was . . . so good, Agnes,' he says, kissing me on the forehead. 'So good.'

I lie on his chest, stroke his bicep with my fingers. It's nice to lie with someone. Maybe it could actually be something, Christian and I. 'So do you want to make this like a fortnightly thing?' I ask him.

'Mmm, I prefer a date-by-date basis,' he says, 'because I travel so much.'

'Oh, okay, sure.'

'Do you prefer cash or bank transfer?' he asks me.

'Um . . . cash is fine.'

He reaches for his trousers that have been flung by the side of the bed, takes his wallet out of the pocket. Hands over twenty £50 notes. I take them from him, feeling awkward.

'Err, thanks,' I say, knowing that I won't be able to see him again. That even I, in my hardened state, am not cutthroat enough for this—sex that shatters me followed by an exchange like something out of a McDonald's Drive Thru.

'Pleasure,' he says. 'Let me call you a car.'

*

I'm not in London. I'm in a cool desert, walking on a sand dune. Dragging my feet through sand blown into ridged mounds by the wind. I look down at my hands—no manicure, no acrylics, the nails bare and bitten down. Over the horizon, I can see a dark silhouette that looks to have the swaying gait of a large animal, maybe a group of camels. I approach, shielding my eyes from the intense light of the sun.

'Agnes!' a woman's voice calls out to me.

'Yes? Who are you?'

I'm closer now, I can see that rather than a group of animals it's just one enormous, monstrous creature, with a scaly red reptilian body and seven heads on seven necks as long and thick as tree trunks. They're like camels or horses but with sharp fang-like teeth that overhang the soft wrinkled flesh of their lower jaws. And on top of the animal is a woman wearing a tiered crown, long thick hair that curls down her back. She turns to look at me, and it's my face, eyes shining, mouth smudged with blood drying to chalky scarlet dust in the corners.

The woman is me but sharper, wilder, darker. She's laughing at me. One hand around the reins that control the beast, with the other hand she takes out a silver chalice from her fur-trimmed robe. 'I am a mystery,' she says. She tips the chalice to her lips and a drop of red streams down her lovely long neck, staining the white fur robe trimming.

'. . .'Scuse me?'

'I am Babylon the Great, mother of prostitutes and abominations of the earth, with whom the kings of the earth have committed fornication.'

Fucking fantastic. So I've graduated to having visions about the mother of prostitutes now. Look at me, Mum, I made it.

She/I holds out the chalice towards me. I look down into the well of the silver cup.

'Is it blood?' I ask her.

She/I throws back her head and laughs, the crown wobbling on top of her head. The laughter reverberates around inside my skull like an echo in a cave. I put my hands to my ears to try and block it out but that only makes it worse, louder, stronger . . .

'Hey—' Sara shakes me awake—'are you okay?'

'What?'

'I know you're not supposed to wake someone up from a dream but you were really freaking out. You kept calling for help.'

I check my pulse. Definitely alive, but I'm drenched in sweat and my heart is racing.

'Fuck. Christian gave me some kind of pill last night, I think maybe acid, and it's just kicked in,' I tell her.

'I never remember my dreams,' she says, yawning. 'What was it about?' Her face looks sort of green-tinged, and her eyes are revolving like carnival pinwheels. That damn Christian, giving me hallucinogenics and not even having the decency to keep me around until I came up.

'Some fucked-up Narnia shit. I think it might have something to do with the sugaring?' I purposefully leave out the Whore of Babylon stuff. 'I used to have these weird hallucination-dream-things a lot—religious guilt, you know? That's why I never normally want to take anything.'

'God, you poor baby. I hated Narnia as a kid—that White Witch always gave me nightmares.'

I chuckle, but the truth is I'm panicking and can't see straight.

'Do you want to try some of my sleeping pills tonight?' she asks, the darling. 'I stole them from my mum while we were in St Barts. Worth a try, right?'

'Sure, yeah, why not.'

I swallow three down with a glass of milk, put my eye mask on and sleep.

When I pull up the blinds the next morning I'm astonished to be met with sunshine and warm weather. I feel the pieces of a plan assembling: a trip to Tesco Express to pick up milk chocolate Magnums, tacky celebrity magazines and Cherry Cokes—the kind of trash you can't buy in a WholeFoods. I want to spend the day in the park watching the neighbourhood Pomeranians trotting after tennis balls and people performatively reading literary fiction, draped over blankets on the grass. When I was a cleaner, I used to enjoy slacking off, kicking back in the kitchen of some suburban mansion when the clients were out, nosying around in their fridge-freezer, eating the contents of their biscuit tins and knowing their kids were going to take the blame for it. It's the little things, isn't it?

A minor spanner in the works is that all the girls are out except Kiki. I haven't spoken to her much since she came back from holiday. But my desire for a day of wholesome fun overpowers my fear of her, gorgeous and terrifying as she is, and I knock on her door.

'Yes?' Kiki answers, calling out from inside her room.

'It's just me.'

'Sara?'

'No,' I say.

'Yomawu?'

'No.' I accept defeat. 'Agnes.'

'Come in.'

I open the door and the sight that meets me almost knocks me off my feet. Kiki is set up underneath a phosphorescent ring light, wearing nothing but red sequin nipple covers and a red lipsticked pout.

'Ah, Agnes, you've come at the perfect time,' she says. 'You can help me record?'

She starts to fiddle with the phone holder built into the ring light.

'I can never get the best angle with this piece of shit.'

I look down at Kiki, her wasp-thin waist, the protrusion of her ribs above her belly button.

'Sure.' I take the phone from her. 'What's this for, anyway?'

'OnlyFans,' she says, turning her head to the left and then tossing her hair over her shoulder. 'Let me see.'

She snatches the phone out of my hand and then storms over to the mirror, pulling the skin on her face tight and smouldering at herself.

'Oh . . . Well, I wondered if you wanted to come and have a picnic with me out at the park?' I say.

'To meet a man?'

'No . . . just to enjoy the weather.'

'I don't think so,' she says. 'I have a date at five.'

'Okay, yeah, no worries.' And then I have an idea. 'Well, can I . . . can I take a picture of you on my camera?'

'For your Instagram project? Sure,' she shrugs.

It's really a crime I don't put the Leica to more use. I took a smattering of shots in Paris, some half-hearted portraits of Sara getting dressed up for a dinner date. As I fiddle with the settings, doing my boxing ring-side shuffle across the floorboards searching for the right angle, I ask Kiki questions. Her bluntness, I think, is a lack of pretence rather than a purposeful rudeness.

'Do you ever worry about your OnlyFans stuff getting leaked? Like your mum or someone finding out?'

'When I was little my mum could barely afford to buy milk,' she says. 'We grew up in the favelas—you know favela? I make more money than she saw in three months by selling a bikini picture. A bikini picture!'

I snap a picture of Kiki in her nipple covers, her hand stroking tenderly at her own shoulder, expensively maintained olive skin. The look in her eyes is one of openness, of defiance.

'Let me show you something.' She takes a little photograph out of her bedside table drawer. 'That's my niece Francisca. I send her money for food, school books, whatever she needs. If I don't make use of this face and body, Agnes, then God wasted it on me.'

'You think God's okay with it?'

'I think God's a realist.'

I look at the little girl in the dark, underexposed school picture. Her hair is a scruffy black halo, her smile is wide and missing teeth, she's maybe six or seven. I think of Marlena and the phone call I keep avoiding, and my heart aches.

'And if God has a problem with it,' Kiki adds, touching up her scarlet lipstick in the mirror, 'then I think he should reassess his priorities, no?'

Nineteen

Tsunami Danger Zone

The weeks go on and I establish a routine, collect a few regulars, Jake the Marketing Guy, Tristan the Writer, Derek the Lawyer (an overwhelming percentage of these guys are lawyers), Tony the Tech Entrepreneur. They're decent-looking men whose company I can stand and who don't have any out-of-left-field fetishes—Tristan's request for me to wear a schoolgirl uniform on his birthday was as wild as it's gotten and yes, I declined. The actual sex is the least complicated part. When it's over, I'll take a taxi to meet the girls at Tape or Cirque or Reign or somewhere else and we sit up in our free booth and drink mouthful after mouthful of free champagne.

I get the girls to model for me. Although Yomawu and Emily are the most beautiful, I find Sara more interesting to photograph. She has a vulnerable liquid kind of quality in front of the camera. Yomawu wants to be photographed in her specially curated outfits, with her cherub mirror in the background. Emily pouts, preens and smoulders like a Playboy bunny and Kiki tells me that if I want to take her picture I'd better email her agent and agree a rate. Last time was a one-off, she says.

There have been times in these past weeks I've felt more alive than ever. Last Friday, on our way into a bar, we passed a gorgeous, gleaming white Wraith parked outside on the street. It had four bodyguards who stood around it, one at each corner, like Greek columns. The owners saw us looking and escorted us to the car, then turned the music up all the way and took us on a tour of that lusciously lit city, light reflecting off the polished white of the car like moonbeam. We glided along the streets with the roof down, part of it all, the night and its vibrations, its music. I felt magical, like I was going to turn into a blaze of flame. I was hysterical. I wasn't worrying about anything.

I wasn't thinking at all.

But then the morning comes and I draw on my face in the bathroom mirror and if I have a lunch date and I'm feeling a bit sluggish I dip a licked finger into Yomawu's stash of Molly. It's no longer opening night, it's a performance I've given a hundred times before.

*

Emily is drunk tonight—she never gets drunk. The two of us have spent the night at Hades, drinking crack babies and eating cheese toasties in the kitchen. The night air is fresh, a dawnish purple tinge hanging overhead.

'I'm gonna call us an Uber,' I tell her.

Emily can barely stand upright, teeters on her heels.

'Here—' I hold her—'sit down here. Stay on the pavement, all right?'

She sits down on the kerb, heeled feet on the road, crosses her arms over her knees and rests her head on her forearms. I sigh—four minutes until the taxi gets here—and sit down next to her on the cold concrete.

'You're hurt,' she says, looking down at the deep scratch on the side of my ankle. 'I'm sorry.'

I scuffed myself on the side of the stairs trying to drag her out of the club.

'It's nothing,' I say. 'You're just wasted, that's all.'

'It's really fucking bad,' she murmurs.

I put my hand on her back. 'You just need some water and a bit of bread,' I tell her, 'then you'll sleep it off.'

'No,' she says. 'Clive.'

'Clive?'

'Mum's Clive—' she lifts her head up from her arms but her eyes are closed—'he . . . I kissed him.'

'Your mum's fiancé?'

She slaps herself on the hand. 'I know,' she says, 'Emily's a bitch.'

'When did this happen?'

'Three—' She hiccups. 'Three years ago on . . . on Christmas Eve.'

'Did you tell Camilla?'

'Never,' she whispers. 'She's gonna be so mad, she's gonna blame me and maybe . . . she's right, it's my fault. But when I look at him, every time I see his face I just picture him . . .' She makes her fingers into a gun shape and holds them out at the street, softly mouthing, *Bang, bang, bang*, and then lets her head roll softly onto her forearms, eyes fluttering closed.

'Come on, hun—' I rub her back gently—'our ride's here.'

*

The next morning I hover around in the kitchen, hoping to catch Emily alone when she eventually rouses herself from her alcohol-induced slumber. She comes out at half-eleven in a pair of Gucci sunglasses and a feather-trimmed nightdress, drinks a glass of water in three gulps over the sink.

'Hey, how are you feeling?'

'Nothing that can't be fixed,' she says, jaw tense as she rifles through the cupboard where she keeps the supplements, filling up her glass with water and dropping in a dissolvable Vitamin C tablet.

'And how are you feeling about that thing you told me?'

She freezes, hands either side of the sink.

'While we were waiting for the Uber,' I continue.

'I don't know what you're talking about.'

'Emily . . .'

'Please, can we just . . . It was too much alcohol, that's all.'

She takes a sip of her concoction, turns around and smiles weakly at me. 'Right, I'm going to go and finish this,' she says, 'and then I'll do a facial steam and have a shower, I think.'

'This is going to be my wedding song,' says Yomawu dreamily. We're lying on Yomawu's bed, my head on Sara's stomach, Kiki's legs over mine, Emily's feet pressed up against the railing at the foot of the bed.

'Which wedding?' asks Emily, tapping ash into the lid of the heart-shaped jewellery box. 'First, second, third?'

'Oh, come on,' says Yomawu. 'When I get married it's gonna be for ever.'

'How many married guys have you fucked?' Emily asks her. 'You know better.'

'No one wants to grow old alone,' says Yomawu.

'We're not alone,' Sara pipes up. 'We've got each other.'

'Well, I'm never going to get old,' says Emily, stubbing out her cigarette in the glass dish. 'I'm gonna die at fifty. I'd rather die than get all wrinkled and saggy.'

'Emily, that's so sad,' I tell her.

'Well, why's it sad?'

'Because . . . it just is.'

'Not really,' she says. 'I've done a lot of living.'

Kiki picks up Emily's right hand and looks at the inside of her palm. 'Short lifeline,' she says.

'See . . .' Emily reaches for her packet of cigarettes and lights up another, feeling vindicated. 'I told you—I'm going to die beautiful.'

Sara's cold bony hand feels for mine across the duvet cover, and I entwine my fingers with hers.

'Stop being so morbid,' I say to Emily. 'You've just got the summer blues, that's all.'

'The mean reds,' says Yomawu.

*

I'm alone in the smoking area and the girls are in the bathroom bumping coke. I don't want any right now, don't want to sober up. I'm absorbed in the smoking of my cigarette, the satisfying click of the lighter, the faint, almost non-existent sound the cigarette makes as it's singed by the flame. I lean against the wall for support, tilt my head up to look at the night sky. I blow out smoke like a dragon.

'Do you have a light?' says a voice.

I turn my neck to look at him. Early-forties, round brown eyes that make his face look boyish, one of those young-old faces like Leonardo DiCaprio, a babyface that's crinkling around the edges. He's tall but not lanky, he's solid, like a tree. An oak tree in a pale pink shirt.

'I do,' I say.

Our hands touch as he takes the lighter and his fingers linger on mine. He has a sunny warmth that makes you want to latch on to him, go around everywhere tucked up under his armpit like a baby bird.

'Thank you.' He has a strange accent, lilting and tough at the same time. 'I'm Sergei.'

Russian. Must be. But then I'm no expert at accents.

He has a way of smiling in which one corner of his mouth turns up and there's a flash of teeth. I follow him inside to where he orders six shots of vodka, calling the bartender by name, and we take them together, one after the other. People clap him on the back like he's some kind of mafia don, and he smiles broadly, passes thrusting handshakes around in all directions.

'Are you . . . famous or something?' I ask him, as more men jostle around to shout their greeting at Sergei, competing to be heard against the booming nightclub music.

'I know the owner,' he says.

It's not much of an explanation but I sense it's all I'm going to get for now.

'You're married,' I say, spying the ring. I am starting to become an expert at spotting wedding bands, I can spy out that flash of carat gold in the lowest lighting.

'It's complicated,' he shouts into my ear above the music, still grinning.

I put down the shot-glass I've been holding. 'That's original.'

But he seizes my wrist. 'Don't go, please. You're divine.' And there it is. The thing that gets me every time. An adjective, a sweet, flattering adjective, in the mouth of the right man at the right time. I'm such a fucking loser.

He presses his hand to his chest. 'I'm a good guy.' There's a sparkle of irony in that upturned corner of his mouth which somehow helps me to believe the next words he says. 'You can trust me.'

'The Good Guy, my favourite myth,' I quickly reply. Still, his voice makes me want to stay, or maybe it's just the vodka taking effect. He puts his arm around me, and the way he holds me carefully, my shoulder fitting into the hollow of his armpit, feels just like I imagined it would—like I'm fragile and delicate, something to be transported home with care. Any time someone passes he puts his arm out to keep them from getting too close, like a bodyguard, as though I'm someone important. I dance, pressed up against him, although he doesn't move, just stands rooted to the spot, my solid oak tree, his hand hovering by my waist to steady me. I hold onto one of his fingers. It takes one more shot for me to make up my mind, look at Sergei's round brown eyes and decide I'm definitely going to sleep with him, married or not (fucking sue me). I can't reach him but he lifts me up, arms around my waist—my heels are off the floor, and I wrap my legs around him. He kisses me, puts me down gently.

'Are you okay, darling?' Gold watch on his wrist.

I nod, I'm fine.

'Let's go back to my hotel,' he whispers into my ear. 'I want you.'

The alchemy of those three words. I—want—you. It starts something in the pit of my stomach.

I remember the swipe of a key card, soft lounge music playing as his hand strokes up the middle of my spine under my jacket, in full view of the night receptionist. Then we're in a lift, there's a walk along soft carpet, another key card. A dark room. I feel his hands in the darkness. The foil of a condom wrapper. He takes my dress down like he's undoing the wrapping paper on something precious and breakable. He stands back to look at me and I'm suddenly desperate for him to touch me again. He puts his fingertips against my lips, traces my profile, the bridge of my nose, my lips, chin, neck, with his index finger.

'Close your eyes,' he whispers, kisses each of my eyelids, my jawbone, my neck, my earlobes, lifts up my hand and kisses my fingers, holds them to the warm softness of his lips.

I open my eyes and look at him. 'What is it?'

'My wife's in the other room.'

'*WHAT?*'

He smiles his one-sided smile, a hand around the back of my waist, the way he strokes my skin makes me shiver. He pulls me in to him. I'm confused. He presses his forehead gently against mine, his shining eyes confront my confused ones.

'Would it be okay with you if she joins us?'

He's stroking at the inside of my arm.

'Join us . . . like a threesome?'

I mean, I'm already here. The idea is intriguing, not unappealing. The more I look at Sergei's mouth the more I think I might actually enjoy it (the threesome, I mean). Fucking hell, are we doing this, Agnes? What do we have to lose?

'Mhmm, have you ever had one before?' I look into his warm brown eyes and that slightly ironic sparkle reassures me.

'No.'

I already feel as though he's someone I don't want to disappoint. Not that I see him as a client because I don't, in fact for the first time in a while I'm actually desperate *not* to get paid. No, I'm doing this because I want to. No faking, no pretending, no routine.

His hand is at my breast, my nipples harden under his touch.

'Have you ever been with a woman?' he asks me, pressing his lips to mine.

'No,' I say, between kisses, 'never.'

'Do you want to try?'

'All right.'

I wonder what it will be like having sex with a woman. Probably not all that different from having sex with a man once the lights are off. Maybe she and I won't actually touch each other at all. Oh my God, I just had a thought, what if she's hideous? If she's hideous I'll have to leave. But what if she's beautiful? Way more beautiful than me? Surely that's okay, like if I'm going to sleep with a woman at least let her be gorgeous.

He withdraws, smiling. 'Wait here.'

Sergei disappears behind the adjoining door into the next room. I hear some murmuring, a woman's voice. I'm suddenly very, very aware of the fact that I'm naked and cross my arms over my middle, feeling childish as I do so. Sergei comes back in, erection straining against his trousers, followed by a woman who looks a bit like Rachel Weisz, a brunette in a black silk slip, heavy breasts, soft stomach under her dress, round hips, arms you want to touch.

'This is Gloria,' says Sergei. He kisses her. 'This is Agnes.'

And she comes towards me. She's taller than me, she smells like sugar and salt and warmth. She brushes my hair back from my shoulder, puts her hand—warm fingers—around the back of my neck. Her eyes are yellow-hazel like a lion's. She kisses me, open-mouthed, I touch her waist, her stomach, her breasts through the silk slip. She's like liquid. I want to sink my teeth into her. Sergei is behind me, kisses my neck, toys with the hem of Gloria's dress before she lifts it up over her head. Her tits are snowy white, nipples the same soft pink brown as her lips, she presses herself against me, soft on soft. Entwines her fingers in my hair.

'Why don't you lie down?' Sergei whispers to her.

She gets down onto the bed, lies on her back, white fingers in her dark hair. She watches me with her yellow eyes, almost smiling, head on the pillow.

'She's incredible, isn't she?' says Sergei.

'She's beautiful,' I say immediately. My voice comes out naturally husky without trying.

'Let me watch you,' he says, settling down into the armchair across the room and loosening another button on his shirt.

I notice something glinting against his chest hair, some piece of jewellery, but then Gloria parts her legs and whispers, 'Come here,' and it's impossible to concentrate on anything else.

It's my first time up close with another pussy, one that isn't mine. I don't know what to do except to replicate what feels good to me. Up on my knees between Gloria's open legs, I look down at the smooth fluid curve of her body, breasts into waist into hips into thighs. I put my fingers inside her, my mouth to her clit. It all comes pretty naturally for something that I was told all my childhood was supposed to be unnatural, an abomination. I want to do it, to please her, to please him, to please myself. Sergei is kneeling by the side of the bed and kissing the soles of my feet. I work at her clit with my tongue, stroke the inside of her, until she clenches around my fingers, back arching up away from the bed like a woman possessed. It's pretty fucking easy to make a girl come, I don't know why guys act like it's cracking the Da Vinci Code or something.

Then I lie down and Sergei fucks me and Gloria leans beside me and the three of us kiss, and then Gloria eats me and Sergei fucks her from behind. It happens easily, smoothly, like a dance, one phase flowing easily into the next. The three of us in sync. It's nice, easier than I thought it would be, better than I thought it would be, and when it's over I'm sated and drowsy.

*

They're already waiting for me with cups of coffee when I meet them downstairs in the hotel lobby. The pair of them look like they're on the executive board of a chic Mayfair start-up. She is immaculately made up and dressed in a black jumpsuit, he is clean-shaven in a fresh white shirt, a crucifix hanging against his chest that he grips in an occasional fist. My God. Literally. How Sergei can bear to wear that thing while he's carrying out these depraved sexual acts I'll never know. Personally, I'd fear spontaneous combustion.

In my black mini-dress and leather jacket, with last night's eyeliner smudged panda-style around my eyelids, I feel like their rebellious teenage daughter.

'Oh, I'm sorry,' I say. 'I thought we were meeting at eleven.'

'A drink?' Sergei asks me, and waves at a server.

'A black Americano, please.'

Sergei and Gloria hold hands across the table. This frightens me somehow, why exactly I don't know. Perhaps because I'm being confronted with the reality of the fact that I'm alone. All the sex, the gifts, the dinners, the calls, the texts. It's not real intimacy, it's a let's-pretend game.

Sergei tells me cheerfully about their plan to return to the States and invites me to stay with them. 'A little vacation,' he says. 'You're more than welcome.'

'We'd love to have you,' Gloria says, a little abruptly, as if Sergei has prompted her with a gentle kick under the table.

'Yes, well. I'll think about it.'

I had fun last night. It was exciting, it was strangely tender, it was as perfect as an unexpected threesome could be. However, the last thing I want is a repeat of the Matthew-in-Paris scenario, failing to live up to the role these people have cast me in. I know what they want: a ditzy little sex-pot with a somewhat scandalous but light-hearted past (no uncomfy trauma that could make them feel guilty for taking advantage), smart enough to navigate their dynamic as a couple, not serious enough to threaten it.

'You know, as our special guest you'll fly First Class, get an allowance,' says Sergei.

The waiter returns with my coffee. I tear open sachet after sachet of brown sugar until I've emptied five into my cup, then I stir it with the teaspoon.

'I don't really know anything about you guys,' I say. I know it's the sensible thing to do with two strangers who offer you a last-minute flight out of London, probe them for homicidal tendencies and criminal records, but I'm hungover and sleepy, and right now all I can think is: a holiday wouldn't be so bad. But on the other hand, I really didn't want this to become a *thing* thing, it was supposed to be a one-off. Fuck, I'm too hungover to really think straight.

'What would you like to know?' Sergei smiles, leans forward like he's in a job interview, bright-eyed, bushy-tailed, eager to please.

'What do you do?'

'What doesn't he do?' says Gloria, answering for him.

'Ah, that would be giving too much away,' he says.

Having already clocked his wedding ring last night, my eyes are now drawn to his gold watch. Just as Emily taught me.

Gloria catches me looking. 'I couldn't talk him out of it. Russian taste,' she says, and I'm not sure if I'm imagining it but I think I hear a note of disdain.

'Gloria is funny about new money,' Sergei says quietly. 'But even new money is better than no money, don't you agree?'

'Yes, Sergei.' Her tone is strained.

'All about money, honey,' he says. He swirls whatever's left in his cup and knocks it back.

'Talking this way is vulgar, darling,' says Gloria.

They smile at one another. Maybe this is all part of some elaborate foreplay.

Gloria crosses her arms and leans forward. 'Are you sure you're not hungry, sweetie?'

This is all a little bit weird and tense. Yes, even for me. I make the decision that I'm finished with Gloria and Sergei.

'I'm fine,' I say. 'Actually, I might head off home.'

Sergei's anxiety is signalled by a twitch in the corner of his lip. It's clear that I'm disappointing him, he really doesn't want me to leave and I suspect he's the kind of man who's used to getting what he wants. He takes a slip of paper out of his inside jacket pocket and hands it to me.

'You will send us your details, won't you? We'll book your flight, First Class,' he's all bright and chipper again, a salesman pitching overseas holidays to unsuspecting hungover young women.

'First Class,' echoes Gloria.

I pocket the slip of paper, pick up my bag and start for the door.

Back in the white streets of South Kensington with its slow-moving vintage cars, stumbling up those dozen flights of Victorian stairs, I let myself into the flat and am confronted with an indigo Slenderman (you know that creepy cartoon internet phenomenon?) figure like a Halloween prop down at the bottom of the hall. All the blinds and curtains are still pulled shut, the house hasn't woken up yet. It's a Western stand-off. I don't think it's a burglar, his hands are empty, and in any case I reckon I could take him—his thighs in his skinny jeans are about the circumference of one of my arms. He could be here to see one of the girls—but we generally don't have men back at the apartment—it's an unspoken rule.

He starts approaching me, I flinch slightly but stand my ground.

'Agnes, it's me,' a man whispers in a plummy English accent.

I squint, trying to make sense of his features in the dim light. 'Freddy?'

'Yeah.'

'What are you doing here?'

No answer.

'See you later,' he says. 'I'm knackered.' He brushes past me and lets himself out through the front door.

I find Sara lying on her bed in a Lovebox festival T-shirt, pant-less, smoking in the dim light. I turn on the switch for the overhead spotlights, and her face screws up into a grimace.

'What are you doing, Ag?' she says. 'I didn't think you were coming back till later.'

'Clearly,' I say, looking around at the mess, empty Pizza GoGo boxes stacked on her dresser together with half-drunk bottles of Corona. 'It smells like sex in here.'

'Oh—' she's fidgety, snatches up some more duvet and turns over like she's going to sleep—'I'm really tired, Ag, can you turn the light off, darling?'

'Sara—' there's a twinge in my stomach, a burning acidic feeling—'did you fuck Freddy?'

A quiet voice from under the covers. 'Maybe.'

'Why?'

Why the fuck would she do that? The thought of Freya's lovely placid face crumpling with tears fills me with such anger at Sara that I don't even want to look at her.

Her fluffy blonde head emerges, her cheeks are red. 'I don't know . . . What are you doing?'

I collect a pair of trackies from my section of the wardrobe.

'I'm gonna chill in the living room,' I tell her.

'Ag . . . I don't . . . It's not a big deal.'

'When you wake up put the sheets in the wash.'

It's a typical Sunday in the flat—a butter-shiny frying pan in the sink, every kitchen surface coated in a thin layer of fag ash—except it's not, it's different. I feel numb, and not in the pleasantly sun-tired, cocktail-drunk, floaty sort of way that I have been all summer. I feel numb like I'm screaming underwater and no one can hear me.

'Where are *you* off to?' Emily asks me, when she wanders by the hallway in her kimono and catches me putting my shoes on at the front door.

'I've got to tell Freya that Freddy was down here.' I feel incandescent, unstoppable. An avenging angel. I feel like the secret is burning a hole in the side of my stomach.

'Are you *insane*?'

'So we just ignore it, keep going upstairs to use their roof and eat their food and drink their alcohol?'

Emily shrugs, a blank expression on her face. 'Well, yeah.'

I shake my head and zip up my hoodie. 'That's fucked up.'

'I'm telling you, Ag,' Emily sighs, 'you're messing up the natural balance of things.'

'She deserves to know.'

'She probably already *does* know.' Emily watches me. 'You think you're friends with her, is that it? With Freya? The *artist*.' She puts a mocking intonation on the word 'artist', soft but unmistakeably cruel.

I'm silent for a moment. 'Look, I don't know what to say to you except I have to tell her Freddy was down here, that's all.'

Emily rolls her eyes. Sometimes I think even if the building was on fire it wouldn't disrupt Emily's perfect calm. Stressing about it wouldn't be worth the wrinkles.

'Go on then,' she says, 'go and save the day.'

Freya answers the door in a paint-covered smock, cut short enough to show the length of her legs.

'Oh, hi, Agnes—' she's frowning—'everything all right?'

'Can I come in? I need to talk to you about something.'

I follow her into the kitchen. She takes her blonde hair down from its ponytail and shakes it out at her shoulders. Fills up two glasses with water from the fruit-infused dispenser. I take two gulps of mine.

'Thanks. Where's Freddy?'

I can't force myself to do the small-talk, chit-chat thing, not when I know what I know. I'm about to send Freya's world into a tailspin.

She shrugs. 'He had some errands, I think, he'll be back later. How's your knee?'

I look down at my leg. 'All healed up.'

Freya strokes my kneecap with the tip of her finger as if she's inspecting it. There's a large canvas spread out on top of her sheets, sunset colours of oil paint mixed up on the palette.

'I . . . I just wanted to tell you, Freddy was downstairs at our place today. I don't know if he stayed the night or . . .' I can't look at her. 'I didn't know if you knew and I just . . . If it was me, I'd want someone to tell me.'

Her hand over mine.

'That's all right,' she says, blushing, 'we're, uh . . . we're actually poly, not that we advertise it or anything.'

Fuck, fuck, fuck. This is so embarrassing. I blather out an indistinguishable string of 'sorry's and one 'none of my business' and some more 'sorry's for good measure.

'It's all right,' she says, still holding my hand.

I can't get out of there fast enough. I tell her I have food in the oven and I've got to be going. I'm mortified at the thought that Emily and Sara knew all along and it was some private joke they wouldn't let me in on. Like I'm some kind of naïve twat from the suburbs, not cultured enough to understand urban couples and their polyamorous ways.

Sara and Emily are sitting on the living-room sofa waiting anxiously for my return.

Emily looks up at me and frowns. 'So you told her, did you? Do you feel better now?'

'Yeah,' I say. I really don't.

She scans my face for weaknesses. 'I was right, wasn't I—about them being swingers?'

'I mean, they're poly but yeah, you were right.'

Sara doesn't look up.

'I'm really sorry, Sara, it was hypocritical and stupid, I don't know why I did it,' I say. Then I repeat, 'I'm sorry.'

'It's all right,' she says softly.

*

After the Freya incident, things feel off in the flat, I feel like the girls think they can't trust me. I sense a subtle hostility when I emerge out into the kitchen for breakfast, like I'm interrupting a conversation whenever I walk into a room, and Sara's feet no longer find mine when we're in bed at night. I find myself thinking of ways to escape London for a while and I wonder if I should go to Miami after all. Three days before they're due to fly out, I send Sergei a text to ask if the offer's still standing. He responds almost instantly with the thumbs up emoji.

It's 4 a.m. when the flat buzzer sounds. I shake awake. It's still dark. Sara is fast asleep beside me, snoring lightly, her peroxide mess of hair reflecting the little light there is.

As I'm on my way out the door, Sara comes rushing into the hall holding my camera.

'Don't you want this?' she asks.

I don't feel like photographing anything or anyone, I feel like passing out poolside but I take the camera, just to appease her.

Then I hug her awkwardly. 'Thank you, I'm—'

'You're sorry,' she says, smiling, 'I know and I'm begging you to *please* stop apologizing.'

'Sure,' I say, holding my free hand up in surrender, 'I can do that.'

'Have a good time,' she says over her shoulder.

From the window I can see a lacquered black Mercedes, waiting outside the apartment building like a slick of pure liquorice. The driver shuts away the case in the boot. He doesn't look me in the eye. I know he's thinking, Whore, whore, whore, when he turns on the ignition. There's a flat rectangular box resting on the seat next to me, tied with an enormous yellow bow. Yes, I think, you're right. And it feels deliciously dark and transgressive to admit it. I'm exactly where I belong, perhaps where I've always belonged, being driven by a chauffeur in the dark.

I push up the aeroplane blind and look down at the grey rain slapping the tarmac at the Heathrow terminal. Gloria emerges from the bathroom in a billowing silk pyjama set, sits down in her First Class pod and closes her eyes. Sergei is next to her with his eye-mask on, and falls asleep instantaneously. I sit back in my own First Class pod with the laminate panelling, where the food comes served behind a screen of plastic. I'm suddenly hungry for Constance's cooking, for the warmth of food prepared in battered metal pans and served on well-used crockery, and my heart aches with loss. Everyone around me is covered up and plugged in and if I scream my lungs out up here, tens of thousands of feet above ground, only a flight attendant in red lipstick will come running.

The air in Florida is muggy and moist, but it thins out as we approach the ocean. As we pass the flat, pastel-coloured architecture on Ocean Drive, there's a man with only one leg, no shirt and sun-weathered skin, drinking from a street fountain and shouting obscenities at a green Lamborghini. Bachelorettes with sandy knees and garish light-up headdresses stagger past, half of them gawping and the rest of them fearfully averting their eyes.

The Vasilievs own a palace on Mashta Drive. It has the stately beauty of an old-world gallery, full of framed oil paintings and ancient vases, endless marble floors, everything with a trim or a frame or an embellishment that shines.

'Wow,' I breathe, meaning it. 'It's beautiful.'

The last time I was in a place this beautiful I was cleaning it. Scrap that, I've never been in a place this beautiful. There are the Camillas and Matthews of the world, but Jesus, this is a whole other level of money. My hands twitch a little at my sides, and I realize that I'm searching instinctively for a hoover or a washcloth.

A tall Latin man comes hurriedly out of a nearby doorway and calls for someone to bring in our bags. 'Welcome home, sir.'

I've never known anyone who had full-time staff, especially not dressed in a tailored suit and silk tie. The man looks delighted to see Sergei and mildly cautious of Gloria, assessing her mood.

'Come and have a tour,' says Sergei.

He takes me by the hand and leads me through the sprawling complex. We cross an enormous entrance hall and trail a long corridor until we reach the kitchen. It has an entire wall made of glass through which you can see a white outdoor terrace, the winking turquoise sea and a dozen swaying palm trees.

'It's heaven,' I say.

We return down the corridor and cross the entrance hall in a different direction.

'I'm so glad you like it. I chose the décor myself. You don't think it's too much?'

Now that we're alone, Sergei is back to his jovial self, a friendly giant with twinkly brown eyes. I hope he scoops me up into his arms again soon.

'I think it's perfect here, against the sea.'

We climb a spiral staircase—one of four, Sergei tells me—and arrive at a landing covered in pictures, their colours visceral and almost 3-D, seemingly painted with gold leaf and squid ink instead of regular paint. Through the skylight I see the gorgeous, Oscar de la Renta baby blue of the heavens.

My room has a four-poster bed with a gold frame, white chiffon drapes riding the breeze from the open window. A large gold-framed clock is mounted on the plain white walls, with hands that could slice your finger off. There's a balcony that looks over onto the sunbeds and barbecue pit below, but the real treat is the adjoining bathroom, which gleams from top to bottom. I feel for whoever has to clean this place, there's really no room for cutting corners with this many reflective surfaces in the mix. Hope they've got a good mirror spray.

'Do you like it?' asks Sergei.

'It's . . .' I struggle for words.

We share a glance and something is exchanged between us and then he kisses me. This is weird. The last time I kissed him I was definitely not this sober, or halfway across the world.

'It's hot in here,' I say, pulling away. 'I feel a bit dizzy.'

'They should have the air conditioning on in here,' he says to himself. 'I'll tell Carlos.' Then he leans in for another kiss.

'Sergei.' It's Gloria's voice, terse and cautionary.

He freezes. I turn to see Gloria standing in the doorway with an expression I can't decipher but know for a fact isn't one of sexual longing. Sergei clears his throat, pushes past her without a word to either of us. Gloria watches me with her blazing yellow eyes, arms folded across her chest, then she turns on her heels and leaves.

What the fuck is going on?

I get up, shut the door and turn the lock, feeling as though I've just done something irreparable.

* * *

When I wake up the air conditioner is on, whirring through the vent. The room is cool, almost too cold to be comfortable. I lie for a while and stare at the ceiling, until a knock at the door makes me jump. I'm naked, last night's clothes lying all twisted up in a tangle in the corner.

'Just a minute!'

I wrap the bedsheet around me.

The maid who's brought my luggage to the door is about the same age as me. I wonder what she thinks now, finding me wrapped in Egyptian cotton in the guest suite.

'Thank you,' I say, smiling broadly to show my appreciation and hoping to distinguish myself from the usual guests who I assume are dismissive of the staff.

'Can I get anything else for you, ma'am?'

'It's Agnes,' I say.

'Oh, can I get anything else for you, Agnes?'

'No, thank you. Um, what's your name?'

'Xiomara.' A tiny smile.

'Xiomara,' I repeat. I want to say something nice so she doesn't think I'm another stuck-up bitch. 'That's beautiful.'

'Thank you,' she says, perhaps a little bored of hearing compliments like this one.

'Oh, um, actually, Xiomara,' I say, feeling a little weird about asking, 'if you wouldn't mind, an espresso and an ashtray? Or . . . or if you tell me where to get them, I can go myself.'

'Miss Gloria is out on the decking if you wanted to join her? I could have your espresso and ashtray sent there?'

There's a disconnect between the extreme politeness of her tone and the cool detachment in her eyes. I get the sense I'm not the first 'lady guest' staying in this guestroom and probably won't be the last.

I don't want to join Miss Gloria at all, in fact that's probably the thing I least want to do in the world. But I'm a guest and the sooner things are smoothed over the better.

Inspired by the beauty of the place and feeling as though I'd better take something to occupy myself with in case Gloria doesn't want to talk, I grab my camera, follow the sound of the sea and find myself downstairs in the open-plan kitchen with the glass all along one side, which opens onto an outdoor seating area with the sea beyond that. Gloria sits on a gold chair at a gold table like a queen, alone, a pale blue scarf wrapped around her hair. She's playing solitaire, red nails against the blue backs of the cards. I take a few pictures and silently thank Sara for getting me to bring my camera.

'Mind if I sit?' I ask her.

'Sure,' she says, not looking up.

She scoops all the cards into a pile and begins to shuffle them again.

'It's a beautiful house,' I say, feeling like an idiot for even using the word 'house' when this place could easily host a village.

I take a picture of Gloria, her red-tipped fingers hovering over the pile of cards. These pictures are going to come out so beautifully, the colour contrast of the red and the blue, the aristocratic disinterest in Gloria's gorgeous face.

'Don't do that,' she snaps.

'I'm sorry,' I say, 'I should have asked.'

Gloria has the power to make me feel small, to make anyone feel small probably. I can practically feel myself shrinking.

'*Yes*, you should.'

There's such an icy chill emanating from her that she cools even the Floridian heat.

'Your espresso, ma'am.' The maid places the miniature coffee cup and the glass ashtray in front of me on the table.

'Oh, and a lighter?' I feel like a bitch ordering her around, 'if you . . . if you wouldn't mind?'

'Of course.'

Gloria puts her cards down and peers at me over the top of her cat's-eye glasses. 'Blow that out downwind, will you?'

'Yeah, of course,' I say, angling my chair slightly away from her before I light up. I exhale and then, out of an obligatory feeling that I should make conversation, I say, 'It's absolutely gorgeous here, I've never seen a place like it.'

'It's vulgar, it's excessive. Sergei is . . . excessive.'

I can't disagree with her there. This place is a literal goldmine. I don't say anything, maybe I'm paranoid but I feel like the slightest word against him would find its way back to him, purred into his ear by Gloria. We sit in silence a while.

'My husband likes women,' she says, and then adds in a stern voice, 'but we *don't* have an open marriage.'

'Sorry?'

Oh my God, this is so uncomfortable I debate the consequence of getting up and jumping in the pool. I hesitate to remind her that I was just an innocent girl in a nightclub before Sergei took me back to his hotel room and got me wound up in all this mess. The cheek of this beautiful bitch.

'Agnes, if you want to stay on my good side there will never be a private meeting between you and Sergei again, do you understand?'

I nod. Whatever, this is getting boring.

'I'd hate to be forced into making things difficult for you.'

'Sorry?'

What the fuck is she talking about? Is she *threatening* me?

'But it won't come to that, will it, Agnes?'

'No, Gloria, it won't,' I say, somewhat sarcastically because she's certainly laying down the law for someone who actually invited their three-way unicorn on vacation. But still, I'm a little scared of her, I can admit it.

'Well, good, I'm glad we understand each other.'

I heed Gloria's warning and stay out of Sergei's way. It isn't hard because I'm mostly left to my own devices, no one seems to go anywhere and I don't particularly want to venture out into a strange place on my own. I want to ask Xiomara to join me for a meal, or to watch a daytime game show with me but I don't. Her politeness is tempered with propriety, with a certain distance. I watch so much daytime TV. A booming Hollywood voice announces a car-leasing deal, then a limited-edition fast-food-joint burger. It seems that no matter where I go or who I meet, I'm inevitably going to end up sitting on my arse watching television alone. The Wasteland, London, Miami.

It's almost like I don't exist at all, except in the deep quiet night when Gloria arrives, at my door in her robe like an apparition. Her expression is impenetrable during these nights, but the way she escorts me to her and Sergei's suite—hand gently on my arm as we round the ghostly corridors—makes me feel that she is making a concerted effort to be kind. I'm alive for those few hours, with Gloria and Sergei, of which my recollections each morning are as vague and watery as dreams.

Living with the Vasilievs is different. We have markedly separate routines and we move around the house, constantly circling each other but rarely colliding. I see evidence of the others' existence here and there. A half-drunk martini in a chilled glass means Gloria has been and gone. A snuffed-out candle means Sergei has been reciting his catechism. Sergei wakes up with the dawn, Gloria around ten, and I roll out of bed sometime after then and moon about, depending on how late I've stayed up chewing Twizzlers in front of the TV. Sergei has a diet of extremes—green juices, ginger shots, tofu, mixed grains, sea moss—offset with so much electric-coloured, processed crap that it just undoes the whole process. He likes Pop-Tarts and shaved ice with garishly coloured sugar syrup.

By the time I come downstairs he's having lunch, nursing a hot pocket, steaming from the toaster. Gloria survives on coffee and a pastry or two until dinner, eats elegantly and plainly, a steak and greens, a yoghurt, a slice of Brie and a handful of berries.

When I wake up with even the slightest of hangovers all I can do is think, *God, who do I have to fuck around here for a tin of baked beans?* The bacon is all wrong and they only have frankfurtery kind of sausages, though there's some nice bread, pumpernickel, which I eat with hunks of real butter. Aside from that it's just whatever I can grab from the fridge or the cupboards and take back to my room with minimal effort. The days of homecooked food, of big long lunches on Sundays punctuated by laughter and arguments with Marlena about washing up, feel more far away than ever now. I pluck my food from the chef-stocked deluxe triple fridge, then eat it lying down undisturbed on Egyptian cotton and if there are any dirty plates or glasses a maid comes to take them away.

I wander around the house looking for entertainment. There's a gym, small and poorly designed—the air conditioning has to compete with the heat of the daylight beating down through the broad expanse of the sunroof. There's a lot of black, somewhat antiquated equipment—an elliptical, a rowing machine. Sergei just likes to use the treadmill and a set of old weights. Sometimes you can smell the metal on him even after he's showered, little rust particles in the grooves of his palms.

Gloria, I've decided, for all her beauty and sophisticated sense of style, is really fucking boring. She reminds me of a collector's butterfly, wings pinned apart under a glass screen, a beauty to behold but not much to study.

I'm sitting on my balcony, trying to read an awful book I bought at the airport, when Gloria and Sergei's angry words float up from the decking below.

'You bitch, you bitch! You fucking hate me? Leave! See where that gets you.'

'You know I would go if I could.' Gloria's voice is fraught with tears.

'Then go, leave everything, it's all mine. That dress on your back—'

Gloria screams, 'Don't touch me! I don't want any of your filthy things, I know what you do to get them, Sergei. You cunt, Sergei.'

'Ungrateful bitch!'

A glass smashes, a door slams and I hear Sergei's furious breathing, hard and animal-like, as he tries to calm down. I decide to go back inside from the balcony, worried he'll look up and see me. I silently tuck the book under my arm and slide off the chair. My foot knocks the coffee cup on the floor and I watch in horror as it rolls between the bars of the balcony, smashing to pieces on the deck below. Fuck.

'Agnes?' Sergei calls up. 'Agnes!'

'Yes?'

'Agnes, I want to show you something. Meet me in the hall.'

Twenty

Saint Agnes

Sergei's sudden attention unnerves me. He's dressed in his black gym gear, his forehead and neck slick with sweat. He calls me into his office and presses me against the desk.

'Gloria warned me not to see you alone,' I say, raking my fingers through his hair, curly and streaked with strands of copper and gold.

He doesn't answer.

'She scares me,' I say, followed by a bubble of nervous laughter that catches me by surprise.

'I'll protect you,' he says, lips on my skin.

I am wearing the necklace Gloria rejected for their anniversary. It's a dazzling wreath of gems in alternating colours, ruby red, pink, green, and it feels heavy and cold on my collarbone. As Sergei kisses the nape of my neck with slow relish, my fear that someone's going to catch us gets catalysed by lust, becomes pleasure. I watch myself in the glass picture frame hanging on the wall behind the desk, my bare chest and the necklace, lips blood red. Sergei touches me like I'm something sacred, arms, wrists, breasts, fingers, legs, feet, thighs. He kisses my body all over, his eyes begging silently for my permission, brow furrowed softly. I don't know exactly what I'm giving him but it's more than sex, and whatever it is, he needs it badly.

I sit at the ornate gilded dressing table in my room, revelling in the deep pleasure of putting on make-up at a glacial pace. I sip white wine and listen to *Ultraviolence* on my phone. Rock guitar, the blue swimming pool outside the window. It's a gorgeous evening, and I have the rare feeling of my soul, mind and body being in perfect harmony. I think about Sergei, I think about Gloria. I resist the urge to lie down on top of the bedcovers and touch myself. It's been a really long time since I've masturbated without a guy watching. The setting sun projects gauzy light through the translucent white curtains, billowing softly in the breeze from the open balcony doors. I take pictures of the items on the dressing table, of the curtain hanging partway across the window.

*

We eat out at the Villa Casa Casuarina at the former Versace Mansion. The dinner is a blur of intoxication and Medusa heads. Mosaics blurry through crystal water, a lot of influencers with whiter teeth than Ross in that one episode of *Friends*, waiters in waistcoats, ice-buckets leaking onto the white tablecloth, tourists posing in front of the fountain. Wives, husbands, girlfriends, boyfriends. What do people think is going on here between the three of us? I wear the Versace dress Xiomara had delivered to my room as a gift from Sergei, Gloria is enshrouded in black from head to toe. Sergei is more handsome to me than ever. He befriends the waiting staff, and to Gloria's copious disgust helps gather up our finished plates into a pile. Gloria asks for an ashtray while Sergei shoots me lustful stares across the table, holding my gaze as long as he dares. Our proximity to Gloria is a key component in the eroticism of it all. I stroke him up and down his trouser leg with my foot under the table, and he pulls Gloria in towards him. She stares into his eyes, then he kisses her on the neck, his other hand reaching for my foot under the tablecloth. She blows out smoke and she looks like a picture, I think.

'Gloria, please can I take a photo?'

She shrugs, stubs out her cigarette in the glass dish and reaches for another. I take my camera out of the Chanel flap bag.

'Allow me,' says Sergei as he holds out a flame for her.

She accepts it coolly. I capture the moment.

I wake up with a sore neck, soaking wet, in the middle of a gigantic wet patch on top of a blue towel. Did I *piss* myself? My hair is damp, curiously, but my dress lying by the side of the bed is dry. How much did I drink last night, for God's sake? My pounding head is worsened by the metallic clang of machinery outside my window. Loud baritone voices, more metal banging and the laboured sounds of men heaving in unison.

'It's up, boys—secure the pegs!'

I find my towelling robe on its hook in the bathroom and fasten it around my waist, then go out onto my balcony, hoping to catch a glimpse of the activities while remaining unnoticed.

There's a freshly erected white marquee, and the midday sunlight gleaming off the top of it hurts my tired, hungover eyes. Staff members are helping carry white tables and chairs out into the garden. I watch them, a parade of ants. My stomach is growling. I get changed and head downstairs where I pass Carlos in the hallway, holding an enormous vase full of white lilies like a bouquet of funeral flowers. He tells me Mrs Vasiliev is throwing a party this evening.

I pick apart the croissant I swiped from the tray of freshly cooked pastries in the kitchen and watch the chaos from behind the golden threshold of the door frame. Suddenly I have a flashback to the night before, like a cold sting on the warm breeze. I remember the pool, light reflecting in its ripples like the flames inside a sapphire. The lapping of the water against the edge. Water up to my neck, against my lips, water on my naked skin, Sergei's hands, one on my throat and the other on my stomach, holding me in to him. My arms spread against the tiled edge of the pool, back arched, Sergei between my legs. Brown hair, brown eyes, his smile. How did we get there? Did we stay up talking after Gloria had gone to bed? Did we kiss passionately in the car on the way back and fuck with abandon for everyone to see, Gloria included? Surely not. I feel embarrassed. Frightened. It doesn't make sense.

'You're biting your lip,' says Gloria.

'Oh, sorry,' I say.

She stands beside me with her arms crossed, her eyes shielded behind large black-framed Dior glasses, surveying her kingdom and its busy workers with a critical eye.

'Carlos said you were having a party.' I flick flakes of pastry off my fingers.

She smiles. 'That's right.'

If she knows about last night she doesn't let on. Or maybe nothing happened, maybe I'm finally losing my mind for real.

'Oh, cool, who's coming? Are they . . . work friends of Sergei's?'

'Some—old friends mostly,' she says.

Later Gloria sends Xiomara up to my room with a bottle of champagne and a garment bag. The dress is blood red like a bullfighter's cape, and a size too small. It hugs my ribs like it wants to crush them, a malicious piece of fabric. It pulls me in, pushes me up, makes indents in the flesh of my breasts. I examine the damage in the gilded full-length mirror. As uncomfortable as it is, it looks good. The champagne makes me a little dizzy, so I sit down on the edge of the bed until the feeling passes.

I rinse my left-out hair at the top of my weave in the basin before blow-drying it and burning it pin straight with my ghds, too lazy to shower again. I neglect the champagne flute and drink from the bottle, feeling uncivilized and decadent. There's something strange in the air, but then everything's felt surreal since I arrived in Miami. I feel more alone than ever before, perhaps it's the new country or living in a married couple's home like a spare part.

It's a full moon tonight, pale, watchful, whole. Reminds me of my mother's face. It's dignified, you know, it doesn't shout like the daytime sun, it whispers. I think of Constance's hushed voice whenever we were cleaning together. *Once some things get dirty they can never be clean again and once some things are broken they can never be fixed.* She talked quietly even when we were alone, trod lightly, always mopped up where she'd just stepped even though she hadn't left a mark behind.

Soon there are more voices, different accents, excit- able, bellowed greetings, heavy footsteps on the decking below. I think maybe they've forgotten me—no one comes to get me, no one calls me down. I reach the bottom of the stairs and see that it looks like less of a party and more of an international mafia conglomerate meeting type of thing. A lot of men with well-pruned facial hair in smart dark clothing, standing around like they're waiting for something to happen. The air smells like salty sea breeze and the scented candles lit in the hallway are jasmine and incense. The frankincense and myrrh scent that brings back memories of churches at Christmas, sombre, tuneless singing and foil stars pasted onto card.

There are maybe twelve guests who've arrived so far. I can only assume from the grand set-up that more are on the way but then again we've already established that Sergei is excessive. Too much is never enough. They are all men except a little Italian woman who is whip-thin with a deep orange tan and platinum blonde hair. She has a little dog on a spindly pink lead, a chocolate-coloured little thing with bug eyes. I approach the group, kneeling down to pet its bulbous head, and grin despite myself when it nudges its tiny wet nose into my palm.

'What's his name?'

'Hers. Bambi.'

The woman looks down at me. Close up her face is hard, wide nostrils in a thin face. I shield my eyes from the glare of the overhead lights.

'Greeting the most important guest first, I see.'

A hand extends down towards me. I grab hold of it and find my feet. The man is medium height and heavily built, he has black hair slicked back to the side with gel and a well-groomed beard. The parting in his hair is so crisp and severe I question whether he's wearing a lace-front. I remove my hand from his and clear my throat.

'I'm Agnes, pleased to meet you both.' I kiss the man's cheeks and then the woman's. He smells like expensive aftershave, vetiver and pepper, she like Chanel No 5 and biscuity spray tan.

'What brings you to Miami?' he asks me.

The woman says nothing, just presses her thin lips together and hoists the dog up into her elbow. Around us there's some hushed conversational buzz, as though everyone's sitting around in a darkened theatre room waiting for the show to start.

'I met the Vasilievs in London, and they invited me to come and stay.'

'Lucky, lucky you,' he smiles. 'Are you staying long?'

'I don't know.'

'Do you work?'

'Not currently.'

The woman yawns.

Operatic music wafts out from the indoor sound system, and Carlos whisks by whispering furiously into a walkie-talkie, 'Too loud, too loud, someone turn it down from the main control!' The woman puts the dog down and tugs it along on the lead for a lap of the pool. The man sidles up closer towards me, puts his arm around me. I remove it, he replaces it, I give up.

'What was your name again?' I say. 'I'm sorry. My memory.'

'Antonio, darlin'.'

I couldn't be less interested in Antonio to be honest with you, even though he's the authoritative older-man type I would have been desperate to please not too long ago. I am, however, sort of fascinated by what these people have to do with Sergei.

'Antonio,' I repeat and try to smile. 'How do you know the Vasilievs?'

'Business. Oh, I love those tiny snacks—over here, mister!' He waves over to one of the extra waiting staff Gloria has hired to help with the event, who offers us a silver platter full of salmon and cream cheese canapés. Antonio grabs up three or four and chews them hurriedly with an open mouth. I take one and, now feeling slightly repulsed, toy with it in my hand and look for somewhere to discard it. Where's the dog?

'Do you know the other guests?' I ask him.

He nods that he does, reels off some names. '. . . Mikhail, Stefano, Albie. Oh, over there that's Gregory, he's British like you.'

I spot Gregory immediately. He's vaguely interesting, a pale, bespectacled figure who stands out among the tanned and muscled men shuffling about in twos and threes. They seem ready at any moment for a fight to break out, their sizeable fingers hooked through belt buckles and buttonholes, brushing close to the gunmetal waiting there below the surface. Where's Sergei? Where's Gloria? A warm, purple-tinged darkness seeps through the air, the sun disappears completely, leaving only the moon. The woman sits at one of the white podiums alone with her dog on her lap, feeding her bits of shrimp off the canapés.

'Who's this you've got here, Antonio?' Two men approach us.

'This gorgeous piece of ass—' he winks at me—'is Agatha.'

'Agnes.'

'Like the saint,' says one of the men.

They are Mexican brothers. One has a protruding stomach that he uses to support his glass of whisky, the other is tall and thin with a moustache and puffs on a cigar.

'Miss Agnes here is British.'

'British, eh? Good evening, my good lady, pip-pip and cheerio.' The one with the cigar looks pleased with himself.

Antonio looks up. 'I'd better watch out, it's a full moon.'

'What does that mean?' I ask him, staring at the blob of salmon stuck to the prickly stubble of his beard.

'A full moon is for releasing,' says the one with the glass of whisky. 'That's what our mom used to say, for endings. You know what it was like,' he says to his brother. 'Catholics by day, *brujas* by night.'

'Well, I'm always wary of a pretty girl on a full moon,' says Antonio.

The Mexican brother with the cigar says, 'She's not a werewolf.'

I say, 'Maybe I am, maybe I'll rip your throat out.'

Bored out of my brain, I smile and excuse myself then chase down a waiter with a tray of champagne flutes, drink alone by the pool. When I turn over my shoulder they're all staring. Staring like they want something from me.

Sergei and Gloria emerge into the garden arm in arm, the picture-perfect couple. Antonio and his wife, the Mexican brothers and the men I haven't yet met gather around their hosts at the other end of the garden under the white awning. The staff finish lighting dozens of tiki torches that illuminate the marquee with a perimeter of fire. Gloria basks in all that attention, she looks beautiful in the flame's glow. Am I missing something? Is this some kind of elite blood sacrifice?

'So what brings you out here to the lion's den?' Gregory asks me.

'Champagne, please,' I say to the passing waiter. At Gregory's insistence I clink my glass with his.

'Curiosity mostly,' I say. 'Or . . . stupidity, I haven't decided. Or maybe I was just bored,' I say, 'of life in London. And I've never been to the States.'

His smile has something sinister in it, sharklike, and he's looking at my cleavage in the red dress, his hand suspended in mid-air like he's had to stop himself from reaching out and touching me, from petting me like a magician's rabbit at a child's birthday party. His dark eyes on me give me goosebumps. He's creeping me out.

'I think I need some water,' I say.

'Oh, well, let's ask a waiter, shall we?'

'No,' I protest. 'I'll get it myself.'

I start towards the house.

'Uh, miss, can I help you with something?' A young waiter in a white waistcoat hurries in my direction.

'I live here,' I say, pushing past him.

Gregory watches me go—I actually feel his stare burning the back of my neck.

I pour myself a glass of tapwater in the kitchen and lean against the counter to drink it, then I go to the nearest toilet and reapply my lipstick in the gold-edged mirror.

On my way out I almost collide with a white-haired man, tall, wearing a black shirt, black suit trousers, eyes the colour of a frozen pond. 'Oh, I'm sorry,' I say. Instead of stepping aside he moves directly into my path to block me from leaving. 'I'm sorry,' I repeat, 'is there something I can do for you?'

'Certainly,' he says. I can't place the accent. He puts his hand under my chin and strokes it. 'Why don't we go upstairs to one of the guest bedrooms?'

'Excuse me?' I can't help but laugh.

'You don't have to pretend,' he says. 'Gloria told me about you. So come on.'

'I don't understand.'

What the fuck did Gloria say? Immediately, I know that whatever she's said, whatever she's done, is payback for my secret meetings with Sergei. I was stupid for thinking that she wouldn't know, that she'd let it slide.

'Or we can do it right here.'

'What the fuck are you talking about?'

His hand grips my arm as he pushes me towards the bathroom. 'You can just suck it. We don't have to fuck.'

'Let go of me!'

He twists my arms around, forcing me to face him, burning the skin on my wrists. His mouth comes close to my face and his breath is stale. I'm ready to hurt him, my right ankle twitching as I prepare to knee him in the balls.

'Relax, relax,' he says, feeling in his pocket for something. 'You want one?'

He produces a doggy bag of pale green-coloured pills, an American dollar sign pressed into the front of each. He shakes the plastic packet at me. A peace offering. I nod, all right, fine, why not? I'll get to Gloria in a minute. He puts the pill into my waiting palm.

Again, his hands on me. This time they tug at the hem of my skirt, try to force themselves between my legs.

'Stop it.' I swat him away. 'I don't know what you've heard but you've got the wrong idea, pal, and if you put your hands on me again I swear I'll . . . I'll break your fingers.'

'But Gloria said—'

'Where is she? What did she say?' I tear from the bathroom in a rage that eclipses any fear I felt of Gloria before. I'm so angry that my hand shakes and I have to put it on my hip to steady it. The incense smell is overbearing, the heat is cloying. I see her outside, engaged in conversation with the Italian woman, the bored dog wriggling in her matchstick arms. I shout, 'Gloria!' as I approach her, anger strangling my voice. Breathe, Agnes, breathe. 'Gloria, I need to speak to you.'

I try to draw her away from the group but she stands stubbornly in place. The Italian woman hauls her dog off in the opposite direction, leaving the two of us alone, like she's scuttling out of a tsunami danger zone.

'What is it, Agnes?'

'A man just, well, he just grabbed me outside the bathroom. He said you told him . . . I don't know, but what did you say to him? What have you been telling people about me?'

'I've told them the truth.'

'What do you mean?'

'That you're an escort, Agnes,' she says, a touch too loudly and with so much mean-spirited relish that I have an incredible urge to push her in the pool.

'But I'm not. You invited me here and you're not paying me.' I will myself not to cry but tears sting my eyes and my cheeks grow hot.

'You're getting an allowance.' Gloria is as cool and stoic as ever, a flicker of pleasure in her deep brown eyes as she watches me disintegrate in front of her. 'I warned you, I asked you politely. But if you want to act like a whore I'll be happy to treat you like one.'

I knew this was about Sergei. I'm a fucking idiot. I can't do anything except stare at the ground, my lips twitching with protestations and denials I don't have the gall to spit out.

'Oh, stop pretending to be so innocent, Agnes. Fifty thousand dollars,' she says breezily, appearing to pluck the sum out of thin air as if to emphasize how little it is to her, 'don't tell me you'd turn that down?'

I shake my head. 'What for?'

'Your job. Entertain, relieve, whatever. Please the guests, if they ask you. I'll pay you at the end of the night.'

'And if I don't?'

'You can leave tonight,' she shrugs, 'without the money. It doesn't matter to me.'

'I don't have any guarantee that you'll actually pay me,' I say.

Gloria laughs. 'I don't lie Agnes, and I have ten times that amount in my handbag collection upstairs. If for whatever unforeseeable reason I don't make the transfer, you have my permission to go into my wardrobe and take a couple of Birkins.'

Sergei. Where is he? He's laughing with the Mexican brothers, his arms moving wildly as he regales them with some anecdote or another, the gold watch shining on his wrist. He hasn't glanced in my direction since the party started.

Perhaps I should just leave, cut my losses. But something makes me stay. It's a lot of money, like buy-a-car-and-put-down-a-deposit-on-a-flat kind of money. A cigarette. A cigarette and then I can think.

A cigarette and a drink. It's straight-up, no-frills prostitution, cash for sex, but it's also nothing I haven't already done when you really boil it down. Though before, I tell myself, I was taken on dates, given presents. But what difference does that make really? I chose the guy, someone articulate, someone I fancied at least a little bit, I decided who, I was picky. I never fucked someone I wouldn't have fucked for free. I debate myself in circles as I tap my cigarette into a white ashtray propped on one of the empty podiums. I arrive back at the primary point: it's a lot of money, and who would know, except the people here tonight? *They've got way more to lose than we do*, I hear Emily's voice in my head. But it was never supposed to get to this stage, it was always supposed to be planned out, under control. Does it really matter? Does anything? I'm already so intoxicated that my ears and eyes feel all out of sync.

'Come on, then.' I go up to the white-haired man, grab him by the hand and take him up to one of the guest bedrooms. 'Leave the light off,' I say, closing the door behind us. It's no big deal, I can get it over with in a few minutes and live the rest of my life denying to myself that it ever happened.

'At least one of the lamps,' he says, fiddling with the switches until the bedside lamp flicks on. 'That's better.' He's looking me up and down, grinning like he can't believe I've come around.

But if I'm going to do this I'm going to do it my way; no five Ms, no pretend passion, no fake moaning and certainly no mimed orgasms. He puts his arms around me, and I smell his stale salmony breath as he insists on kissing me. This is gonna take for ever. I was hoping for a one-pump-and-done kind of scenario.

'Let me look at you,' he says, like a gynaecologist. 'Take this off.'

I tug at the zip of my dress, stand there naked apart from my thong. I hold his jaw in the grip of my acrylics and gaze at him with Emily's look which has become mine, a glazed, hypnotic siren look that bores into his pond-water eyes. I kiss him, bite his lower lip, not hard enough to draw blood but enough to hurt.

He recoils, complaining, 'You kiss with your eyes open?'

'I can't look at you?'

'That look could kill.'

I grab at his dick in a way that says shut up and fuck me. That's what we're here for, right?

I hunch over the basin and splash cold water on my face in the bathroom, dab my running eyeliner on the hand towel.

'Will you help me?' I ask and the white-haired man zips up the back of my dress.

He's a little wary of me, a little intimidated perhaps by my directness.

He's gone all bashful. 'More?' he asks, offering me the pills, I don't think the first one's kicked in yet. 'You know your dress is a little ripped at the seam. I'm sorry if I did that.'

'Is it? Oh, fuck, never mind. Have you got any coke?'

He shows me another baggie.

'Your nose is bleeding,' he says.

'Shit.'

Embarrassed, I shut the ensuite door and snatch up swathes of toilet paper.

'I'll leave you to it,' he says. 'See you downstairs. Er . . . thanks.'

He's remembered his manners then? Joker.

A few drops of blood fall down the front of my dress and soak into the thick material where they blend in without a trace. When the bleeding's stopped I rejoin the party.

Dinner is served on a long table in the marquee covered over with a white tablecloth. Steak cutlets with glistening pink middles are laid neatly in a row. The Mexican with the round belly stands beside me to peruse the buffet.

'You not eating?'

I shake my head. 'I would but I'm vegan.' I'm not, obviously, just something about the meat on the table is turning my stomach.

'Me too.'

'He's lying,' says his brother, his plate piled so high it's become a precarious tower of meat and potatoes.

'Wait here,' says the short one, and he stalks off to the other end of the garden.

Sergei stands in the opposite corner of the marquee, a glass of whiskey in hand, talking to Antonio and a woman standing next to him.

The short man returns. In his hands he holds a cluster of waxy white lilies, stems still dripping wet, which he's plucked from one of the vases.

'I stole these,' he explains, 'for your hair.' He's drunk. He pulls my hair, trying to secure the flowers in place.

What a fucking freak.

'Ouch,' I protest loudly.

'Oh, my darling, forgive me.'

He insists on a second flower, and then a third.

'There,' he announces, 'now you are ready.'

'Ready for what?'

'Ready to dance!'

I explain that I've had too much to drink and can't possibly dance now but he ignores my protestations, snatches my hands up into his and proceeds to twirl me around.

'Dance, dance, dance,' he's chanting.

It's a blur of blood and incense and lilies, candles and animal flesh. I must be coming up, finally. Fuck, there was a time I said no to drugs, it was easy when I wanted to resist being swallowed up in The Wasteland, but here in this luxurious palace it seems futile to refuse. Why would I want to be sober when I can be so fantastically out of my skin? Where's there to go now but down, down, down? Burning flowers, burning hair, laughing, fur with blood soaking into the white trim, choir-song, Gloria's jewelled necklace, a silver chalice filled with blood. A baby born, the full moon, an umbilical cord, the first blood, the pool like a black lake, the sea like oil on tarmac. I go over on my ankle in my high heels.

'Take them off,' he croons, and I do. 'Let's go up- stairs.'

'Okay,' I say, thinking, at least I can lie down.

It's late. I feel sick, nauseous from the alcohol and the drugs and the sex. The party is lively, the opera has been replaced with Gatsby-ish jazz, the chatter of the guests is louder than before to compete with the noise. More people have arrived, among them a couple of mode-lesque women around my age or just slightly older, in slinky backless dresses and halter-neck floor-length chiffon, who look at me with interest but don't approach me. I'm not part of the group. I sit at the pool's edge and dangle my feet in the water—it feels nice, swinging them back and forth, feeling the cool resistance. Across the black void of ocean the city glitters like a utopia. I think about what I'm going to do with the money.

'Another drink, madam?'

'Yes, thank you.'

I go to find the white-haired man for another pill. It's magic, it gives me the feeling of a warm tingle from my head to my toes and when it gets to be too overwhelming I can calm the effects with a line of coke. He looks a little worried at the state of me but I convince him that I do twice as much on the regular and always look much worse than I am. The buzz is worth it. I'm almost scared to confront myself in the bath-room mirror. My eyes and nose are red, a halo of dried blood around each nostril, which only seem to get more aggravated the harder I try to wipe them off. One lily has survived, wilting in my hair. I splash more cold water on my face. My make-up is long gone, but it doesn't matter. No one is looking at my face, not really.

Someone knocks on the bathroom door. I dust away any remnants of white powder from the basin.

'Who is it?'

'It's Antonio.'

Lucky me, another customer. I open the door a small way and see an inch of Antonio's black beard and oiled hair.

'Yes?'

'Is now a good time? Maybe we can have a chat, in private.'

'Sure,' I say and open the door wide enough for him to come in.

'We could go to your room?'

'Here is good,' I say.

He turns the bolt to lock the door and starts to kiss my neck. The hair of his beard is coarse and scratchy, it's going to leave my skin red raw.

'Who's the woman you're here with?' I ask him.

'My wife,' he says.

'Don't you fuck her?' I say provocatively.

The fire inside me is reaching a crescendo and I am ready to surrender to it, I'm ready to burn and everyone who has enjoyed the heat of the fire will also suffer. Agneselations chapter 21 verses 1–3. In other words, I'm feeling violent. I can please this man if I choose to, I know how, I also know how to crumple up his ego like a bit of used tissue. I am *so* tired of acting and pretending and performing for these soulless buffoons.

'Of course I fuck my wife—' there's irritation in his voice—'enough talkin'.'

He lifts me onto the basin. I spread my legs for him.

'Quit starin' at me,' he says, uneasy.

He pushes his little cock into me and I laugh, 'Is that all of it?'

He grabs me by the throat. I stare into his bloodshot eyes steadily—go on, I dare you.

When he leaves I catch sight of myself in the mirror and do a double-take. For a few seconds it looks like there's ruby blood leaking out of my tear ducts. Am I tripping? I wipe my eyes with a fistful of tissue and see that my eyes are fine, perhaps just a trick of the light.

*

I miss Gloria's speech but make it out in time for dessert. It's served in the form of a gigantic croquembouche pyramid, the whole thing alight with sparklers, quite the spectacle. The party is a grim and horrible circus and Carlos is the ringleader, wheeling around the edible tower with a delighted look on his face.

'Enjoying yourself?'

Finally. I'm face to face with Sergei—his round brown eyes are gleeful, and he looks around at the party with such delight you'd never believe he actually owned the place.

'Having a blast,' I say, smiling so widely that my cheek twitches and I feel what I realllllly hope isn't a drop of blood rolling out of my right nostril.

I don't know how to tell him I've been providing sexual favours for most of the party at his wife's behest. Maybe he already knows about it. Still, seems like the kind of thing best discussed while sober.

He claps me on the shoulder. 'So glad you're having a good time,' he says, then chases after Carlos.

Shoeless, I wander inside for some water, having to focus on putting one foot in front of the other. I look up at the pale moon and think of my mother and feel the old familiar shame. You know it's so weird to think that I ended up as me, even with a mother as saintly, pure and perfect as mine. I wonder what happened during the cosmic conception of my soul to make me this way—what buried seed of secret ancestral shame chose to pierce the soul and bloom in me?

Ha, I really am wasted. Someone give me a cold shower and put me to bed.

'Are you okay?' It's Xiomara, who's come into the utility room for more hand towels.

I'm embarrassed that she's found me crying.

'I, uh . . . I've ripped my dress.'

She looks down at the side seam of the lethal red dress, the tear spewing loose thread, the puckered red underskirt.

She bends at the waist, scrutinizes the rip up close. 'It's not too bad,' she says softly, 'tomorrow we'll have it—'

'No, I want to fix it now,' I say, voice trembling and well aware that I sound like a bratty four-year-old, only the ripped skirt makes me feel sick to look at it and right now the only thing that matters is fixing this skirt by any means necessary.

'Uh, I think there's a sewing kit in here somewhere,' she says, looking at my face, my smudged lipstick. 'Give me a minute.'

Xiomara stitches up the rip so it's less noticeable but certainly not as good as new.

'Thank you.'

'Don't mention it.'

I feel a little lighter.

'I'm going up to bed,' I tell her. 'Thank you.'

'It's fine,' she says. 'You're okay, right?'

'Fab, thanks,' I say, holding my thumb up and stretching my smeared red mouth into a ghoulish approximation of a smile. 'Just need some sleep.'

I pass out in my bed and dream of the white-haired man, eyes like the silvery ice on a park pond, my hand grabbing at the scruff of the grey hair at the back of his thick neck. I hold his head in my hands, his severed head, warm rubber-like skin, a slit of yellowing eyeballs visible under half-closed lids.

Thou didst treat me as a harlot, as a wanton . . .

I still live, but thou, thou art dead, and thy head belongs to me.

I can do with it what I will . . .

'You want me to kiss you? Of course I'll kiss you, my love, I'll even close my eyes to do it.'

I put my tongue into the slack of his mouth. He tastes of death. I look at him, the blackheads on the thick skin around his nostrils.

'Look at me, look at me, look at me,' I tell him.

Nothing.

I kiss his lips again.

'Do you like that?'

Nothing.

*

When I wake up, my brains are rattling around inside my skull like I'm a human maraca. I look out from my balcony and see that the guests are gone, though the party hasn't been fully cleared away. I put on my dressing gown and go downstairs to the kitchen to pour myself some water. The enormous back door has been left open. The sky is white, streaked with cotton pink, and the amber light of the city across the water seeps into the cloud like one of Freya's paintbrushes left to soak in a cup.

The lights are on at the bottom of the pool. It's the chemical smell of chlorine that attracts me—I have the urge to be clean, disinfected inside and out. I take off my dressing gown, get into the swimming pool via the silver stairs. I start swimming.

Twenty One

No-one goes to Rome at this time of year

The mansion is still and sombre in the aftermath of the party, nothing but day staff in monogrammed tabards clearing up empty glasses, dirty plates, name cards like gravestones from the garden table. I am sitting on the pool furniture in my underwear, hair still a little damp on my shoulders, stringy and brittle from the chlorine. The shadows are blue-tinged and the arm of the chair under my fingers is coated in a salty crust that I can scrape off with my nails.

Around ten o'clock Sergei comes rushing out onto the decking, curly hair slicked back against his head with water, eyes round and bulging out of his skull in a froggish way. He's babbling about Rome.

'We're leaving for Italy at lunchtime!'

'Italy?'

'*Si, amore!*' He's shouting out jubilant morning greetings at a terrified-looking member of staff, some kind of cook or chef I haven't seen. 'Two coffees as soon as you can, my love.'

He pulls out the other chair at the table and sits down, foot bouncing against the floor. Tap, tap, tap, tap.

'Have you . . . been for a swim?'

'Yes,' I say. It's now or never, so I put down my half-smoked cigarette. 'Do you know what happened last night . . . ? What Gloria asked me to do?'

He puts his hand over mine. 'My dear, you're so nervous, you're shaking.'

He smiles in his usual way, one corner of his lip lifting to show his teeth.

'She offered me money to have sex with the guests and I took it.'

He smiles, takes a cigarette from the packet on the table and lights it up. 'That's your right,' he says, frowning out at the ocean. 'Mmm, when we get back I think I'm going to charter a boat,' he exhales, tapping ash. 'It's decided. Right—' he hauls himself up from the seat—'do you need someone to help you pack?'

'Wait, Sergei—' I touch his arm—'you mean you're fine with it, you're not . . . I don't know, angry with me?'

'Darling, why would I be angry?'

'Because I had sex. For money. With your friends . . . in your house.'

This has got to be it, this has got to be the part where I finally get a bollocking, the shaming I've been waiting for, dreaming about.

'I'm in no position to judge anyone,' he says.

'I've *sold* my body,' I tell him slowly. Maybe he's misunderstanding me.

'You're so beautiful, so valuable, so desired that a man sees you and he wants you. We're human-beings, no? Or you think you should be shamed for taking the money? That doesn't make a lot of sense to me. Everyone is selling something of themselves, Agnes.'

'Maybe you're right.'

I know it's just my desperation to be soothed by anything half resembling parental validation but my whole body floods with relief. Maybe

Sergei is going to be the one to show me how to do it, how to unite all the parts of myself and finally be at peace.

There's no discussion of last night, and with nowhere to put my simmering hatred of Gloria, I simply swallow it.

'I haven't forgotten about your money,' she tells me when we meet in the hall with our packed bags, and then she asks me politely whether I've had a chance to have any breakfast and whether I want someone to bring me a coffee. This is her way of letting me know I've redeemed myself. Sick bitch.

Gloria sulks in the car on the way to the airport. 'No one goes to Rome at this time of year,' she says. 'It's going to be empty apart from the tourists who are too stupid to know any better—we're going to look ridiculous.'

We fly First Class on an American airline, but I spend the whole time clutching a sick bag, sunglasses on, earbuds in, senses numbed. I'm glad we're leaving Miami, and I'm interested to experience Rome. I think a lot about what Sergei has said. When I get up to go to the toilet I pass a woman reading the Bible in her seat, which I find quaint and unsettling. I can't remember the last time I saw someone reading a Bible out in the wild.

A black Mercedes collects us outside the airport in Rome. The driver, who has chin-length, red-brown hair, is wearing a grey suit, blue tie dangling from his neck as he staggers around with our luggage. Gloria complains that it's too hot and I have to agree with her—it's a wearying heat, the kind that demands ice and air conditioning. Gloria has been wilting steadily since we landed at Ciampino, her Dior concealer settling into shiny creases in the fine lines around her eyes, and she insists on wearing all black even now—it's a hill she's willing to die on, quite literally, based on the reddening colour of her throat.

I look out of the car window at the cherubs on every corner, the Holy Mother, the saints, the crucifix. Rome is more than I imagined. More beautiful, more Catholic, more Roman. The Holy Mother and baby Jesus in their blue, yellow, red and gold, framed pictures high up on the building ledges, smaller postcard-sized pictures hanging above shop doors, stone cherubs carved into the corners of buildings. A woman in a dove grey nun's habit is stooping to guide water from a street fountain in the shape of a stony lion into her mouth with her bare hands. I see more nuns who wander in twos or threes, prostitutes too, sitting on benches in well-worn micro-shorts and leather heeled boots in the heat, side by side in a way you would never see back home.

We're staying at the De Russie hotel right by Villa Borghese. I take a shower in my room, meet Gloria out in the garden for a glass of wine.

'Where's Sergei?'

'Preparing to ask God's forgiveness,' she says, rolling her eyes. 'A part of me really thought we were going to evade the whole circus this year but ah, well, we'll try to make the most of it.'

'I didn't know he was actually that religious,' I say.

'Oh, really, you mean between the orgies and the drugs and the alcohol you couldn't tell? He's got a Catholic conscience.'

'So . . . how does that work?'

'He binges and then he purges,' she says, fishing around in her bag for a packet of Sobranie cigarettes and a vintage gold Cartier lighter. She slots a cigarette into a shiny black holder, puts it between her lips. 'There's nothing that enough Hail Marys or Our Fathers can't fix,' she says, lying back in her chair as she tilts her chin up to look at the sky, which is blue in every direction, and then closes her eyes, 'but it still eats him up inside. I blame his mother.'

'His mother? Why?'

'For the whole Virgin Mary act she put on for him. Now he has these freak-outs, starts panicking, thinking he's desecrated the reincarnation of the Holy Mother with his cock and he needs to atone and be cleansed before he can go back home and do it all over again.'

'That doesn't make any sense whatsoever.'

She exhales. 'You're telling me.'

'You're smoking more than usual.'

'It's a necessity in Rome,' she says.

'So what happens now?' I ask her.

'Now he'll go to a spa,' she says, 'to clean his body, and then he'll find a priest for confession to clean his mind, and then he'll want to go to the Vatican.'

'Do we go with him?'

She looks at me. '*You* can do whatever you like,' she says. 'I'll be at the Prada store. God, it's hot.'

When Sergei returns from the spa his skin is pink raw and so are his nerves, judging by the way he can't seem to sit still, his foot bouncing over the other in his navy loafers. He joins us outside for a drink, calls over one of the bartenders with a wave of his hand.

'Tanya! Tanya! This is my friend Agnes. Agnes, darling, tell Tanya what you'd like—whatever it is she'll make it for you. Tanya was the World Cocktail Making Champion of 2019. She's incredible, *incredible.*'

'Ah, um, something a bit bitter,' I say, 'like a gin sour maybe.'

'Sure.' Tanya throws Sergei a suspicious side glance.

When the cocktail arrives Sergei hunches forward to the edge of the seat to watch me sample it.

'Do you like it?'

'It's nice,' I say.

'But do you *really* like it? I want it to be perfect for you, I want you to have whatever you want.'

'It's fine, thanks.'

'Don't worry about offending me,' Sergei goes on. 'We can get you another one, keep going until we find you something you love.'

Gloria snaps, 'For fuck's sake, she told you it's fine.'

We are going to the Vatican (Sergei and I) and Gloria is going to the Prada shop near the Trevi Fountain. We visit the Sistine Chapel and I feel the same nerves I used to feel at church, a flush of the same guilt on entering a holy place and feeling marked, unclean. I think you can probably be religious and not believe in God at all, you can like the tradition and the art and the lore of it. Like people are just in it for the aesthetic, you know? They're into lighting candles, eyes closed, praying fervently, and the smell of beeswax and ash. I reach for a candle, feel it cold and brittle in the palm of my hand. It begs to be cracked, so I roll it under my fingers and feel the wax warm, the outer layer becoming pliable to my touch. I have the urge to put the candle into the deep loose pocket of my sundress but I resist it, and then the phantom grip around my core loosens and releases, my lungs expanding out in either direction from my spine.

A woman is praying beside me. I would really like to be able to believe like that, I would like to be able to feel something when I pray but I don't. Maybe looking for God is just looking for something to be in awe of, something to tremble before, a standard to uphold. Perhaps religion is a way of punishing oneself, a manifestation of the shame built into the human experience.

On our return I take a nap up in my room before dinner. I have another dream in which I'm in a glass box behind a church altar, wearing all white. The seats are full, people are kneeling at the pews. A man in a priest's robe is standing in front of me and as I start to panic, banging on the glass, begging someone to let me out, he interprets my movements for the congregation.

'She says there will be a great flood,' he says. 'The sacred one has spoken.'

'Let me out, you prick!' I bang on the glass.

'She says the time is drawing near, her faithful followers will be saved.'

'Fuck you.' I hit the glass with a balled-up fist. 'Fuck you, fuck you.'

'All hail the Divine Feminine, the life-giving goddess.'

They're all singing and shouting and praying so loudly they can't hear me and I'm starting to suffocate.

We sit out in the courtyard garden of the De Russie, with the high shuttered walls of the hotel all around us. Sergei is frantic-eyed,

Gloria is miserable, and I am sitting here with them at the table like a spare part. Threesomes are for the fiery passion of the early hours, not the tepid light of day. The sexual passion in this trio has dried out like a sponge in the sun and I am haunted by images of the three of us doing a weekly shop at Morrisons or arguing back and forth about where we left the car.

Gloria doesn't want to eat, she isn't hungry, she wants to drink martinis and then go to some rooftop or other. The basket of bread in the middle of the table is like a powder keg, and Gloria eyes it wearily. Sergei reaches for a slice, tears it in two in his bear-like hands, starts chewing.

'You want some?' he asks her.

She shakes her head, says quietly, 'No.'

'What?'

'NO.'

Sergei is smiling or maybe he's gritting his teeth, lower jaw protruding, top lip pulled up in a kind of snarl that shows his front teeth. 'Have some bread,' he says. It comes out like 'Don't you dare.'

Gloria reaches for the basket and takes a slice of bread. Staring steadily at Sergei, she stuffs the whole thing into her mouth so her cheeks bulge around the crust. When she's finished it, she pushes her chair back away from the table and waves down a waiter, orders a margarita with mezcal and then crosses her arms over her stomach.

Every now and again the buzzing of an insect close to my ear makes me flinch. The metallic cutlery is absorbing the heat from the sun and practically burns at the touch, so I can hardly grasp the fork. I push away a bowl of glistening carbonara and reach for the salmon sandwiches, take a small bite. It's too hot to eat at all. I think of Emily and her habit of massaging bread back into a dough. The sandwich is grit in my dry mouth, the crust absorbs any moisture left on my tongue. I reach for the slice of blood orange bobbing around in the sunset-coloured glass of Aperol spritz, and greedily suck the juice from it.

'I'm going to build a chapel in the Miami house,' Sergei announces. 'It's decided.'

'You most certainly will not.' Gloria crosses her arms and looks moodily at him across the table.

'I miss going to church every Sunday,' he continues. 'A bit of spirituality is good for the soul.'

'Go to church if you want to,' she says, through gritted teeth, 'just don't expect me to come with you.'

Sergei drops his fork onto his plate of pasta and claps his hands together. 'Why are you being like this?' he demands.

Gloria sighs. 'Being like what?'

He waves his hand at her. 'So . . . negative.'

Gloria throws her napkin on the table. 'I'm not going to sit here and watch you spiral out of control again.'

'SIT DOWN.' The tone in Sergei's voice gives me goosebumps. 'I'm your husband, Gloria.'

'I'm aware,' she says, beckoning the waiter for another margarita.

'I'm going to the loo,' I say, taking the opportunity to escape for five minutes.

The staff inside are staring at me, talking in hushed voices about the summer of '09. *Do you think he's 'o9ing again?* I can't tell what any of it means, only that judging by Sergei's growing franticness, and Gloria's irritation, it's not good.

When I return, I can see that Sergei's ordered dessert. Everything on the menu by the looks of it. Some kind of deconstructed tiramisu, candy-coloured scoops of gelato, crème brûlée in a shallow dish, raspberries and strawberries in a tall glass, topped with fluffy cream and crumbled pieces of meringue. We are held in polite bondage to each other and to our seats at the table although I can feel Sergei quivering at the edge of the abyss. The tension is palpable. The whole thing's in danger of becoming a Tony Montana and Elvira restaurant showdown kind of situation. *Is this what it's all about? Eating, drinking, fucking, sucking.* I feel that any minute Sergei's going to start yelling at Gloria about her polluted womb.

Gloria's martini arrives and she drinks it in a couple of gulps and orders another.

'Are you happy, Gloria?' Sergei asks her, leaning across the table. 'You can't really tell me that you're happy, and you know why?'

She wipes her mouth with the back of her hand. 'Why, Sergei?'

I am being terrorized by a mosquito. I feel too sick to eat the rich custard of a crème brûlée.

'Because we've been living like godless animals,' he says, 'and when I think . . . when I think of my mother, God rest her soul . . .'

'I've just about had enough,' Gloria says, too loudly—compared to her normal sultry whisper she's practically screaming. 'You will *not* do this again. You will not do this to *me* again. Agnes, get up, we're going upstairs.'

I don't know what the fuck is happening and quite honestly I think that I, too, have had enough of this particular chapter.

Sergei follows us, puts his arms around us both as we take the lift up to the top floor. Gloria is stiff and resistant to his touch. I want to go home. Like now.

'Come to our room,' he pleads into my hair. 'Come to our room for a couple of hours.'

I look to Gloria for guidance but she only stares at the floor. I go with them. I sit on the bed with Gloria while Sergei locks himself in the bathroom.

'Two minutes,' he says.

I can hear him weeping softly. Oh my God, he's really crying.

'This is fucking mad,' I whisper.

Gloria looks at the closed bathroom door with a glimmer of pity in her yellow eyes. 'Yes,' she says. 'He can't help himself.'

I can see now that Sergei is caged in by his own lust and a part of me, a devious, vengeful part, is glad about it. If I'm going to be trapped into this cage of femininity then it's only right he should be trapped as well, brick by brick until he's caged in, starved and without oxygen.

Sergei eats pussy reverently. His arms spread, I could picture him nailed to a cross and weeping even though he bears basically no resemblance to the concave-stomached crucified Jesus. Sergei is paunchy under his clothes which adds a little vulnerability to him. The extra flesh makes him seem almost breakable. More delicate. Sweat, hair, eyelashes, tears, the soles of feet, moist palms. So many candles, tall and white. Gloria's mouth tastes like the ocean.

It's over and Sergei rests his head on Gloria's soft mound of a stomach, my head by her legs, my arm on Sergei's thigh. 'Do you forgive me?' Sergei's wide, round eyes. 'Tell me you forgive me, Agnes.' He reaches for my leg and strokes it.

'Nothing to forgive,' I say. 'It's all right.'

It is all beginning to make sense; the gifts he gives like offerings, the golden temple of a Miami house. Oracles, orgies, lusty Greek and Roman gods, apples and pomegranates. Ceremonial robes as designed by Versace. The candles, the incense. I want to go home.

The next morning, Gloria orders two *caffè*, which are espresso, little sachets of brown granulated *zucchero*. When I tell her I want to leave, she doesn't flinch. She'll book me two nights in another hotel and then a flight back home, and she's wired me the fifty thousand. 'You should see some of Rome, at least, after *everything*.' It's an unexpected act of sorority. I don't know if Gloria is capable of guilt but I think she believes in karma. She can't stand Sergei, that much is clear, but she thinks she deserves him.

The mosquitoes are swarming on account of Gloria's perfume which she wears to spite Sergei and ultimately herself. She picks the mosquito bite on her shoulder until it bleeds.

Twenty Two

Spilt Milk

I'm staying at the Milton hotel which is right by the central station. Smart and functional. The white bedsheets are tucked so tightly over the mattress that I have to wrestle them out, almost dislocating my shoulder in the process. I feel as though a significant chapter of my life is over, like it's the end of a series and next season there will be new cast members, accompanying me on zany misadventures.

I am so tired. I spend the rest of the day in bed scrolling TikTok and peeling slices of prosciutto out of a supermarket packet and cramming them into my mouth. I guess maybe I should be traumatized after the party at the Vasilievs'—and maybe I am, and it's going to come bubbling up out years later in a plush psychiatrist's office in answer to a mundane question about how I handle stress, but for now I only feel tired. My eyelids are heavy and sore, and there's the embryo of a headache burgeoning at the right side of my temple that's already making my eyebrow twitch. I promise myself I'm going to make steps towards a maintainable future when I get back to London. A regular job with normal hours.

I could enrol in a college, try and get another gig with a photographer. Nothing in film or TV under *any* circumstances. I've decided acting isn't for me.

I fall asleep without trying and wake up feeling rested and excited to explore the city. After having a quick shower, I take myself out for a wander, Leica camera in tow. My phone is stacking up with floods of Instagram notifications, the pictures from Miami building on the success of my Paris posts, and people are waiting to see what glamorous place I'm going to visit next, which designer it-bag I'm going to carry.

I pass a small café, advertising a deal on aperitifs. The Marilyn Café it's called, with a poster of Marilyn Monroe on the stand outside. The place is small, about big enough for a counter, and there's no indoor seating, just a few small tables covered with plastic blue table- cloths outside.

> **Jess:** Hey Ag, is everything all right? What are you up to at the moment?
> **Jess:** My mum bumped into your mum in town and she seemed really worried about you
> **Jess:** Everything's fine, yeah? X

Quite why this makes me nervous as hell I have no idea, but I feel as though I'm about to dissolve into a panic attack. Constance is worried about me? That's good, that means she cares, that she's been missing me. Right? But I also have this terrible, sicky guilt feeling that maybe she's been suffering because of me. My God, am I the world's worst daughter?

> **Me:** Hey sorry I haven't responded sooner, I'm all good, I'm in Rome
> **Me:** I know, I know, quick trip lol
> **Me:** Be home soon
> **Me:** Weird, I'll tell Lena to let her know I'm totally fine

'*Pronto!*'

A little woman, with skin like sunburnt leather and wearing a mauve visor, waves at me from behind the counter. She has heavy eyeliner flicks and pink-painted nails. I look through the glass screen at the jam-filled pastries. Sandwiches made out of fluffy white bread and wrapped in clingfilm.

'*Cornetto?*' she asks me.

'I, uhh, no thanks,' I mumble, still trying to emo- tionally process the text from Jess. The hope that I might, against all my previous concerns, actually still have a friend.

'English?'

'Yeah, sorry.'

She smiles—it's a pretty smile, and in it I see her past. Dinner dates in satin-sheen puffed dresses.

'I'll take an Aperol, please.'

The wall behind the counter is pasted with hundreds of pictures of Marilyn. Her glossy, lipsticked pout, plunging Hollywood dresses, sultry bedroom eyes. Strangely there's a picture of the Virgin Mary too, hanging from a nail in the centre of the wall.

The little woman slides the glass across the counter and I hand her a €10 note.

'What's your name?' she asks me.

'Agnes, what's yours?'

'Maria,' she says.

Mary, Marilyn and Maria.

I take my drink outside and she follows me. 'You on vacation?'

I must look too approachable. Now I won't be able to enjoy my Aperol in peace.

'Kind of,' I say, forcing a smile. Wouldn't you like to know, lady. Oh, the stories I could tell. Better go and get your rosary.

She pulls out a chair and sits down at the table with me, her knees apart, leaning back in her chair.

'Ah,' she says, and clucks her tongue. Her eyes are so wise I have a sudden moment of irrational panic that she can see inside my brain. 'Did you come alone to Roma?'

'No,' I say, with a sigh, 'but I'm going home alone.'

'Ah,' she nods knowingly. Imagining the argument I must have had with my sensible but smothering boyfriend, the two of us shouting at each other in the square while a street performer plays Disney songs on the violin in the background. 'Well, you are young, it happens, you will be all right. How long are you staying?'

'Two more nights,' I tell her. 'I moved out to another hotel.'

She sits with me while I drink my Aperol spritz, tells a wasp to 'Fuck off!' I laugh. Maria's easy to like. It makes me feel good and human to like someone and not want anything from them.

She invites me back to hers for dinner and says I can use the pool, that her daughter will be there. 'It's not good to be alone,' she says.

'What about the café?'

'Ah—' she waves a hand in the air—'one day won't make much difference.'

I rest my head on the inside car door while she drives us in her silver Peugeot to her place in La Rustica. She apologizes for the air conditioning; the vents are blowing out stale-smelling warm air into the heat.

It's snowing pollen, which collects as yellowy-white scum on the surface of the swimming pool. Fire ants swarm in the dust and every time I cross the terracotta tiles to get another drink, I hear them crack, ancient and sun-dried as they are, and feel like a giant. The dried leaves falling heavily from the tree sound like bats' wings when they meet the stone driveway. The house and its grounds are in a state of disrepair, but there's still something kind of glamorous about it.

A white cat licks water out of a now-defunct fountain full of lily pads, with a white conch shell floating in the centre. It comes and goes silently between this garden and the next, crawling under the silver Peugeot and between potted cacti and ferns.

Maria hands me a new swimsuit, a black one-piece with the tag still on. It was bought for her daughter but she will only wear a bikini, she says, rolling her eyes, and I roll mine in sympathy. 'Teenage girls can be hell, eh.'

We bob around in the pool under the midday sun. Maria's a tiny woman, loose skin hanging from her hipbones, sagging around the knees. Her swimsuit is that vivid purple colour that only existed in the eighties. Water droplets run along the bridge of her nose and drop down her front.

Angelica, Maria's daughter, is eighteen, with a wide skull and flat dark hair in a middle parting tucked behind her ears on each side. She has a boyish look to her. There's a cluster of red bumps on her smooth jawbone. She dips her feet in the pool and complains about mosquito bites.

'You used to go naked,' Maria teases her.

Angelica tuts and says, '*Ai*.' Slouches down into her spine, squints at her phone screen in the bright sunlight.

'You celebrate your name day?' Maria asks me.

I tell her I'm not Catholic.

'Ah,' she says, 'that makes sense. But you know about Saint Agnes?'

I tell her I don't.

'You don't know the story of your namesake?'

I shrug. 'Do you mind if I smoke?'

Maria fetches an ashtray made of flint stone.

'Saint Agnes . . .' Maria holds out her hand for a cigarette. 'I don't normally,' she says, 'but I smoke with you.'

I light it for her, notice the slight callous on the side of her index finger as she holds the cigarette, the deep ridges in the surface of her fingernails painted with pink shimmer. There's a new bird somewhere up there, maybe on the roof—it sounds like a frog call, throaty and multisyllabic.

'She was a virgin,' she says.

Of course she was.

'Who refused marriage, so they took her—' Maria snatches at the air with her free hand—'and they put her in a brothel and they strip her and none of the Romans will touch her.'

'Why not?'

I turn over my shoulder and see that Angelica has wandered off somewhere.

Maria's eyes widen, little blue veins in the whites of them like the hairline fracture in an X-ray—Marlena had one on her forearm before. We rode our bikes down a steep hill and she lost control of the thing, came tumbling off it. I remember fear, the taste of blood I got in my mouth when I bit my tongue running after her. The sting on the back of the legs from where Constance smacked me. *She's your little sister? You supposed to take care of her and you lead her into danger?*

'. . . He went blind.'

'Hmm?'

I realize Maria's still been talking while I've zoned out. I feel the same breeze I felt the day Marlena was injured, the chill in the air like I'm there now, her little brown legs in scuffed trainers, tangled up with the bike wheels, her hand feeling at the back of her braided head, face creasing into hysterics as the shock wears off.

'The one who touched her, tried to assault her, he went blind,' Maria repeats. Dabs her cigarette out on the side of the pool, black ash between the cracks of the white and grey stone. She breaks into a leisurely breast-stroke, with the kind of bougie, arched-back posture that a cartoon cat might have when swimming, keeping her head out of the water. She reaches the other end of the pool, rests back against the side of it with her arms out over the edge, and lets her legs float, her feet poking out of the water, toes wrinkled. 'They try to burn her but the fire won't catch, so they stab her instead and when her blood spills out everywhere, other Christians come and—' cupping the pool water in her hand, she lets it run out through her fingers—'they collect her blood.'

'Cool story,' I nod. 'But I mean, what's the message of it except stay pure and don't get raped?'

She considers this. 'I think the point is to show that purity doesn't protect you. Any woman can be abused but in the eyes of God the abuse doesn't desecrate you. Saint Agnes is the patron saint of rape survivors and they bless two lambs on her feast day. You know that's what your name means in Latin? Lamb.'

'Did you grow up in a very religious house?' I ask.

She shrugs. 'I'm Italian.'

'Do you have what they call a Catholic conscience?'

'I think God is more forgiving of the human condition than we give him credit for. All the rest is about people controlling people.' She wafts her hands around in the water.

'My mother is religious,' I tell her, 'like, devout, fire-and-brimstone kind of stuff.'

'And you don't believe.'

'I want to,' I tell her. 'I'd love to be able to pray, to feel faith. If God is real then I must just be too fucked up for him to talk to.'

'Have you tried?'

'I've tried, trust me,' I say, leaning my arms out of the water and picking at the grass at the edge of the pool. 'I've prayed about it, cried about it, beaten my head against a fucking brick wall. I hate myself for not *wanting* to be pure because you've got to really want it, haven't you?'

Maria says nothing, just looks at me, encouraging me to keep speaking.

'You know, when I was younger I got really obsessed with the last book of the Bible. Revelation. It scared me and the fear felt real and made me feel like I was closer to God. My mum's friend from church, this awful woman called Phyllis, she showed me and my sister a YouTube video about the End Times, how Jesus will come back for the good people and the rest of us are doomed.' I push with my feet against the side of the pool, pawing at the water to pull myself further down. I bob straight back up to float on my back. 'Well, I think I'm doomed. I'm not . . . I'm one of the bad ones, one of those parasitic birds that eats all the other chicks in the nest when they hatch. Destined for hellfire and nothing can save us.'

'You think you were born bad?' Maria says in her gentle voice. She's stopped to tread water and is looking at me with a soft intentness.

'I've done things, thought things . . .' I start and then stop. 'I just don't have it in me to be saintly.'

'My dear,' Maria smiles, 'there's a reason the saints are called saints and not humans.'

'Some people really are saints,' I say, with gritted teeth. 'Trust me.'

She cocks her head to the side like she's considering it and then she smiles. '*Non è possibile.* This kind of perfection, it is a myth. And besides,' she says, 'there are people dying, people killing—you think God cares about your little mistakes? Hold yourself to that kind of standard, you'll end up—' she twirls two fingers at the side of her head—'crazy. Crazy and angry. Just try your best to be a good person, help other people where you can, enjoy life, that's it.'

We come out of the water and lie flat on our backs on towels thrown over the grass, surrendering to the sun as it dries our bodies. There's a warm breeze, the steady white fall of pollen from the trees, the birds, the flowers.

Maria sighs. 'This is just as good,' she says, 'as praying.'

*

The morning I'm due to fly back to London, a slender green-speckled lizard shimmies across the stone step. Two other lizards crawl over each other high on the garden wall, their tails entwining like aged rope. It's early, the sun has barely broken, and Maria is asleep. I take my Leica camera out of my handbag. It's probably too dark to get a decent picture but I try anyway.

Me: Heyyy Jess, heading home today
Me: Wanna meet for a catch up? Xx

I decide it's time to fix things with my friend. I've let her squirm for long enough. I don't know if we can ever get back to how we were before, but I'm willing to try.

On the plane back, I have a dream about my mother, about Constance. Constance as Saint Agnes in a gold robe with a sword and a lamb in the crook of her arm. And she's hiding the lamb, growing frantic—she hooks her robe around it, whispers into its soft grey ear. And then I blink and she's not dressed in a gold robe any more, she's wearing her pink overalls from Mrs Finch's and she's holding a duster instead of a sword and the lamb is gone.

Twenty Three

I'm Rich, Bitch

T he first thing I do is send my film off to be developed and transfer
Marlena £1,000 via bank transfer. Summer is over, the supermarkets advertise 'Back to School', displaying acrylic pencil cases and electric neon binders, while people start talking about Halloween. There's
a sense of finality hanging in the air. The warm optimism I felt on the
flight home and the taxi ride and the first night back in bed beside Sara
has started to dwindle a little bit.

> **Marlena:** Thanks for the money sis xxxxx
> **Marlena:** It's Mum's birthday in a few weeks
>
> **Me:** You're welcome my love
> **Me:** I know

She doesn't nag me for a phone call anymore, I think she's lost faith on
that count.

> **Marlena:** So I think maybe it's a good opportunity to reach
> out and make amends

Me: Lena

I start typing out a vague excuse about having to prioritize my needs right now then put my phone down. She has a point. If I ever want to make things right with Constance, now's the time. I can wish her happy birthday, buy her a new angel statuette for the living room, show up with a smile on my injection-plumped lips and hope for the best. The thought that she could shut the door in my face with all the force of her delicate wrists is too scary for words. But I consider it. And though the idea frightens me, I promise Marlena I'll think about it.

Marlena: More promises 😬

Me: Hey, I really mean it

Marlena: We'll see

I had no reason to anxiety spiral about things being awkward when I got back to the flat. The Freddy, Freya, Sara saga is so far gone it's like it never happened. Today, everyone's buzzing about Emily's news—she's booked a big modelling campaign for Nivea. I buy her a celebration cake from an extortionately priced bakery, grateful that they're all too preoccupied to ask me any probing questions and that things are so frantic in the flat I'm not left alone with my own thoughts for half a second.

'Thanks,' she says, poking at the slice of fluffy sponge I've cut for her, 'but I can't eat this. I've got to take care of my skin.'

I mean, I didn't expect she'd polish the thing off unaided but she could have managed a polite nibble.

She strides over in the direction of the mirror as if some of the sugar might have gotten into her system by osmosis and caused an instant break-out. Sara eats her slice then Emily's, hovering around the cake like a bee, putting her finger in the icing.

'When are you leaving?' I ask Yomawu.

'Two weeks, Friday,' she says, and I can see she's a little sad beneath the gracious smile she's touting.

It seems that the end of summer signals the end of sugaring, too. Yomawu's parents have got her a real job as a conveyancing paralegal at a private equity-backed legal marketing firm. They're moving her into some kind of shared working and living space for young professionals. She doesn't seem especially pleased about it.

'I probably can't take the ribbons,' she says, 'or the mirror, it's already furnished.'

'I'm sure it will be really nice,' I tell her.

I hope she can't tell I'm a little bit jealous, not just of her new career but of the support from her parents.

She hangs her head. 'I'll be in grey and black suits from here on in.'

'You could make anything look good.' I mean it, she could.

'*I know*,' she says, matter-of-factly, and then, 'sorry, thank you.'

Her smile is fading.

'It's all right.' I know Yomawu by now. She's not stuck up but she can come off that way at times, sensitive about her beauty, defensive, perhaps anxious about the privilege and wanting to handle it correctly.

'Hey, on the bright side, maybe you can take my room when I leave?'

'Makes sense,' I say, hating the fact that my first thought is that they'll probably want to charge me full rent if I have Yomawu's room. I've got Gloria's money, sent without comment via bank transfer, which was a surprise because after Rome I felt certain I'd been taken for a ride. I'M RICH, BITCH. Maybe I'll finally enrol in that course at the college or even go to Central Saint Martins like Freya.

I feel less obsessed with making my winged eyeliner as sharp as a knife, or with walking like I'm hanging from a cloud or whatever. Obviously I still notice if men turn to look at me on the street, but I don't feel the same glow of satisfaction any more, I've stopped collecting each sidelong glance like it's a meal token. I'm not feeling that interested in being seen at all, these days.

I think I'm realizing that what I really want is to get other people to see the world from my point of view.

'How's the job search been coming?' Yomawu asks me. 'Any interview yet?'

She's talking about the dozen applications I dashed off yesterday for part-time nanny, supermarket cashier, barista. I shake my head.

'Well, I'm sure you will,' she says.

'You should definitely take Yoyo's room,' Sara pipes up. 'As long as you won't miss our night cuddles too much.'

I squeeze her on the shoulder. 'I'll be sneaking back in, don't worry.'

'We should go out tonight,' says Sara, her arm around my waist. 'We need to celebrate properly, pop some champagne.'

Emily scoffs. 'No, thank you. I won't be doing anything that doesn't hydrate my skin and minimize my pores for the next three weeks.'

Everyone deflates a little bit. She controls the temperature of the room, like she always has.

'Your skin is flawless,' I tell her.

'They'll be shooting in ultra-HD for the advert,' she says, flicking open her pocket mirror by way of impulse and examining the size of her pores, her non-existent under eye circles and her recently injected lips.

'All right, well, I'd better be going,' I tell them, checking in my handbag for my keys, purse and phone. It occurs to me that I have a significant cash reserve in these handbags—the Chanel bag I'm about to bash around on the Underground is a solid five figures.

'Where are you going?' Yomawu asks me.

'Meeting a friend from home.'

'Didn't know you had any other friends,' says Emily.

Jess arrives five minutes late, striding through the coffee shop door. 'Ag! Back from your jet-setting? Still looking like a beauty pageant contestant, I see.'

'Yeah.' I feel a little embarrassed. I'm aware that Jess's perception of me has changed, perhaps permanently. Her opinion of me is one that, annoyingly, still matters.

But she has a big bouquet in her arms—peach-coloured roses and baby's breath dangle over the edge of the brown paper.

'Are those for me?'

'Yep.' She's looking intently at my face. 'You've got a bit of a tan. Lucky bitch. I've just about managed to stop the peeling from Thailand. Aloe vera, that's what I've . . .'

I interrupt her. 'Jess, you're doing that thing where you keep changing the subject.'

'Oh yeah,' she chuckles. 'Sorry, I'm working on that. Here, take these.'

I take the brown paper-wrapped bouquet, touch the velvet head of a rose. 'Thanks, they're beautiful. You shouldn't have.'

'Yeah, well, I wanted to make it up to you after last time.'

'Not necessary,' I say, shaking my head vehemently.

We sit down opposite each other and smile awkwardly for a few seconds.

'No, I think I was harsh,' she says with a deep exhale of breath. 'I didn't *really* think about how difficult it might be for you to see the old school lot again, not properly. The way they ambushed you with all that . . . it was horrible.'

'Yeah,' I say, flinching at the memory. 'It was. But . . . that's over now.'

'And I could have been more understanding about the whole secret sugar baby insta thing.'

A shudder down my spine.

'Let's forget about it,' I tell her. 'I deleted it anyway.'

'Okay, well.' There's a sudden desperate look in her green eyes as she watches me across the table. 'I want you to know that you're my best friend and I would never judge you for doing something like that. It hurt my feelings that you thought I would and didn't tell me.'

I sigh. 'That's not the only reason. I guess I didn't tell you because I knew you'd have concerns and I knew some of those concerns would be valid and I'd already made up my mind that I was going to do it no matter what.'

She's nodding, taking in what I'm saying and listening closely.

'I didn't want a voice of reason,' I said.

'That's fair enough,' she says. 'And are you still . . . ?'

I shake my head. 'No, I gave it a fair shot. On balance, I . . . I don't think that life's for me.'

'But it *was* fun, wasn't it?'

'So fucking fun,' I tell her. 'I'm not going to lie to you.'

We laugh, and get up to order our drinks. In the corner, a resident florist gathers pastel tulips and rosebuds into bunches. This café is the type with enormous windows, exposed beams and bookshelves everywhere—Jess chose it, she said she likes to come here to study, and I see why.

'So, Miami?' Jess stirs sugar into her coffee as we settle back down. 'What was that about? If you . . . if you don't mind sharing.'

'A mistake,' I tell her with a shrug. 'I met a guy.'

'And it didn't work out?'

'He had a wife,' I say, and suddenly, from somewhere deep inside, I erupt into loud, spontaneous laughter.

'God, Ag.' She's watching me with an expression of horror on her freckled face. 'Why are you laughing?'

'I don't know,' I tell her, my cheeks twinging, jaw aching, eyes blurry with tears.

The laughter goes on for another couple of minutes, like a sudden downpour of rain. I can't do anything to stop it.

'Sorry,' I say, shaking my head and gasping, 'no idea what that was about.' I slurp the foam off the top of my cappuccino.

'I actually do know you, Agnes,' Jess says with a curious smile. 'I know you laugh like a maniac when you get uncomfortable.'

I glow inside and squirm awkwardly in my seat. 'I . . . I wanted to thank you again for sticking up for me, to Olive and that lot. I know they're your friends as well.'

She groans. 'Oh, come on, Ag, you're number one, you know that.'

'Thanks,' I say. And then, 'You've learned to separate the curls, I see.'

'Shirley Temple,' she says, smiling at the memory. 'What are you going to do now?'

'Get a normal job, I guess.'

She laughs. 'You don't sound too excited about it.'

'It will take some adjustment.'

She tells me all about Thailand, the full-moon party on the beach, the turtles' eggs. Shows me the Instagram profile of this German guy she met. 'Hans,' she says dreamily, holding her phone against her chest, and I feel this wave of relief washing over me. Shirley Temple is back.

Twenty Four

Complications May Apply

My pictures arrive in a paper envelope. The first half-dozen are a murky mess. But there are some good ones in there, I think. I spread them out across the kitchen table, run my eyes over them. There are lots of Emily—Emily home after a date, collapsed on the sofa, gold hair a veil over her face, revealing the tiniest tattoo in the nape of her neck, and then some close-ups of her feet, showing raw cuts on her ankle bones, bandaged little toes, scars pinkish and brown, left over from her high heels. Emily blotting her lipstick, eyes focused intensely on her reflection. I see something there in the frame that I've never noticed in real life—desperation. There's Kiki looking defiant in her red lipstick and nipple covers. Sara in black cotton underwear, her arm across her bare chest, looking fragile even when she's smiling, light through the fraying edges of her blonde hair. The pictures I took of Yomawu dancing to Lana in a pastel yellow nightdress with a matching robe, her lips parted, singing along.

I've photographed the cupboards, haphazard collections of mugs and glasses we've accumulated on the way. Our little commune always had an expiry date. We never 'gave the cat a name', so to speak.

'They're beautiful,' says Kiki. She holds up the photograph of a woman bending to smell a bouquet of flowers in a Paris market. 'I love this. You took these?'

'Yep. You sound surprised,' I say, laughing nervously.

'Well, yeah,' she says, adding in typical Kiki fashion, 'I thought you were gonna be a useless amateur, but these are actually good.'

'Ha, you really think so?'

'I believe you're talented, Agnes,' she says. 'Look at me, I'm not one for blowing smoke up people's arses, I'm being serious.'

'Thank you, Kiki.'

'Don't mention it,' she says. She picks up the photo of Gloria's red manicure on the blue playing cards. 'Who is this?'

'Long story,' I say, clearing my throat.

I look over the table—a lot of what I've experienced since I left home is here. Matthew's hands gripping tight to the edge of the table in the yellow Parisian light, his jacket and shoes on the hotel sofa, a tangled mess of white sheets. My black lingerie with pale pink rosebuds screwed up on the hotel carpet. The blue Miami ocean, empty champagne bottle, the rip in my red dress. Mary, Marilyn and Maria. A stone lion water fountain. A lizard in the dark. My life in the model apartment—moody and blue, faded beauty of lipstick smudged around the mouth.

*

I wake up restless and aching. Stepping over a pair of lacy black knickers that someone's abandoned on the bathmat, I stand on the cold tiles in front of the mirror, picking sleep out of my eye. The sink glitters with purple make-up dust, and leftover bubble-bath scud languishes at the bottom of the tub like stiffened meringue. When I run the tap a kind of ominous groaning emanates from the plughole, some sort of piping issue. We've told the landlord but no one's come to fix it yet.

I bundle up in my dressing gown, fill up the moka pot. When I sit down at the kitchen table, I feel the coffee curdling as soon as it makes contact with my nervous, acidic stomach. I take a few deep breaths, try to fix my eyes on a point on the wall, and find them wandering to the little quote plaque above the fridge. *Love makes our HOUSE a home.* It's not ours, of course, it came with the flat. The type of thing that you get when you become a mum, buy a slow cooker and join the local WhatsApp gossip group. I never really paid it much attention before but now it's grating on me. Everything about it, from the chubby little hearts to the frankly psychotic random capitalization.

Home. Today's the first time I'm going back since the day I stormed out.

After the party, I had it in my head that neither hell nor high water could ever get me to step foot back in The Wasteland again. But as it happens, Lena trumps them both.

'You're not going away to uni for another three weeks,' I'd told her on the phone, stalling, avoidant as usual. 'Let's wait a bit.'

'No,' she'd said, 'you'll change your mind about coming to the house.'

'*Haunted* house,' I'd said, under my breath.

She replied without missing a beat. 'Haunted house, crime scene, the only home we've ever known.' There was a note of challenge in her voice.

'What's the big deal? Can't we just go to Starbucks or wherever?' I feigned nonchalance but something about the words stung. I thought about Maria's crumb- ling place in Italy, her daughter with her feet in the pool. The way everything in the house, the columns, the gateway, the cups, had a kind of vibration to them. They were rooted.

'It will be . . . *nice*,' she'd insisted.

Yeah, nice like Paris was nice. Nice like Miami was nice.

'Whatever you want, Lena,' I'd said, as Sara came and crushed up against me on the sofa, her shoulder jabbing into mine, which helped distract me from the horrible visions I was having of bumping into Constance.

South Kensington's leaves are turning brown already, everyone in neutral-coloured knitwear. I've got a plastic tote full of things for Lena to take with her to uni—I went a bit manic in the stationery shop and couldn't resist an extortionate hardback notebook with an iridescent scaly cover. I'm taking a stack of my photos, I want her to see I'm sort of good at something other than fracturing the only small family unit we've ever had.

When I pass Emily's door, I can hear her singing 'Happy Birthday', Marilyn-to-JFK style, to some guy on the phone. She's never going to give this life up. She's too set on the idea of her beauty as a commodity, something to be acted on with urgency, to be frantically spent before it runs out or goes to waste. I think about Marilyn and the roles we cast her in—fragile victim, unacknowledged genius, shimmying sexpot—and wonder if maybe she was as shrewd an operator as Emily is. A woman with a plan. A steel fist in a beautiful, hand-finished velvet glove.

I've reached the point in the train journey where yellow and green fields start blurring past the windows and everyone's conversations have diminished to a background hum. At this point I'd normally expect to feel my eyelids getting heavy with sleep but I'm wide awake, can feel the blood pumping through my body like I've taken something. Even though Lena promised me that Constance was out at prayer group, I am fucking nervous. I can't shake the thought that I'm about to return to my own religious reckoning, that it's time to pay for my sins. *God sees everything. God's always watching.* Agnes Green, get a fucking hold of yourself.

I can feel my phone buzzing in my pocket.

Emily: Hey Tracey Emin
Emily: What do you think of this?

It's a JPEG. The cover for her long-awaited eBook. A pale pink background with white capital letters trimmed with silvery white glitter. *10*

Easy Ways to Get a Man to Do Anything You Want by Anonymous. It looks appealing, though really it needs a footnote added as a disclaimer:

*Requires substantial denial of self and the projection of a false image that may ultimately contribute to low self-esteem and difficulties developing genuine connections with men. Additional complications may apply.

I'll respond to her later and tell her how pretty it looks, how seductive the title sounds. For once, I'll be telling the truth.

We're pulling into the station now. I get out and jump in a taxi. He takes the long route, probably assuming that I'm an out-of-towner. The Wasteland looks even smaller now. Has it always been like this? It's like I could cross from one side to the other with a couple of strides. I almost feel guilty for hating it so much. Almost. There are signs of tragic misguided optimism all over the place, like the faded yellow paint on the wall of what used to be an independent bakery but only lasted two months before it folded, or the multicultural mural they painted on the underpass, smiling faces in a spectrum of shades, which survived untouched for about forty-eight hours before someone with a spray-paint bottle added rapper hats and face tattoos reading '69'.

Constance opens the door. Well, this is horribly fucking awkward. She's not supposed to be here, Lena promised me. Advice about what to do in an emergency starts flashing through my brain, like, STOP, DROP and ROLL!, DON'T FIGHT JUST FLOAT! and SHOUT FIRE!

'Hello, Aggie,' she says. Her voice is low, not unkind, but she has an eyebrow raised.

'Hi, Mum,' I squeak back at her, in the small, childlike voice that seems to come out of nowhere because even if I'm towering over her in heeled boots, I always feel like a little kid in Constance's presence.

My throat is almost too tight to speak. Marlena is hanging around behind Constance by the kitchen entrance looking all sheepish and avoiding my eye contact because she's tried to *Parent-Trap* us. For someone so smart she really can be stupid. Constance turns back towards her for an explanation and I shuffle from side to side in the doorway and mentally debate running away.

Marlena shrugs at us both. Constance turns back to me and this time she smiles, a little uncertainly.

'So you remember where your home is?'

'I didn't know I was welcome.' And I didn't want to fucking come, I think, slipping back into angsty teenage mode like I always do when I'm standing on the threshold of this house.

Her eyes glide over my face, my scrubbed, polished, micro-needled, derma-fillered, baby-botoxed face.

'Come in, then.'

She's still as beautiful as ever, maybe a little tired. I pull the door closed behind me, kick off my shoes, linger around waiting to be told what to do next. I glare at Marlena as I deposit her bag of uni supplies, propping it up against the wall. I can smell my own armpits, the sweat coming through the slightly mildewed fabric of my long-sleeved dress, probably a shitty polyester blend—which is annoying because it wasn't cheap. It's a mistake to assume that the more expensive something is, the better the quality. These days you're paying for the label.

'Lena, the little schemer. Why don't you make yourself useful and put on the kettle?' says Constance quietly.

'Sure,' says Marlena, her voice a little too cheerful for my liking given that she's just submitted me to an act of grievous deception.

Constance turns over her shoulder to look at me as she makes her way into the kitchen. 'Don't tell me you're really waitin' for an invitation to sit down in your own house?'

I sink into the sofa like a well-trained dog. My quilted Lady Dior bag is starkly out of place against the baggy, blanket-covered arm of the sofa. Now that the shock is wearing off, my other senses are starting to function again and I realize the house smells delicious. There's something doughy and salty baking in the oven, something wonderful bubbling in a pot on the stovetop.

'So how have you been, Mum?' I ask her. 'Everything okay?'

She doesn't respond. Ah, the silent treatment. The immigrant parent's favourite punishment.

'Mum,' says Marlena as she pours hot water into mugs.

'No need to show me fake concern, Agnes,' she says. The smile has disappeared from her face and she's not making eye contact with me anymore.

'It's not fake,' I say, pleadingly.

She doesn't respond to that either.

Marlena brings me my mug of tea and puts it down on the coffee table, whispering, 'Sorry, I really thought this would get you guys talking again. It's been so long, I just . . . I thought as I'm leaving it's kind of like a fresh start.'

'It's rude to whisper, Lena,' Constance says.

'Sorry, Mum,' she says, and the genuine distress on her face makes me feel sorry for her. *Sorry*, she mouths at me.

I reach for her hand and squeeze it. 'It's all right,' I tell her. 'No point crying over spilt milk. I'm here now.'

There's the noise of crockery, plates, bowls and dishes as Constance fumbles around in the cupboards and starts laying the table.

'Girls, come and give me a hand.'

We roll our eyes at each other out of habit and for a brief shining moment, it's like nothing ever happened, like I never left. We stand in the tiny kitchen await- ing instructions. When Constance opens the oven, the hot air blasts up at me and my arm jerks from the elbow as I pat the tendrils of hair around my face back into place.

'What are you panickin' for, Aggie,' Constance says, turning back from the oven and chuckling. 'You look like one of them Barbie dolls you used to play with.'

'Oh, thanks,' I say, my mood momentarily brightening.

'One of the white ones,' she says flatly.

'Oh.'

'Grab that for me, will you?'

I hold a serving dish that's so heavy it makes my wrists ache and Constance uses a pair of kitchen tongs to transfer runner beans into it from her big metal saucepan with the scratched scoured bottom.

The table is bountiful with everything I've missed since I left home. There's a round dish of macaroni and cheese with the cheese toasted brown on top and bubbling hot at the edges. Bakes, or dumplings, fried golden—I pull one apart in my hands and the inside is as fluffy and white as snow. Baked chicken, with the skin on, coated in honey and barbecue sauce and sprinkled with parsley. Constance's home-made coleslaw. Rice, yellow from turmeric and butter, scattered with soft brown peas.

I sit down with my mouth wide open and practically watering.

Constance looks like she's trying to stop herself from smiling. 'Enjoy,' she says.

I can see the little flame of hope in Marlena's face. She can barely allow herself to believe we're really sitting here and not fighting with each other.

'Can you pass me a napkin Judas?' I say to her, hoping that if I sound irreverent it will delay my sudden urge to burst into tears. Constance raises an eyebrow at the biblical reference but says nothing.

I take the paper napkin and flick it over my lap in that same smooth singular movement I learned from Emily. Constance and Lena look at each other and smirk.

'What?' I scoff, self-consciously.

'It's like *Downton Abbey*,' says Marlena.

I have missed so many small details about home. The weight of the honeycomb-moulded glass in my hands, the acrylic floral tablecloth. Maybe that's why all the objects in Maria's home felt so singular to me, shot through with this electric charge. They weren't just pretty things for the sake of ornament, they were signs of a life being comfortably lived.

Constance is looking at me kind of strangely. 'Your teeth, Aggie.'

My hand jolts upwards instinctively to cover my mouth.

'What about them?'

'They're so *white*.'

'Oh, ha. Yeah, I guess they are.'

'We can probably use them like a nightlight in the dark,' Constance says seriously, but her eyes are kind.

When we're finished eating I raise my glass of orange juice in a toast to Marlena going off to Cambridge.

'Good idea,' says Constance. 'A toast to my darlin' girl.'

'I'm so proud of you,' we say in unison and I feel heat spread up from my neck and warm my cheeks, embarrassed for some reason to be caught in a moment of solidarity with her, as if it somehow undermines all the anger and resentment I've been feeling over the last few months, years, life.

'She dance for joy when that computer show up,' says Constance softly when Marlena's gone to the loo. 'She been missin' you.' She doesn't look at me but keeps her eyes fixed on her plate. 'If you want to come back home, you're welcome.'

I'm not so certain that she really means it. She thinks it's the right thing to say.

'Thank you, Mum,' I reply, 'I really appreciate that.'

I don't tell her that I could never move back now that I've left. The thought is comforting but slightly oppressive at the same time, like being held a little too tightly.

After we sip tea and eat malted milk biscuits, I give Marlena the bag of stationery and tell them I'm going to the bathroom, then turn straight into my old bedroom, gently close the door behind me. It smells like dust and old blankets. I look at my face in the wardrobe mirror, the same dull, smudged glass that I used to scrutinize every inch of my body in before I went out to see Toby—front, profile, behind. Toby who I wasn't good enough for and then Matthew, who only thought I was good when I stuck to the script. It's crazy to think about those years when I felt so unsure, a walking catalogue of deficiencies. Then, this summer, I finally mastered it. I made men my business.

There's some satisfaction in performing, reading the script, wearing the costume, after all. And on the other side of the satisfaction there is rage. The deep and exhausting rage of having fallen for a scam. Because when all is said and done, being beautiful only offers you a temporary haven. A pedestal to fall from.

Anyway, I'm not sure if I ever really liked either of them, Toby or Matthew. I think they just represented something that at the time I had convinced myself I desperately needed.

I open up one of my photography books, fan out the middle pages. The model lies on an elaborate dining table amongst the glassware and the crockery, in a plunging gown with a slit up the thigh, like she's ready to be eaten.

I can admit it. It feels good to be wanted, to be delectable, delicious. But if I've learned anything it's that I don't want to be consumed. I have teeth of my own.

A knock on the door jolts me from my trance. Marlena hovers in the doorway, a plastic wallet full of photos in her hand.

'You left these in the bag with my stuff,' she says. 'I looked at them.'

I snatch them from her hand with mock irritation. 'Because you haven't done enough to piss me off today? All right, Peeping Tom, let's hear your verdict then.'

'Well,' she says, 'you know I'm not artistically inclined.'

'True,' I say, 'but you're brutally honest.'

'True,' she repeats, and then she grins. 'God, look at you, you're actually nervous.'

I bump my fist against her arm.

'All right,' she says, rolling her eyes and taking a deep sigh as though the admission physically pains her. 'They're magic. Okay?'

'They're what?'

'You won't get it out of me again,' she snaps. But before she leaves, she pauses in the doorway to smile at me.

ACKNOWLEDGMENTS

Firstly, to Artie, my biggest supporter and my best friend. I'm so sorry you passed away before we had the chance to see this book in print together. It's your achievement as much as mine and no understatement to say I never could have done it without you. For getting me my new laptop, for listening to my ideas, for never letting me give up, for supporting me in every single sense of the word, for being my safe place in the world. We did it together. Your impact is woven through these pages and carried with me always. Rest peacefully my love, thank you for everything. I hope I've made you proud.

Thank you to my brilliant agent Hattie Grünewald for believing in me and this book, and for having faith in me as a debut writer. I'm so incredibly lucky to have you and excited for what the future holds. Thank you for encouraging me when I've needed it and for all you do on my behalf.

Enormous thanks to an incredible editor Sarah de Souza for your wonderful insight and for pushing me to develop Sugar, Baby into the book it never could have been without you, I couldn't have dreamt of a better editor to be with me on this journey.

Thanks also to all the talented and hard-working people who've worked on my behalf and had a hand in bringing Sugar, Baby into the world at The Blair Partnership and Corvus, Atlantic.

With thanks to the whole team at Bloomsbury USA. A special thank you to my editor Amber Oliver, I am so grateful to have an editor and publisher who I feel have understood the essence of my work so completely. Thank you for giving me such an incredible platform from which to share this story with an even wider audience.

Thank you to Artie's parents: Eni and Artur, for your love and support and for raising such an incredible human being. We've been through so much together and this book also belongs to you both.

Mum, Dad, Jack, Nana and Grandad, aunties and uncles- there aren't enough words to say thank you. To the OGs, Iaya, Gill and Emily, thank you for being there when I've needed you the most and always supporting my little projects and writerly dreams. Iaya and Gilly, going to Spain in November was a lifesaver, I'd be completely lost without you, you have a friend for eternity in me.

To all who've helped me through a year I didn't think it would be possible to get through, I love you all so much. Also, if we're related, please use this book to decorate your coffee table or your bookshelf, please don't actually read it.

A NOTE ON THE AUTHOR

CELINE SAINTCLARE is a Buckinghamshire based writer of Caribbean and English descent, born in 1996. She has a degree in Social Anthropology. *Sugar, Baby* is her first novel.

Follow her on Twitter @CSaintclare